Rogue with a Brogue

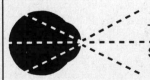

This Large Print Book carries the
Seal of Approval of N.A.V.H.

ROGUE WITH A BROGUE

SUZANNE ENOCH

THORNDIKE PRESS

A part of Gale, Cengage Learning

GALE
CENGAGE Learning·

Farmington Hills, Mich • San Francisco • New York • Waterville, Maine
Meriden, Conn • Mason, Ohio • Chicago

GALE
CENGAGE Learning·

LIBRARY OF CONGRESS CATALOGING-IN-PUBLICATION DATA

Enoch, Suzanne.
  Rogue with a brogue / by Suzanne Enoch. — Large print edition.
    pages cm. — (Thorndike Press large print romance)
    ISBN 978-1-4104-7752-1 (hardcover) — ISBN 1-4104-7752-5 (hardcover)
    1. Large type books. I. Title.
  PS3555.N655R64 2015
  813'.54—dc23   2014047548

Published in 2015 by arrangement with St. Martin's Press LLC

Printed in Mexico
1 2 3 4 5 6 7 19 18 17 16 15

For my very good friend
and fellow author
Karen Hawkins, who voluntarily
added a ten-hour drive
to a cross-country flight
just so I wouldn't have to
drive alone, and who liked
my driving playlist.
And the snacks.

CHAPTER ONE

Clan MacLawry had an old saying that through the years had become, "If ye want to see the face of the devil, look at a Campbell."

There was another MacLawry saying about London and the weak-chinned Sasannach who lived there, Arran MacLawry recalled, but as he currently stood in the center of a Mayfair ballroom, he would keep it to himself. A gaggle of young lasses, all of whom had donned elegantly arching swan masks, strolled by in a flock. He grinned at them, disrupting the formation and sending them, honking in feminine tones, toward the refreshment table.

"Stop that, ye devil."

Arran glanced over at his brother, seated a few feet away and in deep conversation — or so he'd thought — with an elegant owl mask. "I didnae do a thing but smile. Ye said to be friendly, Ranulf."

Ranulf, the Marquis of Glengask, shook his head. Even with his face partly obscured by a black panther half-mask, there wasn't likely a single guest at the Garreton soiree tonight who didn't know precisely who he was. "I said to be polite. Nae brawls, nae insults, and nae sending the wee Sasannach lasses into a frenzy."

"Then likely I should've worn a cow or a pigeon mask, instead of a fox." Or perhaps he shouldn't have attended at all tonight — but then who would keep a watch for Campbells and other unsavory sorts?

The owl beside his brother chuckled. "I don't think the disguise would matter, Arran," she said in her cultured English accent. "You'd still make all the young ladies sit up and take notice."

"I suppose that to be a compliment, Charlotte," he returned, inclining his head at his oldest brother's Sasannach fiancée, Charlotte Hanover, "so I'll say thank ye." At that same moment he spied a splendid peacock mask above a deep violet gown and smiled, but the expression froze as the green and gold swan beside the peacock came into view. *Damnation.* The two young birds joined arms and turned in his direction, but he didn't think they'd spotted him yet. "Yer bonny sister wouldnae be a swan tonight, would she?" he asked Charlotte, slowly straightening from his lean against the wall.

"Yes," Charlotte returned. "Poor thing. I don't think she realized so many others would be wearing swan masks tonight, as well."

"Well, if ye see her and Winnie, tell the lasses I said hello," he said, turning for the door to the main ballroom. "I spy Uncle Myles, and I ken he wanted a word with me."

"Liar," Ranulf said. "And dunnae go far. The Stewarts are expected tonight, and I want ye to make Deirdre Stewart's acquaintance."

Arran stopped dead, though he did duck a bit to stay behind the clutter of masks between him and the green-gold swan. "Deirdre Stewart? The hell ye say."

His older brother didn't look like he was jesting, however. "I've heard she's pleasant enough, and she's but two-and-twenty. And she's the Stewart's niece."

So that was the other reason his brother had told him to stay in London, even after the brawls and his obvious . . . impatience with the rather English way Ranulf had been conducting himself. "That's my duty now, is it?" he asked, unable to keep the growl from his voice.

9

"We've nae met Lord Allen's daughter, so I suppose we'll find oot." The marquis glanced beyond Arran's shoulder. "Yer pretty bird is close by."

Jane Hanover was more like a vulture, circling and waiting for him to succumb to her relentless charm, but Arran wasn't about to stand there and argue while she closed in. He didn't need to wear a fox mask to sense trouble, and Charlotte's eighteen-year-old sister was nothing but. His own sister Rowena's dearest friend or not, she was a debutante, a Sasannach, and a romantic. Arran shuddered, glancing over his shoulder. Devil take him before he let himself be caught up with that.

And then, evidently, there was clan Stewart. There'd been no open warfare between the two clans, and now that he thought about it, over the past week his brother had mentioned them more often than he had the Campbells. And though this was the first time Ranulf had spoken about him and Deirdre in the same sentence, Arran had had more than a hunch it was coming. Politically an alliance would likely fare better if Ranulf himself offered for Deirdre, but as the chief of clan MacLawry had gone and fallen in love with a Sasannach, Arran supposed that left to him to be the sacrificial

MacLawry. And so he could only hope the lass more resembled her mother than she did her frog-faced father, and he could be grateful that no other lass in particular had caught his eye before now.

Off to his left the music for the evening's first waltz began, shaking him back to his present peril. Damnation. Jane Hanover would track him down, inform him that she had no partner for the dance, and he would have to be polite because they were about to become in-laws. Before the music finished he would find himself betrothed — and that would throw a bucket of sour milk into Ranulf's plans, not to mention his own.

A peacock and swan hurried through the doorway behind him. And by God he wasn't yet fool enough to end up leg-shackled to a fresh-faced debutante who found him "ruggedly handsome." Saint Bridget, he didn't even know what that meant. Sidestepping between two groups of guests, he turned again — and walked straight into a red and gold vixen half-mask.

"Sir Fox," she said, a surprised smile curving her mouth below the mask.

"There he is, Jane!" he heard his sister, Winnie, exclaim.

"Lady Vixen," he returned, matching her smile with one of his own. "I dunnae sup-

11

pose ye'd care to dance this waltz with one of yer own kind?"

Shadowed green eyes gazed at him for a half-dozen heartbeats, while his doom moved in behind him. One of his dooms. How many of them was a man of seven-and-twenty supposed to shoulder? "I'd be delighted, Sir Fox," the vixen said, saving him with not even a moment to spare.

He held out his hand, and gold-gloved fingers gripped his. Moving as swiftly as he could without dragging her — or giving the appearance that he'd fled someone else — he escorted her out to the dance floor, slid his hand around her trim waist, and stepped with a vixen into the waltz.

His partner was petite, he noted belatedly, the top of her head just brushing his chin. And she had a welcoming smile. Other than that, she might have been Queen Caroline, for all he knew. Or cared. She wasn't Jane Hanover, and at the moment that was all that mattered.

"Are we to waltz in silence, then?" she asked, London aristocrat in her voice. "Two foxes among herds of swans and bears and lions?"

Arran grinned. "When I looked at the dessert table I was surprised nae to see baskets of corn for all the birds."

12

She nodded, her face lifted to meet his gaze. "Poor dears. Evidently Lady Jersey wore a particularly lovely swan mask to this same soiree last year, and it prompted something of a frenzy."

As she glanced about the crowded ballroom, he took her in again. Petite, slender, light green eyes, and hair . . . He wasn't certain what color to call it. A long and curling mass straying from a knot, it looked like what would result if a painter ran a brown-tipped brush through gold and red in succession — a deep, rich mix of colors that together didn't have a name.

He blinked. While he'd been known to wax poetic, he generally didn't do so over a Sasannach lass's hair. "Why is it that Lady Vixen didnae already have a partner fer a waltz?" he asked.

"I only just arrived," she returned in her silky voice. "Why was Sir Fox fleeing a peacock?"

So she'd noticed that. "I wasnae fleeing the peacock. That bird's my sister. It's the swan who terrifies me."

The green gaze held his, and he found himself wishing he could see more of her face. As a Highlander and a MacLawry, his ability to assess someone's expression swiftly and accurately had saved his life on several occasions. An abrupt thought occurred to him. Ranulf had said the Stewarts were attending this evening. What if this vixen was Lady Deirdre? Was she taking his measure as much as he wished to take hers?

"All swans," she countered, "or just that one? Do they not have swans in the Highlands?"

Of course she knew where he was from; even if all of Mayfair hadn't been buzzing about the MacLawrys brawling their way through drawing rooms over the past few weeks, his brogue would have made it fairly obvious. Unlike his sister, Rowena, he made no attempt to disguise or stifle his accent. Being a MacLawry was a matter of pride, as far as he was concerned. "Aye, they do have swans there, though nae many. It's easier to avoid them in the Highlands, where a lad knows the lay of the land and there's more space to maneuver."

"I had no idea swans were so deadly."

"Aye. They'll catch hold of ye when ye're nae looking, and they mate fer life."

She laughed. "Unlike foxes?"

Did foxes mate for life? He couldn't even recall at the moment. After a fortnight spent hunting for more human dangers, both male and female, a discussion of wildlife — even an allegorical one — seemed . . . refreshing.

14

"This fox is nae looking for a thing but a partner for the waltz," he returned, smiling back at her. There. If this was Lady Deirdre, she now knew he wasn't pursuing some other lass. "And the vixen?"

"I was looking for a friend of mine. An interlude with a fellow fox is an unexpected . . . distraction. And if you say something flattering, I won't even be insulted that you only asked me to dance in order to avoid a bird."

Was that a cut? Or a jest? The fact that he couldn't be certain of which it was intrigued him. Sassanach lasses in his experience and with very few exceptions knew all about the weather and could discuss it for hours, but he couldn't give them credit for much else. "Someaught flattering," he mused aloud, trying to decide how much effort to go to. He meant to approach a marriage agreement from a position of strength, after all. True, perhaps he didn't dread the notion as much as he had five minutes earlier, but he wasn't ready to surrender. Not by a long space. A MacLawry didn't beg for an alliance. "Ye dance gracefully," he settled on.

She laughed again, though it didn't sound as inviting, this time. "Well. Believe it or not, you aren't the first Scotsman to say so.

You measure quite equally with the lot of them."

Arran was fairly certain he'd just been insulted. He hid a scowl, not that she'd be able to see it behind the fox mask. If she *was* Deirdre, perhaps he needed to be more . . . charming, or some such. Though she might have introduced herself before she began pecking at him. "I've known ye fer two minutes, lass," he commented, pulling her a breath closer. "I weighed saying ye had a lovely pelt and gracefully pointed ears, but I didnae ken ye'd appreciate that."

"And why wouldn't a vixen like to hear that a fox admires her pelt?"

"Because ye're nae a vixen, any more than I'm a fox. Ye chose nae to wear a swan mask, which at least sets ye apart from a dozen other lasses here tonight, but I'm wearing a fox mask because my sister handed it to me. I reckon I'd rather be a wolf, truth be told." Yes, the family generally called him the clever one, and Rowena had seemed pleased enough at the choice that he'd gone along with it, but it was a well-painted piece of papier-mâché — and nothing more.

"I wanted to be a vixen," she said after a moment. "My father wanted me to be a swan."

Now *this* was interesting. "And yet here

ye are, nae a swan." She also was a young woman, perhaps three or four years older than Rowena — the age he knew Deirdre Stewart to be — with an attractive mouth, lips that seemed naturally to want to smile, and shadowed green eyes that he imagined crinkled at the corners. If Arran hadn't had both hands occupied with the waltz, he would have been fighting the urge to remove her mask, so he could see the whole of her face, to know if the parts were equal to the sum.

Her lips curved again. "And *that* is a compliment, Sir Fox." She tilted her head, the gold lights in her hair catching the chandelier light. "Or do you wish me to call you Sir Wolf?"

"I'd answer to Arran," he returned, grinning back at her. She didn't react to his name, but then she likely already knew who he was. London Society didn't boast many lads fresh from the Highlands.

"Tell me why the swan — the one pretending not to gaze at you from over by the refreshment table — terrifies you, Arran," the vixen said.

He shrugged. "She's my sister's closest friend, and my oldest brother is betrothed to *her* sister."

"Ah," the vixen returned, her lush gold

17

and red gown swirling against his legs. "The moment she discovered her future brother-in-law had an unmarried brother, she began dreaming about a double wedding."

"Aye. Someaught like that. I've nae wish to break her heart, but I'll nae end up marrying her to avoid seeing her pout, either."

"You must be quite the dancer, if your waltz causes ladies to become spontaneously engaged. Someone should have warned me."

"Tease if ye like, lass, but I'm nae here to get tangled into a debutante's fairy tale." God and Saint Bridget knew there were more than enough bonnie lasses awaiting his pleasure in the Highlands, and none of them with silly Sasannach sensibilities about romance and danger. When Ranulf, the chief of clan MacLawry, married his English bride, the family would have more than enough gentle southern blood brought into the mix. And evidently he was to be aimed at a Stewart, anyway.

"If you're not here to marry, then what brings you to London? The mild weather?"

Arran snorted. "If it's nae someaught that can knock ye to yer knees, it's nae weather. I'm only here to keep an eye on my brother and sister. And to be polite."

He sent a glance over where the big black

18

panther waltzed with his owl. With Ranulf distracted by a pair of pretty hazel eyes and Rowena enamored of everything English, one of the MacLawrys needed to keep a wary eye open for Campbells. That was why he'd left their youngest brother, Bear, behind to see to Glengask while he rode down to London. Because William Campbell declaring that clan Campbell would recognize a truce with the MacLawrys was just words. Very fragile ones. Arran had seen enough bloody deeds to recognize the difference.

" 'To be polite'?" she repeated. "An . . . interesting goal. Are you generally not polite, then?"

It likely wasn't a coincidence that she'd several times now decided to comment on the most barbed portion of his various statements. She was needling him — and on purpose. He liked it. "I'm a very polite lad," he said aloud, "except to those who dunnae deserve a kind word."

Amused green eyes looked up to meet his gaze again. "And where do I fall in this hierarchy?" she asked.

Whoever this lass was, she was no timid flower. "Ye've some Highlands blood in yer veins, do ye nae, lass?"

She lowered her head for a heartbeat. "I

do, at that. But what makes you say so?"

With a crescendo the waltz ended. Arran stood there for a moment, briefly wishing he hadn't named himself the designated watchdog of his family. Then he would have been free to continue this conversation somewhere more intimate. "Save me a quadrille or someaught, and I'll tell ye," he offered instead.

She belatedly untangled herself from his arms. "I would, but there are enough men here that that wouldn't be . . . seemly. Another time, perhaps?"

"Aye. Another time. But at least tell me yer name, lass."

A slow smile curved her attractive mouth once more, and this time the muscles across his abdomen tightened in response. For God's sake, he hoped she would say Deirdre Stewart. Then he could put this odd heightened awareness to instinct. Taking a step closer again, she put a hand on his shoulder and lifted up on her toes. "I think, Sir Fox," she murmured, her warm lips brushing his ear, "that you should call me . . . Lady Vixen."

With that she moved back, then turned and walked away. She sent him a single glance over her shoulder before she vanished into the sea of sparkling masks. *Hm.* Whatever the devil that had been about, he felt in need of a cold swim in the nearest loch. His nether MacLawry felt nearly at half-staff, just from having his ear nibbled on. In public. Striding to one side of the room, he captured a glass of vodka from a footman and downed it.

"Who was that, Arran?" his sister asked, appearing beside him to grip his left arm.

He shook himself. If Winnie was here, then Jane Hanover would be directly on her heels. "An old friend," he improvised, inclining his head as the swan hurried up behind the peacock. At least he'd avoided waltzing with her. "Did anyone write his name on yer wee card fer this quadrille, Lady Jane? And do ye have a country dance left fer yer own brother, Winnie?"

Jane flushed beneath her ornate mask and yellow hair. "Well, I — yes, but — Actually, I . . . was hoping you —"

If he didn't stop her floundering, she was likely to injure herself. "Hand over yer card, then, and I'll scribble doon my name," he offered, trying to decide to whom he would say he'd promised the damned second waltz when she asked about it — and she *would* ask.

With an audible sigh the younger Hanover sister handed him her card and pencil.

She'd been claimed for nearly every other dance, he noted, including the second waltz. Thank Lucifer. No wonder she'd been in such determined pursuit of him earlier. Evidently he owed Lady Vixen more of a debt than he'd even realized.

Stifling a sigh of his own, he wrote down his name and returned the card to her, then did the same with his own sister. Rowena still wore the excited smile she'd donned almost from the moment she'd handed him his fox mask yesterday. She had to know that he wasn't interested in her young friend. Why, then, did she seem to be encouraging Jane's pursuit of him? He was going to have to have a chat with her — and soon. The last thing he needed was two of his siblings throwing women at him, especially when he felt obligated to favor Ranulf's selection.

"I still don't understand how *she* could be an old friend," Jane said, her voice a touch shrill. "Winnie said the MacLawrys don't like the Campbells."

Arran jolted back to attention. *What was this?* "What are ye talking aboot, lass?" he demanded.

Jane took a half step backward. "The . . . your friend in the vixen mask. You said you were friends. *You* said it. Not me."

22

"I —"

Winnie nudged him in the ribs with her sharp elbow. *"Bràthair."*

He ignored that. There was a time for him to be polite, and then there was the Campbells. "Do ye know who she is, Jane?"

"Everyone knows that's Mary Campbell. Her grandfather is the Duke of Alkirk."

Rowena gasped, but Arran clenched his jaw against the roar that wanted to erupt from his chest. The charming, intriguing Lady Vixen wasn't Deirdre Stewart. She was a Campbell. And not just any Campbell, either. She was the granddaughter of William Campbell, the chief of clan Campbell. *The* Campbell.

No wonder she hadn't given her name.

But she *had* danced with him, and jested with him. From her point of view, the petite thing likely thought she was making fun of him. She'd certainly made a fool of him.

"What's afoot?" Ranulf's deep voice came, as he and Charlotte Hanover walked up behind them. "The Stewarts have just arrived. Who was the vixen, Arran?"

Arran took a breath. "If ye cannae be bothered to be concerned over the Campbells," he returned, unwilling to be called a fool by his brother, "ye leave it to me to keep an eye on 'em. The vixen was the

Campbell's granddaughter."

He'd rarely seen Ranulf surprised, but that did it. The oldest MacLawry sibling shoved his panther half-mask up over his forehead. The face beneath was perhaps more agreeable, but at least as fierce. Dark blue eyes narrowed, and he lifted his hand as if he meant to seize Arran by the lapel. "I told ye to behave," he said evenly, his voice low and hard.

Arran held his brother and clan chief's gaze until Ranulf lowered his hand again. Neither of them was known for backing down, but this felt more like a mutual decision not to make a scene — another scene — in the middle of a Mayfair ballroom. "Ye told me to be polite," he countered, "and so I was."

"I dunnae recall giving my permission for any of my kin to dance with a Campbell," Ranulf retorted.

And this from a man set on something at least as scandalous as dancing with a Campbell — taking an English bride into the Highlands. Yes, Charlotte Hanover had more spleen and wit than most Sasannach, but before this wee holiday in London, Ranulf would have burned his own bed before he'd share it with an English lass.

"Ye're the one who went and made a truce

with the Campbells," Arran pointed out, reflecting that a few short weeks ago he would have been choosing his words much more carefully. Evidently he owed Charlotte some thanks for improving his brother's temperament, now that he considered it.

"So we could stop killing each other, Arran. Nae so ye could waltz with one of 'em."

"And do ye know a better way to test the Campbell wind? Because I dunnae believe this peace'll last the week, myself."

Of course his argument only worked as long as Jane and Winnie didn't blurt out that he'd had no idea who the vixen was. Shaking his head, he held out his hand to young Jane as the music for their quadrille began. Evidently he preferred being accused of doing something wrong to doing something foolish.

At the same time, he truly *didn't* think the truce would last. None ever had before now. And so he'd made a point of learning which of the Campbell men were about, their appearance, and their disposition. He knew their allies, and he generally knew when any of them was within twenty feet of his brother or sister. But then the trouble had come from somewhere he didn't expect.

And vixen, fox, wolf, or Campbell, tomorrow he meant to go hunting. Mary Campbell was not allowed to think she'd made a fool of a MacLawry. Especially not when he was in London to look after his family. Especially not when for a moment he'd thought her smile and her wit attractive. That was when he'd thought her someone else.

"Where's this Deirdre Stewart ye want me leg-shackled to, then?" he asked brusquely. "Let's get on with it before blood begins spilling again."

"What?" Rowena asked, wincing as Jane made an abrupt sound like a wounded cat.

"I didnae say ye had to marry her," Ranulf countered, covering half his frown as he lowered his panther mask again. "Nae until I've a word or two with Viscount Allen, anyway. Go dance yer quadrille, and stay clear of Campbells while I go speak with the Stewarts."

At least Ranulf hadn't said he should bare his legs or show his teeth so Lord Allen and his daughter could view him to best advantage. If the two clans required a marriage to seal an alliance he would give them one. But at the same time he wondered if waltzing with Mary Campbell and then tracking her down tomorrow would be the last independent act permitted him. *That* didn't sit particularly well. As a man accustomed to action, he felt far more comfortable with the idea of giving Lady Mary a piece of his mind than with having tea with his little finger held out for Lady Deirdre's benefit. But the clan came first. It always did.

"Your aunt Felicia even commented that you put all the other young ladies to shame last night, Mary," Joanna Campbell, Lady Fendarrow, said with a smile, as she strolled into the breakfast room. "Even with her own Dorcas attending. Thank heavens I convinced your father that a swan mask would never suit you."

Smiling back, Mary tilted her cheek up for a kiss as her father joined them. She didn't recall that particular conversation, and likely neither did Walter Campbell, the Marquis of Fendarrow, but if her mother wanted credit for such a small thing, she, at least, was quite willing to let her have it. "It was a grand evening," she agreed.

Her mother paused at the sideboard. "That's all you have to say?"

Mary busied herself with pouring her father a cup of tea. "What else should I say?"

"Well, for instance, who was that tall, broad-shouldered gentleman with whom you waltzed?"

Drat. "Do you mean Harry Dawson? You

know him, Mother." She sipped at her own cup.

Her father sat at the head of the table and leaned forward to pull his tea closer. "She means the man in the fox mask. Arran MacLawry."

The tea she swallowed went into her lungs. Mary began coughing, choking, trying to draw in a dry breath until Gerns the butler came forward to pound her between the shoulder blades. Her mother stood frozen, a slice of toast held delicately in a pair of tongs, while her father coolly sipped at his own tea.

"Thank you, Gerns," she rasped, motioning the butler away again.

"Of course, my lady," he intoned, returning to his station at her father's shoulder.

"MacLawry?" the marquis prompted.

"He . . . surprised me," she finally managed, still sputtering.

"Hm."

Mary scowled at her father. "He *did* surprise me. I was crossing the room to see Elizabeth, and he ran into me. When he asked me to waltz, I couldn't refuse him without . . . insulting him."

"You could easily have said you already had a partner," her mother countered, slight color returning to her generally pale cheeks.

"I daresay your father or any of your cousins would have been pleased to dance with you if you'd so much as wiggled a finger at them. And what about that handsome Roderick MacAllister? You know your father expressly wanted you to dance with Lord Delaveer."

"I *did* dance with Roderick. I dance with him quite frequently."

"A country dance. That barely signifies."

"And I certainly have no qualms about insulting a MacLawry," her father put in. "Particularly in favor of a MacAllister."

"I do, Walter. The MacLawrys are dangerous beasts. Didn't you see that brawl they caused at the Evanstone ball? They nearly killed Lord Berling. Your own cousin."

"My second cousin," Lord Fendarrow amended. "And a fool. But yes, you are correct, my dear. You didn't need to insult him, but you shouldn't have danced with him, either, Mary."

Mary nodded. "There is a truce, though, is there not? Arnold and Charles and all my other cousins aren't going to murder Arran MacLawry for dancing with me, are they? Because I don't think he had the slightest idea who I was."

And she'd rather enjoyed that, actually. To him she'd been Lady Vixen, and they'd

29

simply chatted. Yes, she'd needled him a bit, but then he was a MacLawry. He hadn't become flustered or annoyed or defensive at her barbs, though. Rather, he'd shown more wit and humor than she'd expected — after all, she'd grown up on tales of the goat-faced, hairy-knuckled MacLawrys.

She wished she could have seen more of his face, because his mouth with that cynically amused quirk of his lips, the way the lean fox visage seemed to fit his features — he didn't seem remotely goat-faced. In fact, he intrigued her, just a little.

"To be perfectly clear," her father said, shaking her out of thoughts of black, wind-blown hair and a lean, strong jaw, "you aren't to dance with Arran MacLawry or Ranulf MacLawry, or Munro MacLawry if he should venture down from Glengask. Nor are you to befriend Rowena MacLawry. Or the Mackles or Lenoxes or MacTiers or any other of their clan or allies."

"I —"

"I know you're aware of your place, Mary," he continued over her interruption. "I know you've been told a hundred times that as my daughter, as your grandfather's granddaughter, you have a value to both allies and enemies. It wasn't as . . . vital when the MacLawrys kept to the Highlands, but they're here in London now. And simply because my father decided we should at least pretend some diplomacy with the Marquis of Glengask doesn't mean *you* need to do so."

"I understand, Father," Mary said hurriedly, hoping to avoid being bombarded by the entire speech. Because she hadn't heard it a hundred times; she'd heard it a thousand times. "Truly."

"Good. Because the present circumstances have provided us with an opportunity we don't mean to let pass by."

"An opportunity that hinges on you," her mother put in, finally taking a seat. "Even though I was married by one-and-twenty, it seems your . . . stubbornness and your grandfather's indulgence have now actually benefited us."

"Indeed," the marquis resumed. "Your previous reluctance to marry hasn't helped ease any clan tensions. But your grandfather agrees that this truce can be used to our advantage."

So far it didn't seem to be much of an advantage for her, except for one waltz with a man she would otherwise have been forbidden to look at through a spyglass. Then she realized just which opportunity they must be referring to. "You're setting me after Roderick MacAllister," she stated, her heart bumping into her throat.

"This truce won't last," her father returned matter-of-factly. "The Campbell's favorite granddaughter marrying the MacAllister's son will give us the numbers to challenge the MacLawrys, and the MacAllisters wouldn't make that bargain, sweet as it is, without this cease-fire. We must strike now." He leaned forward, putting a hand over her teacup before she could lift it for another sip. "And that is why you are not to risk upending this truce by waltzing with Arran MacLawry."

Ice trailed down her spine. Yes, she could have avoided a dance with a MacLawry — if she'd wished to do so. When she'd realized he had no idea who she was, she'd felt . . . excited, as if she were doing something forbidden and dangerous. As opposed to something . . . disquieting. Roderick MacAllister was pleasant enough, and she supposed at the back of her thoughts she'd known he was one of her beaux, along with every male cousin in the Campbell clan. But that didn't erase the fact that there had been something stirring about waltzing with a rogue.

Her father released the cup of tea and sat back again. "We likely should have had this conversation three years ago when you had your debut."

"We did," the marchioness countered, a fine line appearing between her brows. "But who would ever have expected the Mac-Lawrys to come down from the Highlands? Not I, certainly."

"Not to argue," Mary said slowly, "but if we are attempting to keep this truce with Lord Glengask and his clan, should we not be more . . . friendly toward them? Perhaps with a dance or two we can avoid any future bloodshed. Surely that would be worth the risk."

"Didn't you hear your father? If Charles Calder or Arnold Haws sees you partnered with a MacLawry, you'll be causing a fight. If you're seen favoring that rogue over Lord Delaveer, you will be jeopardizing the most significant alliance of the past hundred years."

There had already been a fight — several of them, actually — between the Campbells and the MacLawrys this Season. In fact, she had no idea how Lord Glengask and her second cousin George Gerdens-Daily had managed to converse long enough to decide they should attempt to avoid killing each other. But they had, and now no one seemed to know quite what to do. Or rather,

her family had decided to use the few moments of peace to nearly double their strength in anticipation of when the truce fell apart. And she was the linchpin.

She pushed to her feet. "So I am not to dance with a MacLawry, and not to be rude to a MacAllister. I believe I can manage that." Mary came around the table to pat her father on the shoulder. "I'm off to find a new hat, then, and I will be going to luncheon with Elizabeth and Kathleen."

"Oh, give my best wishes to Kathleen for her mother, dear," the marchioness said. "I do hope she'll be recovered enough to attend the Dailys' recital on Thursday."

"I'll tell her." Mary kissed her mother's cheek, then made her way out to the foyer to collect her maid, Crawford, and the blue bonnet that matched her walking dress.

"Are you certain you don't want to take the coach, my lady?" Gerns asked, as the butler helped her with her matching blue shawl.

"We're only walking to Bond Street," she returned with a smile, deciding she could use a few moments to clear her head. Because if her parents couldn't stop talking about one silly waltz with Arran MacLawry, her friends would wish to discuss nothing else.

Of course she knew that logically she shouldn't have danced with that lean, dark-haired fox half-mask. But for heaven's sake, to say that she wasn't allowed to waltz with a gentleman she'd never even met before simply because some man she hadn't yet agreed to marry might be angry? Ridiculous.

Of course marrying her would be a political coup, a way into clan Campbell's higher echelons. She'd known that for what seemed like forever. Just the same way she knew that her male cousins and the potential Campbell allies paid her special attention because of her bloodline and not because she was particularly charming or lovely. But Arran MacLawry had danced with her for the simple reason that they'd worn matching masks. It was utterly . . . mad that everyone had begun roaring and stomping because of a coincidence of costume.

Perhaps next her father would decide she couldn't waltz with anyone dressed in blue. Or black. Or would it be her husband who dictated that? For heaven's sake. She hoped she would at least have the chance to chat with Roderick before her family dragged her to a church. All she knew about him at the moment was that he danced tolerably and had a weakness for stinky cheeses. There was a vast difference between amiable chatting and attempting to discover whether a man would make a husband.

"Lady Mary, are we late?" Crawford panted from beside her, her skirts clutched in one hand.

Mary immediately slowed her pace. "I'm so sorry, Crawford. My mind was elsewhere."

"Was yer mind on a masquerade ball, by any chance?" a deep, rolling brogue asked from off to her left.

Starting, she whipped around. "Arran."

He leaned against a tree trunk, calm and still as if he'd been there for hours. A predator waiting for his prey. Black hair lifted off his temple in the light breeze. With the fox mask on, his parts — jaw, mouth, shadowed blue eyes — had hinted at a handsome face. Without the mask, adding in high cheekbones, a straight nose, and slightly arched eyebrows, he was a dream — a dark Highlands prince who likely ate wildcats for breakfast.

"Aye. Arran MacLawry," he affirmed, finally straightening. "And how do ye do this fine morning, Mary Campbell?"

CHAPTER TWO

Finding Mathering House, the Mayfair residence of the Marquis of Fendarrow, had been a simple matter even for a relative stranger to London. It stood large and white and proud on the corner of Curzon Street and Queen Street, directly across from the even larger Campbell House. Arran briefly wondered if the Campbell's eldest son and heir enjoyed seeing what he would one day inherit, or if he resented that the Campbell showed no sign of being ready to turn up his toes.

But whether the Campbell was presently in the Highlands or not, Arran could tell just from the pricking of the hairs at the back of his neck that he was not in friendly territory. In fact, it was entirely possible that he'd lost his bloody mind. For the devil's sake, he was supposed to be on his best behavior while Ranulf negotiated him into a marriage, and instead he'd deliberately gone looking for a Campbell.

He had his reasons, of course; last night Mary Campbell had made a fool of him. She'd taunted him and teased him, and had likely reported to her father how easily a MacLawry could be led about by the nose. That could not be allowed to stand. It put him — and every MacLawry and ally — in a position of weakness. Without a balance of power, there would be no reason for the Campbells to continue the truce, and no incentive for the Stewarts to ally with the MacLawrys. And he was not about to allow clan MacLawry to be brought down by a pair of pretty green eyes.

Even if in the sunlight those eyes looked the color of moss beneath a waterfall. Even if her long, curling hair took on a golden bronze that continued to defy description. He drew a breath. She looked like a princess of some fairy realm, a lass about whom Shakespeare would have waxed poetic. *Sweet Saint Bridget and all the heavenly angels.*

"I thought we might walk in the same direction fer a bit, if ye've no objection," he drawled, mentally shaking himself. This was about what she'd attempted to do, not how she looked. Deirdre Stewart had perfectly pleasant features and fine dark hair, and he'd been relieved to discover that she didn't squint or stammer. *That* was what — who — he needed to keep in mind. His almost betrothed.

Mary glanced over her shoulder as if looking for reinforcements. As he'd followed her down three streets before making his presence known, he was fairly assured that other than her well-seasoned companion, she was alone — a position in which no one would ever find a MacLawry female. He couldn't imagine permitting his sister to venture into public without at least one armed man to protect her. The lapse made the Campbells all the more foolish.

"Well, lass?" he pursued. "Dunnae ye at least have a slap or a good set-down for a MacLawry? Or is the joke nae as amusing now that I ken who ye are?"

Mary tilted her head as she studied his face for a long moment. He had no idea what she thought to see; everyone in the Highlands knew that the second MacLawry was the current heir to the Marquis of Glengask, that he'd served four years in the British army on the Continent, that he was a crack shot, that he wasn't to be trifled with. Except that she had trifled with him, damn it all.

"I'm on my way to Bond Street to meet

some friends," she said after a moment. "You're welcome to escort me. Do Mac-Lawrys purchase bonnets?"

"Nae me personally," he returned, hiding his surprise and falling in beside her when she started off again. "My sister's been known to wear them with some frequency."

"Your younger sister, yes? The peacock mask from last night."

Arran clenched his jaw, fighting the deep-rooted mistrust in having a conversation with a Campbell. Especially when the conversation turned to his family. But *he'd* approached *her* — twice, now. "Aye," he said aloud, nodding. "Rowena. The youngest among us. She turned eighteen just a few weeks past."

"And there's your oldest brother, Lord Glengask. Are you the second or the third brother?"

"The second. Munro's between Rowena and me."

"He's the one they — you — call Bear."

"Aye. And ye're the only child of Fendarrow, who happens to be the heir to the Duke of Alkirk." There. He could recite her lineage, too, now that he knew who she was. When he glanced sideways at her, she was already looking at him, a half smile on her oval face. "What do ye find so amusing

40

then, lass?"

"It's just that this conversation feels a bit like a saber dance."

"Ye're the one who didnae tell the truth last night," he returned. Perhaps she wasn't accustomed to conversations as careful as chess matches, but *he* was. "I gave ye *my* name."

"And if I'd given you my name, we would never have finished that waltz. Something would have happened, and you would have ended up in a fight with my cousins. So I saved you by withholding the truth, Arran MacLawry."

"That's the way ye mean to view it, then? That ye did me a favor by flirting with me and naming yerself Lady Vixen?"

She stopped to face him, jabbing a finger into his chest. "*You* called me that. I simply chose not to disagree with you. Don't try to turn this into a battle, when all I did was try to avoid one. On your behalf, I might add."

Hm. He'd expected a wilting flower, a lass who would be cowed and frightened once she realized he'd discovered her identity. But Mary Campbell had her chin lifted, and her forefinger still stuck into his ribs. For such a petite thing she had better than a full portion of courage, to stand toe-to-toe with him.

Arran tilted his head. "Then ye want me to thank ye, I suppose?"

The finger she had dug into his sternum twitched, then abruptly retreated. "No. You don't need to thank me." Slowly she turned to face the row of shops again and resumed her walk. "I was only attempting to explain why I deceived you. Or rather, neglected to tell you the truth."

He caught up to her, sending a glance at Mary's older, frowny companion. "So ye had my best interest in mind, did ye?"

"I —"

"I appreciate it, I suppose, considering how many of yer cousins were at the party last night. I might have got my nose broken. That would make the lasses at home weep."

"Oh, please," she retorted, a chuckle bursting from her chest.

His own mouth curved in a smile before he even realized it. "But the question I have fer ye, Lady Mary Campbell, is why?"

She actually looked startled. "Why would I wish to keep a brawl from beginning?"

"Aye. I've spent my entire life spoiling fer a good fight with a Campbell or a Gerdens or a Daily. I've thrown my share of punches. And I know fer a fact that most of yer kin would dance a jig on my grave."

42

"There's a truce," she said, though she didn't disagree with his statement. "Your own brother arranged it with George Gerdens-Daily, and my grandfather agreed to it."

Arran wished he were facing her so he could see her expression more clearly. "So if I'd stumbled across ye a fortnight ago ye would have stomped on my toe and told me to go to the devil?"

Mary Campbell stopped again, putting her hands on her slender hips and glaring at him with her moss-colored eyes. "I'm tempted to do that at this very moment," she snapped. "Not because you're a Mac-Lawry, either. Simply because you're being rude and provoking."

He narrowed his eyes. "I —"

"How should I know what I would have done a fortnight ago?" she continued over his protest. "Everything's different now. What would *you* have done if you'd danced with me a fortnight ago and realized I was the Campbell's granddaughter?"

For a long moment he gazed at her. The answer should have been clear and simple. Whatever truce Ranulf had managed, the Campbells had burned out their own cotters, bullied their allies to do the same, and used the profits they'd made by turning the vacated land over to sheep to build new alliances in England. Their sway in the Highlands might have waned, but elsewhere they were as strong as ever. And they were the enemy.

But was she the enemy? He looked at all five feet and a few inches of her. Aye, she was a Campbell, and one with a temper, too. At the same time, she was also a very pretty young lady with an air of confidence about her that most ladies seemed to lose when confronted by an actual Highlands male. Deirdre had barely looked him in the eye during their brief conversation last night. He couldn't even recall what color her eyes were, and he had a reason to remember that.

"I'd have danced with ye, I ken," he answered, then grinned. "And then tossed a few of yer cousins over my shoulder later fer fun."

Her shoulders beneath her pretty blue walking dress lowered. "Well. I suppose hat shopping to be a poor substitute for Campbell-thrashing, but if you'd care to join me, I shan't object." She gestured at the door of the small shop behind him.

Mary half expected Arran MacLawry to announce that he'd had his fill of bantering with a Campbell for one day, and that he'd

44

truly only tracked her down to inform her that he knew who she was. She half hoped he would, because she had other things to consider, and he was . . . distracting. Instead, he turned around and pulled open the door, holding it for her and a clearly concerned Crawford. Her maid wasn't Scottish, but she certainly knew to whom Mary should or should not be speaking. This tall, lean, black-haired devil was clearly in the "should not" category. In fact, he was at the very top of that particular list.

Moving past him into the shop and hoping that it was indeed a milliner's, for a moment Mary wished he would close the door on Crawford so she could ask him some questions without worrying over whether every word of the conversation would be reported to her father. But for heaven's sake, she'd never met a member of a rival clan before. She'd been raised in southern England for that very reason. And now she found herself excessively curious, even when she'd been expressly ordered not to be.

"I thought all the MacLawry men had cloven feet and breathed hellfire," she noted, stopping to peruse some hair ribbons. That was a lucky thing; for all the attention she'd paid, this might have been a cutlery shop. And the two of them in a room

45

filled with knives would be unwise.

"Nae," he returned. "It's ten toes and air fer the lot of us." He spoke with the same deep, teasing brogue he'd used during the waltz — when he hadn't known who she was. Did that mean they were on friendly terms again? She rather hoped so, because she didn't generally converse with men about whom she knew so little. Or ones as fierce as Arran MacLawry was reputed to be.

"That information might have spared me some nightmares as a child." She held up two ribbons. "Which do you prefer?"

"The light green one," he said promptly. "It matches yer eyes and brings oot the red in yer hair."

Something about the way he said it — along with the fact that this man had no reason in the world to flatter or humor her — sent pleasant little shivers down her spine. "You seem to have thought that through very thoroughly," she commented, draping the green ribbon over Crawford's arm and discarding the yellow one.

"It's the truth. How long should a man take to consider it?" he said, shrugging. Then he grinned. "Aside from that, my sister says I'm the only brother with taste in other than what goes down his gullet."

Mary laughed. He said it so matter-of-factly. "We'll see about that." She produced a swatch of yellow and white muslin from her reticule. "I need a hat to match this. It's for a walking dress." She sent him another glance. "Unless this isn't manly enough for you."

His smile deepened. "The more manly a lad, the less likely he is to complain over toting a lass's reticule." He took the material, their fingers brushing as he did so. The touch unsettled her, like the moments before lightning struck on a stormy day. She'd felt it last night, as well, when they'd waltzed. But today it seemed more pronounced. Perhaps because now they both knew to whom they were speaking.

Behind her Crawford made a choking sound, and she realized they both still held the muslin. Swiftly she released it, wiping her fingers into her skirt, and turned to see the maid staring at her. "We should be getting back, my lady," Crawford said in a too loud voice. "Your dear mother, Lady Fendarrow, will be wondering where you've gotten to."

It was more likely that Joanna Campbell would be wondering whether her only child had lost her mind. But from the expression on Arran's face, he was aware as she was

47

that it would be an excuse to escape his company. And she certainly didn't wish to be seen as a coward. She was a Campbell, after all. And so her desire to remain had nothing to do with the fact that she was enjoying herself, that most men of her acquaintance didn't challenge her wits or question her reasoning, that here she felt a certain . . . thrill both at the notion of speaking with a MacLawry and at the way this lean, tall, devilish-handsome man had gone well out of his way to find her.

"Mother isn't expecting me until after luncheon," she said. "And we've only just arrived here."

"So ye're nae afraid of me?" she heard him murmur, and she shook her head.

"Should I be?"

"Today? Nae."

"But you're to lunch with Lord Delaveer, my lady. Your father would be most angry if he —"

"I am not," she returned firmly. "You know quite well that I'm lunching with Lord Delaveer on Thursday."

"Delaveer?" Arran took up, his brow lowering. "Roderick MacAllister." He paused, assessing her again. "Ah."

Mary glared at Crawford. She should be furious that the maid had revealed a Campbell alliance before it was finalized, but at this moment she felt more annoyed that Arran would likely leave now. "That is Thursday," she said succinctly, her gaze on his face. "It has nothing to do with today."

Arran sent a glance between her and Crawford, then squared his shoulders. "Well, then. Let's find ye a hat, lass."

It meant something that he'd elected to remain rather than run off to tell Lord Glengask that the Campbells and MacAllisters were negotiating an alliance — because he had definitely realized that something of the kind was afoot. She could see it in his eyes. But he *had* stayed, and she liked that. Blinking, she turned to the rack of bonnets.

She spied one she liked almost immediately, a straw hat with a narrow brim and a flourish of yellow silk daisies with green silk leaves. Instead of selecting it, though, she made a show of trying on a dozen different unsuitable chapeaux.

"So are ye avoiding that hat because ye wish me to discover it," Arran finally asked, indicating the one she'd been trying not to look at, "or because ye cannae think of another way to keep me aboot this morning?"

He certainly wasn't at all timid about speaking his mind. "You went to the trouble

49

of finding me. I thought it impolite to give the impression that your assistance wasn't appreciated."

With an amused snort he took the hat down from its peg and handed it to her. "Then I suppose I feel appreciated."

Trying on the hat, Mary faced the large mirror that stood in the corner. At the edge of the reflection she caught him gazing at her. For a long moment they simply . . . looked.

For heaven's sake he was handsome, with that unruly black hair that badly needed a trim, light blue eyes that couldn't quite disguise the sharp intelligence behind them, and that mouth that seemed to want to smile far more often than she'd thought possible for a MacLawry. Her cousin Charles Calder had once accused the Mac-Lawry brothers of strutting about like the last Highland princes. They were that, she supposed, admitting to herself what no other Campbell ever would.

After all, the MacLawrys had the largest property in the Highlands. And where most of the other clans, hers included, had been forced to sell off their land, turn out their own cotters, and exchange their people for Cheviot sheep, the MacLawrys had resisted. They'd paid for that stubbornness, as well,

50

with the death of Arran's own father, school-houses burned down, and of course the hostilities between them and the surrounding clans. Her grandfather had called the MacLawry lads "arrogant, stubborn rogues" who would rather spill blood than admit to being wrong.

"Have ye ever been to the Highlands, lass?" he asked abruptly, blinking and then turning away from her reflection.

"Of course I have. I spent a fortnight there, spring before last." She'd wanted to stay longer, but her family had deemed it too dangerous. Pulling off the hat and rather annoyed at her own contrary line of thought, she handed the thing over to Crawford and fixed her hair.

"But ye were raised English."

She couldn't tell if he meant to imply that she wasn't truly Scottish, or if he was genuinely curious. But she didn't like it, regardless. "I was raised outside of Scotland," she said slowly, "because my parents and my grandfather were concerned over my safety. Because Alkirk is but fifteen miles from Glengask."

"So the Campbell feared the devil Mac-Lawrys would harm ye?" he returned, stepping around to block her path.

Mary met his gaze. "I grew up hearing

frightful tales about you and your kin. One of my cousins once told me that you captured the son of one of our chieftains, and you roasted and ate him."

His sensuous mouth twitched. "Nae. He was too scrawny. We threw him back."

A laugh passed her lips before she could stop it. "I'll grant you that the tale was perhaps a bit absurd," she conceded, still grinning, "but surely you have similar tales about the Campbells."

"Oh, aye." He pulled out his pocket watch, clicked it open, and frowned down at it. "I'll tell ye some of them when we meet fer luncheon tomorrow at . . . Where do ye like to eat luncheon?"

Her favorite eatery in London was a small bakery just east of Bond Street, but it was likely to be stuffed with her friends and acquaintances. And perhaps Lord Delaveer, as well. "The Blue Lamb Inn on Ellis Street," she said instead. No one she knew would be there, since it was owned by a distant relation of the MacDonalds. The Campbells hated them nearly as much as they did the MacLawrys. Aside from that, it was south of Mayfair, directly on the north bank of the Thames.

He nodded. "Then I'll see ye there at one o'clock tomorrow, Mary Campbell."

Before she could either affirm that or come to her senses and claim she had a previous engagement, he left the milliner's and vanished back into the streets of Mayfair.

For the first time Mary realized that there were three other ladies in the shop, and that all of them had to have seen her with Arran MacLawry. He wasn't a man someone could set eyes on and not remember. How had these ladies escaped her notice? Yes, Arran was rather . . . compelling, but for goodness' sake. If any of her friends or family discovered with whom she'd been conversing, especially after last night, she wouldn't be able to go anywhere without an armed escort.

She'd seen Arran's sister on a handful of previous occasions, always from a distance, but that was how Rowena went about London — either with one of her brothers or an armed groom or footman or someone from their clan.

Since her entire childhood had been arranged so she could avoid needing that sort of protection, to call it down on herself now would be worse than ending locked in a cell somewhere. The care her parents and grandfather had used in keeping her well away from Highland politics and Highland rivalries had always seemed ironic, because even back then she'd known that whoever married her would be doing so in order to raise and solidify their standing in clan Campbell, or to ally themselves with the clan. This was the first time she actually felt like she was in the middle of something. It was exciting, really — or it would have been, if she hadn't known about Roderick MacAllister and that her future had already been decided.

But at this moment it was more important that she figure out in how much trouble she could be from the other shoppers. The first woman, three or four years older than herself, she didn't recognize at all. From her simple gown and very practical shoes she might well have been a lady's maid, come to pick up a purchase made by her mistress.

The second two were a mother and daughter, Mrs. John Evans and . . . oh, what was it? Flora? They attended some of the same parties, but she didn't think they knew anything about her family's politics. Thank goodness for that.

Before any of them could notice her staring, she returned to her perusal of baubles, selecting two more hair ribbons she didn't particularly need. There. Everything was as it should be, with no flirtatious encounters between rival clan members or any other such nonsense.

"My lady, do you truly wish to purchase the hat that . . . man favored?" Crawford asked, interrupting her thoughts.

"I'm purchasing the hat *I* favored," she countered, trying to gather her scattered thoughts. "It's merely a happy coincidence for him that he liked it, as well."

"But you're meeting him for luncheon tomorrow. I mean to say . . ." The maid flushed, her pale cheeks turning a blotchy red. "What I mean is, you say you don't care for his opinion, but you're spoken for."

Mary forced a smile as they approached the shop clerk. "At this moment I'm being spoken *at*. Nothing's been settled. And I wasn't about to make a scene here," she returned. "That wouldn't have benefited anyone."

"I — yes, my lady."

She knew perfectly well what Crawford wanted to say but didn't dare do so. That a surprise waltz was one thing, a surprise shopping companion another, and a pre-arranged luncheon quite a different matter entirely. "I'm aware of your concerns, Crawford," she said quietly. "I haven't forgotten my duty. And I have a day to consider the wisdom of a third encounter."

"Very good, Lady Mary."

What Mary couldn't explain aloud, or even to herself, really, was why she meant to meet Arran MacLawry for luncheon, whatever anyone else's objection. The maid saw trouble, a mistress behaving contrary to her parents' well-known wishes. And *that* was the point of it all — partly, anyway. The devil MacLawrys had been flung at her practically since she was born. They were why she'd been cautioned not to begin an acquaintance with anyone until her father or one of her uncles or cousins deemed him or her acceptable. They were why her father had entered into talks with the MacAllisters, and why she would now be expected to marry Roderick.

Arran MacLawry hadn't looked or acted anything like she'd expected. He was different, not beholden to the Campbell or Lord Fendarrow, and that intrigued her more than she'd expected. They'd made a truce, so technically she supposed that in the strictest sense she was doing nothing wrong. Except that it felt wrong, and wicked, and very, very exciting.

The shop door flung open. "Oh, thank heavens!"

Her blond curls bouncing in time with her hurried steps, Elizabeth Bell crossed in front of the other, openly curious shoppers and hugged Mary. Returning the embrace, Mary frowned at the relieved expression on her friend's face.

"What's amiss, Liz?" she asked, patting Elizabeth's shoulder and taking a half step backward, guiding her friend away from the exceedingly troublesome onlookers.

"We expected you at Madame Costanza's nearly an hour ago!" her friend exclaimed. "What are you doing . . ." With a glance around her, Elizabeth stepped closer so she could whisper. "What are you doing here? Cyprians purchase their hats here, you know."

Oh, dear. How was she supposed to explain that she'd merely seen a lady's hat in the window and stumbled inside because she couldn't risk staying on the streets any longer? Not with her very large male companion attracting everyone's attention. "Do they?" She managed a giggle. "How scandalous!"

"Never mind that. We have to hurry. Kathleen is to wait until eleven, and then go alert your mother about your disappearance."

Mary felt all the blood leave her face. "Where is she?"

"We're to meet up at the Biscuit House.

Come along."

If Mary hadn't been so concerned that her parents were about to discover to whom she'd been speaking just a few minutes ago, she would have been congratulating herself for deciding not to meet Arran tomorrow at the Biscuit House. The Blue Lamb would be much more discreet. Though of course the wisest course of action would be for her to remain at home for luncheon tomorrow. The question was, how wise did she wish to be?

CHAPTER THREE

When Arran returned to Gilden House, the very proper Sasannach manor settled directly in the middle of Mayfair that his brother had seen fit to purchase, half the household was out on the front drive. Perhaps they'd discovered where he'd gone off to, and meant to thrash him for blatant stupidity. He might fight back, but he wouldn't blame them for it.

His second thought was that someone had set fire to something again. The new stable was half completed, but Ranulf was still betrothed to an English lady — and some of his Sasannach rivals still didn't like that.

He didn't smell smoke, though, and no one looked particularly alarmed. When he spied one of the footmen Ran had brought down with him from Glengask, he made his way over. "Owen, what's got the hoose emptied?" he asked.

"The dogs, m'laird," the stocky former

soldier and newly minted butler answered. "Peter took 'em oot fer a run, and they flushed a badger. The *amadan* brought it home fer the pelt, only it came to life again."

Arran lifted an eyebrow. "So we've a badger and two deer hounds loose in the house?"

"Aye. The laird yer brother said we were making it worse with all the yellin' and running aboot, so he booted us all oot and said he'd see to it."

So they'd left the chief of clan MacLawry, the Marquis of Glengask, alone in the house with a likely angry badger and a pair of excited, waist-high Scottish deer hounds. For a brief moment Arran wished his younger brother Munro wasn't still in the Highlands, so he could enjoy the fun, as well. Then he grabbed a broom one of the maids clutched and shoved open the front door, closing it firmly behind him.

The frantic barking of Fergus and Una echoed from somewhere upstairs toward the rear of the large house, so he headed up in that direction. "Ranulf!" he called, hefting the broom and wishing it were a wee bit more substantial. He'd never been bitten by a badger himself, but he'd seen it happen. They had jaws like a vise, and the temper of a demon.

"Block the north billiards room door!" his brother bellowed.

"Aye! Give me a moment! I'm still on the stairs!"

The second he stepped into the adjoining hallway a low, dark thing charged at him, snarling. With a curse he swept the broom out, turning the badger past him and toward the main hallway. A heartbeat later Fergus slammed into his left leg, twisting him sideways. When Una pounded into him with the next breath he went down, sprawling into a chair with dogs leaping over him. Then with a crack a chair leg gave way, dumping him onto the floor.

Ranulf strode in, sent him a disgusted look, and followed the dogs. The noise rambled down the hallway toward the rear bedchambers — including his own. *"Ya bas,"* he cursed, clambering to his feet. He'd spent four damned years in the British army. He was not going to be tossed into a chair and laughed at by a bloody badger.

Grabbing up the broom again, he followed the sounds of barking, Ran yelling, and things breaking. Of course the badger had made its way into his bedchamber. Arran sighed. It crouched in a corner, growling, while the massive dogs took turns trying to get past its formidable jaws.

His brother had a pistol in one hand, and a rapier in the other. "What, no claymore?" Arran said, frowning. "This hardly seems sporting."

"So says the fellow knocked to the floor by the wee beastie."

"That wasnae the badger. It was yer elephants there that nearly killed me." He edged closer, trying not to alarm the animal into fleeing — or emptying its bowels. "And dunnae shoot it in here; ye'll get badger all over my bed."

Ranulf sent him a sideways glance. "And yer suggestion would be . . ."

Arran looked about the room, then went over to empty the brass wastebasket that sat by his small writing desk. A silver tea tray lay on the floor just outside the door, broken teacups scattered around it. Handing the tray to his brother, he hefted the wastebasket and slowly advanced again. "Call Fergus back, will ye?" The dogs would listen to him, but not while Ranulf was there.

"Dunnae get eaten," his brother said cynically. "Fergus, off. Here, lad."

Lowering his tail, the larger of the two dogs slunk backward and then padded over to sit beside the marquis. Edging closer, Arran waited until Una had the badger's full attention. Then he lunged forward over the edge of the bed, scooping up the animal and shoving the wastebasket hard against the wall. After a surprised second of silence, the badger began thrashing, thudding into the wall and the round sides of the brass bucket.

Kneeling down, Arran leaned into the container, keeping it hard against the wall. "Are ye going to stand there and look pretty, or hand me the damned tray?" he grunted at his brother.

Silence. At least from Ranulf — the dogs and the badger were making enough racket to give a banshee a fright. Shifting to keep his weight against the wastebasket, he looked over his shoulder. Ranulf stood close by the writing desk, one hand gripping the tea tray, and the other holding a wrinkled scrap of paper.

Arran frowned. There'd only been one or two things in his damned wastebasket — and one of them was the note he'd made this morning when he'd cornered the rag and bone man and asked him if he knew where the Campbells resided. *Bloody hell.*

"Ran?" he prompted, deciding to feign ignorance until forced to do otherwise. "The badger'll be through the wall and into the sunroom in aboot a minute."

The marquis lifted his gaze from the paper. "Why do ye have the Marquis of Fendarrow's address here?"

"Is that what it is?" Inside the wastebasket the badger must have lunged backward, because the container nearly ripped out of his hands. "Fer Saint Bridget's sake, Ran, bring me the damned tray!"

His brother didn't move. "I know this is Mathering House, because I made a note of all the places I'd nae tread, and this one was at the top." His brows lowered. "Ye went to see the lass, didnae? Mary bloody Campbell?"

Inwardly Arran squared his shoulders. Had the question come from anyone else, he would have simply refused to answer. But Ranulf was not only the head of his family, he was the chief of the entire clan. And he would have an answer. At the same time, as Arran didn't wish to be ordered back to Glengask, he was going to have to lie. And he didn't like that, either. His siblings were the only immediate family he had, except for their uncle, Myles Wilkie, but the Earl of Swansley was a Sasannach.

"She made a fool of me," he returned, shoving back at the bucket. "I wanted to be certain the lass knew that I knew who *she* was, and where I could find her."

"And so ye told her all that?"

"Aye." More or less, anyway.

"Did ye happen to consider what might've transpired if Fendarrow or any of his brothers or nephews were aboot? I'm attempting to make a new alliance, not have ye trample a truce that's nae a month old."

"I'm nae a fool," Arran retorted. "I waited until I could speak just to the lass." And at least that part was true.

"And if she tells her dear papa that ye hunted her doon, ye idiot?"

He drew a hard breath, surprised at his abrupt reluctance to speak. Clan first. Not an enemy lass he barely knew. Not even if what he needed to say didn't particularly benefit her. "She'll nae say a word, or she'd have to explain how we discovered her family wants to marry her off to Roderick MacAllister."

Ranulf regarded him for a moment, eyes narrowed and ignoring the growling and barking and jumping going on all around him. "Dunnae venture into Campbell territory alone again. Truce or nae truce."

"Ye couldnae know about the MacAllisters already," Arran countered.

"Nae. But as we're after the same thing with the Stewarts I'm nae surprised, either. Give me yer word, Arran."

"Ye have my word." And the Blue Lamb Inn was nowhere near Campbell territory, thankfully. "Now if ye dunnae bring that tray here, I'm going to set this beastie loose again. And he smells rather foul."

Pocketing the paper rather than discarding it — no doubt his way of pointing out that he had no intention of forgetting the incident — Ranulf hefted the tea tray and held it flat against the wall just above the wastebasket.

"Ready?" Arran asked, beginning to feel the ache in his arms from the effort of keeping control of the trapped animal.

"Aye. Ready, and . . . now."

Arran tilted the top of the bucket away from the wall. Moving at the same time, Ranulf slid the tray down, turning it into a lid. A paw with massive digging claws jabbed out, catching Arran's sleeve, and then he pushed the container closed again.

Still moving together, they turned the wastebasket upright and set it down on the floor. Arran sat on the tea tray with the badger snarling and rocking beneath him. "Some rope, do ye think?" he asked.

Straightening, Ranulf nodded. "I'll fetch some." He flashed a grin. "Dunnae go anywhere."

"I'm near dying from laughter. Take the dogs with ye; they arenae helping anything now."

The marquis whistled both dogs to his side, and the three of them trotted for the staircase. Almost immediately the badger began to quiet, and aside from a few half-hearted snarls, it seemed fairly content to be there in the close dark.

Poor fellow, out hunting for someaught, then flung about by Scottish deer hounds and carried back to a proper London house to be skinned. It wasn't much of a stretch to see his own situation reflected in the badger's. After all, he'd only left Glengask after Ranulf's letters from London began to speak of a troubling obsession with a Sasannach lass.

His presence hadn't stopped Ran from falling in love and proposing marriage to Charlotte Hanover, nor had he done anything to help this truce with the Campbells along — except to get a pistol pointed at him and his sister; the very thing that had prompted Ranulf to make a cease-fire agreement with old enemies.

And now that he'd been designated a part to play, he found himself reluctant to take on the role. He wouldn't have liked being forced into a marriage, regardless, but now . . . He'd waltzed with Mary Campbell by accident. And whatever his original reason for hunting her down this morning, he'd lingered because she was . . . unexpected. As for tomorrow, at the moment he could put that down to curiosity. It was more a test of her courage than his, and why he'd decided that was important, well, he'd figure it out later. It wasn't as if a conversation or two with her would keep him from doing his duty by the clan and marrying pleasant Deirdre Stewart, after all.

"So, Master Badger," he drawled aloud, "what should we do with ye? I dunnae suppose, if given the choice, ye'd prefer to be turned into a lady's wrap or work gloves."

The tray under his arse bumped.

"Nae, I didnae think so. Ye shouldnae have gotten yerself caught, then. Once ye're caught, yer fate's nae yer own."

"Are ye finished chatting with the beastie," his brother asked from the doorway, "or should I leave ye be?" Without waiting for an answer he squatted down beside the wastebasket to run rope through the tea tray's handles.

"I was only pointing oot the risks of handing his life over to someone else." Arran slid off the lid, holding it closed with both arms so his brother could bind it to the bucket.

"Deirdre Stewart's a pretty lass," Ranulf said, rising again.

"Aye. Ye should marry her," Arran retorted. "A shame ye went and followed yer heart. But then ye can always throw yer obligation at someone else, so all's well."

The marquis tilted his head. "Is yer heart leading ye somewhere?"

"Nae. Of course not," he answered, hoping he hadn't answered too vehemently.

"Then shut yer mouth and stop making trouble."

Arran hefted the snarling, wriggling wastebasket and carried it down the hallway, down the stairs, through the foyer, and out the front door. Setting it down on the drive, he sat on it again to keep it from tipping over and rolling away. His older brother looked at him for a long moment, stone-faced, then faced the milling servants.

"The excitement's done with," the marquis said, "though there's a bit of a mess upstairs. Back inside with ye."

Owen began urging servants toward the front door. "What do ye mean to do with that thing?" he asked.

"Why didnae ye shoot it?" Peter, the footman, seconded. "Damned thing near frighted me to death, coming back to life like that."

"Do ye remember where ye and the dogs flushed it, Peter?" Ranulf asked the footman.

"Aye, I reckon I do, m'laird. Ye want me to find more of 'em fer ye? Though if ye mean to carry them aboot in buckets, I dunnae know why ye want them."

"Hitch up a wagon and take it back."

Peter stared, clearly baffled, at the marquis. "Are ye mad, m'laird? If ye dunnae want to ruin the pelt, I'll droon it fer ye."

Ranulf sent another glance at Arran. "Nae. Arran's gone and named it Munro. We cannae kill it now."

"After yer own brother, Laird Arran?" Now the servant seemed concerned that at least one of the MacLawrys needed to be carted off to Bedlam.

"Aye," Arran answered, caught between surprise that Ranulf wasn't suggesting *he* be hauled away and drowned, and reluctant amusement. "If ye please, take wee Munro back to where ye found him."

The footman sighed. "I'll do it fer ye, m'laird, but I'd nae be yer true and faithful man if I didnae speak my mind."

The marquis nodded solemnly. "Say yer piece then, Peter."

"I think ye've been in London too long, m'laird. The madness of these Sasannach is seeping into yer brain."

"Ye may have the right of it," Ranulf returned, sending a glance at Arran. "But

I'll nae leave here withoot Lady Charlotte. Ye'll have to keep a close eye on us until we're safely back to Glengask."

Peter drew himself up even straighter. "Aye, m'laird. I'll see to it ye keep to the Highlands way." With that he claimed the wastebasket and hauled it off in the direction of the stable.

"And what is the Highlands way?" Arran asked, trying to decide whether attempting to slip the note from Ranulf's pocket would be worth the additional scrutiny if he was caught at it. More than likely he'd explained it away well enough, and the next time Ranulf looked at it he would simply discard it rather than bring up the topic of Mary Campbell again. Best to leave well enough alone.

"I dunnae. Kilts and brawling and nae saving badgers, I suppose."

"The badger didnae mean to end up at Gilden House with deer hounds nipping at his heels." Arran looked over at Ranulf as they walked back to the house. "I dunnae see myself as the badger, ye know. I killed my share of men over in Spain and France, so I'm nae squeamish. Ye know I'll hunt fer food, but I've nae eaten badger. The —"

"You made a good point, Arran," his brother interrupted. "I likely should have been the one to marry a Stewart. But I'll nae have any lass but Charlotte. And there wasnae a chance fer an alliance anyway, until ten days ago."

"As ye say."

Owen held open the door as they entered the house again. From the look — and smell — of the morning room just off the foyer, the badger had visited there, as well. Several footmen and maids were in there already, removing torn couch cushions and sweeping up broken vases and candy dishes. The whole room was so . . . English that Arran tended to avoid it. The smell of badger piss might even make for an improvement.

"Ye'll be able to tell Rowena aboot it tonight," Ranulf continued. "She and the Hanovers are meeting us at the theater."

Damnation. "All the Hanovers?"

As he turned toward his office, Ranulf paused. "Jane thinks ye handsome and charming."

Arran narrowed his eyes. "Ye cursed me, didnae? All I said was fer ye to be certain ye wanted to bring an English lady to live in the Highlands." He'd thought it a valid question, given the way their own lives had gone.

"And all *I* said was that I hoped ye found a lass who agreed with yer every word and nae gave ye a moment of trouble. Mayhap ye should be grateful I found ye someone else."

It wasn't an improvement. At the time it had sounded deathly dull. Now, after having firstly become the focus of eighteen-year-old Jane Hanover's infatuation, and then having an equally bland Scottish lass thrown at him, the idea of being married to just such a creature gave him nightmares. Nightmares that would soon become real.

"Ye're nae a nice man, Ranulf," he said aloud, as his brother would be expecting some kind of response.

"A word of advice, *bràthair:* never advise a man nae to marry the woman he cannae live without."

"Is this Deirdre shite revenge, then?"

"Nae. It's survival."

As Arran went upstairs to assess the damage done to his bedchamber and wall, he had to admit to himself that what Ran had said truly surprised him. Not the last bit, but the part about Charlotte. Yes, he'd heard his older brother say he loved Charlotte Hanover, and heard her profess the same to him. But Ranulf was one-and-thirty, four years his senior. He'd become marquis and chief of the clan when Arran had been eleven.

All the younger siblings knew their brother to be iron-willed, independent, and unwavering. To hear him say he couldn't live without Charlotte — it spoke of a need, a vulnerability, that Arran hadn't expected. In a sense, it was even unsettling. They'd all become so accustomed to relying on Ranulf, who relied on no one but himself. And yet after only a few weeks in England Ran had found an outsider, a Sasannach lass, and declared that he needed her.

Shrugging off his disquiet, if not his frustration, Arran shed his jacket. He pulled a few coins from his pockets, and then a piece of pretty yellow and white muslin. Mary's walking dress. For a moment he looked at it, turning the fabric over in his hands. He could discard it if he still had a wastebasket, but considering what had already happened with that, keeping it someplace safe would likely be wiser. With a glance at his half-open door he went to his wardrobe and tucked it beneath a pile of cravats. He wasn't being sentimental. Not over a Campbell. He was merely being cautious.

That done, he sat down to write Munro. Bear, as he'd been known since their father had prophesied that he would grow to be the size of one, had remained at Glengask

74

to oversee the estate and the clan. He hadn't wanted to do so, but being the youngest brother — and the youngest sibling excepting Rowena — had to have some sort of penalty attached to it. Considering that Ranulf had thrown Deirdre at the nearest brother, Bear should count himself lucky that he'd stayed behind.

As he reported about the progress of Ranulf's engagement, his own soon-expected betrothal, and their luck thus far in keeping Rowena from falling for the charms of some weak-chinned Sasannach lordling, he left out any mention of Mary Campbell. Mary was . . . interesting, and she could possibly give him some insight into the Campbell clan. And that, he told himself, was the beginning, middle, and end of it.

Finally Owen knocked on his door. "Ye're to leave fer the theater in an hour, m'laird. Do ye wish help dressing?"

If he'd learned one thing about the English during his sojourn in the army, it was that they changed clothes every time they changed seats. "Nae, Owen. I'll see to it."

"Ye know Laird Glengask gave me leave to hire ye a valet." He scowled. "I'm certain that Ginger fellow valeting fer the marquis knows some others like himself."

Arran grinned. "I'll manage. And ye may as well get accustomed to Edward Ginger. We'll have Lady Charlotte in the hoose, and ye can nae have only one Sasannach. They multiply, like toadstools."

The old soldier laughed, then abruptly glanced behind him and sobered again. "I'll see the coach readied then, m'laird."

"Thank ye, Owen," Ranulf's voice came, and the butler fled. As Arran cursed beneath his breath, the marquis stopped in the bedchamber doorway. "Toadstools, are they?" he asked, folding his arms over his chest.

"Ye ken that I still have behind me twenty-seven years of hating everyone south of Hadrian's Wall, do ye nae? Whatever happened to change yer mind hasnae happened to me." There. He was damned tired of walking about on eggshells where Charlotte Hanover was concerned.

Ranulf stepped into the room and shut the door behind him. "I'm nae asking ye to love the Sasannach. I'm telling ye that Charlotte is now a MacLawry, and so are her parents and her sister. Ye'll treat them as such. And if ye dunnae like that, ye'll still behave in a way that nae gives any of them — or me — any idea of that fact. Is that understood?"

He'd be a fool to disagree. "Aye," he said

aloud. "The Hanovers are a part of clan MacLawry. And so will the Stewarts be, I assume."

"They make sense fer us, especially with Fendarrow going after the MacAllisters."

"I ken, Ran. I dunnae like it one damned bit, but I ken."

With a nod, his brother pulled open the door again, then hesitated and shut it more quietly. "I rely on yer counsel, Arran. Dunnae let me down. The times . . . everything is moving forward fast as the wind. We need to understand that, and to make the changes that help us survive."

Evidently one of these changes was Ran falling for an English lass, while him dancing with a Campbell lass was not ever going to be acceptable. It all seemed hypocritical in the extreme, but Arran inclined his head. "As ye say, Ran."

His brother didn't look convinced. "I never know what's rattling aboot in that clever head of yers, but fer my sake, know Charlotte better before ye decide she will-nae do fer me. Ye've only been here a few weeks."

That, at least, seemed fair. "I said I would, Ran, and so I will."

"Good." The marquis opened the door again. "Get yerself dressed, then. I expect ye're the only one who'll enjoy *Hamlet* tonight, anyway. Damned Danes."

It was clearly meant to be a jest, so Arran forced a grin. Once Ranulf left, he dropped the expression. He'd always, *always* supported his brother and his vision for the clan. Schools, farms, mercantile to be sold to Highlanders who'd been pushed off their lands all the way to America — it had all been about bettering the clan and staying out from under the thumb of the English.

Their own mother had been English, and she'd swallowed poison rather than live on in the Highlands with four children. For years after that they'd never even mentioned her; to this day Ranulf referred to her as Eleanor rather than as his mother. The rest of them followed suit.

And now Ran had changed the rules because it suited him to do so. That was his prerogative as the clan's chief. But it served to make Arran feel not a whit of guilt about going to luncheon with Mary Campbell tomorrow, and not telling another soul about it.

CHAPTER FOUR

"Were your parents furious?" Elizabeth Bell whispered, sitting beside Mary and taking her hand. Behind them two sets of parents chatted, evidently highly amused that their daughters had claimed the front seats of the box — as if they hadn't been encouraged to sit there all along. They couldn't show well from the dark rear of the theater box, after all.

"Yes," Mary returned in the same tone, and sighed as she tried to push back against her increasing cynicism. Whatever was wrong with her, she wasn't certain she liked it. "I explained that Lord Arran surprised me and that I was trying to avoid a scene, but they still wanted to yell."

"You can hardly blame them. What if your cousin Charles had realized with whom you were waltzing?"

She'd thought about that, actually, and in a brawl she wasn't certain which of the two men would have emerged victorious. Charles had a certain sharp meanness about him, but Arran MacLawry seemed very . . . capable. And extremely confident. Or at least he'd been so both last night and this morning.

Not even Liz knew about him accompanying her to the milliner's, though, and she'd sworn Crawford to secrecy. Because while he'd surprised her with his presence twice now, she could easily have declined to spend time with him this morning. And she couldn't explain at all why she'd agreed to meet him yet again tomorrow.

"I told you crimson was your color," Elizabeth pointed out, gesturing at the heavy, embroidered silk gown Mary had chosen to wear tonight. "You look very dramatic."

"Thank you. Mother thinks it makes me look forward, but as no one's allowed near me without a half-dozen people's approval, that hardly signifies." And aside from that, the gown made her feel decadent. If she was to be forced to wed Lord Delaveer, she wasn't likely to have another chance to indulge herself.

Liz giggled. "No wonder everyone's in a panic about you running across Lord Arran, then. He couldn't possibly be on the approved list."

Yes, they were in a panic, and that was why she'd done her best to be tolerant of it. If not for the niggling thought that her family was more concerned that she'd done something scandalous than they were worried she'd been in danger, she would likely have been a great deal more understanding. Of course the clan came first — but she was part of the clan, for heaven's sake. Why had she been chosen as the Campbell sacrifice? Because her grandfather didn't think she was a drooling half-wit like he did most of his other grandchildren?

Elizabeth squeezed her hand, shaking her back to the present. "Oh, look! The Duke and Duchess of Greaves. I didn't even know they were in Town. And the Earl of Westfall. The new one. It was so sad that his brother was killed in that silly duel."

Mary sat forward, looking across the theater at the opposite row of boxes. Since Greaves had married a commoner, he and his wife spent most of their time in York. Sophia Baswich had flaming red hair and a reputation for speaking her mind, and she'd reportedly once worked at The Tantalus Club — a gambling club for gentlemen and staffed solely by females. Mary wondered how in the world the two of them had managed not only to meet and to fall in love,

81

but to have the courage to marry. Even with half the theater staring at them, they looked happy, sitting close to each other, her arm tucked around his.

As she looked at the rest of the boxes, her breath caught. In the fourth box from the stage the Marquis of Glengask stood greeting the pretty blond woman she knew to be Lady Charlotte Hanover. Mary didn't know her well — she was four years younger than the earl's daughter, after all — but to marry Lord Glengask, the chief of clan MacLawry, seemed exceedingly daunting.

Nor were they alone in the box. Charlotte's parents, Lord and Lady Hest, had joined them, and so had the other daughter, Jane. Next to her sat Lady Rowena Mac-Lawry, moving her hands animatedly as she chatted about something with the fourth young lady present. Mary frowned. With her dark hair and pale skin, there was no mistaking Lady Deirdre Stewart. Her father, Lord Allen, was there, as well, speaking with Glengask. What were the Stewarts doing with the MacLawrys? That thought, though, vanished as *he* left the gloom at the back of the box. Arran MacLawry.

Where his brother had a certain mountainous presence, Arran seemed more like a wolf than a lion — sharp, predatory, and alert for weakness. Except that he'd been charming and clever at the masked ball and even this morning, after he'd learned who she was. Yes, she was wary in his presence, but if she'd been truly frightened, truly concerned for her safety, she would have made her entire family aware of his activities. And she never would have agreed to meet him tomorrow.

At that moment he turned, meeting her gaze. From across the theater she couldn't make out the color of his eyes, though she knew them to be a light blue. Nor could she see any details of his expression, but a warm shiver ran down her spine, regardless. If he'd been other than a MacLawry, she would have called herself intrigued, and interested.

"Oh, my goodness," Liz whispered from beside her, shaking her out of her thoughts. "Lord Glengask. And he's seen you, I think. Lord Arran has, I mean."

"Well, he's not likely to attack from over there," Mary returned, deliberately and with some difficulty turning her gaze toward the stage at the front of the large room. Quite likely it was only the fact that she'd been ordered to stay away from him that left her so conscious of his presence. It made him a dangerous rogue, and what woman wouldn't notice someone like that gazing at her? Or inviting her to luncheon?

"The Stewarts, eh?" her father muttered from behind her. "So the MacLawrys don't have any more faith in the truce than I do."

"The Stewarts must be desperate for Mac-Lawry resources if they're willing to hand their prettiest gem over to Glengask's brother," an additional voice said from behind Mary, and with a carefully hidden scowl she turned to look. The son of Malcolm MacAllister stood there shaking hands with her father and Mr. Bell, and complimenting the two mamas. *Oh, dear.*

"Thank you for inviting me tonight, Fendarrow," Roderick MacAllister said warmly.

Then she noticed the man standing slightly behind him, and her frown deepened. Charles Calder, the son of her father's youngest sister, smiled at her as well, though the expression didn't quite fit his face.

That wasn't her cousin's fault, she supposed, since Charles had simply been born narrow. Narrow shoulders, lidded eyes, thin lips — they'd all called him Otter until he'd turned sixteen and bloodied his older brother Adam's nose over it. Which made him narrow-minded, as well. Still, if he'd wanted to distance himself from the nickname, he likely should stop slicking back his straight, black hair and wearing nothing but black clothing.

"You know you're always welcome to join us, Roderick," her father returned. Lord Fendarrow glanced at her, his smile too rushed. "I know you enjoy a good *Hamlet,* so we've saved you a front row seat."

So *that* was why her father had suggested she would be able to see better from the middle seat of the three in the front row. So Lord Delaveer could sit beside her. At least he wasn't trying to match her with Charles. She certainly didn't view Roderick . . . romantically, but at least she didn't feel the need to bathe after speaking with him. In fact, she didn't feel much of anything. Was that because she'd only seen him as part of the pack of potential beaux? If she set her mind to it, could Roderick stir her pulse as . . . Oh. No, no, no. That . . . No. She wasn't smitten with Arran MacLawry. That feeling was only nerves, because she wasn't supposed to be anywhere near him.

Roderick took the vacant seat beside her, and she jumped. "Good evening, Mary, Miss Elizabeth."

"Hello, Lord Delaveer," Elizabeth returned, smiling. "I didn't know you enjoyed Shakespeare."

"I enjoy the company."

"I enjoy Shakespeare," Charles put in from directly behind Mary. "Especially the tragedies."

The light, mostly absent brogue in his voice annoyed her. Previously she was certain she'd barely even noted it, but tonight it sounded as though he couldn't decide whether he was English or Scottish. "What an odd thing to say," she returned.

Perhaps that accent indecision was what made her hesitate about Roderick, as well; wherever she lived, she felt like a Highlander down to her toes. Arran, even if he hadn't had a deep, delicious brogue, could never be mistaken for anything but a hot-blooded, fearless Highlander. There was nothing mild or hesitant about him. On the other hand, Roderick had likely never unsettled a butterfly. And Charles probably pulled off their wings.

Charles furrowed his narrow brows. "How so?"

"Saying you prefer the tragedies is the same as saying you prefer death and murder and betrayal to love and happiness."

"Perhaps it's merely that I find the tragedies more realistic." He sank back in his seat, turning his gaze not toward the stage, but in the direction of the boxes at the far side of the theater. "You waltzed with Arran

MacLawry."

Her first thought was to tell Charles that who she danced with was none of his business. It wasn't really, but her cousin had already had several run-ins with Lord Glengask this Season, before the truce. And she had no intention of ruining that days-old truce by saying something flippant. "We were both wearing fox masks, and he had no idea who I was. I wasn't going to cause a scene."

"Don't dance with him again."

Mary took a breath and held it until she could hear the beat of her heart. "I don't know why I would," she returned. "Out of curiosity, though, are we not at peace with the MacLawrys?"

"We're not killing them. That's a pause in battle. Not peace."

She was still debating how to respond to that when Roderick chuckled. "Don't mind your cousin, Lady Mary. I enjoy peace. It provides some surprising — and welcome — opportunities."

"Aye," Charles countered, his voice lower and flatter. "Whereas war favors other individuals."

Now that was interesting. And disturbing. Was Charles Calder so against this truce with the MacLawrys because of what her father had mentioned — that the MacAllisters would help bolster their ranks, but they didn't wish to be pulled into a conflict? Because if the Campbells and MacLawrys drew blood again *Charles* would be the one the clan wanted her to marry? A shiver ran down her spine.

So she seemed to be doomed either way, truce or not, and it was only a narrow window that made her groom Roderick rather than Charles. Who, though, was pushing her and Roderick together? Her father, or her grandfather? The Campbell himself seemed a more likely force, as he was the one who'd agreed to the truce. Which meant, she supposed, that she had another reason to be grateful to her grandfather. Because while neither Roderick nor Charles interested her, she easily preferred dullness to cruelty. Though if given a third choice, it would be to not have to marry either of them.

On the tail of that thought, the curtains opened. A more appropriate play would have been *Macbeth,* but she wasn't certain the several hot-blooded Highlanders in the audience would have been able to tolerate that.

On the other hand, she wasn't certain she could tolerate *Hamlet* tonight. Aside from the presence of a very troublesome man just across the stage from her, there were the plots within plots, lies, deceit, betrayals, murders, suicide — given all the soul-wrenching mayhem, this was likely Charles's favorite play. After forty minutes or so, she found herself once again gazing across the darkened space toward the MacLawry box.

Were the MacLawrys doing the same thing to Arran that her own clan had in mind for her? Or had he already been in pursuit of Deirdre Stewart before . . . heavens, was it only last night that they'd met? The Stewart's niece was considered a great beauty, after all. But if Arran was after Deirdre, what had he been doing asking a vixen mask to waltz? And what about this morning? And luncheon tomorrow?

"Excuse me," she whispered, standing. "I'll be back in a moment."

"I'll go with you," Roderick said, starting to his feet.

"Nonsense. You'll miss a murder."

"Mary," her mother chided.

"I apologize. It was Charles who likes the murders. I will be back in a moment." Evidently she'd convinced him that she didn't need his assistance to find a privy closet, because inclining his head, he sat back again.

With another murmured apology to the rest of her box mates, Mary made her way to the curtain at the rear and slipped into the hallway beyond. A few other audience members wandered past her, outnumbered by footmen toting drinks and opera glasses and warm wraps — and even a small, fluffy dog.

Leaning back against the wall, Mary closed her eyes for a moment. Yes, she was one-and-twenty, and yes, even with her grandfather's indulgence she'd always known she would eventually have to marry according to the clan's will. But not yet. For goodness' sake, if anything the truce with the MacLawrys should have removed any urgency from her impending union, not created it.

She took a deep breath and opened her eyes again — then let it out with a barely stifled squeak as she spied the man topping the stairs and heading in her direction. He was not a footman, and he was not carrying a dog. He was, however, wearing a splendid kilt of black and white and red. Before he could approach her parents' box; she straightened and hurried toward him.

"What are you doing here, Arran?" she whispered, starting to reach for his arm and then stopping herself. They weren't friends;

they were . . . they were new acquaintances who were never supposed to have met. And she happened to find him somewhat, barely, attractive.

"*Hamlet* seems a bit too close to my life," he drawled in his deep, rich brogue. "And I keep wanting to yell at Hamlet to kill his uncle and stop all that lunatic talking to himself and the play-within-a-play nonsense." Light blue eyes regarded her. "What sent ye fleeing, lass?"

"The same thing, I suppose. Too much subterfuge. I prefer the comedies."

"Aye." He glanced past her at the closed curtains of the Campbell box. "Calder wasnae blaming ye fer dancing with me, I hope."

Had he come all the way around the theater into enemy territory just to see if she was well? "*You* blamed me for it, as I recall."

That wicked grin touched his mouth again. "Ye're nae a shy lass, are ye?"

She edged closer, wishing he would lower his voice just a bit more. For heaven's sake, her cousin Charles was twenty-five feet away. And her almost betrothed, only twenty-seven. "I can be diplomatic. But I prefer to be direct. It makes for fewer misunderstandings."

"Direct it is, then. Has Delaveer offered fer ye?"

Mary lifted an eyebrow. "Have you offered for Deirdre Stewart?"

"Nae." He shifted his feet, glancing beyond her in the direction of her parents' box. "Between ye and me, lass?"

He was asking for her discretion. She should have been shocked and surprised, but she wasn't. The entire time they conversed was only for the two of them. "Yes. Just between us."

"Then I'll offer fer her, once her father and uncle decide how much of their grazing land they'll return to their cotters, and Ranulf decides it's enough of a concession."

"Do you want to marry her?" It was a stupid, silly question, but she asked it anyway.

"Nae. She's . . . pleasant, I suppose, but she's nae warm-blooded enough fer me." He glanced down. "And Delaveer?" he continued, meeting her gaze again. "Ye didnae answer my question."

"He and my father are negotiating," she said slowly. "Along with his father and my grandfather."

"Do ye want to marry him?"

"No," she returned, in the same tone he'd used, realizing that there was no one else in the world with whom she could — or would — have this particular conversation. "He's not warm-blooded enough for me. If the Campbells and MacLawrys were still fighting it would be Charles Calder after me, though, and that would be even worse."

Arran scowled. "Calder? That dog needs to be put down."

Mary gazed at him. With the gray coat that couldn't hide his broad shoulders, the trim black waistcoat, and the bold MacLawry plaid of his kilt, he looked magnificent, no matter which name he carried. She wondered what he might be thinking about her. "I don't like Charles, but he *is* my cousin."

Arran shrugged. "I ken who ye are. I also reckon I may have caused ye trouble withoot meaning to. And yet, I dunnae intend to apologize fer it." He took a slow step closer. "What do ye say to that?"

"I don't know what to say. And I don't think it matters, anyway. We marry who we're told to marry, do we not, Arran Mac-Lawry? For the good of our clans?"

He tilted his head. Then, before she could move, he closed the short distance remaining between them, leaned down, and touched his mouth to hers. He tasted of warmth and whisky, and sin. It was surprisingly delicious.

Realizing she had a hand splayed against his chest, Mary swiftly lowered her arm, curling her fingers into her palm. "You . . . You just kissed a Campbell," she whispered, her voice sounding husky to her own ears. "Lightning may just strike you dead."

He shook his head, a lock of his wavy black hair falling across his brow. "I nae kissed a Campbell. I kissed *ye,* Mary." With a half grin he backed away, then turned on his heel. "And I say, let the lightning come if it will. I'm nae married yet. And neither are ye." Arran glanced over his shoulder at her. "I'll see ye fer luncheon tomorrow, lass."

Mary gazed after him, then belatedly touched her fingers to her lips. He was a MacLawry, and she was a Campbell. They were *not* friends. But whatever it was they were, she was abruptly beginning to find it very interesting.

Ranulf met Arran on the front drive as he returned from his morning ride with the dogs and his quick-footed black Thorough-bred, Duffy. Though calling it a ride was somewhat of a stretch, since even Rotten Row had been packed with gentlemen seeking the morning air. Or to be seen in their fine riding gear. He wasn't certain which.

"Ye're going to have to wear someaught

else to White's," Ranulf said, taking Duffy's bridle. "They'll nae admit stableboys."

As Arran dismounted, nearly as breathless as the dogs and the horse, he took a moment to study his brother's easy expression. However he felt about the chief of his clan — his own brother — marrying a Sasannach, Charlotte did make Ranulf happy. And he could be grateful for that. "I'm nae going to White's," he returned. "I'm meeting Fordham for luncheon." Or at least that was what his old army comrade would vouch, since he'd arranged for it during his ride.

"Have him join us. Charlotte's father issued the invitation, and Uncle Myles will be there. Allen's attending, as well. And Tollifsen. I'm attempting to show a proper front."

"I have plans," Arran repeated, with more heat than he intended. "Ye can be proper and English withoot me. And ye dunnae need me fer Allen until ye settle on how much land I'm worth." He handed Duffy's reins over to Debny, the head groom Ran had brought down with him from Glengask.

Ranulf blocked his path to the house. "Allen and Tollifsen have good merchant contacts here in London, and they'll nae do business with men who're naught but dragon-wrestling Highlanders."

"Who won't? The Stewarts, or the merchants?"

"Neither of them."

"Well, it's yer good fortune, then, that ye've been turning yerself into a Sasannach fer the past two months, isnae?" Arran moved around his brother, stripping off his riding gloves as he did so. "I recall a few months ago when ye didnae care what the Sasannach thought of ye. And when the clan MacLawry was strong enough to stand against any family in the Highlands withoot bringing in pinky-lifting tea drinkers fer support."

"Which tea drinkers? The Stewarts, or Charlotte's family?"

"Both of them."

"Arran."

"If ye want to prove ye're civilized, why dunnae ye have luncheon with the Campbell? Or Lord Fendarrow?"

"That's enough."

He kept walking. "Then stop my flapping gums with yer damned fist, Ran."

"It's nae yer gums I'm trying to convince, Arran. It's yer mind."

"Then dunnae bother. I'm nae the chief. Do as ye will."

If Ranulf wanted to disregard or excuse

centuries of conflict with the English, excuse Highlanders being forbidden to carry weapons or wear kilts or play the damned pipes, or even being burned off their land by other Highlanders, he could do so. But at the moment Arran was the heir to Glengask — at least until Ranulf married Charlotte and she gave him a son — and he refused to let his brother forget who was paying the price for his new, proper ways. It seemed he wasn't going to be granted that luxury himself, and fair was fair.

Owen pulled open the front door as he reached it. "Did ye have a good run, then?"

"Aye, Owen. I very nearly kept heading north."

The footman-butler chuckled. "If ye decide to do that, make certain ye take me with ye."

So he wasn't the only one growing uneasy in London — though Owen had been there several weeks longer than he. Handing over his hat and gloves, Arran trotted upstairs. Yesterday afternoon he hadn't been certain Mary would actually meet him today. And then he'd defied his brother's orders and his own better instincts and not only sought her out last night, but kissed her.

Why, he wasn't certain, except that she'd

looked lovely and sinful in scarlet and he'd wanted to do so. They'd found themselves in very similar situations, but that kiss hadn't been about commiseration. The actual truth would have to wait until he'd deciphered it. Because all he knew for certain at that moment was that he meant to keep his rendezvous at the Blue Lamb Inn, and that he'd lied to and insulted his brother in order to do it. All for a luncheon with a Campbell. All when he should likely be planning a luncheon with Lady Deirdre.

Still without a valet, he pulled off his sweaty riding clothes and stepped into the bath of cold water he'd requested. Chilly as it was, it still seemed less breath-stealing than a swim in Loch Shinaig. Then he dressed in a plain gray jacket, brown waistcoat, and buckskin breeches tucked into some impressively shiny Hessian boots. There. Suitably English, but not fancy enough to warrant a second glance. Or so he hoped.

"Hail me a hack, will ye, Owen?" he asked the butler as he headed back downstairs.

"Aye, m'laird. Do ye nae want one of the lads with ye, though?"

"Nae." He took his gray beaver hat and set it on his head. Until last week he'd never worn such a useless thing. "We've a truce, didnae ye hear?"

"I heard. Dunnae believe it'll last, though."

"Good. Ye keep that up, Owen." He followed the new butler outside, waiting on the front steps as Owen walked to the end of the drive and signaled a passing coach.

A moment later he returned, the hack trundling up beside him. "Yer brother the marquis says to trust a wee bit more than we have been," he said, as he pulled open the door. "The Sasannach, I mean."

"Ye do that, then. I'll be keeping both my eyes open." With a smile he didn't feel, Arran climbed into the short, narrow vehicle. "Crane House, on Madox Street," he said loudly enough for Owen to hear, naming William Crane, Viscount Fordham's, address for effect. He'd hire another hack from there to take him to Ellis Street and the Blue Lamb.

If Ranulf learned anything about this, his brother would likely attempt to bloody his nose and put a boot in his arse, then order him home to Glengask to wait for his bride to be delivered. But Ran couldn't have it both ways; either they were the MacLawrys who trusted and relied on no one but themselves, or they were half-English lads making alliances and friendships with every

Highlander who wasn't a Campbell and every Sassanach who wished them good morning.

And until the Marquis of Glengask decided who they were and when he was to marry a Stewart, Arran meant to do as pleased him. Since he'd kissed Mary Campbell last night, it pleased him to see her today. It was also necessary, on the chance she'd taken offense and told Charles Calder or her father. That would mean the end of the truce. If she hadn't taken offense, well, that would be much more interesting.

"I have no wish to be sacked, my lady." Crawford wrung her hands together as they stood beside a stable yard, around the corner from the Blue Lamb Inn.

"You're doing as I ask. No one's going to sack you. I won't allow it." She only half paid attention to the conversation; most of her was occupied with listening for church bells, waiting for them to chime one o'clock.

"It's not the doing as you've asked part that troubles me," the maid returned. "It's the me not informing your parents that you're doing something dangerous. You're practically engaged to another man, Lady Mary."

In ragged unison across London, bells

began ringing in a single, discordant note. One o'clock. Her last chance to regain her sanity and return home. To be a dutiful, obedient daughter who would never have a carnal thought about a MacLawry — not even one as handsome as Arran. " 'Practically' means not yet. And I'm not doing anything dangerous, Crawford. Now please, go purchase something pretty for yourself. I'll meet you back here at half two, or you can come in and fetch me."

The maid looked halfway to tears, but she nodded. "Very well, my lady. Please, please be careful."

"I will be."

She watched the maid cross the street toward the shabby shops lining the way. Crawford looked back over her shoulder every few feet, like some sad pup being told to leave home without supper. When she disappeared inside a milliner's, Mary took a slow, deep breath.

London — not the best part of it, of course — bustled around her, but for the first time in what may well have been ever, she gazed at it alone. The maid had told her to be careful, and here she actually needed to be so.

Perhaps she didn't generally have guards surrounding her, but she was never on her own outside of Mathering House. She should likely be nervous now, or even frightened. But she wasn't. What she felt most, in fact, was an unsettled anticipation.

Of course if she didn't go inside the Blue Lamb Inn, this would all be for nothing. An enemy was waiting for her inside. A very roguish, attractive enemy she'd yet to find any real reason to dislike. A man who kept her thoughts occupied so she didn't have room to dwell on her impending doom. Because that was what the idea of marrying Roderick felt like. Doom.

Mary squared her shoulders, walked up to the inn's peeling blue door and pushed it open. A dozen men and half that many women sat at various wooden tables in the main room. It rather reminded her of the inns where they changed horses on the way up to Scotland, in fact, except for the strong London accents chittering around her.

Toward the back of the room a figure stood, and her heart skittered, her mouth curving upward before she could even think to stop it. This was the moment, she realized. The moment when she chose to misbehave, when she chose to think of her own interests above those of clan Campbell — at least for one afternoon. Moving as gracefully as she could with all her insides jittering about, she joined Arran at the table.

"You came," she said, sitting on the bench opposite him.

He resumed his seat again. "And so did ye."

For a brief moment he looked down at his hands, and she wondered if he meant to tell her that they were tempting trouble for no better reason than it *was* trouble, and that meeting for a stupid luncheon simply wasn't worth the risk if they were discovered. All that was correct, but she didn't wish to hear it. Not when it had made her feel so wicked and bold just to be here.

When he looked up again, his face bore the half smile that made her knees feel just a little wobbly. "I've an idea," he drawled.

"And what might that be?"

"What if we begin from the beginning, as if we'd never heard of each other, of our families? What if I'm Arran, a lad from the Highlands, and you're Mary, a lass from Wiltshire, neither of us with any other commitments, and we just . . . become acquainted?"

She offered her hand. Without a hesitation, he reached out and shook it. She could swear that where their skin touched felt electrified, though that might have been her nerves. "I agree," she said. "I'm Mary.

103

Pleased to meet you, Arran."

His grin deepened. "So, tell me aboot yer-self, lass."

CHAPTER FIVE

"I can't imagine what it would be like to lose your father at such a young age," Mary said, selecting another of the absurdly delicate and delicious tea cakes Arran had requested after their luncheon.

"It upended everything," he returned, then motioned the innkeeper for another pot of tea.

She wondered if he'd patronized the Blue Lamb before, because he certainly seemed to know which foods to order. On the other hand, he'd likely spent a great deal more time at ramshackle inns than she had. "You must've been so angry. At my grand—"

"Nae," he said, putting up a hand. "None of that."

Considering how deeply their family histories were intwined, it had been surprisingly easy to refrain from mentioning Mac-Lawrys or Campbells, or MacAllisters or Stewarts. She certainly knew at whom the majority of his suspicion and anger had been aimed over most of his twenty-seven years, just as he was obviously aware how many times his family's name had been sworn at by hers. And words were the least of it. Mary nodded.

"Is this your first time in London, then?" she asked, deciding to change the subject before things became testy.

The glance he sent her from beneath long, dark lashes was amused. "Nae. We all attended Oxford, though there's some debate over whether Bear actually opened a book. I came doon a few times with friends, but nae fer long. And I had to march in a parade before Prince George once, when my regiment came back from the Peninsula."

"So you served in the army?"

They both reached for the same tea cake, their fingers brushing. And neither of them gave way. If this was purely a friendship they were beginning, it was an odd one; she didn't get shivers when she held hands with Liz or Kathleen. Finally he turned up her palm and placed the sweet into it.

"Aye. Fer four years."

"But the Mac— you, I mean — stayed in the Highlands to avoid the English, I thought. Why fight for them?"

He shrugged. "It was encouraged that we

prove our loyalty to the Crown. If I hadnae gone, Bear would have. As his head is better suited fer being a battering ram than fer thinking, I'm fairly certain he would've gotten himself killed."

"You're very close to your brothers and sister, aren't you?" She knew they were a feared and united clan, but for some reason the idea that they felt affection for each other had never really occurred to her — not that she'd spent much time thinking about the MacLawrys at all, except as the people who prevented her from visiting her grandfather in Scotland on all but the rarest and briefest of occasions.

"Did I give that impression?" he returned with a slow grin. "Aye, we wouldnae have survived withoot each other. They're my dearest friends. Are ye and yer cousins close? Ye seem to have at least forty of 'em."

Mary chuckled. "My father has two younger brothers and three younger sisters. At last count I had thirteen first cousins."

"But ye're yer father's only bairn?"

"Yes." She nibbled at a cake to give herself a moment. "I had an older brother, William — named for my grandfather — but he died before I was born. Only a few days old, I think. They don't talk about him much. And because Mother got so sick when I was born, they didn't want to risk having another child."

"Ye know, considering how much I thought I knew about ye, Mary, nearly everything ye tell me is a surprise." He moved in closer to the table and reached out to tap his forefinger against her knuckles. The gesture looked innocent enough, but as he met her gaze with those light blue eyes of his, it felt surprisingly sensuous. *Oh, my.*

"Likewise," she returned, attempting to keep her mind on the conversation. "You and your brothers were bedtime stories my uncles and cousins told me to keep me awake and shivering under the covers. You're supposed to have a needle-thin dagger in your boot, for instance, that's still red with the crusted blood of . . . my kin."

"Oh, aye, I do."

She blinked. "What?"

Reaching beneath the table, he produced an old, sharp-looking knife. It looked very clean, just the sort of tool a Highlander would use for skinning the deer he shot. "More or less, anyway." His gaze growing serious, he sheathed the blade again. "It's nae spilled a drop of yer kin's blood. My fist has; I split Charles Calder's lip just last week, as I recall. But nae my knife. And nae my rifle."

"I believe you," she said, wondering why he so obviously wanted to assure her that he'd never done permanent harm to any of her family. Was he trying to tell her that she was safe with him? Because while she did believe that he wouldn't harm her, she didn't feel safe. She felt wicked.

The inn door opened again, as it had every few minutes since they'd sat to eat a rather fine roasted chicken and watered-down Madeira. She'd had the Madeira, rather; Arran had gone from whisky to tea. The common room seemed to be a popular place for luncheon with local merchants and bankers, which suited her perfectly well. Because while she and Arran seemed to be finding more common ground than either of them expected, if anyone of their acquaintance saw them together, this little tête-à-tête would be finished — and the day would end with her being married either to Roderick MacAllister or Charles Calder, depending on whether her father declared open war on the MacLawrys again or not.

Arran looked past her. His abrupt frown alarmed her to her toes. "Yer maid's here," he murmured, starting to his feet. "Will she use yer name?"

Oh, no. Was it so late already? "Yes. I

didn't give her a dif—"

"Mrs. Crawford," he called, motioning the servant closer.

"Oh, thank heavens, my l—"

"Mrs. Fox has been waiting fer ye," he drawled. "Ye'll see yer daughter home for me, willnae?"

Mary flashed him a quick grin. Now she had a faux mother and a faux name. Fox. She liked it, for obvious reasons, but it was also forgettable — which had no doubt been the point. "Yes, Mama. Thank you. Mr. Fox needs to return to work. At the mill." She stood, sending the servant a warning look to keep her from blurting out something they didn't want overheard.

"I . . . Yes, of course," Crawford stammered. "It's time we get you home, daughter."

Arran tossed some coins on the table, sent the innkeeper a nod, and took her hand in his as they walked to the door. "I reckon we should do this again," he said in his low brogue.

"Why, Mr. Fox, are you attempting to lead me astray?" she asked, her voice unaccountably breathy.

"Aye, I believe I am, Mrs. Fox."

"You are a rogue, sir."

He grinned. "Aye, that I am. Do ye have

an objection?"

"Only that we're both slated to marry other people and our families will murder us if they find out." And likely a million more that logic dictated she consider, but she would do that later. Now was the moment for courage. Until a few days ago, she would never have thought that danger had an appeal. Now, it was all she could do to keep from laughing in delight.

"Then we'll stop when we've said our vows, and in the meantime we dunnae let them find oot." Drawing her up against his chest, he lowered his face to hers.

This time she expected the warm touch of his mouth against hers, the pull between the two of them, but the kiss still stole her breath and sent warm electricity swirling down her spine. Oh, this — he — was trouble, trouble, trouble. And no good could possibly come of her attraction to him. And yet she could scarcely think of anything else.

"I'll be attending the dinner party at Lord and Lady Penrose's house on Friday evening," she murmured against his mouth.

He kissed her again, then with a breath took her hand and placed it around the dour-faced Crawford's arm. "Now there's a coincidence," he drawled. "I believe I've been invited, as well. Or my brother has, rather, which is the same thing."

She wanted to kiss him again, but now that Crawford had hold of her, the maid wasted no time in dragging her out the door and onto Ellis Street. "You — this — I — you —"

"Crawford, you cannot say anything," Mary broke in sternly, abruptly alarmed that her lady's maid was about to suffer an apoplexy.

"But he . . . he *kissed* you, my lady!" she blurted out, then put a hand over her mouth.

"Good heavens. Keep your voice down. I am Mrs. Fox at the moment, and you are my mother." Mary lifted a hand to hail a passing hack.

"I wouldn't be doing my duty if I didn't tell you that that man is a . . . a rogue and a blackguard and a *MacLawry.* What will your father — oh, goodness, or your grandfather — say? He doesn't mean you any good, you know."

"No one is going to know, and we are being discreet. Our families have been warring for centuries. Don't you think it's time two of us became acquainted?"

"I think you'd be better off becoming acquainted with Lord Delaveer, begging your pardon. This MacLawry could mean to ruin you and then tell the world! Bless me, that would kill your mother."

It would do more than that. It would explode the truce, and open the road to a full-out war between their clans. Could that be his goal? To seduce her and then publicly humiliate her? To stop her family from allying with the MacAllisters?

From what she'd learned about him thus far that didn't seem likely; if anything, the Arran with whom she'd chatted seemed honorable, and not just for a MacLawry. Still, she might feel mad and wicked in his presence, but she was not a fool. Or she tried not to be one. Before anything went too far — if it hadn't already — she would need to call a halt to it. They both had obligations to their clans.

But none of that would stop her from going to that dinner party Friday evening.

For someone who spent as much time as he did taking steps to protect Ranulf's various progressive policies and innovations, assessing what their neighbors' reactions were likely to be and heading off the worst of the trouble, Arran couldn't begin to explain what he was doing. Not even to himself.

In the Highlands, when a pretty lass caught his eye, he invited her to share his bed. More often than not she accepted, and then after a night or two or three he found himself bored and sent her on her way. They both wanted a bit of fun, satisfied a mutual desire, and moved on.

That method had served him well enough, and it mostly avoided the chore of him having to converse with the lasses beyond a few pleasantries. They'd all grown up in the same set of valleys, had heard all the same gossip, and none of the ladies had ever seen a larger town than the village in which they lived.

And then there was Mary. Yes, he'd kissed her twice now, and since the hat shop yesterday he'd been imagining unbuttoning her pretty, fashionable muslin gown and licking her soft skin. He shifted, abruptly uncomfortable in the ill-sprung hired hack.

It wasn't just a physical attraction, though. He'd chatted with her. They had talked, the two of them — and he likely already knew her better than he did any other lass save his own sister. More than that, he *enjoyed* talking with her. He liked the way she viewed the world, even if it was contrary to his own way of thinking. He liked *her.* And that, he hadn't expected.

She interested him a thousandfold more than Deirdre Stewart and her "yes, Lord

Arran" and "no, Lord Arran" politeness. They said Deirdre was a great beauty, and he could see it, he supposed, in a porcelain doll sort of way. But the porcelain doll had no passion that he could detect — especially when compared with an autumn-haired, clever-tongued vixen.

By the time he arrived back at Gilden House it was well past three, and he half expected Ranulf to be waiting on the front drive to bellow at him for being contrary. As frustrated as he felt after naught but a kiss with Mary when he'd been fantasizing about a great deal more, a brawl might well be just the thing. Or it might knock some sense into his skull so he could forget the lass before something happened that they would all regret.

Instead of Ranulf, however, the familiar face waiting for him in the foyer belonged to his sister, Rowena. "There you are," she said with a merry smile, still burying her lovely Highlands brogue beneath the passing fair southern England accent she'd picked up from the Hanover sisters.

"Didnae Owen tell ye I was oot at luncheon?" he returned, kissing her on the cheek and using every ounce of willpower he possessed not to look into the neighboring room for Jane Hanover. "What brings ye here, Winnie?"

"You do." She hugged his arm, pulling him into the morning room.

Arran held his breath until he could verify that she hadn't brought anyone else with her. When she seated herself primly on the couch, he settled down beside her. Before she'd fled Glengask for a London Season, the youngest MacLawry sibling had confided in him frequently. Even with the chaos of the past weeks, he'd missed that.

"Well, here I am," he drawled. "What's in yer heart, *piuthar*?"

Her shoulders rose and fell with the deep breath she took. "Firstly, why don't you like Jane? She adores you, and if you married her, we would be sisters."

"Ye're supposed to ease yer way into a question like that, ye know," he said with a short smile. "A bit of 'how was yer day' and 'isnae the weather fine today' first."

She grimaced. "Not with you, I'm not. Answer the question."

"As ye wish, then. I *do* like Jane Hanover. She seems a fine, friendly lass, and she talked her family into taking ye in when ye ran from Glengask and appeared on their doorstep."

"That was Charlotte, actually, but go on."

Had it been? Ranulf's betrothed? That was

interesting. "I thought ye didnae know Charlotte before ye arrived."

"I didn't. I never corresponded with her. But she was so nice, and then when Ran burst in to drag me home she walked right up to him, put her hands on her hips, and told him no."

"And they fell in love because she argued with him?"

"I think that's part of it," she returned, "but you'd have to ask Ranulf. I'm talking about you and Jane, though."

"Lass, completely aside from clan politics ye ken I cannae marry yer friend just because it'd be fun fer ye to call her sister, I hope. Ye'll have Charlotte fer that."

Her face fell. "But she's pretty!"

"Aye, she is. She's also nae but eighteen."

"I'm nae but eighteen. Ranulf wants me to marry stupid Lachlan, so eighteen is nae — not — too young."

So Lachlan had in a few short weeks gone from being her knight in shining armor to being stupid. He was going to have to tell Ranulf about that — if they were still speaking. But perhaps Lachlan MacTier could be of some help, after all.

"Winnie, do ye recall how Lachlan reacted to ye tagging aboot after him everywhere? And sighing and making doe eyes?"

"I did not —"

"He ran the other way as fast as his wee legs would carry him."

"Lachlan does not have wee legs. He's as tall as you are, Arran."

Arran grinned. "So ye do still like him."

Sending him an annoyed look, she rose to pace from the couch to the fireplace and back again, while he wished someone could have this same chat with him about Mary and remind him why he needed to stop tempting fate as he was. That would entail telling someone about her, though, and he knew better than that.

"I don't like Lachlan," Rowena retorted belatedly. "He hasn't even bothered to write me a letter since I left the Highlands. I was merely stating the fact that he was tall."

She paused at the mantel to run her finger along the spine of a porcelain dog there. Arran didn't know where it had come from — but then Ranulf had purchased the house fully furnished so he wouldn't have to go to the trouble of searching out English knick-knacks. Personally Arran would rather have looked at bare walls and empty shelves, but then he wasn't trying to become a Sasannach.

"Ye see my point, though," he continued. "Jane's been chasing me like I'm the last rabbit in winter. She's too young, too agreeable, and too naïve. And I think ye know we'd both be miserable together, even if Ranulf hadnae decided we need the Stewarts aboot to keep his Charlotte safe."

She sighed. "Yes, I suppose so. It still would have been fun."

"Nae fer me. Or fer her, after she realized I'm nae as nice as she thinks." As he spoke, it was another young lady's face who entered his thoughts, and it wasn't that of his nearly betrothed. He barely knew Mary. And if a MacLawry ever married a Campbell, the earth would crack open and swallow the Highlands. That was the legend, anyway.

He shook himself out of the ridiculous daydream. Of course his mind went to making a match with Mary, because it was so absurd. Nothing meant for rational thought, anyway, and far outside the future being laid out for him. "Ye said 'firstly.' Was there someaught else, then?"

"You and Ran are arguing. I don't like that, so stop it — whatever it is."

"It's nae that simple, *piuthar*. Ye can pretend nae to be Scottish, but I cannae. I dunnae want to be a Sasannach. And Ranulf . . . Since when do we consider Sasannach opinions before we do someaught?

119

Since when do we make alliances with clans we've had nae to do with for three hundred years just because now they bolster our numbers in Mayfair?"

"Times are changing, Arr—"

"Aye, they are," he interrupted, warming to the argument. "Because Ranulf and ye are changing them! The only difference between now and six weeks ago is that ye left Glengask, Winnie, and he followed ye."

His younger sister stared at him. Then, putting her hands on her hips, she stalked up to him. "So you'd rather we were still all alone in the Highlands without any allies but those who owe us loyalty because their great-great-great-grandfathers bent a knee to ours? Ye'd rather we didnae have any friends or allies outside the village of An Soadh? Perhaps Maggie at the bakery there could show Ran how to manage English politics."

"Winnie, ye —"

"Perhaps ye'd rather have had Lord Berling shoot ye last week when he aimed his pistol at your head, but I'm glad Ran could arrange a truce. Times *are* changing, Arran. And because Ran's in London and nae far away in the mountains, he can see to it that we profit rather than perish. Here and back home."

She stood there, breathing hard and glaring at him, tears rising in her pretty, dark gray eyes. "Ye've made yer point," he snapped. Being lectured to by a lass nine years his junior wasn't something he'd ever tolerated before. Some things were definitely changing, then.

But other things weren't changing. Ranulf could dine with English fops, but *he* wasn't permitted even to dance with a Campbell lass. Not even when their meeting had been completely by accident. And he couldn't explain any of that to Winnie.

Unless he could. For a long moment he gazed back at her. "What if I told ye someaught?" he went on in a calmer voice. "Could I trust ye with it?"

"Of course you can. You're my brother." She must have said her piece and done, because her brogue had disappeared again. A damned shame, that.

She would likely keep her word to him, then, whatever he told her. But saying anything aloud to anyone felt like he was putting voice to something that was too nebulous to be touched. If it became a real, solid *thing,* it might well shatter and break — like a piece of blown glass cooled too quickly.

And really, he'd only seen Mary Campbell

— Saint Bridget, was it four times now? — and he wasn't certain he had anything to confess, anyway. Burdening his sister with that kind of knowledge for no good reason wouldn't be fair to either of them. "Another time," he said aloud, pushing to his feet.

"Are you certain? Jane didn't want me to say anything, but Deirdre Stewart likes you, you know. She told me you're very handsome, and have a Highlands way about you."

"What the devil does that even mean? I'm a Highlander. Of course I act like one." Then again, Deirdre had Highlands blood, but he damned well didn't see it in her. Mary Campbell, now . . . Wherever she'd been raised, she was a Highlander.

"I don't know," his sister returned. "Do you want me to ask her?"

"Nae. Now. Are ye expected back at Hanover House, or do ye care to try me at billiards?"

Rowena flashed her customary charming grin. "I have time for a game, and then you can see me back to the Hanovers after I thrash you."

He followed her to the door, wishing all his troubles and concerns could be resolved as easily as his sister's frown. "So ye say. I have my doubts."

■ ■ ■ ■

With a muffled curse Ranulf ducked backward into his office and slipped behind the half-open door, where he stood silent and unbreathing until his siblings had passed by and gone upstairs. He wasn't accustomed to sneaking or snooping about, and he could admit that he didn't do it well. But his family was supposed to come to him with their troubles. That was the way it had always been. He wasn't supposed to have to track them down and eavesdrop to discover what bothered them.

If he'd had any doubts that Rowena was becoming a keen-sighted young lady, her fine argument in favor of learning more about the English had answered them. Now he only needed to worry that she would use the same logic of changing times against him and announce she'd found a Sasannach lordling she wanted to wed.

Perhaps ordering Lachlan MacTier, Lord Gray, to remain at Glengask as Bear's lieutenant had been a mistake. But the viscount's lack of attention had been one of the reasons Rowena had decided she required a proper English Season in London. And he'd ultimately agreed to it because his sister did need to view the people her own clan had spent so long fighting against. And of course because he'd met Charlotte.

The idea had been that distance would make Rowena's heart grow fonder — after all, she'd spent the total of her first seventeen years telling all and sundry that she meant to marry Lachlan, until she'd abruptly realized that she was the only one doing the pursuing. For Lucifer's sake, he hoped this was one problem that would settle itself.

It was Arran who worried him more at the moment. Something was afoot, and he didn't like not knowing what it was. Low as he'd stooped to convince Rowena to come and chat with the middle MacLawry brother, and as little as Arran had said, it did mean something that he wouldn't confide even in his sister. Whatever it was that troubled him, it was serious.

And whatever did bother him, he couldn't continue going about London without telling anyone his destination. Truce or not, Ranulf didn't trust the Campbells or the Dailys or the Gerdenses any further than he could throw one of them. Arran could handle himself, and well, but the MacLawrys and their allies were badly outnumbered here. Arran certainly knew that, and yet he continued to vanish on a regular basis.

Was he trying to stir up trouble? That made no sense, unless he meant to escape a match with Deirdre Stewart by setting the MacLawrys and Campbells after each other again. They all knew that only a fool would ally himself with a clan in the middle of a centuries-long feud — and the Stewart was no fool. But that made no sense. Yes, Arran detested the Campbells, but he was also fairly logical. They needed peace, and they could certainly make good use of the Stewarts, both for their trade connections and to keep all the damned Campbells from attempting something unwise now that it looked like the MacLawrys would be spending more time in London.

The last resort would be to send Arran back to Glengask for his own safety, and make him wait there until Deirdre Stewart could be delivered. Before any banishment happened and caused a rift even Rowena couldn't heal, he wanted — needed — more information. And as soon as possible, before one or the other of them said something they couldn't forgive.

"Crawford, you know you look ridiculous," Mary commented, turning her mare, Alba, in a tight circle around the maid. "You can't think to escort me on foot."

"I will be close by, at least," the maid returned. "Davis will escort you." She gestured at the groom, a few feet behind on one of the numerous horses Mary's father kept in his London stable.

"Davis always escorts me when I go riding. I don't even know why you're here."

She did know, of course. All the previous times she'd gone for a morning ride in Hyde Park, she hadn't yet made the acquaintance of Lord Arran MacLawry. Now she had, and suddenly Crawford needed to be present. And Mary tolerated it, because at least the maid hadn't tattled about her luncheon with him.

"Just enjoy your morning, my lady. I'll be close by."

Before Mary could decide whether it was even worth going out this morning with the maid traipsing after her, she spied Elizabeth Bell and her older sister, Annabeth. "Liz," she called, waving, and urged Alba down the path.

"Good morning, Mary. Is that Crawford?"

Mary sighed. "Yes, she detests horses, but she's decided to follow me, anyway."

"You could just send her away, you know."

"Yes, but then she gives me a look like a

126

little lost puppy. And she means well." She reined in to trot beside them.

The park was crowded this morning, likely because the weather was so fine. Within ten minutes her cheeks felt tired from smiling greetings at all her friends and acquaintances, from uttering admiring pleasantries to all the young bucks cantering about to show off their horsemanship and sterling riding attire. It was like a great parade, where each person knew their role and played it each and every time the weather was agreeable enough for the cavalcade.

And then she spied someone riding against the tide. A splendid black Thoroughbred sidestepped gracefully around a barouche and continued forward — toward her. And the man riding him didn't look as though he would willingly be a part of any prerehearsed pageant. Unruly black hair tossed by the breeze, sharp, light eyes that practically crackled with humor and intelligence, and a lean, strong jaw and steady gaze that simply radiated confidence and power and pride. Highlands pride.

While Liz and her sister stopped to chat with an acquaintance in a phaeton, Mary backed Alba around and turned the chestnut mare toward a thick stand of trees. She didn't hurry; that would certainly attract attention, and that was the last thing she wanted. The black changed course to intercept her.

"What are you doing here?" she asked in a low voice, ducking beneath a low-hanging branch.

"I'm observing the Sasannach," Arran returned with a grin. "Ye look rather splendid this morning."

Her cheeks heated. "Thank you. You look fine, yourself."

"Do I? Winnie says I should wear a hat more, but I've never seen anything more useless than those tall, narrow-brimmed things the fops swear by."

"It isn't just the fops," she countered, but personally she agreed with him. Not that hats were useless, but that he looked exceedingly fine without one. For a MacLawry, of course.

"Tell me someaught," he said, urging his black closer. "Is it just me?"

"Is what just you?"

"Us. Is it just me? Because when I woke this morning, the first thought that popped into my head was that it would be grand to see ye today." He reached over and brushed a finger down her arm. "What did ye think this morning when ye woke?"

Considering she'd awoken from a dream

128

that Arran MacLawry had been standing in a forest with her, kissing her senseless, she wasn't certain she should answer that question. But then he would be the only one with any courage, and she would be . . . well, just who she was supposed to be. "I thought it would be pleasant if I were to catch sight of you this morning," she said aloud. "And that perhaps you might kiss me."

Arran stood in his stirrups, leaned sideways, and captured her mouth with his. Heat rushed through her veins, exciting and heady. His very capable mouth molded against hers, making her think of things she was certain young ladies should not be considering.

"I'm beginning to wish you weren't a Mac-Lawry," she murmured.

He backed away from her a little, and for a moment she thought she'd insulted him. Then a slow smile touched that mouth of his. "We're only a Campbell and a Mac-Lawry to the rest of the world, lass," he returned in a soft, low brogue. "To me, ye're Mary. And if ye go riding tomorrow, I'll meet ye here again. And every day until I see ye at the dinner on Friday night."

"And what about the . . . other people with whom we should be spending our time?" she countered, reluctant to speak of them at all, much less name them.

Brief frustration crossed his handsome features. "Are ye married yet, lass?"

"No. Of course not."

"Neither am I. Ye keep answering that same way, and I'll keep kissing ye."

She sighed, taking him in all over again. "Then I hope it doesn't rain tomorrow."

It would likely be better for both of them if it rained, thundered, and hailed, but at the same time, what harm could a few delicious kisses be? Especially when they were wicked and forbidden and very, very arousing.

CHAPTER SIX

"What kind of question is that?" Lord Fendarrow asked, lifting an eyebrow.

Mary sat back against the plump coach cushions, concentrating to keep the curious half-smile on her face. "It's been on my mind, with the truce and Roderick MacAllister. So do you know? How this feud began, I mean."

Lady Fendarrow beside her husband folded her hands into her lap. "Speaking of Roderick, I heard that he had a jeweler call on him two days ago."

A lump of coal settled into the pit of Mary's stomach. Of course everyone was in a hurry, determined to solidify alliances before the truce collapsed again. But she wasn't ready. She'd kissed Arran every day for a week now, after all, and it still wasn't nearly enough. Unless someone could remind her why she was supposed to hate him, she meant to kiss him again tonight, as well.

"Delaveer can purchase all the jewels he wants, but he'd best not give any of them to Mary until my father sends word that he's agreed to the terms we've set."

"So . . . you've come to an agreement?" Mary asked, trying to keep her voice level.

"Ah, so now you're interested?" Her father sent her a cynical look.

"Why wouldn't I be?"

"You've spent nearly every day since I suggested the match out riding and shopping with your friends. I know Roderick called on you at least twice while you were out. Did you even bother to send him your regrets?"

She'd meant to. Putting pen to paper and writing his name, though, made the pending match seem too real. She much preferred the present daydream. "I will write him tomorrow," she said aloud, to avoid any further argument on the topic. "But the feud? It's caused so much trouble, and I've realized that I really know nothing about how it began."

The marquis narrowed his eyes. "You'd get a more thorough answer from your grandfather. Why don't you write him when we get home?"

Bother. "I will. But you're making it sound as if you don't know."

"Don't stick me with your needles, Mary," he retorted, eyes narrowing. "There wasn't one argument or one slight that caused the feud, so I've no easy answer for you. Five or six hundred years of war and politics and kings and land caused what we have now. And be grateful you didn't live a hundred years ago, when the Campbells and Mac-Lawrys went out hunting for each other instead of clashing when we accidently meet."

"Haven't some of these things been resolved or forgotten by now?"

"We never forget." Her father took a breath. "And as sure as the sun rises, an old argument is replaced by a new one. They have the largest standing army in the Highlands, you know. And they are constantly unsettling our cotters with their absurd ideas about providing schools and employment to their own.

"They make it sound as if we enjoy having to turn our ancestral lands away from farming and hunting. But England needs wool, and that is what England purchases — not heather and fish and bagpipes. And they try to hold themselves up as better than anyone else, when everyone knows they're

133

all scoundrels and rogues. All of them."

Perhaps she should have saved her questions for her grandfather, after all. Nothing in her father's voice or his words gave an indication that he would be willing to alter his opinion of the MacLawrys even if presented clear evidence that they were all saints. And they were far from being saints.

"I wish all of them had just stayed in the Highlands. Next thing you know, the giant one — Bear, they call him — will be down here, and none of us will be safe." With an exaggerated shudder, her mother gathered the shawl she wore more tightly around her shoulders.

It was on the tip of Mary's tongue to defend the MacLawrys — or at least Arran. The Gerdenses, her own clan's kin and closest allies, had instigated at least two fights with the Marquis of Glengask over the past weeks. Someone had even burned down his stable, and as far as she knew not even his enemies thought he had done that to himself.

Over the past days she'd begun to wonder just how much of this feud was due to rumor and pride. She'd hoped — well, *almost* hoped — an actual, concrete event that had begun all this existed somewhere in the past. That it would be something so heinous that all her father would have to do was mention it aloud and she would immediately understand why the two clans detested each other. She would no longer think about Arran MacLawry at all, much less want to kiss him and enjoy the sound of his voice and his laughter. She would be proud and pleased to marry Roderick MacAllister and give the Campbells even more sway in the Highlands.

"The fact is, my dear," the marquis finally said in a milder tone, "you are my father's favorite grandchild. You will be lavished with money and land when he passes on. That makes you very marriageable. It also dictates who, precisely, is in pursuit of your hand. The Campbells don't want your property to leave Campbell hands. But this truce provides us with an opportunity we don't mean to pass by."

"Yes, the MacAllisters."

"Yes. The MacAllisters. Otherwise it would be one of your cousins. You are *not* heir to my — or your grandfather's — title and fortune, but you *do* have a significance as part of the direct line of Campbells."

She knew all this — because she happened to be female, the titles of Alkirk and Fendarrow and the clan leadership would go to one of her father's brothers, or her oldest male cousin, Gerard. For heaven's sake, she didn't want any of it; evidently she had just enough importance to warrant a miserable life with a man not of her choosing.

"Better Roderick than Charles, Mary," her mother, always more matter-of-fact than her father, said briskly. "And better Charles than someone who gains us nothing. Or worse, you might go about with your friends until you're on the shelf, and no one will have benefited."

Mary chuckled, though she didn't feel much amused. "Well, we can't have that."

"No, indeed. You might as well marry a . . . a MacLawry!" The marchioness shuddered. "Can you imagine the uproar? Goodness."

Before she could even begin to decipher a way around all this mess, the coach stopped and a red-and-black-liveried footman handed her down to the cobblestoned street. All the windows of Penrose House glowed with yellow-orange light. The earl's — or rather, his wife's — idea of an intimate dinner party didn't precisely fit the dictionary's definition, but it remained exclusive enough to still make the invitation a coveted item.

Given Lord Glengask's reputation for brawling at Society to-dos, she was rather surprised he and his brother had been invited, but then Penrose — not his wife — did have a penchant for welcoming the company of "interesting" persons. And even her father would have to acknowledge that Glengask was interesting. His brother, in her opinion, was even more so.

They entered the house and climbed the wide staircase to the first floor where the drawing room and formal dining room blazed with the light of still more candles. Mary found herself wanting to smooth her violet gown and find a mirror to check the tumbling, twisting knot of her light brown hair, but she resisted both urges. Arran would either be there or he wouldn't, and in either case she wouldn't be acknowledging him. In fact, it was entirely possible that she wouldn't be able to say a single word to him all evening — even if her father didn't make the family's excuses and bundle them home again once he realized the MacLawry brothers were in attendance.

This year at least sixty well-dressed aristocrats crowded into the large drawing room and spilled into the hallway outside. As she squeezed her way in among the tightly packed guests, Mary began to wonder if she'd be able to even see her own feet, much less anyone more than an arm's length away from her. Their hostess, the Countess of Penrose, used a footman to push her way through the crowd so she and Mary's mother could carefully hug without causing any wrinkles or out-of-place hairs. The two women began chatting, as they usually did, about the latest Paris fashions. They'd had luncheon together three days ago so Mary didn't know what new innovations could possibly attract their interest, but she fixed a smile on her face and stood there, trying not to be trampled.

Neither Kathleen nor Liz would be in attendance tonight, but several of her other friends would be. As would Lord Delaveer. And more than likely, Lady Deirdre Stewart. Wondering just how many conversations about fashion any one person could listen to before her head fell off, she turned around — and looked up to see dark blue MacLawry eyes gazing down at her.

"Lord Glengask," she said, swallowing her surprise. The marquis and Arran were clearly brothers, but Arran's face was leaner, the lines and angles less . . . hard. As to which brother was more handsome, that had been a subject of much debate this Season, but it was an argument that for obvious reasons mostly took place out of her hearing. If anyone had asked, she would have placed her wager on Arran.

"Lady Mary Campbell," the marquis said in his deep-voiced brogue.

A hand touched her shoulder, pulling her backward a step. "Glengask," her father's voice came, clipped and cold. *Oh, dear.*

If anything could be worse than one clan coldly shunning the other, it was an open argument between them. These two men were not going to talk about fashion. They both stood not quite square, but right side slightly forward, duelists but for their empty hands. Being attracted to Arran was difficult enough. This could make things so much worse.

"Lord Fendarrow," a more familiar brogue drawled, and Arran stepped around his brother. "I dunnae think we've been introduced." He offered his hand. "Arran Mac-Lawry."

Mary held her breath. Her father was not a rude man, but he *was* a Campbell. One day he would be *the* Campbell, the chief of the clan — as Glengask was the chief of his. Arran kept his gaze steadily on her father, but she looked at him, at his calm expression, the slight, open smile on his face. At this moment he didn't look at all like the rogue he was reputed to be. What he looked like was a Highlander, tall and strong and fearless.

After a hesitation that everyone within sight had to have noticed, her father reached over and shook hands with Arran. "Mac-Lawry," he grunted, letting go and lowering his hand as swiftly as he could do so without looking like he found the deed distasteful. "Come along, Mary," he continued, wrapping his fingers around her arm. "Your mother is looking for you."

"Thank ye fer dancing with me the other night, Lady Mary," Arran continued, and her father froze in his retreat. "I know I must have surprised ye, but there's nae one of us who wants a truce broken over a fox mask."

She nodded, trying to hide her approval. Was he actually attempting to . . . Heavens, she had no idea. To impress her father? To make it known that the MacLawrys were committed to the truce? Perhaps imply that there was no need to rush into new alliances? And now she had to say something, in front of her father and Arran's brother, that wouldn't cause the Penrose drawing room to erupt into open warfare. That would mean pride-driven death, and her pushed at Charles Calder. "You dance a fine waltz, Lord Arran."

Her father gripped her arm hard enough to leave a mark. "This way, Mary."

She had to go with him, or be dragged off her feet. When she managed a parting glance at Arran, he was looking right back at her. And smiling.

Mary had worn a deep violet gown that hugged her fine curves, and no amount of willpower could have kept Arran from lowering his gaze to her swaying hips as her father hurried her away. Her lovely autumn-colored hair was coiled into an intricate tangle of braids and beads, soft curls framing her oval face and bringing out the green of her eyes. She made him hungry, and for something more primal than food.

Ranulf grabbed his shoulder. "What the devil was that?" he murmured, moving around to face Arran directly.

Only an inch or so separated them in height — which was odd, because in his mind Ranulf had always been larger than life. But standing there before him was simply . . . a man. A big man, but then so was he. And Bear was bigger than both of them. He followed the law of the clan because Ranulf asked him to do so. But now for the first time, he found himself unsure that his brother was on the correct path.

Did that give him leave to carve his own trail?

"I asked ye a question," Ranulf hissed, his grip tightening.

"We have a truce," Arran returned with a one-shouldered shrug. "Ye looked ready to pummel him, so I stepped in."

"I'm nae talking aboot that. Ye thanked the lady fer the dance."

"Should I have spat at her, then?"

His brother took a half step closer. "Ye told me that ye hunted her down the day after the masquerade and warned her nae to take ye fer a fool."

Damn it all. "Aye. I did. And now she and her father know we can be civil," he returned, thinking quickly. Since when had his wish to see her rendered him blind and witless? "That's what we're aboot these days, isnae? Showing all and sundry that we're safe with their children and wee animals? That we're merchants and nae warriors now?"

"Why do I think what's best fer the Mac-Lawrys has naught to do with this?"

"I dunnae, Ranulf. I shook the man's hand so ye wouldnae have to do it, so we look like we're keeping to the truce and ye can still be fearsome. Or ye and Fendarrow could've glared at each other till the moon sets." He stepped backward out of his brother's grip. "It nae makes a difference to me."

"That might suffice," his brother returned, his voice low and level, "if I believed ye had naught else in mind. Ending a truce is the devil of a way to escape a marriage."

Arran shook his head. "I've nae wish to fight the Campbells."

"And why, *bràthair,* is that? A week or so ago ye were playing a different tune."

Time, then, either to confess that he'd struck up a friendship with Mary Campbell, or to lie about it. "Ye're the clan chief. Ye figure it out." If Ranulf hadn't unilaterally decided that they were to alter their way of life based on who his in-laws would be, Arran might have answered differently. As things stood, he met his brother's gaze squarely, his fists coiling for the inevitable brawl. Before one of them could throw the first punch, though, their uncle Myles stepped between them.

"Good evening, lads," the Earl of Swansley said with a warm smile. "I wanted to warn you that Lady Penrose is particular friends with Lady Fendarrow, so the Campbells will likely be in attendance tonight. I seem to be tardy in that."

Ranulf sent Arran a last, annoyed glance.

"Aye. Next time ye might warn us *before* we agree to attend. Arran shook Fendarrow's hand."

Myles lifted both eyebrows. "You — you did?"

"Aye. Ran says we're civilized now."

"Well. Speaking of which, Ranulf, I managed to arrange that meeting you wanted with Kerns-Stanley and Dryden. We're to lunch together on Tuesday, so if you can bring Allen to the table, we may have that agreement you've been after. The . . ."

Arran took the moment to slip into the mass of milling Sasannach. Ranulf would be safe with Uncle Myles beside him, and the two of them could discuss their strategy for befriending English bankers and anglicized Scotsmen to their hearts' content. There were basketfuls of other weak-chinned, round-shouldered Englishmen for them to flirt with tonight, if bankers weren't enough for them.

At least Rowena had had other plans; she and Jane Hanover had asked half of London's debutantes to Hanover House for an evening of dinner and charades. It sounded like a lace-covered nightmare. Even Ranulf had looked relieved when Charlotte had informed him that men were not invited.

Whether that would keep his brother from

going out later and climbing the trellis beneath Charlotte's bedchamber window was another matter entirely. Privately he hoped it would keep Ranulf home, because he was growing tired of sleeping with one eye open so he could hear his brother slip out of the house. If Ranulf had known that his clandestine evenings were anything but a secret, much less that he was being shadowed whenever he left the house at night, he would have been furious. Disagreeing or not, though, they were brothers. And whatever else happened, he would still protect his brother with his last breath.

A footman edged his way by, a tray of drinks in his hands. Arran took one and downed it without tasting it. He wanted to go see where Mary might be, if her father was far enough away that they could risk a moment of conversation. It was ridiculous, of course; any of half a dozen lasses present tonight would be happy to find a private room with him. And none of them were Campbells.

Whatever madness had seized him, he didn't feel inclined to fight against it. He liked being in her company, and as far as he was concerned, he hadn't spent enough time there. A bit of a tease, a taste, every morning had only served to whet his appetite. Beyond that — well, no damned body seemed inclined to give him a moment to figure that out.

"Good evening, Lord Arran," a soft coo of breath came, barely audible over the din of the room.

He tried not to flinch as he turned around. "Lady Deirdre," he returned, inclining his head. Her dark hair was pulled up into a knot, her pale skin nearly translucent above a deep blue gown. "You look lovely," he continued, forcing himself to stop searching the room for Mary.

She curtsied. "Thank you. I've heard there may be music later. Will you sit with me to listen?"

That seemed like one of Dante's lower levels of hell. Arran hid his frown. None of this was her fault. He supposed he owed her an attempt at congenial conversation. "What do you think of the two of us being pushed together?"

Large brown eyes almost met his, then lowered again. "You're very handsome, my lord, and of course we must do as our families think best."

"Aye, but what about *you*?" he asked, emphasizing the last word. "Do ye have other wishes?"

She offered him a demure smile. "I wish

to do my best," she returned.

"At what?"

"At . . . whatever my family and my husband require, of course."

Of course. And now he felt ready to stab himself with a fork. "Will ye excuse me fer a moment?" he bit out.

"Oh, certainly, Lord Arran."

Good God. A mere five minutes of that could well kill him. A lifetime was unimaginable. For the first time it wasn't annoyance and frustration digging at him as he thought of being leg-shackled to that. It was dread, and a fair bit of horror. He turned around, making for the far side of the room.

Finally he spied Mary, standing with a small group of young people all chatting loudly about something, and the knot in his chest loosened. Unlike her friends, she wasn't gabbing. Instead, her moss-green gaze roamed the room like she was looking for someone. Looking for him, he hoped.

Snagging another drink, he rounded the fringe of the room until he was close by one of the windows overlooking the street below. A step behind him stood Mary, facing in the opposite direction. He took a breath. "This is nae what I had in mind fer tonight," he murmured.

Silence. From her, at least; the room fairly

vibrated with the cacophony of voices. He drew another breath, wondering how loudly he could speak to the window before people began to notice. Or if she *had* heard him, and decided she wasn't willing to risk anyone seeing them speaking to the air in the same vicinity.

"It's very crowded this year," Mary's voice came softly, a sweet note amid the chaos. "Lord Penrose acquired a Donatello sculpture last month. I think he wants to make certain everyone sees and admires it."

"So he's showing off? Do all these people know it?"

"Most of them do. But an invitation to this dinner is generally very difficult to come by. So when someone is invited, they accept."

"I didnae come here to see a piece of marble." A lordling close by sent him a sideways glance, then abruptly found somewhere else to be when Arran looked back at him.

"There's a fish pond in the garden," she returned, her voice barely more than a soft breath. "I'll attempt to take a stroll there after dinner."

Thank God. "Then ye'll find me there, as well."

"I hoped you'd say . . . Your brother's

148

coming. And, oh, dear, so is Lord Delaveer."

"Go then, lass. There's naught fer ye to worry over." He, on the other hand, had to fight the abrupt urge to punch mild Roderick MacAllister in the face. Shifting the curtains aside with his fingers, he took another drink. For the first time he realized the glass was vodka. He generally detested vodka. Whisky at least had some character.

"What's so interesting oot there in the dark?" Ranulf asked, stopping beside him.

"There's air oot there," Arran replied. "More than I can find in here."

His brother nodded. "Nights like this do make me long fer the Highlands."

Arran faced him. "Then let's go home. Bring yer Charlotte with ye — all the Hanovers, fer that matter — and let's be gone from here, before someaught happens," he returned, sudden desperation thinning his voice. Disaster loomed from every direction, and most especially from where he most wanted to turn. Toward a Campbell, of all people.

"I'm nae having this discussion here, *bràthair*. And I'll nae flee trouble."

"What trouble? There's a truce. And we shouldnae be so far from Glengask when it ends." And he had the distinct feeling that if they didn't leave London, hopefully tonight, he would be the one to end that truce. Because he couldn't seem to stay away from Mary Campbell, even after knowing her for only a week. Because he wanted more than kisses. He wanted her.

"I'm nae ready to leave yet," his brother responded coolly. "If ye're homesick, then go. I dunnae need ye here if ye've nae a mind to do as I ask ye. But dunnae think that leaving excludes ye from yer duty to clan MacLawry."

"Fer the devil's sake, Ranulf, have ye spoken to Deirdre?" Arran asked, sotto voce. "She has the brains of a rock. A wee rock."

A gong rang at one end of the room, loud as the bells of doom. "Dinner is served, ladies and gentlemen," Lord Penrose said grandly, as if no one had ever eaten before. "We do not stand on ceremony here, so take a seat where you like. The only rule is that you not sit beside a spouse or family member."

For some reason the guests seemed to find that amusing. In Arran's limited experience with Sasannach dinners, though, it wasn't uncommon. Evidently at a to-do where everyone was supposed to be clever, laughing at the host's humor was a way to be invited again next year. He didn't plan to be in London next year whatever happened with the Stewarts, and he'd only come here tonight to see Mary, so he didn't bother to pretend a laugh.

As the guests flowed from the drawing room to the dining room with its yards-long table, Ranulf put a hand on his shoulder. "Dunnae even think of sitting near the Campbells," he whispered. "I'll nae have ye making a stir to overturn this agreement with the Stewarts. A wee rock fer brains, or nae. Mayhap I'll inquire if the Stewart has a brighter niece fer ye."

Arran shrugged free. "Mind yerself. There's more than one way fer a man to be a fool."

"Ye and I are going to have a discussion when we get back to Gilden House tonight." This time Ranulf's voice was flat and tone-less — a certain sign the marquis was not amused.

"I look forward to it."

Without a backward glance Arran walked around to the far side of the table and claimed a chair between a pretty blond lass and an ancient-looking lady with white hair pulled into a bun so tight its purpose seemed to be to keep her eyes open. Good. He didn't feel like engaging either his wits or his patience over roasted duck and summer pudding. All of his attention focused on the autumn-haired lass two-thirds of the way down the table and seated between a round, bald fellow and a hatchet-faced older man. If she'd been joined by Lord Delaveer he wasn't certain what he would do — but he knew he wouldn't have liked it. At all.

"Are we supposed to introduce ourselves?" the younger lass asked, her voice high-pitched and breathy. She actually lowered her head to gaze at him through her eyelashes.

"I shouldn't bother, dear," the tight-faced woman replied, leaning her ample bosom in front of Arran to do so. "You're here to be gazed upon. Leave the cleverness to the ugly people."

"But —"

"Never mind her," the fellow past the lass countered, then offered his hand. "Thomas, Lord Addent."

"Oh." Looking mollified, the blond lass shook his fingers. "Lady Constance Overton."

Arran returned his attention to the white-haired woman. "I'm nae inclined to introduce myself," he drawled, "because I reckon ye'll call me ugly."

She barked a laugh. "You can be the exception, young man." With a baleful glance at the chinless fellow on her other side, she held out her hand, wrist limp.

Taking her pale fingers, Arran bowed over them. "Arran MacLawry," he intoned.

"Ah. Glengask's brother. Why not *Lord* Arran?"

"It sounds pretentious. I've nae anyone I need to impress tonight."

Retrieving her hand, she cackled again. "I like you. Lady Forsythe-Hendley, and I *am* pretentious. If people don't bow and scrape before you, what's the point of being titled and paying all those taxes?"

He grinned. "At least ye admit to it."

"I insist on it."

While Lord Addent charmed breathy Lady Constance Overton, Arran spent most of the dinner chatting with the sharp-tongued dowager countess. He knew precisely where his brother was seated, close to the head of the block-long table with Uncle Myles only a few chairs away. He'd found Mary's parents, flanking her on the opposite side of the table, likely as watchful for Mac-Lawrys as he generally was for Campbells. And Deirdre sat closer to him than he liked, and only one seat down from Roderick MacAllister — two unwanted pawns in an unwanted game.

"You're unmarried, I hear," Lady F — as

she'd insisted he call her — commented.

"I am." For the moment, anyway. "Why, do ye have a granddaughter to set after me?"

She slapped her hand on the table. "Heavens, no. The girl's a complete imbecile, just like her parents. I plan on having her marry Lord Pettigrew. That'll show him."

Arran laughed. "Ye're a cruel woman, Lady F."

"Indeed, I am. So who is she?"

He lowered an eyebrow. "Beg pardon?"

"You're young, unmarried, sitting beside one of the Season's beauties, and you're chatting with me. Either you fancy the bearded set, or someone's got your attention."

If it was that obvious to a complete stranger, he was going to have to be more cautious. Turning now to flirt with Lady Constance would be far too obvious, so he kept the grin on his face. "I'm a Highlands lad. Only a Highlands lass will do fer me."

"Then you are in the wrong place, Arran MacLawry. You won't find any of those here."

There were two, actually, even if they'd been raised English. But only one had the Highlands spirit. One of them he had no wish to engage in conversation, and the other he was forbidden to approach. "Hence me chatting with ye, my lady. And ye've kept me from nodding off into my onion soup."

"Likewise. It's only a shame I'm not fifty years younger, or I'd show you the merits of English ladies." She put a hand over his, but the gesture felt friendly rather than amorous. "I was at the Lansfield soiree when you and Glengask wore your full Scottish regalia. Even *my* heart went pitter-patter, I think. My great-grandmother was a MacDonald. You made me proud of that."

Arran wasn't certain anyone should boast about being a MacDonald, but he understood the sentiment, and nodded. *"Alba gu bràth."* Scotland forever.

A few years ago just saying that might've seen him thrown in prison, but Lady F only smiled and nodded. Very well, not every Sasannach was a fool. He did have friends among them — men like William Crane, Viscount Fordham, with whom he'd served in the army. But outside of that, he hadn't even bothered to consider he might find a friendly face. Much less an interesting one. Of course she was part Scottish, which could explain it.

Beyond that, he did his best not to rush through every course. He couldn't force everyone to eat more quickly so he could go strolling in the garden. Whoever said that anticipation was the best part of a reward deserved a clout to the back of the head. Both he and Mary had already skirted rules and orders. They would be outright defying their family patriarchs if they went out to meet by the pond — and whether she appeared or not was the only thing that concerned him. And he knew what that meant. He was becoming obsessed with the last woman in the world he should ever be approaching, and he was willing to risk his own safety and that of his clan just to see her.

Deirdre Stewart looked from Arran Mac-Lawry, as close by her as she could manage to sit, to Lady Mary Campbell, halfway down the table. It didn't make any sense. She'd done everything right, just the way she'd been taught. Let a man know of her interest, smile and laugh, flirt and be nothing but pleasant and mild.

In addition, her father had said that her marriage to Lord Arran would gain the Stewarts more ships for trading, more crops to sell, and more stability in the Highlands without them having to be there. It should have been her he'd been whispering to behind the crowd tonight. It should have been her meeting him down by the pond for . . . whatever it was they meant to do there.

She could imagine, of course. He would kiss her, and she would smile at him and tell him how handsome and wicked he was — at least that was how she'd imagined it would be when he asked *her* to meet him somewhere private. Oh, she could almost swoon just thinking of it.

Except that it wouldn't be her. From the way he'd looked at Lady Mary when he thought no one else noticed, he might agree to marry someone else — her — but it would be a misery. Her, being made to look foolish by a Campbell and a MacLawry. The Stewarts and the MacLawrys were supposed to be forming an alliance, through her and Arran. How could they do that when he was sneaking off to see someone who was supposed to be his enemy?

If Lord Fendarrow discovered that they were somewhere together, Mary Campbell would likely be sent home to Fendarrow for the rest of the Season. And then perhaps Arran would do as he'd been told, and turn his gaze to her. She was one of the Season's beauties, after all. Everyone said so. And Mary Campbell had been out for three years, and Deirdre couldn't recall if anyone had ever called her a beauty.

As the ladies finally rose to leave the table she found Lord Fendarrow, seated several chairs away. Lord Glengask had been so adamant that nothing happen to disturb this truce they'd somehow arranged so she could tell *him,* of course, but then he might send Arran away. All the MacLawrys would vanish back into the Highlands, and would have no need of the Stewarts. No, the Marquis of Fendarrow would know just what to do — and she would be helping the Stewarts, the MacLawrys, the MacAllisters, and the Campbells, all at the same time. And when had anyone ever accomplished that?

CHAPTER SEVEN

Mary followed her mother out of the dining room as all the ladies left the gentlemen behind to their brandy and cigars. Servants had opened the double doors at the far end of the drawing room to reveal an additional sitting room. Why they hadn't done that earlier when everyone was crowded together like potatoes in a sack, she had no idea. Of course she didn't intend to spend much time in there, regardless of whether there was room to exhale or not.

"Mother," she said, touching the marchioness's powder-blue sleeve, "please excuse me. I'll be back shortly."

Her mother nodded, most of her attention on Lady Penrose and the story she was telling about the massive dining room table. "I'll save a seat for you, dear. Don't be long."

With her heart pounding, she retreated downstairs and left the house through the servants' entrance across from the stable yard. She would be in *so* much trouble if her parents discovered what she was doing and who she was seeing. It thrilled and terrified her all at the same time. A heady combination indeed, and that wasn't even adding in Arran and his intoxicating voice and kisses.

Torches lined the garden paths, and she found the pond with no difficulty. Golden scales flashed orange in the firelight, and she sat on a bench in the shadows to watch. Crawford had been convinced that Arran meant to wait until she was alone and then set half of clan MacLawry on her like wolves. Well, she was alone now, and he knew it. If he did mean trouble, she would much rather know it.

Except that she did feel like she knew already, or she wouldn't have ventured outside at all. To herself she could admit that she felt like the danger, the thrill, surrounded her and excited her, but she herself was safe. Because she trusted Arran. But was it that excitement that made him so alluring, or the man himself? It certainly wasn't thoughts of the future, because the two of them didn't have one. Not together.

"Did ye know they pass a pot aboot fer all the men to piss in, so no one has to leave

160

the table?" Arran rounded the back of the pond and ducked into the shadows to sit beside her.

She hadn't even heard him approach. "How did you make your escape, then?"

"I stood up, nodded at my brother, and walked oot the door. He's being civilized, so he'll nae leave his new friends to look fer me." He took her right hand, lifting it to look at her fingers. Slowly he twined his own with hers.

"You shook my father's hand."

Arran smiled, the expression heating her insides. "I didnae want him and Ranulf coming to blows. And he has a fine daughter."

Well, that was very nice of him to say. But she still had some concerns, and if he began kissing her, despite the fact that she was not the sort of lady who swooned at the idea of romance, she would likely forget them. "It occurs to me," she said slowly, "that we're not doing anything but preparing to cause ourselves pain. More pain."

He cocked his head in that alluring way he had. "Has Delaveer offered fer ye, then?"

"No, but evidently he's had a jeweler call on him. And his father will be in London on Sunday."

"That's two days from now."

161

"I know. What about you and the Stewarts?"

"There's a luncheon tomorrow. It's nearly settled."

Another chill ran down her spine. "I'm not ready for the end of . . . this."

For a moment he met her gaze, light blue eyes dark in the torchlight. Out here, even in formal English clothes he looked wild — a Highlander to the heart, merely wearing a civilized jacket and waistcoat because it suited him to do so. Someone who didn't care for the Campbell's approval or a taste of his power, because he had his own. And that was very intoxicating, indeed.

"I dunnae want this to be the last time I set eyes on ye, either, bonny Mary. I dunnae want this to be the last time we talk, or the last time we kiss." He firmed his grip on her hand. "Will Delaveer be good to ye?"

Mary nodded. "I think he will. He's not cruel, just . . . dull."

"I'll nae release ye to someone ye dislike or fear. Nae matter the consequences."

She knew he meant it; she could feel the truth of it in her heart. And the idea that he would soon be married to lovely Deirdre Stewart troubled her as much as did the thought of her own impending marriage. Would he think of her? Would he miss her?

162

She wanted to ask him, but it felt unnecessarily cruel to both of them. "Well, I daresay we both know married people who live completely separate lives," she offered, trying to sound lighthearted. "That will be tolerable, I suppose."

"Tolerable," he repeated, more harshly. "I've known ye but a short while, and I cannae seem to shake ye from my thoughts. I feel like . . . I feel like a traitor to my own brother, but then I tell myself that if he can make friends with all the Sasannach and call it reasonable, I can kiss one Campbell and call it desire." That slow smile touched his shadowed face again. "We'll settle fer 'tolerable' tomorrow."

She wanted to lean against his solid shoulder, and sternly stopped herself. That would only make parting from him more difficult. It seemed impossible that a fortnight ago he was just a name, a rogue who brawled, who seduced and abandoned women, and who stood against everything the Campbells favored. Stories about a faceless monster who in person was nothing at all like she'd feared.

"I know precisely how you feel, Arran, because I keep having that same conversation with myself. I wish . . . I wish . . . something."

"Well, then." He tilted her chin up with his fingers and kissed her. Heat spun down her spine, delicious and welcome. Part of what they said about him must have been true, because he kissed like sin itself. But they weren't her kisses. She was stealing them from another woman.

Mary blinked her eyes open and put the flat of her free hand against his chest to push him back. "No more kisses," she announced, though her gaze didn't leave his mouth, his slightly parted lips. "This is only making it worse."

"I know." He squinted one eye. "I'm bloody frustrated, Mary. And so if ye have an idea, I'm listening."

She had several ideas, but most of them seemed to end with him being shot on her front step and her being forced to wed Charles Calder. "We shake hands and wish each other happiness."

"I have a different idea," he drawled. "We save the fare-ye-wells fer tomorrow, and now I kiss ye again. Ye taste like honey."

"That's probably from dinn—"

She couldn't finish speaking because he covered her mouth with his. Mm. Mary slid her hands around his shoulders, wanting to be closer to him. Abruptly he lifted her to sit across his thighs, and she leaned into his muscular frame. Beneath her bottom he stirred, and heated electricity jolted through her again. Arran MacLawry didn't want her because of her pedigree; he wanted her in spite of it. And that was very arousing. *He* was very arousing. And he was correct; good-byes could wait until tomorrow.

"Damn you, Arran MacLawry! Get your bloody hands off my daughter!"

Arran set Mary on her feet and stepped between her and the voice before he even consciously noted who was shouting. One hand moving toward the knife in his boot, he faced the Marquis of Fendarrow — and the pistol in the marquis's hand. The truce was broken, then. Thanks to him. Slowly he straightened. With the way the marquis's hand was wavering, Mary might be injured by accident.

"Mary," Fendarrow hissed, motioning at her with his free hand, "come here. Now."

"Father, please put that down before something terrible happens," she said, her voice tight. Arran felt her palm touch his shoulder then abruptly drop when her father flinched.

"Lass, ye need to move away," he said calmly. Or he hoped he sounded calm; his mind flew through a dozen different possible outcomes, several of which ended with him dead in a fish pond. "Nae need fer both of us to get shot."

"There's no need for *anyone* to get shot. Father, for heaven's sake, put that pistol away! Why do you even have one here?"

The lass did move, but only to stand directly beside Arran. He appreciated the united front, but at the same time she likely wasn't helping matters. This wasn't the part her family wanted her to play. When shouting began on the carriage drive, Arran clenched his jaw. The only thing worse than being discovered by her father would be adding his brother into the mix. For a brief moment he considered making a run for it; Fendarrow likely hadn't shot at anything but grouse for years, and that wasn't done with a pistol. But that would leave Mary to face this mess alone. And a MacLawry didn't run from a fight.

"Arran!" Ranulf bellowed, skidding into the garden with Uncle Myles on his heels. The entire guest list trotted and skipped and waddled out of the house behind him, Lord Allen and Deirdre with them. And Lord Delaveer. *Bloody wonderful.*

"What's all this?" the Earl of Penrose demanded, their host's stern tone somewhat undercut by the way he stopped several yards away from the fracas.

"Put that damned pistol doon, Fendarrow!" Ranulf ordered. Unlike their dinner party host, he moved directly into the line of fire. His gaze moved from Arran to the Campbell's granddaughter and back again. "Arran," he murmured, "ye bloody f—"

"Get yerself back, Glengask," Arran interrupted. "This has naught to do with ye." By himself, he could likely disarm Fendarrow before the marquis had a chance to pull the trigger, but Ranulf would jump in if he moved — and he damned well wasn't going to risk his brother's life. Although as he'd just trampled their fragile little truce, he'd already put Ranulf in danger.

"I don't give a damn about either of you," Fendarrow growled. "Mary, come here. Now."

"I'm so sorry, Arran," her soft whisper came from behind his shoulder. "I don't know wh—"

"Go to your *athair,* lass. We cannae settle anything here tonight," he murmured back, keeping his hands well away from his sides and his gaze steady on her father. Abruptly he wished he knew more about the man; once a Highlander left the Highlands for England's softer ways, though, the MacLawrys tended to ignore him.

Slowly Mary moved around him and walked toward her father. Arran had read about scandals similar to this one in the London newspapers that had made their way up to the Highlands. They all ended with either the father shooting the rogue who'd tried to despoil his daughter, or a quick marriage between the two parties concerned to quash any further scandal. The latter would never happen. Not between Mary and him.

He risked a glance at Mary's straight, stiff shoulders. Because he'd been unable to think straight, or in fact to ponder anything beyond having her in his arms and hearing her clever laugh, he'd put them in this position. And now the best he could do was try to salvage enough peace that Roderick MacAllister wouldn't withdraw from the negotiations.

"Do ye mean to murder my brother now, in front of all these witnesses?" Ranulf demanded, in the same tone that had once sent an armed Adam Daily rolling backward down a hill rather than confront him.

Fendarrow lowered the pistol, then shoved it into his pocket. "No," he said clearly. "Nor do I want this . . . aberration to affect our dealings. In return, however, I want *him*" — and he jabbed a finger in Arran's direction — "gone from London."

As angry as Ranulf likely was, being ordered to do something that concerned his own family wouldn't sit well with him. Especially when the order came from the Campbell's oldest son. Arran braced himself, ready to step between the two men.

"I'm agreeable to that," Ranulf said with a curt nod. "He'll be gone by sunset tomorrow."

Arran stared at his brother's profile. Jaw clenched, fists clenched, eyes narrowed and icy, the Marquis of Glengask didn't look inclined to concede anything, much less banishing his own brother at a Campbell's request. And yet not even a Sasannach could have misunderstood his words.

Fendarrow grabbed Mary by the arm and yanked her back toward the house. They headed in Delaveer's direction, as if the marquis meant to hand her over to Roderick right then and there. The viscount, though, shook his head and walked away. *Damnation.* Now it was worse. Mary's already pale cheeks went even grayer, but she didn't fight her father's grip. Instead, her pretty, moss-green gaze fixed on Arran's face, she backed away from the garden.

Once she went through the door into Penrose House, he would never see her again.

169

He knew that with an ice-cold certainty that made his lungs feel like they were filled with sand. It would have happened soon enough anyway, but not yet. He wasn't ready. "Ranulf."

His brother faced him. "I dunnae want to hear another damned word from ye," he snarled. "I dunnae even want to look at ye. Get in the coach and go back to Gilden Hoose."

"Ran —"

"Now."

With a curse Arran turned on his heel and strode for the stable yard and the street beyond. He passed by the coach, ignoring Debny's attempt to catch his attention, and continued down Hill Street. If he sat in the coach like a naughty lad sent to his bedchamber for poor behavior, he would combust.

As he turned the corner another coach trundled by, the horses under the whip. The Campbell coat of arms glinted on the door panel in the lamplight. Mary had been sent home as well, to take responsibility for . . . for whatever it was they might accuse her of. His first instinct was to charge after them and claim responsibility for whatever ill deeds they chose to fling in his direction. If he showed his face at Mathering House, though, he would be doing more harm than good.

And realistically, what would he do, anyway? Promise he wouldn't make more trouble so she could be wed to dull Delaveer, after all? He didn't want her to marry the viscount. He didn't want her marrying anyone — at least not until he'd figured out what the devil *he* wanted, himself.

Damn it all. So much for his reputation as the "clever" MacLawry brother. Even Bear had never been caught by a lass's parents. And the worst part of it was that for the past few days, and especially tonight, he felt like something had begun, like they'd been on the precipice of something that could have been — would have been — extraordinary, if only she hadn't been a Campbell and he a MacLawry.

Now, because beneath everything else he was Ranulf's brother and heir to clan MacLawry's chief, he would take the thrashing he was handed, and then he would go home. Go north to the Highlands, return to Glengask. The incident finished and if not forgotten, then never to be discussed again. Ranulf the master negotiator would make some additional concession to the Stewarts, and he would still have his alliance. The

171

remainder of his own life would be filled with the dull prattle of Deirdre Stewart. Mary, however, was likely to be confronted with something even worse. And it was all his own damned, arrogant fault.

Scowling and half hoping some thug would accost him, Arran reached Union Street, hesitated, and then turned north when he should have turned south. If he was wrong about what would be in store for Mary, he was about to cause even more trouble for himself. But he needed to know. He needed to know she would be well.

And so he kept walking. Turning another corner, he climbed the steps to the modest-sized house in front of him and swung the brass lion's head knocker against the door. He hadn't precisely been full of good ideas this evening. And he could only hope this would be the exception. Or it could be the first — or last — nail in his coffin.

The door swung open, an elderly, liveried man moving into the opening. "Lord Arran," he said, inclining his head. "Was Lord Fordham expecting you? He isn't in this evening, I'm afraid."

Arran nodded, still attempting to gather his thoughts into something coherent. "I wondered if I might write a note oot fer the viscount."

"Certainly, my lord." Stepping aside, the butler ushered him into the morning room. "You'll find paper and pen in the writing desk. May I bring you some tea?"

What he wanted was whisky, but he was going to need all his wits over the next few hours. "I'd thank ye fer some tea." This was going to take some time he likely didn't have, but at the moment he was finished with weighing regrets. And taking action weighed less than leaving all his questions and hopes unanswered.

"I should have him arrested, is what I should do," Lord Fendarrow snapped, pacing a tight line in his office.

Mary and her mother sat in the chairs facing the desk, the marchioness following her husband's stalking with her head, and Mary doing her best to keep her gaze on her folded hands. It was the only way she could keep them from clenching, and the only way she could keep from doing something as stupid as stomping her feet and shouting that if anyone would just take a moment to listen, they might understand.

"Accosting *my* daughter," her father continued, the pitch of his voice rising as he ranted. "The Duke of Alkirk's granddaughter! Rogues, all of them! I'm sending word to Alkirk. This will mean war."

"No!" she broke in, all the blood leaving her face. "You can't do that, Father! I was kissing him just as much as he was kissing me, for heaven's sake! I told you that."

"That's enough, Mary!" her mother said sharply. "He is the man; this is all his responsibility. He tricked you. He led you astray. You are very nearly betrothed. This is . . . inexcusable."

"Mother, y—"

"That's it, isn't it?" her father took up, snapping his fingers. "The end of the truce. That's the MacLawrys' aim. Why else would Glengask have sent his brother after you? And why would he have arranged for me to discover you at so opportune a moment and at so crowded an event? He doesn't want the Campbells allying with the MacAllisters."

"Father, I —"

"They may have men in place, just waiting for word that we've broken the truce so they can murder us all." He stalked to the window, peered outside, then pulled the curtains closed as if he feared assassins could be lurking in the shrubbery even now.

"Arran and I stumbled across each other, and we've become friends," Mary insisted, raising her voice when her mother tried to hush her again. "There's a truce, so what's the difficulty?"

"The 'difficulty,' as you call it, Mary, is that you are Lady Mary Campbell, for God's sake. Why do I need to state that you do not kiss random men? Especially men from a rival clan?" The marquis snapped his mouth shut. "You only kissed him, didn't you? You're not despoiled? By a Mac-Lawry?"

"*What?* Of course I haven't — we've only been acquainted for a week!"

"Which is evidently long enough for you to embarrass us and put all of our futures at risk. Roderick wouldn't even look at us as we left the dinner, and what do you think Charles is going to say when he hears that Arran MacLawry kissed you?"

Mary began feeling ill. Not because of what she'd done, but because they'd stopped her. Because Charles Calder had clearly endeared himself to her parents more than she'd realized, in case of just such a fiasco. Because Lord Glengask had said that Arran would be on his way back to Scotland by tomorrow night, no doubt with Deirdre Stewart on his heels.

She couldn't even explain it. For goodness' sake, she was one-and-twenty. He was not Romeo, and she was most certainly not

Juliet. This wasn't love at first sight. But there was something. They'd begun something, touched something, she and Arran. They'd said they would end it when the time came, but given the way she felt at this moment, she wasn't certain how she would have parted from him.

"Go up to bed, Mary," her father finally ordered, pausing his pacing. "For the world at large I blame MacLawry. Privately, I am most disappointed in you. And some things are going to alter. This indulgence we've shown because of your grandfather's fondness for you stops. Clearly you cannot be trusted not to act in ways that weaken this family."

That sounded even more ominous. Protesting now after she'd already stated that she'd become friends with Arran would only make her father more furious. With a stiff nod she stood and walked to the office door. "Good night, Father. Mother."

They didn't answer. In her entire life she'd never seen them so angry. Certainly she'd never given them cause to be disappointed or even annoyed with her before. But this *was* her fault. She couldn't say she was proud to be a part of clan Campbell, because she'd never truly felt challenged about it. She was proud of her grandfather and how well respected he was, and she was proud to be his granddaughter. For the most part her parents did as he requested, which made them seem almost like an extension of him. Would the Campbell be as angry as they were? Was he truly the one who'd pushed the alliance with the MacAllisters? What would he say now that she'd ruined it? Would he not wish to see her or write her letters or send her bits and baubles from the Highlands any longer?

Crawford waited for her upstairs and helped her change out of her fine violet evening gown and into her night rail. The maid was clearly near to bursting with "I told you sos," but Mary didn't give her the opportunity to use them. Of course she knew better. The risk had seemed worth it. It still did, actually.

She spent most of the night awake, half hoping that Arran would climb through her bedchamber window — not to ravish her or help her run away, but so she would have someone with whom she could discuss what had happened. So they could attempt to make sense of events and figure out what they needed to do to fix things.

He didn't appear, and then Crawford began throwing open curtains shortly before eight o'clock in the morning. "We need to hurry, my lady," the maid said, pulling a rather plain green and brown muslin from the wardrobe.

"Why are we hurrying?" Mary asked, brushing the night's restless knots out of her hair. "No one will be out and about for hours."

"I don't know, my lady. Your father the marquis said you were to come down to breakfast at once."

So she would be spending the day being reminded of her ancestry and her duty and the history of the clan's rivalry with the Mac-Lawrys. Or perhaps he'd managed to convince Roderick that the truce, more rickety or not, remained, and that the Campbells and MacAllisters still had an alliance. She frowned. Roderick. Yes, he was likely waiting for her just downstairs. After she'd kissed and chatted with Arran. A life of dull and mild, with a hundred might-have-beens up in the attic where she could dwell on them endlessly.

Even with all that, though, she couldn't regret meeting Arran. Without him she would have missed a handful of the most interesting conversations of her life. She would have missed the sensation that her feet weren't quite touching the ground when he smiled at her. She would have missed knowing him — and that would have been a tragedy even greater than the one currently opened at her feet.

"Oh, you have a letter," Crawford exclaimed, making her jump. The maid produced a crisply folded missive from her pocket and handed it over. "I nearly forgot, with all the goings-on this morning."

Mary frowned as she turned it over. " 'Lady Joan Crane,' " she read aloud, not recognizing the name. The address was a respectable one on Reeves's Mews, so with a shrug she broke the wax seal and unfolded the note.

"Dear Lady Mary," she read to herself. "Though we aren't well acquainted, I would very much appreciate knowing that you are well. If for any reason you find your present circumstances untenable, please feel free to inform me."

What the devil was this? She opened the last fold of the short note, and a small scrap of yellow and white muslin fell to the floor.

Heat and understanding jolted through her. Swiftly she bent down to retrieve the scrap, and curled her fingers hard around it. Arran had kept this, from that morning at the hat shop. She hadn't even realized. And he'd managed to find a way to contact her. He was still thinking about her, still concerned about her — just as she was about him.

Almost immediately the chill of reality swept in to drive the warmth of those thoughts away. Because able to contact her or not, he was still a MacLawry. He was still leaving for Scotland by sunset, and she still had Roderick MacAllister awaiting her downstairs. And so she would write him via this Lady Joan, and tell him that she was well, that she wished . . . that she wished *him* well, and that this — whatever it might have become — was over.

Once Crawford finished pinning up her hair, Mary put the note and the scrap of muslin in the drawer of her writing desk and went downstairs to be lectured.

In the breakfast room doorway, though, she stopped dead. Her parents sat in their usual places, their expressions as grim and somber as she'd expected. But the reason she couldn't catch her breath was seated in *her* usual spot at her father's right elbow. And it wasn't Lord Delaveer.

"Good morning, Mary," Charles Calder said with a smile.

The fact that he was smiling when he should have been plotting revenge against the blackguard MacLawrys horrified her. Because she could only think of one thing that would make him smile this morning. The MacAllisters had fled the alliance, after all.

"Have a seat, Mary," her father said flatly. "We have some things to discuss."

CHAPTER EIGHT

"Dunnae bother, Winnie. His mind's made up." Arran threw the new pair of Hessian boots he'd acquired into the traveling trunk along with the ridiculous beaver hat the Sasannach required their men to wear out of doors.

He'd arrived in London four weeks ago in such a hurry that he hadn't packed anything but a clean shirt. Everything going into the trunk now had been purchased here. More than likely he'd never need any of it again, but perhaps the church in An Soadh could make use of the clothes if they ever put on an English play.

"But he's arranging his wedding," his sister countered, tears skittering down her cheeks. "We'll all be heading home in a few weeks. Ran would be better off with you here."

Arran held up a small porcelain fox that had somehow found its way onto his dressing table. "Is this from ye, or Ranulf?" he asked.

"Me."

"Thank ye, then." He wound it into the small pile of cravats he'd also acquired, then tucked it into one corner of the trunk.

"Couldn't you simply apologize?" Rowena insisted. "Tell him you were spying on the Campbells for us, to see if they truly mean to honor the truce."

He shook his head, setting aside the thought that he'd considered telling that very lie just so he would have an excuse to be seen in Mary's company. If that tale had ever had its moment, it had now passed. "Nae, *piuthar.* It's only Ranulf who can decide to make peace with an enemy because he wants a woman. The rest of us wed who and when we're told. So watch yourself, Rowena. I hear the Cameron has an unmarried son. And he's naught but fifty-seven, only twenty-nine years yer senior."

"You shouldn't say such things, Arran. Especially about Charlotte. And the Hanovers are very nice, too."

"Aye, they are. And I have no quarrel over a friendship with the Hanovers. It's Glengask shaking hands with all the Sasannach and all the Scots who've fled the Highlands that grinds my teeth. But he can do as he wishes. I cannae, obviously."

"This is ridiculous!" she argued, stomping one foot. "Just talk to him! We are family. We don't send each other away."

"Ye have that wrong, Winnie," Arran returned, waiting until his sister's back was turned before he slipped a pistol into the pocket of his hanging jacket and set the other one into the trunk. However he felt about Mary, he was not popular with the Campbells at the best of times. By now the lot of them were likely frothing at the mouth to be after him. "Ran banished Uncle Myles fer three years fer being pleasant to the Donnellys."

"Because it ended with Bear being shot. This isn't the same. And he forgave Uncle Myles."

"Aye, he did. The moment Ranulf needed him to navigate through the Sasannach."

She folded her arms across her chest. "So you're just leaving London. You're running away like a scalded dog."

Arran walked around his bed and sat on the edge of it to face his sister. "Whatever anyone thinks, I dunnae want trouble with the Campbells. I didnae intend fer this to happen. So aye, I'm leaving. Like a scalded dog."

"I don't like this."

Frequently Arran had been put into the position of being the diplomatic MacLawry, the one who soothed over some of the more radical of Ranulf's decisions. Like when he'd decided to build schools in the two villages on Glengask land, and require every child under the age of twelve to attend them. Well, with the mood he was in, Ranulf could be his own diplomat.

"The only one who's allowed to like the way of things is Ranulf. Dunnae ye see that by now? Do ye think I'd be aboot to marry Deirdre Stewart if I had a choice? Saint Bridget. I've had more interesting conversations with a hammer."

Rowena furrowed her brow, dark gray eyes searching his. "Arran, you aren't in love with Mary Campbell, are ye?"

Since her brogue kept slipping into hearing she must have been truly surprised, and truly distraught. On another occasion he might have teased her about it, but this morning he didn't feel amused. He wanted to know that Mary wasn't paying an even higher price than he was for this disaster. That was the only thing that would make leaving London acceptable — if by doing so he was helping her. Of course helping Delaveer *to* her didn't sit nearly as well, but he was a better choice than Calder.

He'd done what he could when he'd had Fordham forward that letter to her. Answering it would be up to her. And if she didn't respond, he would never know if she was simply relieved that the decision of what they would do next had been removed, or if she felt as at sea as he did. Milling currents, muddled feelings, that sense of loss without ever having grasped what it was they might have had.

"We'll never know now, will we?" he said aloud, knowing his sister expected some sort of response. "I'm pledged to Deirdre. Or near enough."

"But did ye tell Ran? If he knew, he might —"

"Who do ye think ye're talking to, Rowena? Now go downstairs and be nice to our *bràthair* before he decides ye need to go home, as well."

That evidently made an impact on her, because after favoring him with a tight, damp hug she fled his bedchamber. Arran blew out his breath, then stood to resume packing. He might have been more positive, more circumspect, he supposed. He might have offered his sister some hope that he and Ranulf would reconcile.

Except that he didn't think they would. Ranulf hadn't spoken a word to him since they'd parted at the Penrose dinner. But more than that, this trip down to London had changed the marquis. Whatever it was, Arran didn't understand it, he didn't like it, he didn't see a reason for it, and he didn't think it was in the best interest of clan Mac-Lawry, no matter who else they brought into the fold.

Finally he shut the trunk and buckled the leather straps to keep the lid locked down. Every ounce of will he possessed fought against the desire, the need, to go to Mathering House and discover for himself how Mary fared. But he'd arranged for her to get his note. If he went to see her in person, several people would likely end up dead.

"M'laird," Owen said from the doorway.

"Aye. Come in."

The butler stayed in the hallway, as though he were worried he might catch the plague if he stepped into the room. "I'm to tell ye Debny's hitching up the heavy coach fer ye, and that ye're to be gone in thirty minutes. He'll drive ye home."

"I sent Peter oot to hire a coach fer me. I'll nae take that monster with the Mac-Lawry crest on the panel. And I've nae need of bodyguards." Arran furrowed his brow. "I'm lyin' in the bed I made." Of course soon enough he and Lady Deirdre would be lying in the bed Ranulf had made for them.

"I — As ye say, m'laird. I'll inform Lord Glengask." The servant nodded, then cleared his throat. "Ye've a letter from Lord Fordham, as well."

Arran just resisted launching himself at the door and snatching it out of Owen's hand. "Aye? I left him a note last night to tell him I was leaving London." Walking up to the door, he held out his hand. "Are ye allowed to give it to me, or do ye have to get Glengask's leave first?"

Owen straightened. "I'm only supposed to catch notes ye send oot."

Ranulf didn't trust him not to make more trouble, then. He wasn't surprised, and he was more thankful than ever that he'd stopped by William Crane's house last night. Arran took the missive from the butler's fingers, then retreated to his writing desk to read it, intentionally leaving the bedchamber door open as he did so.

Taking a breath, telling himself his hands shook from anger, he opened the letter. Across the top of the page in Fordham's distinctive handwriting, he read, "This arrived at 2:17 this afternoon. And write me when you're safe at Glengask, you idiot."

The rest of the note had been written in a different, more elegant hand. For a heartbeat he shut his eyes. Mary had sent him an answer, and he had no idea what he hoped it would be. Or rather, he did know what he wanted to read, but there was no way in the world any good could come of it.

He opened his eyes again. "Dear Lady Joan," he read to himself, hearing her voice in his head, "I regret to tell you that I won't be in London to better our acquaintance, though I dearly wish that wasn't so. My parents have decided it is time I marry. I will be leaving Mathering House first thing in the morning, and returning to Fendarrow in Wiltshire by the main road. There, in two weeks' time, I am to be wed to Mr. Charles Calder, my cousin."

Arran stopped reading. Anger pulsed through him. The MacAllisters were out — and that was his fault. Even if he hadn't known about Mary's dislike for her cousin, Charles Calder was a clever, cruel man whom he wouldn't want to see wed to his worst enemy — which he supposed Mary was. She didn't feel like an enemy, though. And unless in the next few lines she could convince him that she'd made her peace with the idea of marrying Calder, he was not going to allow it to happen. The strength of that thought actually surprised him. But he bloody well meant it.

He looked down again. "If you have any words of hope or wisdom for me, Lady Joan, I would welcome them. And please know, I do not blame you for the fact that we are not better acquainted. Indeed, our friendship was just begun, and as far as I'm concerned, our friendly sentiments were mutual. Or so I choose to believe."

"Damnation," he muttered, his jaw clenched. "Damn, damn, damn."

"I have no expectations from you, but as you asked after me, I wanted to answer completely and truthfully. Yours in fond, fond recollection, Mary."

She hadn't wanted to let this . . . moment between them end, either. At least he hadn't been wrong about that. But knowing her feelings didn't help anything. It didn't help *her.* Arran walked over to the nearest window. Calder, MacAllister, Stewart — he wanted nothing to do with any of them. Who the devil gave a damn if they gained a few more bodies fit for glaring across the valley at the Campbells? Especially now that the Campbells weren't allying with the MacAllisters. All this nonsense was for nothing. And he and Mary still had to pay for it.

The window frame beneath his fingers splintered. He unclenched his hands from the wood, but the fury and frustration continued burrowing its way into his chest. Arran smoothed out the crumpled letter and read it again.

Mary had been very specific about when she was leaving and where she was going. She hadn't precisely asked for a rescue, but she *had* asked if he — or Lady Joan, rather — had any suggestions, because she was about to become desperately unhappy. As was he.

A knock sounded at the half-open door, and he turned around. "My clock has struck, I presume?" he drawled.

"Aye," Owen answered, his expression even more dour than it had been earlier. "The coach ye hired is doonstairs. Debny saddled Duffy, so ye could ride if ye wanted."

Arran nodded, then motioned at the two footmen with Owen. "Just the one trunk, lads, and my satchel."

"I'm to send Peter Gilling north with ye, m'laird, to watch over ye until ye're back at Glengask, and then to be certain ye . . . behave until Lady Deirdre arrives."

"Nae. I go alone. I fought the French fer four years, the same as you and Peter. I can keep clear of a few Campbells, if need be."

Owen's scowl deepened. "Laird Glengask willnae like that."

Walking up to the butler, his mind spinning already with a dozen different scenarios that would be impossible with another member of the household in tow, Arran pointed a finger deeper into the house. "Then Laird Glengask can tell me that himself. Because I dunnae give a damn what he likes or doesnae like."

"I — Aye, m'laird."

The footmen disappeared with his luggage, and Arran made one last tour of the bedchamber he'd occupied for the past few weeks. The wall remained torn up where he'd cornered the badger, but other than that it might have been any Sasannach's room in any Sasannach's house. It wasn't home. Nowhere was home but Glengask. And if Ranulf's temper didn't cool, he likely wouldn't be welcome there after the rest of the family returned.

Of course if he did half of what he was beginning to contemplate, he might find the entire Highlands rising up against him. Slowly he pulled on the old hunter's jacket he'd worn when he'd ridden down to London. He'd been in a damned hurry, concerned that Ranulf had lost his mind over an English chit and was about to get himself killed. *Ha.* He should have stayed in Glengask.

"Peter goes with ye," Ranulf said from the doorway. "Ye've done enough to bloody up things with the Campbells. I'll nae have ye killed when that would mean open war. And I'll nae have ye marrying some farmer's daughter to avoid yer obligations."

Damnation. If he protested or argued now, Ranulf would assume — and rightly — that he wasn't finished with making trouble. So instead he gave a curt nod. All the things he wanted to say, explanations, decisions, his intentions, Ranulf wouldn't want to hear. And actually, if Mary was leaving London tomorrow, he didn't want to stay either, so he no longer had any reason to argue against it. "He can ride with the driver, then."

The two deer hounds pushed past Ranulf into the room, their tails down as if they sensed the tension in the house. He gave each of them a brisk pat. "Guard Glengask," he instructed them, and moved by his brother without touching him or meeting his gaze.

Downstairs the footmen finished loading his trunk onto the back of the coach and fastened the satchel to Duffy's saddle. Arran paused in the foyer for a moment, waiting for . . . Hell, he didn't know what he was waiting for. The earth would open and swallow the lot of them before Ranulf would bend.

As he stepped outside Rowena ran out of the morning room and threw her arms around him. "I'm so sorry, Arran," she sobbed. "I dunnae want ye to go."

He tilted her chin up with his fingers. "Dunnae weep, *piuthar*. I'm nae dying; I'm going home to the Highlands."

"I know that. But Ran's so angry with you."

There remained a wide chasm between what he wanted to say to Ranulf and what he would say to Rowena. "As in every argument," he drawled, extracting himself from her grip and walking over to swing up on Duffy, "I ken there's more than one side. He has his. I'm nae certain it's the correct one. He doesnae seem like a man who puts his family first, any longer. So mayhap it's time fer me to look after myself."

"What does that mean, Arran? You're worrying me."

He forced a half smile. "It doesnae mean anything. I reckon I'll grumble fer a time, then do as Glengask asks."

Or perhaps he wouldn't. With that he nodded at Peter perched up beside the one-eyed coachman and kneed Duffy in the ribs. Ranulf didn't like the choices he'd made. But with this method of punishment, Ran had given him what he wanted: time. Even if it did come with a nanny named Peter Gilling. But Arran could guarantee that his brother wouldn't like what he meant to do with the opportunity. Whether Mary Campbell would like it or not was a question for tomorrow.

What a difference forty hours made. Just two nights ago Mary had been enjoying the most interesting, arousing moments of her life, even if she did know it would be short-lived. Part of her remained baffled that every moment since had gone so wrong.

She kept her gaze fixed on the changing scenery outside the coach window, but it could have been a moonless midnight for all the attention she paid. Arran had left London sixteen or so hours ago, heading in the opposite direction she was going now. Disasters for both of them.

"Mr. Calder was very pleasant this morning," Crawford said, shifting on the opposite seat.

"Of course he was," she retorted, her stomach roiling again at the mention of her newly betrothed's name. "He's gotten exactly what he wanted. I wouldn't be surprised if he was the one who told my father I was out by the fish pond."

Whether her parents were angry with her or not, Mary couldn't fathom why they'd decided she should marry Charles. She found none of her cousins particularly appealing, but she could see this as nothing other than a punishment — one that would literally last a lifetime.

"Perhaps you could reason with them after they've had a chance to see that with Arran MacLawry gone from London, the talk has subsided." Crawford sent her an uncertain smile that was likely meant to be hopeful. "And no blood was spilled, so perhaps Lord Delaveer will return to the table."

"Even if my father hadn't already placed the announcement in the newspaper, according to Roderick's letter he will have nothing to do with a woman of my low character, whatever the incentive."

"That seems an ungentlemanly thing to say."

"Yes, but then Charles's argument was that if I didn't agree to marry him, he could well feel the need to extract from the MacLawrys the price of the damage Arran and I did to the Campbells. Not a gentleman to be seen." She clenched her jaw. Charles had clearly been anticipating the fragmenting of the truce, and then while it teetered he'd threatened to push it into the abyss himself. And her parents had seemed almost grateful to him for "offering" for their disgraced daughter. If it hadn't felt so tragic, it would have been ridiculous.

As it was, her parents had already placed the announcement in the newspaper and set the date. And she knew why they'd done that, as well. The more quickly they made the arrangements, the less likely her grandfather would be able to intercede. Of course she had no idea if the Campbell would have done anything to save her, given the opportunity; he'd wanted her wed to Roderick, and she'd stomped that plan into the dirt. Aside from that, Charles Calder had licked her grandfather's boots for years, and the Duke of Alkirk couldn't possibly view this mess any less seriously than did the Marquis of Glengask. And Glengask had sent his own brother away. The duke had several granddaughters. Perhaps Beatrice or Mavis would simply take her place as his favorite.

The timbre of the wheels changed, and she blinked the world back into focus as the coach turned into an inn's stable yard. The Giant's Pipe Inn already. They were making good time, likely because she hated every moment that brought her closer to Fendarrow Park.

Thomas the footman pulled open the coach door and flipped down the steps. "Gordon says the roads have been good, so you've an hour for luncheon and to stretch your legs while we change the horses, my lady."

Mary took the hand he offered and stepped down to the ground. "Thank you, Thomas." She turned toward the inn as the footman handed Crawford down. Had it only been two months since she and her parents had last stopped at this coaching inn at the beginning of the Season? It seemed like years. Decades.

Inside, Crawford requested a platter of baked ham and fresh bread, and they sat at one of the scattering of long tables and benches. At midday the inn's common room was crowded, both with travelers and locals stopping in for a bite. Previously she'd enjoyed the light, friendly banter darting around her. Today, it didn't fit her mood.

She was halfway to requesting a private room where she could sulk and close the shutters when she caught sight of the man seated at the back of the room, a floppy straw hat on his head, a pint in his hand,

and light blue eyes gazing straight back at her. Her breath caught.

In addition to the farmer's hat Arran had also donned a worn, patched brown coat, but she recognized him immediately. Her heart began to pound, the twisted knot in her chest to loosen. Perhaps their moment wasn't yet finished. Had he read her return note? Did he merely want the chance to say good-bye in private? To say he wished she'd refused to dance with him that first night? She almost wished for that, herself — she'd had the barest taste of passion and possibility, just enough to make her yearn for impossible things.

Arran angled his head toward the rear door, then stood and left the common room. Mary found herself on her feet almost before she'd decided to move. "I'm going to walk down to the stream," she said. "I need to clear my head."

"Of course, my lady." Crawford climbed to her feet, as well. "Shall I fetch your parasol?"

"No. Stay here and finish eating. I'll be in sight of everyone in the yard." She forced a smile. "I have a great deal of thinking to do."

From Crawford's expression, the maid thought it was far too late to begin considering things logically now. She was correct, of course, but nothing about Arran and the way he swept her into a windstorm was logical. Logically she should never have spoken a word to him. Logically they should hate each other simply because of the surnames with which they'd been born.

Mary stepped outside, and a warm hand pulled her around the corner of the inn. "What are you doing here?" she asked in a low voice, fighting the urge to kiss him right there.

"Nae here," he murmured in that enticing brogue she'd thought she would never hear again. "This way." Taking her hand in his, he led the way into the scattering of trees behind the inn. Down the eroding stream bank, across a questionable bridge of stones, then up the far side again. Finally he faced her again. "I took a bit of a detour on the way north," he drawled. "I wanted to have a conversation with ye, lass."

When his mouth curved in a slight, rueful smile, she couldn't stand it any longer. Grabbing his lapels, she pulled his face down to hers and kissed him. In response, Arran pressed her back against a tree, molding his mouth against hers. Hungry. She'd been hungry, and this — him — was the only thing that could sate her.

"I read yer letter," he said, cupping her face and kissing her again. "Ye asked fer advice."

"Advice that doesn't include murdering my cousin," she returned, a bit alarmed by the determined glint in his eyes.

He backed off just a little. "Did ye agree to marry him?"

"I . . . Yes. He made good use of my parents' alarm. And of course he mentioned shredding the truce, and you, if I didn't agree to his so-called offer."

Arran gazed into her eyes for a long moment. She didn't know what he might be looking for, or hoping to see, but finally he ran the back of one finger along her right cheek, in a way that gave her little shivers. "Tell me if I'm in error, Mary, but I see two doors fer ye. The first door gives ye all this shite yer family decided fer ye."

"We did instigate this, you know."

"Aye. I ken we shouldnae have met and shouldnae have decided we like being together. They made a truce, and still will-nae have anything to do with each other. Instead both sides spent their time looking fer more soldiers to man their battlements. I ken I didnae get asked why I kissed ye. Did anyone ask ye a reasonable question?"

"No. No one did. And they've made

certain my grandfather won't know anything about the wedding until it's too late." Mary tilted her head. "Where does the second door open?"

"It opens with ye going missing from the Giant's Pipe. And then the two of us head north and see what happens with no other MacLawrys or Campbells or MacAllisters or Stewarts in sight."

She'd half thought he might say something like that, but the words sounded so utterly scandalous to her ears that she couldn't help a slight shudder. "What about Lady Deirdre? Have the Stewarts withdrawn?"

He grimaced. "Nae. They want a piece of what the MacLawrys hold. I'm nae inclined to provide it to them. Nae if we've a chance of someaught, Mary."

"I'll be ruined, you know. More ruined."

"Aye, ye will, as far as the world's concerned. But between us, I'm nae here fer an afternoon's mischief, lass. I've known a lady or two, and I've never . . . I feel a bit mad when I'm about ye, Mary, and I think ye feel the same way. I want to know where this would go if we were Mr. Highland and Miss Fox." He took her hand, gripping her fingers. "And I swear to ye, if we decide we dunnae belong together, I'll walk ye up to the Campbell's front door myself. At least ye'll be able to have a word with yer *seanair* before ye're shackled to Calder."

Her heart stuttered. Never in her entire life had she considered running away. Yes, a few times when she was younger she'd imagined taking the mail coach up to the Highlands to see her grandfather — her *seanair,* as Arran called him — but that had been years ago. Later the consequence had always seemed more dire than the moments of anger or frustration.

Mary closed her eyes. Every part of her knew that this was not a decision she could make logically. It was about hope, and attraction, and trust. And whichever clan Arran belonged to, he was still the only one she'd thought about, her only regret. And he was also the only one who'd done a thing to extricate her from an untenable situation.

"If I go away with you, Charles will try to kill you," she said, opening her eyes again.

"The past fortnight is the only time in the past ten years he hasnae tried to kill me. I'd even say I'm accustomed to nearly being killed."

She tugged at his lapels again. "What do you want?"

"I'm here, am I not? I want ye to come with me, lass. I know it's mad, and I dunnae go aboot asking women to run away with me. But every pound of me says I'm nae to give ye up. Nae withoot a word, and nae withoot a fight."

Hearing that sent her heart beating again. "And what if we *are* compatible?"

Slowly, deliberately, Arran kissed her again. "Then the rest of the world be damned." He slid his hands down her hips. "Ye can say all this is sinful, but I say we'll be committing a greater sin if we dunnae walk through that door. Together."

"But it is my decision."

He nodded. "Aye. I cannae steal ye away if ye dunnae wish to be stolen."

If he'd insisted, she would have refused. He'd given her a choice, though. And with a definite Charles Calder on one side and a chance to be with Arran — or at least to talk to her grandfather about all this — on the other, the decision was actually a simple one. In fact, she was half convinced she only hesitated so she wouldn't look too eager.

"Steal me away then, Arran MacLawry."

"Aye. With pleasure, Mary Campbell."

CHAPTER NINE

Arran let out the breath he was certain he'd been holding since sometime yesterday. By God, she'd agreed to come with him. And as far as he was concerned, Deirdre and the Stewarts could all go to the devil. And if Ranulf chose not to remove his blinders, he could follow them.

"We've nae much time, then," he said, taking her hand again and leading her toward the clearing where his rented coach waited — unless Peter had convinced the driver to return to London so he could report to Glengask. When the vehicle came into view he was actually surprised.

"I knew it!"

Swearing, Arran whipped around. Her skirts hiked to her knees, the maid, Crawford, galloped through the meadow at them. "Let's be off," he grunted, moving faster.

"She'll rouse the entire inn with her screeching," Mary countered, pulling against him. "Hush, Crawford!"

The servant stopped squawking, but didn't slow her approach. Instead she jabbed a finger at Arran. "I knew you were that farmer, MacLawry. I knew it!"

He straightened. "Lord Arran," he said succinctly. Whatever Mary chose to do about the maid, he was *not* going to be lectured by a Sasannach servant.

It seemed to have the desired effect, because she stopped short of trying to bowl him over. And though she was a substantial lass, he was far more solid than she. Instead Crawford squared her shoulders, puffing up like an angry chicken. "*Lord* Arran," she snapped, "you will unhand Lady Mary at once, or I shall scream bloody murder."

"Crawford, you will do no such thing." Mary continued to grip his hand tightly, which he found more significant than anything else. She wanted to go with him.

"I will. I swear it."

"Well, we cannae have that, can we?" Arran flicked the fingers of his free hand, and Peter disappeared around the back of the coach. "Ye see, a good part of my plan, such as it is, rests on Mary's family nae knowing quite where to look fer her. If ye squawk aboot her being with me, ye'll nae be doing her any favors."

"Not going anywhere at all with you will be doing her a greater favor."

Peter emerged at the edge of the trees behind them. The footman hadn't forgotten what he'd learned during his time in the army, anyway. A strip of cloth in his hands, he crept up behind the maid. Arran gave a slight nod, and the footman pounced.

The cloth swept around the maid's mouth, and the two of them grabbed her hands and feet and set her flat on the ground. "Get more rope." Arran grunted as she kneed him in the gut. "Damnation! We'll lash her to a tree."

"Stop this at once!" Mary barked, shoving at his shoulders.

"If we dunnae give ourselves a bit of time to disappear to the north, I may as well drive ye to Fendarrow and hand ye over to Calder, myself. And I'll nae do that."

Mary knelt down by her maid's head. "Crawford will come with us, then."

Arran blinked, ignoring the muffled cursing going on by his knee. "Are ye mad, lass? How can we make an escape with her yowling every moment?"

"Because she'll help add some respectability to our party."

Peter began winding rope around her legs, binding her skirt with it. "This was a poor enough idea to begin with, m'laird," he grunted. "Once Fendarrow knows fer certain who has his daughter, all the Campbells will be after us like wolves on a deer."

"Crawford might have told my parents that we met at the Blue Lamb or at the park every morning, and she didn't," Mary continued. "And if you want me along, you cannot treat my maid in this manner." She looked up at him, moss-green eyes narrowed. "You told me you let the badger go, for heaven's sake."

"The badg . . ." He trailed off. *The damned badger.* "Let her up," he said, standing and backing away.

"I can count our allies on one finger," Mary continued. "If she throws in her lot with us, we've doubled our chances."

"Or halved them, if she doesnae cooperate. I said to let her up, Peter."

Giving him a sour look, Peter untied the maid's legs again. "I'm nae an ally, either, I'd like to point oot. Yer brother said to keep ye in sight, and to keep any Campbells away from ye. I cannae keep an eye on ye if I run back to London, so here I am. And these are both Campbells. Ye'll get me sacked, ye will."

"I'm aware of who they are, and no, ye willnae be sacked. Nae fer doing as ye've been asked," Arran returned. He offered a hand to the maid, but she glared daggers at him and sat up in the grass on her own.

Yanking off the gag, she threw it at Peter. "I want no part of you ruining Lady Mary."

"I'm nae ruining her. I mean to marry her." Behind him Mary gasped, and he turned to face her. "Ye cannae be surprised, lass. I'm fairly certain we're compatible, or ye wouldnae have sent me that letter. And I told ye already, I didnae go through all this fer one night in yer bed."

"But . . . I'm not jumping from one marriage to another just for the sake of convenience." Her brow furrowed. "Not that there's anything convenient about you and me."

He slid his hand around her waist and drew her up against him. "Then fer now it's a rescue," he said in a low voice, covering her mouth with his. For Saint Bridget's sake, he couldn't seem to resist kissing her for long enough to make their escape.

"And if you don't sway her to a highly inappropriate marriage?" Crawford said, rolling onto her knees and then climbing clumsily to her feet. "What then?"

"I already gave my word to yer mistress," Arran said, keeping his gaze on Mary's upturned face. "I'll escort her directly to the Campbell. Even if she'll nae have me, I'll nae have *her* marrying Charles Calder because *he* was convenient."

The maid dusted off her disheveled gown. "I'll accompany my lady then, just to see you flayed alive by the Duke of Alkirk."

Well, this should be pleasant. He released Mary, giving her a brief smile. "Well, then. Let's be off, shall we?"

Duffy would have to remain tied to the rear of the coach for now. Tempting as it was to ride off with Mary seated before him, she was dressed like a lady and he like a farmer. People would notice that. And to avoid that, he would tolerate riding in the coach for a time with the beauty and the battle-axe.

"Thank you, Arran," Mary whispered, kissing him on the cheek as he handed her into the coach.

And for another whisper and a kiss, he would hand *himself* over to the Campbell. He knew she would be his downfall; it only remained to be seen if the spell she'd cast over him would be fatal. Belatedly he offered a hand to Crawford, but she avoided him again and climbed into the coach on her own.

Arran stepped into the vehicle, then leaned back out the door, holding on to the window frame in case the maid should try to put a foot to his backside and make off with Mary. "Howard, head us west and south fer a bit, will ye?"

The one-eyed driver doffed his hat as Peter climbed up to sit beside him again. "I'm at your disposal, Mr. Fox."

Once the coach rocked into motion, Arran pulled the door closed and sat back to find two pairs of female eyes gazing at him from the front-facing seats. Making off with a lass and then bringing her maid along. Bear would be laughing at him now — and then his brother would attempt to knock him on his arse. And Munro would be in the right to do it. Alliances and family loyalty thrown into a ditch over an auburn-haired lass promised to another man. Not even Bear would attempt something so foolish — and dangerous.

At least Mary was smiling. "Mr. Fox again?" she said.

"It suits us, I reckon. And ye'll be Mrs. Fox." He glanced at the glaring servant. "Fer the time being, anyway. Fer respectability's sake."

" 'Respectability,' " Crawford scoffed. "You left all of her trunks of clothes behind, you know."

"So ye're on our side, are ye?" he drawled,

taking Mary's hand to draw her onto the seat beside him. "She cannae dress like Lady Mary Campbell if men will be searching fer Lady Mary Campbell."

"We'll make do," Mary took up. "I have some pin money in my reticule." She tossed the small bag onto the seat beside Crawford.

"I'll purchase ye some clothes. And a horse." Arran sent the maid a pointed look before returning his attention to Mary. "Ye'll nae want to be caged in here all the way north, I reckon."

"You reckon correctly," she returned, facing him. "It sounds like you have this all planned out."

If he had, there wouldn't have been a maid or a footman along. He shook his head, hoping he didn't sound like a complete lunatic. "Nae. When I read yer letter yesterday I wanted to save ye, but until I started oot of London I'd nae much of an idea how to do it."

"I couldn't think of anything, either," she returned, her expression growing somber. "Of course I knew I'd be marrying, but I never truly thought my parents would agree to Charles the moment Roderick walked away." She closed her eyes for a moment. "Whatever happens, you've given me a chance, Arran."

"You've given *him* a chance, you mean. A chance you'll marry him instead of an upstanding man like Charles Calder," the maid put in, her face turned toward the window as if that made them — him — invisible to her. "Even with Lord Delaveer removed from the table, you might have been able to simply spend your time apart from Mr. Calder. Participants in arranged marriages do that all the time. Now you'll be apart from everyone you love."

"I'm aboot to gag ye again, Crawford."

He would have continued, but Mary put her palm on his cheek and kissed him. At least she wasn't taking her maid's angry spittle seriously — though perhaps she should. All of them, himself included, knew he hadn't done this out of chivalry. He wanted her. And as she was a highborn lady with a troublesome ancestry, and he an aristocrat with an equal familial burden, matters had to proceed in a certain way. He'd already bent them as far as they could stand without breaking.

"Three hours ago I'd aboot decided to disguise myself as a highwayman to rob yer coach and kidnap ye," he admitted. It had seemed too reckless, but it would've left the maid out of the equation. "Then I reckoned ye'd likely stop at the inn there to change horses."

She gave him a swift grin. "I'm glad you didn't resort to masks and pistols. The footman traveling with me — Thomas — was armed. You might have been shot."

"I'm hoping we'll leave behind more confusion this way. We'll keep to the south and west for today, then head north tomorrow, avoiding the North Road."

"It won't matter." Crawford had evidently decided he wouldn't gag her again, or at least that Mary wouldn't permit it. "Thomas and Gordon will send for the local beadle, who will call out the militia, I'm certain. You've kidnapped the Duke of Alkirk's granddaughter, you rogue."

"I am not kidnapped," Mary disagreed. "I am escaping. *To* my grandfather. And aside from that, Arran is giving me the most daring adventure of my life." She flexed her fingers in his. "You are the most excitement I've ever had, you know."

So she didn't wish to acknowledge that he meant to marry her. Perhaps that was burning one too many bridges even for her. "We've been raised to be suspicious of each other, lass. And ten days is fairly slight when weighed against that. Luckily, though, I'm a patient lad." And she was a rather practical lass with a sharp mind and a logical bent to her thoughts. If he needed to seduce her into deciding that marriage to him was the best solution to their troubles, he was more than willing to do so.

Arran shook himself. However much the maid flapped her gums, he couldn't afford to ignore her out of hand. "Is Crawford talking oot of her arse, or will yer people alert the army before they get word to yer *athair* back in London, do ye reckon?" Because if armed soldiers were going to be riding them down before nightfall, he needed to alter some of his plans.

"No, I don't think they will. First they'll search the inn and the land directly around it themselves. Since Crawford's missing too, they'll likely have no idea what's afoot. Thomas will eventually send Gordon — the driver — back to London to inform my father that I've gone missing."

"And your poor mother will be beside herself with worry," the maid put in. "As will your father."

"Hush, Crawford. They agreed to have me marry Charles, even knowing what sort of man he is. Yes, I embarrassed them. But I'm also their daughter. And so I'm not feeling terribly sympathetic." She returned her attention to Arran. "Father will ride out to the inn and search there himself. When he doesn't find any trace of me he'll likely send word north to the Campbell." She paused, for the first time looking concerned. "They will likely suspect that you're involved. And then my father will call on your brother."

That was the one thing that had made him hesitate. He'd spent his entire adult life protecting and defending his family. The idea that he would be the one everyone blamed for breaking the first truce between the MacLawrys and Campbells in a century haunted him. But at the moment he could blame Ranulf for driving him to it. And given his own choice between clan and family, Lord Glengask would likely do what was necessary to protect his new way of life.

"Ranulf's nearly disowned me as it is," he said aloud. "I imagine he'll curse me and say he has naught to do with any of this, then send word to Munro up at Glengask that I'm nae to be allowed back on Mac-Lawry land. And to the Stewarts aboot someaught." And for Bear's sake he hoped Ranulf wouldn't try to match their youngest brother with Deirdre. They might tease Munro about his thick skull, but he was not a fool. And it would take a fool to tolerate that lass.

"And you still think this is a good idea?"

Crawford folded her hands in her lap, her face as compassionate as a saw blade. "You have nowhere to go, my lady — and no income, no clothes, and no future. And that's if you *do* marry him. If you don't, you'll fare even worse than he will, my lady. For God's sake, we must return to the inn before it's too late!"

Even Mary began to look alarmed. If he didn't want this to become a kidnapping in actual fact, he needed to make a few things clear to Mary — and without the damned maid looming over them like a dour gargoyle. Arran banged on the roof of the coach with his fist. "Stop us here."

The moment the shabby old vehicle rocked to a halt, Mary reached past Arran for the door handle. "I need some air," she muttered, taking the long step down to the rutted road and then striding for the edge of the lane and the small stand of trees beyond.

This morning she'd been desperate. Arran's appearance at the inn would have seemed a godsend even if she wasn't rather enamored of him. But the reality of it all was that she had no idea if she was better off now than she'd been an hour ago.

She couldn't seem to pull enough air into her lungs. Had she gone mad, choosing to flee everything she knew simply because she liked the sound of Arran MacLawry's voice? Had she chosen ruin and poverty and a devilish handsome face over the slim chance that she might be able to change her father's mind about Charles Calder? Over the even smaller chance that they could convince Roderick to return and she could be happy with just . . . ordinary?

"Mary."

Arran followed her into the shelter of the trees. "Go away," she said without heat. "I need a moment to think."

"I'll give ye as many moments as ye want," he returned in his intoxicating brogue, pulling at the shoulders of the shabby coat that was clearly too small for him. Why hadn't she noticed that before? Just how ridiculous was she?

"Then go," she insisted, when he didn't move.

"I have one thing to tell ye first." He leaned against a straight oak trunk, crossing his ankles and regarding her coolly. This was where he fit in, she realized abruptly. Not beneath chandeliers and gilded cornices, but out of doors, where his tall frame and broad shoulders had room to move, where the wind could lift the coal-black hair from his temple.

"I decided to come with you, Arran. I'm merely weighing the consequences. I should have done it before, but I was so . . . grateful to see you." "Grateful" wasn't the right word, actually, but admitting that she'd been excited and elated and aroused wouldn't make her sound any more intelligent.

"And ye're nae so grateful now that Miss Lemon Mouth has soured the air?"

"She made some good points."

"Aye. I reckon she did. And now I'll make some." He plucked a leaf off a low-hanging branch and began shredding it in his fingers. "I may disagree with Glengask aboot nearly everything, these days, but he did make certain everyone in his family would be protected, no matter what might happen to him or to the clan. Therefore, even if we're both banished from our families and clans, I have enough blunt to see ye with a new wardrobe, a horse, a house, and a carriage or two if it pleases ye."

"You rescued me from marrying Charles."

"Aye, after I kissed ye and sent Delaveer scuttling away."

"That wasn't just you doing the kissing," honesty made her admit. "But I don't want to be a woman who jumps from one man's arm to another's. Crawford just made me consider what I would do if my grandfather doesn't want to see me. Or if he decides I should marry Charles, after all."

"I'd be more worried if ye didn't have some serious reservations, lass. I dunnae want ye to see me as the least of three evils, either. I want ye, and I think ye want me. We'll begin with that. It's a long way to the Highlands, and we'll have time to figure oot if we're . . . compatible."

"You're being very reasonable."

"I'm generally a reasonable man." He straightened. "I'll wed ye, Mary Campbell, but now ye've wounded me. If ye want me now, ye'll have to ask me fer my hand like ye mean it." Arran flashed her a jaunty grin and then strolled back to the coach.

Mary kept her gaze on his departing backside, then blinked and turned her gaze elsewhere. No one could dispute that Arran MacLawry was a fine-looking man, but her physical attraction to him had nothing to do with how she meant to resolve her situation. His appearance had helped *cause* her troubles. And yes, she did like him, far more than Roderick and Charles. But if she decided to make a mistake this momentous, she required more than ten days of acquaintance, a handsome face, and a keen wit. After all, he'd fled an arranged marriage just as surely as she had.

And so for the moment it made much more sense to say only that he was escorting her north to see her grandfather. Because everything had been perfectly . . . pleasant before he'd roared into London. Predictable, yes, and even dull, but pleasant. And it could be again, if she could convince the Campbell to do away with the idea of her marrying Charles.

At this moment she felt much more kindly toward a sworn enemy than she did her own clan, but her only hope of returning to her old life lay in not succumbing to Arran's charms and doing something as ridiculous as proposing to him — and then in reaching Alkirk and throwing herself on her grandfather's mercy.

She took a slow breath and made her way back to the coach. Insisting that Crawford accompany them was the most brilliant thing she could have done. The maid would save her reputation, and as a bonus she would certainly take every opportunity to point out what a mistake it would be to succumb to Arran. Even to kiss him, really. Though she'd kissed him several times already just today, and truly there didn't seem to be much harm in it.

Yes, she was grateful to have Crawford

there, she decided. And not at all annoyed.

"So do we go forward, or back?" Arran asked, holding out his hand.

Mary gripped his fingers, intentionally not noting their warm strength, and stepped back up into the coach. It would likely be for the best if he didn't know she'd decided not to be charmed by him. He might decide that setting the MacLawry agenda aside to escape with her into the Highlands wasn't worth the reward. Or the lack of reward, rather. Oh, goodness, he was in at least as much trouble as she was. And yet there he sat, gazing at her expectantly.

"We go forward," she said, and her insides hardly warmed at all at the sight of his responding smile. It was most likely indigestion she felt, anyway.

They drove roughly southwest until late afternoon. Then Arran instructed the driver to find them a respectable inn somewhere off the main road, and shortly after nightfall the coach rattled to a stop in the Twice-Struck Oak Inn stable yard.

"Peter, hire us a pair of rooms fer the night," Arran said, tossing a coin at the rough-faced footman.

"Aye, m'laird."

"Nae more o' that. I'm nae a lord here."

The servant flushed. "Aye, Mr. Fox," he

amended.

Mary took Arran's hand and stepped to the soft ground beside him. She'd initially thought to tell him to save his coin rather than going to the expense of purchasing her a mount; staying inside the carriage with Crawford seemed safer for her heart. But after five hours of being whacked on the bottom every time they drove over a rock or a rut, a horse seemed a heavenly idea. And it had nothing to do with the hours the maid had spent glowering.

He kept hold of her fingers. "I'll go into the village in the morning to find ye some clothes. Have the battle-axe make me a list of what ye both require."

"I could send Crawford to do that."

"Nae." He edged closer to her, lowering his voice. "She reads and writes, aye?"

She nodded. "Yes."

"Then I'll be keeping an eye on her fer a time."

Wrapping her hand around his rough sleeve, Mary leaned into his hard frame a little. It wouldn't do to be impolite, after all. "Do you think she would try to send word to my father?"

"Aye, Mrs. Fox. I reckon she would."

"What about Peter? You sent him off alone."

"Peter cannae read or write. And he figures the only thing worse than what I'm doing is seeing me caught by an angry cavalry of Campbells."

As accustomed as she was to bloodcurdling tales about clan wars and about the MacLawrys in particular, it still surprised her that he could speak so nonchalantly about a happenstance that would surely lead to his death. "If Peter and Crawford weren't along with us, how many rooms would you have requested?"

"One. We're married, lass. Remember that, or people might well remember *us* if someone should come by later to inquire." He frowned. "Crawford'll remember she's yer *màthair,* willnae? If anyone looks here, it'll be fer a Highlander, a lady, and her maid."

"She'll go along with this for my sake. But whatever we do, you're still a Highlander."

"So are ye, lass, even with yer odd accent."

Almost no one called her a Highlander. Only her grandfather ever called her by her Scottish name — the one she'd been born with. Everyone else had anglicized it to Mary, but she'd always felt in her heart that she was Muire. Belatedly she gathered her thoughts back in. "What I mean is, how would anyone mistake you for anything but a Highlander?"

His attractive smile returned. "I've an idea or two."

Heavens, he would be memorable covered in mud or wearing a priest's frocks. Hopefully no females would be inside the inn. And now she had the additional image of him in nothing but mud with which to contend. *Well done, Mary.*

The footman met them at the door. "Secured ye two rooms at the top o' the stairs, m— Mr. Fox."

"Excellent. Fetch our trunk up there, will you, Peter, my boy?" Arran said, in a rather remarkable London accent. Even Crawford was staring at him. "What?" he murmured in Mary's ear, making her shiver. "Ye think I havenae been listening to the Sasannach?"

"No. I . . . Hm. Well done," she whispered back.

"Thank ye." Half turning, he took Crawford by the arm, pulling her up on his other side. "Come along, Mother Graves. Let's get you settled in, my dear."

Mary feigned a cough to keep from laughing. With Crawford's glare she actually looked like a disapproving mother-in-law. For the first time Mary began to think they might actually have a chance of succeeding.

The innkeeper helped Peter haul the

heavy-looking trunk upstairs and deposit it in one of the small, neat rooms they'd claimed. Of course none of Mary's things were in there, but no one in the inn could possibly know that. All in all, and despite having only a few hours to plan a rescue, Arran had done surprisingly well.

"My wife's cooked up a pot roast," Mr. Jessup the in-keeper said, bobbing his head. "We'll be serving downstairs in an hour."

"That sounds perfect," she returned. "We're all famished this evening."

"Well, there's plenty for all."

By dinnertime the Twice-Struck Oak was full to bursting; evidently they weren't the only ones avoiding the main roads. Arran had said that these out-of-the-way establishments on the edges of forgettable villages were always less expensive, but it still made her wonder how many of the other guests might be fleeing unwanted lives.

Not that hers was unwanted; it had merely taken an extremely unfortunate turn. Or turns, rather. She glanced sideways at Arran, laughing easily at some tale spun by the village blacksmith. How odd that a MacLawry had both caused her troubles — with her own ample help — and had turned out to be the only one concerned with helping her escape them.

And how well he blended in here — much better than she did, Mary was certain. These people were well outside of Society. They were accustomed to looking after themselves, to driving their own carts and mending their own clothes. Her peers would look down on them as the unwashed, ignorant masses, but in a sense they had a freedom about them. A way of living in the moment that Arran himself seemed to embody. And it was very, very attractive to a lady who'd known her own role since . . . well, since forever, even if it had lately begun to chafe.

But this was about more than her indulging in fairytale dreams. Poor Thomas and Gordon were likely beside themselves back at the Giant's Pipe, and if Gordon had borrowed a horse rather than taking the coach, he might well have made it back to London by now. Her parents might be aware that she'd gone missing. Would they think she'd run away? That she'd been kidnapped? If she hadn't been so angry at the way they'd refused to listen to her explanation, at the way they'd used her one and only indiscretion as an excuse to hand her off to a clever, cruel bootlicker, she might have felt some empathy for them.

Instead, she sat beside Arran and chuckled at the tale Mr. Billings the farmer told about a very stubborn pig and his wife's turnips. She sang along to "Barbara Allen," and listened to Arran's fine baritone when he joined in. Of course he knew it; it was a Scottish ballad, after all. Tonight it was a simple thing to believe that they belonged together.

Here she wasn't Lady Mary, or the Campbell's granddaughter, or even a Campbell at all. No one tried to gain favor with her or marry her off because of her birth, and when Mrs. Jessup the innkeeper's wife complimented her on her hair, she could believe it was meant sincerely.

Finally Arran stood and offered his hand to her. "We should head upstairs," he said in his faux English accent. "We've an early day tomorrow. Shall we, Mrs. Fox?"

A low, excited tremor ran down her spine. "Certainly, Mr. Fox."

Tonight she wanted nothing more than to feel his mouth and his hands on her bare skin — which did nothing at all for her resolve to resist his charms. If he asked, though, if they shared a bed as a husband and wife did, she knew she wouldn't be able to resist him.

Crawford rose from the table, as well. "Sleep with me tonight, my dear," she said loudly, though she kept Mary between herself and Arran. "You know I don't travel well."

"Oh." Mary stumbled, not nearly as grateful for the rescue as she should likely have been. "Of course, Mother."

With Arran close on their heels, they climbed the stairs to the first floor. Mary could feel the heat of him looming behind her as they stopped by the first door. Nobody seemed to want to make the first move, but they couldn't stand there all night glaring at each other, blast it all. Finally Mary reached past the maid and pushed open the door.

"Go on, Mother," she said. "I'll be along in a moment."

The maid still didn't move. "I'm here to preserve your reputation, my lady, and I intend to do my duty."

Moving with that abrupt, deadly grace of his, Arran stepped forward, lifted the ample-sized maid off her feet as easily as if she'd been a feather, and set her down again inside the doorway. "There," he said.

Crawford's face turned scarlet. "I will not be manhan—"

Arran pulled the door closed on her comment. "That female is trying my damned patience," he said darkly.

The idea of being with him was just

another fairy tale, Mary told herself. Nothing good could come of her being ruined, and certainly not by a MacLawry. Not even this one. "It's for the best, Arran," she returned. "We — you — if we share a bed, then our choices become much more limited."

Light blue eyes studied hers. "I'll nae touch ye unless ye wish it," he finally murmured, lifting his hand to run a finger along her cheek. "Unless *ye* wish it. I dunnae give a damn what Crawford wishes. This is between ye and me, my bonny lass. So open whichever door pleases ye tonight. If the maid tries to interfere like that again, I'll tie her to the roof of the bloody coach."

Serious as his tone was, the image of Crawford squawking on the roof of the shabby old coach made her snort. "She would die of mortification."

Arran narrowed his eyes. "I'm trying to get ye in my bed, Mary, my lass."

Oh, my. "Crawford makes a very good point, you know," she muttered, plucking at his sleeve, "regardless of whether she's overstepping or n—"

He backed her against the wall and tilted her face up with a hard, hot kiss. Good heavens — though heaven had nothing to do with the way he kissed. That mouth of his was made for sin, and she wanted to be a sinner.

A serving woman topped the stairs. Mary would have shoved Arran away, but he kept her pinned between his hard body and the wall. The woman chuckled and squeezed by them. As she went through a door farther down the hallway, Arran shifted to nibble at Mary's ear. "We're married, lass. I'll kiss ye when I choose." His mouth drifted to her jawline. "And I choose to kiss ye now."

Her knees began to feel wobbly. To keep from falling to the floor, she slid her arms around his shoulders. *Mm.* Every part of her felt . . . breathless. Tangling her fingers into his thick, black hair, she drew herself closer against him.

The door at her shoulder squeaked open. "This will not do!" Crawford gasped.

Arran freed one hand and pulled the door closed again. "Come to my room with me, Mary," he murmured.

Oh, this was not the way to make a logical, informed decision about her future. Lust for him had already caused her to do things she would never have imagined previously. And it couldn't possibly solve any of her troubles now. "I should go in there with Crawford," she whispered, hearing the reluctance in her own voice.

He tugged down the high neck of her gown to press his lips against the base of her throat. "Ye shouldnae."

Uttering a half-hysterical giggle she ducked out of his grip, fumbled behind her back for the door handle, and pushed it down. "Good night, Mr. Fox," she managed, and closed herself in the room before she could change her mind.

CHAPTER TEN

For a long moment Arran leaned his forehead against the cool stone that lined the hallway. He was a damned Highlander, for God's sake. A MacLawry. The day a petite lass and a maid could defeat him would be his last.

And yet Mary was there behind her door, and he was still in the hallway. Tonight those circumstances clearly would not change. Even though he'd chosen to risk his own future — and his life — for her. Even though in the space of ten days she'd turned his entire existence on its head. However much he wanted her splayed beneath him, however much he wanted to claim her for his own, tonight he would simply have to be patient.

He glanced down. "Next time, *caraid,*" he told his cock.

Neither of them seemed to be convinced, but he refused to stand in the hallway with a tent at his crotch. Uttering a last curse and trying to shake himself out of his lust, he took a half-dozen steps and opened the neighboring door. He wasn't a damned Sasannach, but he could be a gentleman. Whatever else happened, she'd needed assistance. And he would not ask a price for aiding her, whatever the final cost to himself.

"There ye are, m'laird," Peter said, rising from the chair beneath the window. "I made doon the bed and found ye some clothes fer tomorrow. I'm beginning to think I'd make a fair valet."

"Thank ye, Peter." The last two sleepless nights beginning to press down on his shoulders, Arran sank onto the edge of the bed. "I know ye dunnae like any of this. I cannae even explain it to myself. But I willnae see her handed to Charles Calder."

Peter plunked himself into the chair again. "I'm all fer saving a lass from a dastardly villain," he said. "But ye said ye mean to marry her, yerself. Yer own *bràthair* is likely to murder ye fer that. He says ye're to wed Lady Deirdre."

Arran could try to explain his own frustrations with Ranulf, but as of the moment Mary had trusted him enough to step into that coach, this had stopped being about anything but her. "He can marry Deirdre, then."

"He'll nae give up Lady Charlotte."

"And I'll nae give up Mary. Nae withoot a bloody fight. And he can give murdering me a go if he chooses to do so. But tell me someaught, Peter: have ye ever known me to do a thing withoot first thinking it through?"

The footman shook his head. "Nae. I havenae. And I expect that now ye'll tell me to trust ye. To which I say, I think ye've lost yer bloody mind, and if ye dunnae expect me to tell ye how much trouble ye're stirring up, ye've lost it twice."

While it would have been nice to have someone agree with him, Arran hadn't actually expected it. Not from another Highlander who'd spent his entire life hating Campbells. "I cannae argue with that. Just swear to me ye'll help me keep her safe." He paused. "Even from me, I suppose. I'll nae see any harm come to her."

"That, I can promise ye. As long as ye dunnae expect me to turn my back on ye to do it."

Arran doubted Ranulf would be as reasonable. "Agreed."

With a nod, Peter pushed to his feet. "I'll be off, then. The groom said there's a

235

blanket in the stable fer me. Hopefully it isnae too close to Howard. He has an odor
aboot him, that fella does."

Stifling a grin at the man's pitiful tone,
Arran held out one booted foot. "Help me
get these things off and I'll give ye half the
bed. I'll nae be needing the space tonight."
And at this point he supposed that half an
ally was better than none at all.

In the morning he rose before everyone
else, had Duffy saddled, and rode up the
hill to the tiny village of Crowley. If he'd
known when he left Gilden House that he
would be paying the travel expenses of four
people, he would have brought more ready
blunt with him. He could send bills on to
Glengask or back to London, of course, but
then finding him — them — would be a
simple matter.

Still, if they were careful, they would manage. He spent a few quid on dresses and a
hairbrush and most of the other items on
the list Crawford had written out for him.
The pretty bay mare at the stables, though,
would take most of the blunt he had to
hand. He could forgo purchasing it and take
himself out on Duffy when he couldn't
tolerate Crawford any longer, but truth be
told, he wanted Mary close by him. A man
couldn't convince a lass of anything if he

couldn't even manage a word or two with her.

Finally he hit on a solution, and had the bill for the animal sent to William Crane. Lord Fordham would pay it without question, and then Arran could reimburse his friend when he was able to do so. And when news of Mary's disappearance reached Ranulf's ears, hopefully his brother wouldn't think to call on William and ask about bills.

When he returned to the Twice-Struck Oak, he carried his two sacks of purchases upstairs and knocked on Mary's door. It cracked open, and one baleful eye looked out at him. "Mr. Fox."

"Mother Graves," he returned. "I've brought ye some things. Have Mary doon fer breakfast in thirty minutes, if ye can. I'd like us to make an early start."

"Lady — I mean, Mrs. Fox — cannot possibly be dressed that quickly. I'm certain none of these things will fit her adequately, anyway."

"I'll be down in thirty minutes," Mary's voice came from farther back in the room. "Thank you."

"Ye're most welcome." He returned his gaze to the maid. "I bought ye someaught, too, but dunnae go thinking that means I've a yen fer ye."

"Humph." The maid snatched the sacks and shut the door again.

"Old bat," he muttered beneath his breath, then returned to his own room to wake Peter and get his own things packed.

It was far too early to declare their escape a success, but they'd survived the first night without being run down by a herd of angry Campbells or MacLawrys. And to himself he swore that tomorrow morning it wouldn't be a footman in his bed. He meant to convince Mary they belonged together. He knew one certain way to demonstrate that they were, and it wasn't by sleeping in separate rooms.

Lady Charlotte Hanover sent her fiancé a glance, at least the fifteenth one with which she'd favored him this morning. Ranulf MacLawry was not a man who went about with a grin on his face, but he had been known to smile a time or two — particularly at her. Not today, though. Not for four days, now.

"You didn't have to come with me, you know," she finally said, keeping her voice pitched well below that of the priest standing behind the pulpit several feet in front of and above their seats.

"A civilized man attends church, doesnae?" he returned in the same tone.

"Yes, he does. But I believe I informed you that a sermon from Father Gregory was more akin to torture than anything else."

"Hush, Charlotte," her mother whispered from her left. On the far side of Ranulf, his sister and hers were making even more noise, but then Winnie and Jane weren't betrothed to a Highlands devil.

"I'm looking fer some insight into forgiveness," Ranulf continued, lowering his voice still further.

Of course she immediately knew to what he was referring; she doubted there was anyone in London who hadn't heard about Arran MacLawry being discovered at the Penrose dinner party with the Marquis of Fendarrow's daughter on his lap. At first she hadn't even believed it. Not of sensible, logical Arran. But Ranulf had confirmed it, himself.

"I don't know Mary well, but she's always seemed very nice," she breathed back. "And very prett—"

"I'm nae discussing it," he said flatly. "Arran's marrying Deirdre Stewart."

Father Gregory sent the marquis an uncertain look, then resumed droning on about the sins of excess. Charlotte took a breath, deciding that if Ranulf wanted an argument they would be better off waiting until they were somewhere more private. And with better insulated walls.

Jane leaned around the two MacLawrys, one petite and delicate, and the other mountainous and iron-muscled. "Elizabeth told me that Lady Mary left London at dawn two mornings ago," she whispered. "And I saw the announcement in the newspaper this morning. She's engaged to that Charles Calder. He's her first cousin."

"I ken who he is," Ranulf growled. "No doubt Delaveer cried off — the MacAllisters are a squeamish lot. And her father was right to send such an ill-mannered lass away before she could cause more trouble."

"But Arran likes her," Rowena said, her own expression far less happy than Charlotte was accustomed to seeing. "And he said Charles Calder was a poor excuse for a hu—"

"I dunnae care what Arran said," Ranulf broke in. "Another word aboot him, and ye can take yerself back to the Highlands, too."

Rowena, her expression aghast, folded her hands in her lap and faced forward again. Jane did the same thing, likely more as a show of unity and support than because she thought her future brother-in-law could send her away, as well.

"That was mean," Charlotte stated. If he thought he could banish *her,* he had another think coming. "Winnie loves her brother."

She could practically hear his teeth grinding, his jaw was clenched so hard. "Do ye think I'd risk ye up at Glengask, knowing we'd stumbled from skirmishing into open war with the Campbells? Arran very nearly accomplished that, after only one bloody fortnight of peace. And that doesnae put me in a forgiving mood."

Father Gregory cleared his throat. Loudly. For a moment Charlotte thought Ranulf would walk out of the church. Evidently he'd weighed the satisfaction of escaping the priest's nasal, nonsensical droning against the renewed rumors and whispers about his uncivilized behavior, though, because he sank back on the hard seat and sent the pastor an elegant wave of his fingers. "Go on, then," he intoned. " 'The muddy waters of pleasure.' "

Somehow in the middle of all this he'd kept track of the sermon. She favored his still profile with a slow smile. "You're a remarkable man, Ranulf."

His mouth softened. "If the priest knew what I was thinking right now aboot pleasure, he'd have an apoplexy."

That left her nearly unable to sit still for

the remainder of the sermon. Ranulf had been the one to teach her about pleasure, after all.

Finally they all recited the Lord's Prayer and Father Gregory dismissed them with the admonition to think of others before succumbing to self-indulgent pleasures. Ranulf stood to offer her a hand up. When he offered the same hand to his sister, Winnie took it, but let it go as swiftly as she could do so.

"May we go now?" she asked, looking everywhere but at her brother.

"Aye. I'm aboot out of patience, myself."

As they left the church, heading for Ranulf's barouche, a horse galloped into the yard and skidded to a halt directly in front of them. Ranulf stepped between them and the horseman before Charlotte even grasped that they might be in danger.

"M'laird!"

To Charlotte's surprise, Owen, Ranulf's butler, leaped down from the horse and sprinted forward, unmindful of the other worshipers exiting the church yard. Every single one of them, though, seemed to turn and look at him.

"What is it, Owen?" Ranulf barked, meeting the servant in the middle of the yard. "The Campbells didnae hunt down Arran, did they?" His voice was tight and hard, a fairly equal mix of anger and concern.

"Nae, m'laird. I dunnae ken so, anyway. But ye need to get back to Gilden Hoose to find oot fer certain. They're there. The Campbells, I mean."

Behind them, Rowena gasped. Ice shot down Charlotte's spine. Not now. Not when she'd finally convinced Ranulf that the Highlands didn't frighten her, that she would be safe there.

"Which Campbells?" Ranulf asked, striding for his barouche.

"Laird Fendarrow. And Charles Calder. I wouldnae allow 'em into the hoose, but they're nae too pleased to be left standing in the front drive. I decided to come fetch ye myself."

Nodding, the marquis turned to take Charlotte's hand. "Can ye find another way home?"

"Yes, for the others. But I'm going with you."

"Ye are, are ye?"

"Yes, I am. If they intend violence, having a witness there will give them something else to consider."

"I'm coming, too!" Winnie announced, moving around them to climb into the barouche and towing Jane with her.

"Nae. I'll nae have ye in danger. None of ye."

Charlotte's father stepped forward to hand his wife into the barouche. "You've made us a part of your clan, Glengask. And I prefer to learn of any trouble firsthand."

With a curt nod Ranulf helped Charlotte into the vehicle, as well. "So be it, then. I've nae time to argue with ye."

The driver, Debny, rushed them up the street at far too fast a pace, but it still seemed too slow. The newspaper's betrothal announcement about Lady Mary Campbell had named Charles Calder as the groom. However Calder had ended up in that position, had he taken exception to Arran kissing his betrothed? Had he hunted down Ranulf's sharp-witted younger brother?

Charlotte's heart pinched. If something had happened to Arran, it would destroy Ranulf. He could be angry enough at his brother to spit, but they were still brothers, and the closest of friends. And that meant everything to him.

Two men on horseback waited on the Gilden House drive as the barouche turned in. She immediately recognized the pepper-haired Lord Fendarrow and the sleek, black-clothed Calder. They were alone, but she had no idea if that was a promising sign or not.

"Fendarrow," Ranulf said crisply, stepping down from the open carriage. "What brings ye to my door?"

The older marquis dismounted. "Not out here."

"This is my clan. I've naught to hide from them."

"Where's your brother then, Glengask?" Calder asked. He stayed mounted, presumably so Ranulf would have to look up at him.

"He's nae here." Ranulf took a slow step forward. "Fendarrow and I've made our agreement, and I kept to it. That business is nae yers."

"It is mine," Calder snapped, his horse fidgeting beneath him.

"My daughter and her party stopped at the Giant's Pipe Inn afternoon before last," Fendarrow broke in, his usual swagger missing. "She and her maid did not return to the coach."

Charlotte's breath seized, but Ranulf only narrowed his eyes. "I'm nae acquainted with yer daughter, but I did read aboot her engagement. I thought Delaveer was after her. Did she want to marry ye, Calder, or did ye weasel yer way in at an opportune moment?"

Finally Calder swung to the ground and stalked up to Lord Glengask. That was something of a mistake, because Ranulf was both taller and more broad-shouldered. "That business is not yours," he growled, mimicking Ranulf's words.

"My brother left here at sunset three days ago, just as I said he would. I sent a man with him to see that he stays safe and heading north. If yer daughter's missing, I'll help ye look fer her, but it has naught to do with us."

"I don't require your help, Glengask," the Duke of Alkirk's son stated. "I already have men searching for her. All I ask of you is your honesty."

"And that's what I've given ye."

Fendarrow nodded, then climbed back into the saddle. "I won't defy this truce," he said, "yet. But if your brother is involved with my daughter's disappearance, the Campbells will fall upon you like thunder."

With that he and Calder clattered back down the drive. Winnie's face had blanched to gray, and Jane looked ready to be ill at any moment. Then again, she had had a tendre for Arran. On Thursday she'd even wept at his departure. Charlotte's parents looked as troubled as the girls did — but then they'd seemed to think being adopted by

246

clan MacLawry was quaint. They likely didn't think that any longer.

"Ranulf?" she said quietly, unable to decipher his still expression.

He stirred. "I'm nae troubled by thunder," he drawled, signaling Owen and Debny to approach. "It's naught but noise."

"Aye, m'laird?"

"Debny, go fetch Myles," he instructed, naming his uncle. "Owen, find me a messenger I can send north. A fast one."

The men scattered, and Ranulf strode for the house. Gathering her skirts, Charlotte hurried after him. "What are you going to do? Do you think Arran's involved? Should we ask the Stewarts for their assistance? They have more clan in London than we do."

He turned in the doorway to face her. "I do like when ye say 'we,' *leannan.*"

"Don't sidestep the question, Ranulf."

"Och, but ye're a fierce lass. We'll nae be sending fer the Stewarts. If Arran *is* involved, I dunnae want them knowing yet that he's thrown over the arrangement with Deirdre."

Charlotte gazed at him intently, attempting to decipher what he might be thinking. "What will you do if Arran *has* taken Lady Mary?"

"I'll kill him before the Campbells get a chance to do it." With a dark curse he disappeared inside the house, leaving the rest of them standing on the drive.

Of course he didn't literally mean he would kill Arran — or so she thought, anyway — but the alternative would likely be just as painful for all of them. He'd banished his uncle, Myles Wilkie, from the family for three years for the crime of talking to the Donnellys. If Arran had made off with Mary Campbell, the consequences would be much, much worse.

Rowena hurried into the house after her brother, but Charlotte's parents stayed in the drive. "We should go," Charlotte said, so they wouldn't have to do so. "He needs to figure out what to do."

Her father nodded, handing the marchioness back into the carriage. "Well said. I'll send over a note later asking if he requires my assistance. Jane?"

Janie uttered a stifled sob. "I didn't want Arran to marry Deirdre, but this is so much worse! Why couldn't he have liked me?"

"You wouldn't want all this on your head, Jane," Charlotte replied in her most matter-of-fact tone. "Everything will end as it should. You'll see." She sent a fond smile back toward Gilden House. In the past weeks she'd become a great believer in happy endings. And as she also happened to believe in the idea of someone finding a perfect match, she couldn't help hoping that something miraculous would occur to save them all.

"Good evening, Mr. Fox, Mrs. Fox," the innkeeper said with a jowly smile. Either he was naturally jovial, or visitors were rare enough in Wigmore, Herefordshire, that their arrival late this afternoon — or that of Arran's coin — was cause for celebration.

"Thank you," Arran replied in his very fine faux accent. "I've heard that the roast beef ribs here are exceptional."

Mary kept the smile on her face, despite the fact that for a moment she wondered if he lied about everything as smoothly as he did about inn meals. They hadn't even known what the place was called until they stumbled across it.

The innkeeper, though, was patting his belly. "If I say so myself, Mrs. Castleman — that's my wife — does make a fine roast rib. And a better roast turkey."

"What do you reckon, Mrs. Fox?" Arran asked, looking sideways at her with amusement dancing in his eyes. "Ribs or turkey?"

"The turkey sounds splendid."

"Aha! Grand choice. Sit yourselves close by the fire; we'll have a chill wind coming up tonight. Mark my words. If you're here for the assembly, you'd best take a wrap with you, Mrs. Fox."

Arran's brow lowered a little, and she could practically hear him saying they would be too tired to attend a dance. She stepped forward. "Oh, an assembly! Are you certain they wouldn't mind strangers there, Mr. Castleman?"

"No, no! The more the merrier. It begins at nine sharp. And I'll tell you what: I promised Mrs. Castleman a dance, so we'll escort you over. The hall's a bit hard to find in the dark, with it being behind the cemetery."

"We happily accept," Mary returned, ignoring Arran's arm tightening beneath her hand.

The innkeeper chuckled. "Excellent. We could stand to see some fresh faces around here."

He waddled off to place the request for their dinner. Clearly Arran was about to disagree with her decision, so she released his arm and faced him. "Yes, I know it would be safer and wiser to stay hidden and then leave at dawn. I would like to dance with you."

Arran opened his mouth, then closed it again. "If we're caught, then we're caught," he finally said, a slow smile dancing into his sunrise-blue eyes. "At least I'll have ye in my arms one way or another."

"I thought you would deem an assembly gathering strategically unsound."

"This whole venture is strategically unsound, lass. That doesnae mean it shouldnae be attempted."

Behind them Crawford and Peter descended the stairs, and she stifled a sigh. Yes, Crawford did lend a certain respectability to their group — something which could come in very handy if Mary found herself on her grandfather's doorstep. At the same time, having the maid present made it more likely, she knew, that she would end this adventure at Alkirk rather than in Arran's arms.

For the past two days Crawford had lain in wait like a spider, pouncing out at every opportunity to remind her of everything she would be losing if she continued on this journey. It said something for Arran's patience that he hadn't resorted to tying the maid behind the coach with their mounts, but the constant bombardment had to be weighing on him, as well. For the moment Crawford had a part in this play, but Mary didn't precisely need to be told that going directly to her grandfather and keeping Arran at arm's length would be . . . safer.

That was what she'd originally thought, of course, but the better she came to know him, the less sense all her reservations made. Yes, a lifetime of prejudice was a great deal to overcome. But marriage . . . A chance at something she never would have considered before she met him, but that now she couldn't stop thinking about. She wanted more time alone with him. More time when they weren't on horseback in view of anyone using the old, rutted roads. And definitely more time than they would find riding in the coach with Crawford glaring at him.

Arran took her fingers and kissed them. "I'll dance with ye, lass. There's nae a man alive who could stop me." He sent a glance past her. "Or a woman."

He excused himself to go talk to Peter, while Crawford sat at the rough wood table directly beside Mary. "Are you trying to fence me away again?" Mary asked, shifting closer to the end of the bench to give herself more room, only to have Crawford close the distance again.

"I am a lady's maid," the servant returned. "If he ruins you, I become unnecessary."

"I appreciate your diligence, Crawford. Truly. But you aren't going to keep me from talking to him. This isn't just an escape from Charles and clan Campbell's dictates; it's a chance at a different life." An unexpected life.

Steely brown eyes returned her gaze. "He's a poor chance at anything, if you ask me. With both MacLawrys and Campbells likely after us, he'd make you a widow the moment you became his wife."

"He's the only one interested in knowing what *I* wanted."

"I'm certain that's none of my affair, my lady."

No, it wasn't any of Crawford's affair. But it was hers. Discovering who truly cared about her circumstances and her well-being, people and things she'd taken for granted until they'd all been yanked out from under her — Mary needed to decipher all the pieces of the puzzle before it was too late to do so. Or perhaps she was overthinking everything, and she just needed to take a moment to look at what lay around her. Or rather, at who had just seated himself across from her and favored Crawford with one eye narrowed. "I've a question for you, Mother Graves," he said, straightening as their host brought a loaf of fresh, warm bread to the table.

"And what might that be?" the maid asked tightly. Mary wasn't certain what the servant disliked more — being called Mother, or having to speak politely to Arran.

"You didn't dance at our wedding," he said with a warm smile, reaching across the table to take Mary's hand, "what with your gout and all. But will you dance with your son-in-law tonight?"

"Ah," Mr. Castleman intoned as he paused by their table, "it's a wise man who makes peace with his mother-in-law." He placed some mismatched glasses on the table. "Mine kept trying to hire ruffians to rob the inn and shoot me."

"Heavens!" Mary exclaimed, hoping he wasn't giving Crawford ideas. "She's stopped trying?"

"Aye. A woman had best think twice before keeping company with ruffians." He sent her a broad wink.

"You're jesting!" she said with a grin.

"I can't lie to a lovely lady, Mrs. Fox. She's the one baked the bread."

Arran laughed. And as excellent as his English accent was, for some reason his laugh sounded Scottish. Perhaps it was the fresh joy in it, or the complete absence of fear. Whatever it was, Mary liked it. She wanted to hear it about her always.

She chuckled, and their gazes locked. The two of them alone or in some clan or other, on ancestral land or somewhere new, the idea of keeping that laugh, that joy, in her life held a great deal of appeal. *He* held a great deal of appeal.

"Ye have a fine smile, lass," he noted, as the innkeeper went to greet a new arrival. "It warms my heart."

"No, I won't be dancing this evening," Crawford stated, making Mary jump. Heavens, she'd nearly forgotten anyone else was there.

"Crawford, it's perfectly fine, you know."

"No, it isn't, my lady. Not for you, either. A village assembly? You're the Duke of Alkirk's granddaughter."

At least the maid kept her voice down. "Not tonight, I'm not," she returned. "Tonight I'm Mrs. Fox. And you'd best stay in tonight to rest your foot, Mother."

"What aboot me, m' . . . Mr. Fox?" Peter put in from beside Arran while Crawford continued to look daggers at the lot of them. "I'm nae part of this family, but I do like dancing a reel. Nae that we're dressed fer it, a' course. A man cannae dance a proper reel withoot a kilt."

"That's enough, Peter. I'm a Sasannach at

the moment, if ye'll recall."

The footman's brow furrowed. "Aye, I recall. I dunnae like it, though. I cannae talk like them."

"That's why ye're my Scottish footman. And I'd prefer if ye'd stay here and keep a watch fer trouble."

"That I can do, Mr. Fox."

Despite the fact that the trouble he would be watching for consisted of her relatives and allies, Mary found herself relieved that someone was determined to help them whether he agreed with what they were doing or not. It was more than she could say about Crawford, certainly.

Once they finished dinner, Arran sent a meal outside for Howard, who'd insisted on sleeping in the coach tonight. Evidently he feared someone would make off with it — or her, as he referred to the vehicle. She wondered what the one-eyed coachman made of all this, but thus far he hadn't raised a note of complaint over their selection of less-traveled roads.

The round cook appeared from the kitchens and shed her stained apron to reveal a pretty yellow silk gown. Mary was abruptly grateful she'd gone back upstairs to don the deep green silk and lace gown Arran had somehow procured for her. It was far simpler than anything she would wear in London, but here in Wigmore, it was perfect.

"Let's be off," Mr. Castleman said, and led the way outside and on down the narrow lane lined with spicy-scented summer roses.

With her hand wrapped around Arran's arm, his long stride shortened to match hers and the Castlemans', Mary couldn't help smiling. This was the sort of evening she might have been able to experience in the Highlands if she'd been permitted to spend time there. And being in this tiny, quaint place with a man who'd showed himself to be anything but an enemy made her feel light inside, as if her feet weren't quite touching the ground.

"A penny fer yer thoughts, my bonny Mary," he murmured.

She shook herself out of the fairy tale again. "I'm not thinking anything worth that much."

"Ye were smiling like moonlight."

"And what does moonlight look like when it smiles?" she asked, deciding that talking was better than thinking.

"Mysterious, with a wee touch of magic," he replied promptly.

And now he had her sighing again. It was unfair, to be pursued by a man as charming as Arran. How the devil was she supposed to resist him, whatever her best interest might be? "I do wish you weren't a Mac-Lawry."

He slowed a little more, putting distance between the older couple and themselves. "Are we back to that again? Campbells and MacLawrys?"

"It never left. Do you know what would happen to you if Charles and my other cousins catch up to us? Have you ever seriously considered it?"

"Mary, I've hated yer family fer my entire life, same as they've hated me. The rumor is that my own father was killed by Campbell allies. But from the moment I set eyes on ye, everything upended." He put his hand over hers where it rested on his arm. "So to answer yer question, aye, I know what would happen if the Campbells tracked us doon. I reckon they'll try to kill me, in which case I will try to kill them back. And if the Mac-Lawrys found us, I'd fight them off too before I'd let them step between us."

He said it so matter-of-factly. For a long moment she gazed at his profile, at the nearly shoulder-length black hair lifting from his temple in the light breeze, at his self-assured step and his cool gaze that seemed to notice everything and still stayed focused on her. "You're not the least bit frightened, are you?"

His sensuous mouth curved upward at the corners. "Of yer kin, nae. Of ye finding some reason we shouldnae be together, aye."

They resumed their walk, and a few moments later the church came into view in the moonlight, a dark shape with luminous tombstones surrounding it. The Castlemans crossed the edge of the cemetery, but Arran veered around the low stone border.

"Nae sense walking over some poor lad who's nae done a thing to us," he said by way of explanation. "The innkeeper's likely related to 'em."

"So angry spirits and I concern you." Highlanders were a unique breed, indeed.

"Someaught like that," he agreed, brushing his cheek against her hair.

The intimacy of the gesture warmed her to her toes — unless he was trying to distract her about something. "The men around me travel in packs, you know," she said aloud. "Like wolves. They would never admit it, but they fear being caught out alone by a MacDonald or a MacLawry. And there you are, knowing that half a hundred Campbells could be looking for me — for us — and you're escorting me to a dance."

"They'd nae expect that strategy, ye have

259

to admit," he drawled with a swift grin. Slowly his expression sobered again. "I'll tell ye true, Mary. I'm concerned. I'm concerned they'll find us and drag ye back to marry Calder, and that he'll be worse to ye because of what I've done. I'm afraid ye'll listen to Crawford and nae yer own heart. And I'm terrified that when we reach the Highlands ye'll still ask me to take ye to the Campbell and ye'll nae choose to stay with me." He took a breath, shrugging. "Am I afraid of the Campbells? Nae."

A door opened a short way in front of them, light flooding the evening and the sound of music filling the air. It seemed almost symbolic. If she went inside with Arran, there would be no turning back. It meant something. It meant that she could do as he'd already done, and choose the two of them over her own clan. If she went back to the inn, then she could still claim her old life, whether or not it would include Charles Calder or Roderick MacAllister. But returning to her old life meant that she would have to accept whatever her family decided for her. And whomever her family decided she should wed.

Or she could set all that aside in favor of the utter unknown. Mary tightened her grip

on Arran's arm and stepped into the noise
and joy of the assembly.

Chapter Eleven

Peter Gilling looked up from his seat in the inn's tavern as the large woman slipped into the nearly empty common room. If he'd been a gentleman he supposed he would have stood up and invited her over for a pint, but firstly he wasn't a gentleman, and secondly he didn't like the way she looked down her nose at Lord Arran. The Mac-Lawrys could trace their ancestry back before Hadrian, back to the Vikings and the blue-faced Celts, and the maid sneered at Lord Arran for taking the lass he wanted and making off with her.

Of course he'd chosen a Campbell, which was both daft and dangerous, but Peter meant to follow Lord Glengask's instructions: protect Lord Arran, and see him safely back to the Highlands. Everything else was secondary. Well, almost everything else was. If he'd had a way to inform the marquis about both Lady Mary being stolen away and the route they were taking he would have done so, but he couldn't send the information without telling someone else the words to write down. And Lord Arran was adamant that no one else know what they were about — for good reason.

He finished his beer as Crawford left the tavern and returned upstairs. It was time he went back outside to watch the road for Campbells and Gerdenses and Dailys, as well. Moving past the wide bar, he waited until the one serving lass turned away. Then he reached over to pick up the letter Crawford had left for the morning's mail coach.

He put it into his coat pocket as he left the inn. What the letter said he had no idea, but he could guess. And whether or not he found a way to contact the chief of clan MacLawry, he wasn't about to tell the Campbells where they were, or allow anyone else to do so. Not while he had anything to say about it.

From the way Captain Evers from the local militia kicked up his feet for the country dance, Arran thought the lad might have had some Scottish blood in him. Whose and which clan he had no idea, so he kept as much distance as he could between the half-dozen red coats in the ballroom and himself.

"Mrs. Fox comes from money, I think," Mrs. Castleman noted from several feet away. "I paid Mrs. Noland a shilling to braid up my hair, and it isn't near as fancy as that."

Arran put a smile on his face and turned away from watching Mary dance with the village's baker. "She and her mother were both lady's maids," he said conversationally into the murmur of gossiping, trying not to sound stiff with the stiff Sasannach vowels. "Her mistress didn't allow servants to marry, so here we are."

This seemed to be the best gossip Mrs. Castleman had ever heard, because she closed in to seize Arran's right arm. "That's horrid!" she exclaimed with obvious delight. "Did you work for the family, as well?"

"In a roundabout way," he returned, actually pleased he'd been able to use the tale he'd constructed during their ride today. "I was employed as their solicitor." In tiny villages like Wigmore, the solicitor was frequently the wealthiest, most educated man about, and he'd needed to explain two horses, a coach, a driver, and a footman. As long as no one asked him to solicit anything, he figured the story would suffice. And it was far enough from the truth that it would hopefully do nothing for any pursuers but cause more confusion.

A tall, bony woman clutched his other arm. "Which family was it?" she asked, batting brown eyes up at him. "The Morrisons, I'll wager. Lady Ludlow once chased one of her daughter's suitors down the street with an axe. Or so I heard."

"He couldn't say, Fanny, I'm certain," the innkeeper's wife countered. "If the family found out, poor Mrs. Fox would never find employment again."

"True enough, Mrs. Castleman," Arran said, extricating himself from the females as the country dance squeaked to a finale. At least one of the fiddlers had been drinking too much ale, and they were sadly in need of a piper or two. "And now if you'll excuse me, I'm going to dance with my wife."

Mary met him at the edge of the dance floor. She was out of breath and grinning, and at the sight of her and her sparkling green eyes he decided that being here with her tonight was worth the risk. Worth any risk.

"Were you seducing Mrs. Castleman?" she asked, taking the glass of lemonade he offered her and drinking half of it down.

"Nae. She does make a fine meal, but only one lass will do fer me," he returned, straightening the lace of her left sleeve so he'd have an excuse to touch her.

"Is that why you didn't dance?"

So she wanted to talk facts. Perhaps she was concerned she wouldn't be able to resist him if she listened to his flirting. He liked that explanation better, anyway. "I was jealous that the baker asked ye to dance," he said aloud. "Ye crushed my own dream of plates and platters of free biscuits."

Mary laughed. "I had no idea you'd set your cap for him."

God, he wanted to kiss her smiling mouth. In a quaint Sasannach village like this one, though, such scandalous behavior — even between a husband and wife — would definitely get them noticed and remembered. "Actually, some of the lasses were speculating that ye were a lady, what with yer fancy hair and pretty speech."

She grimaced. "You told them the story, then?"

"Aye. I figured I should say someaught before they stumbled too close to the truth."

"Do you think Crawford made my hair too fancy on purpose? She is accustomed to following the latest fashion." She grimaced. "I should have realized. I'm sorry."

"Dunnae apologize, my bonny lass. I've been imagining taking out the pins and running my fingers through yer autumn-colored hair all evening."

In response Mary found a speck or two of lint on his sleeve that suddenly needed to be plucked at. "Truly?" she murmured, blushing prettily.

"If ye dunnae know by now how very fine ye are to me, then I've nae chance at all to convince ye to marry me."

"I'm beginning to realize that I enjoy it when you flirt with me," she admitted in her usual straightforward manner.

"And do ye enjoy me kissing ye, Mary?" he asked, moving a half step closer to her as most of the village of Wigmore milled around them.

"You know I do. I just don't know if you're the best solution for my troubles."

"If ye dunnae leap, *leannan,* ye'll never know if ye can fly." As if to support his statement, the ramshackle orchestra launched into a waltz. Arran reached out his hand, holding his breath until Mary curled her fingers into his. Perhaps arguing with her wasn't the wisest tack to take, but she valued honesty, and he valued her.

"This isn't leaping," she commented, placing her other hand on his shoulder.

"It is if ye do it right," he countered with a grin, slipping his free hand onto her waist, then taking a long step forward to set her off balance. With a gasp she clutched at his hand, holding tightly as he dipped her backward, then swung her upright and into the energetic waltz.

"I thought we weren't supposed to be doing anything that would attract attention to ourselves, Arran," she chastised, that breathless grin touching her face again.

"Devil take it. I'm waltzing with the lass pretending to be my wife." Or rather, the lass who *would* be his wife if she felt for him half of what he was beginning to feel for her.

As they twirled around the room to the energetic tempo the orchestra had set, everything else faded into the background. Everything but the lass in his arms. When they'd first met she'd had every reason to fear and despise him. They should never have been able to converse long enough to discover they had anything in common, much less that they liked each other.

"Describe Glengask to me," Mary said, her gaze lowering to his mouth. "The house, not your brother."

"It began as a fortress," he answered, fleetingly wondering if he would ever set eyes on his birthplace again, "so the walls are three feet thick. She stands four stories tall, gray and white and overlooking the river

Dee. My grandfather had windows carved into the ground and first floors after Culloden. He said we'd lost the war with the Sasannach, so we might as well be able to watch the sunset."

"That's very Scottish," she observed, her smile deepening.

"Aye. Whether he meant to or not, he made Glengask a lighter place, inside and oot. 'They took our ability to fight, but they didnae take our eyes,' he said." He gave a brief smile. "My grandfather had a great many sayings. Anyway, being set on his arse made him turn his attention closer to home. To our cotters." He hesitated. The way his clan had dealt with those dependent on them remained a major bone of contention between the MacLawrys and the Campbells. Pointing it out now while she swayed in his arms seemed extremely foolish. "Anyway, to answer yer question directly, Glengask is a large, lovely, loud old sprawl."

"But your grandfather didn't decide to fight the Clearances because of some windows, Arran. What happened?"

So much for diplomacy. But then Mary did tend to pursue the heart of the matter — except where her own heart was concerned. "I think he couldnae accept that we'd lost. And unlike the other clans, he'd taken to investing his fortune in Scottish businesses in Aberdeen and Edinburgh. That left us with cash as well as land. We didnae need to graze sheep to pay our Sasannach taxes. He always said the clan had kept us strong, and now we were beholden to keep the clan strong."

"He did have a great many sayings, didn't he?"

"Aye."

"What you just told me is a very different version of the tale than the one I grew up hearing."

"Is that so? What did ye hear aboot the devil MacLawrys, then?"

"That you'd unburied an old Viking hoard and used the gold to keep your army about you, so you could drive out your neighboring clans. That your brother started schools and businesses on your land to encourage the cotters of other clans to rebel against their chiefs."

"We're diabolical, then. Fancy that." He drew her a breath closer.

"But there must be something aside from rumor and myth that makes us enemies."

"Are ye still looking fer reasons ye shouldnae marry me?"

She frowned, then quickly smoothed out her expression. They were far from alone,

270

after all. "I'm trying to decipher why your clan and mine are actually at odds. If it's merely because a MacLawry speculated that the Campbells wouldn't like all the cotters staying put and then the Campbells saying the MacLawrys must be out to ruin other clans because they've kept an army in the Highlands, then . . . Well, a great number of people have died for no good reason."

Arran started to reply that of course there were real troubles between the clans after better than two centuries of feuding, but he stopped the words unspoken. Perhaps she was correct. Perhaps all the animosity had begun when her five-times great-grandfather had accidently stepped on the foot of his five-times great-grandfather and had then assumed there would be some kind of reprisal. Perhaps his own father had been murdered because one of his ancestors had overlarge feet.

"Arran? You're not angry with me, are you? I don't mean to belittle your reasoning."

"I'm nae angry, Mary."

"I mean, even if this did begin because of something absurd, there are actual reasons now for mutual suspicion and anger."

He shook his head. "Nae between us, lass. Dunnae use that fer an excuse. If ye dunnae want me, just tell me, fer God's sake. I'll still see ye safe to the Campbell. I gave ye my word."

"I can't tell you that I don't want you, Arran, because I do. I'm merely not certain we —"

"Stop talking," he ordered, moving them to the edge of the dance floor, firming his grip on her hand, and walking quickly for the nearest door.

"What's wrong? What are you doing?"

"Ye say ye want to chat with me, so we chat. Ye say ye want to dance with me, and so we dance." He pulled open the door and led the way into the cool darkness outside. "Ye say ye want me, and so we're going back to the inn, and ye'll have me."

She made a sound that might have been excitement or trepidation. And he was being a damned fool to drag her off like a lunatic when it was his patience that had gotten them this far. Arran stopped at the edge of the cemetery.

"Ye can change yer mind if ye want, my bonny lass," he made himself say. "If ye mean to turn me away, though, do it now, fer Saint Bridget's sake. Because once I get ye into that room with me, I'll nae let ye go."

Mary kept her grip on his hand. "Let's

go, then. But don't trample any dead villagers on the way. We don't need that ill luck."

No, they didn't. Detouring around the church yard, they continued up the lane to the Fox and Grapes. If he recollected his classical literature, the tale of the fox and grapes was from Aesop, something about the fox being tantalized and unable to sate his hunger. Well, tonight he wasn't going to be that particular fox.

They walked in through the side door and slipped as quietly as they could up the stairs. He, at least, had no intention of allowing the maid to come between them, even given the fact that she'd been surprisingly effective at it so far. Best not to awaken the old battle-axe at all.

Silently he pushed open his door, and Mary brushed past him, her silk skirts tangling around his legs as she tiptoed. His cock twitched, but then the single-minded fellow had been on alert all night. The moment he crossed the threshold Arran closed the door, turned the lock, and then shoved a chair beneath the door handle.

"Heavens," Mary whispered with a chuckle. "She's not a bear."

"Nae. She's worse. Ye can shoot a bear when it charges ye. Her, ye have to give a seat in yer coach."

"It was important that she come."

"Only if ye want yer old life back."

Mary lifted her shoulders. "You're the one who upended my old life."

Arran stayed where he was in front of the door. This wasn't the argument he wanted or the time he would choose to have it, but it needed to be said. "Aye, I am. And ye wanted it upended, or ye never would have danced with me."

"Stop disagreeing with me," she demanded.

"Stop trying to hold on to everything and decide what ye want to let go of," he shot back, sending up a quick prayer that it wouldn't be him. Had he earned enough of her trust, though? Was he pushing her into a situation she truly did not want? He didn't think so. "Yer family tried to shackle ye first to a dullard and then to a bloodthirsty lunatic in the space of one day. And mine wanted me to marry a pretty potato because she has family in London. Do we still owe them someaught?"

She eyed him for a long moment. Then she strode up to him. Arran braced himself on the chance she meant to punch him. Instead, she flung her arms around his neck and kissed him hungrily. "You gave me a chance to change my life," she mumbled against his mouth.

Splaying his hands around her waist, he lifted her so he could meet her mouth more squarely. All he'd done was try to keep her from having to marry a man he knew to be cruel and unpleasant. And at the same time he'd taken her for himself. "And ye've changed mine."

When she pushed at his shoulders, he set her back on the floor and shrugged out of his old, patched coat. Half convinced she would change her mind if he gave her a single second to think, he kept his mouth on hers, teasing at her with tongue and teeth until she groaned. Tangling tongues, hands frantically pulling at clothes, the crack of the sputtering fire in the small, drafty hearth — the sensations planted themselves in his mind so he would never forget.

He swung her up into his arms again, carrying her to the bed and sinking down over her. "Pull off my shirt, ye lovely lass," he managed, reaching for every ounce of patience and willpower he possessed.

Laughing excitedly against his mouth, she lowered her hands to pull his shirttail free of his trousers. Arran lifted his hands over his head, parting from her until the rough cotton slid over his head and she dropped it off the side of the bed.

"Sit up," she ordered, shoving both hands against his chest. "I want to see you."

Narrowing one eye in a half grimace, he complied. She might as well have been a butterfly beating her wings at him, but he'd become helpless to deny anything she requested. Straddling her thighs, he settled upright onto his knees. Mary lay flat on her back beneath him, her autumn-colored hair coming loose from its pins and her face flushed.

"Surely ye've seen a man's bare chest before," he drawled.

"I haven't seen yours." Her hand shaking a little, she ran her fingers from his throat, down his sternum and past his belly to where his trousers cut off the view. "You have scars."

"I have two brothers. And I spent a time fighting the Frenchies." He shrugged. "Nae anything to slow me doon. And now it's my turn to take a look at ye, Mary."

He bunched up handfuls of silk and pushed the dress above her knees, and as she lifted her hips he took his time gazing at her bare thighs, the brown, curling hair at the apex of her legs, her flat stomach and the goose bumps his perusal seemed to raise on her skin.

"Arms up, my lass. I want to see all of ye."

Brief uncertainty crossed her gaze, but without a hesitation she put her arms above her head and arched her back to let the material slide from beneath her. Once he tossed the gown aside, he sat back on his heels to take her in. She had skin the color of fine cream, kissed here and there with a spray of freckles. Her breasts were round and inviting, just the size to fit his hands. With a smile he went down onto his hands and knees over her. His cock strained at his trousers, but for the moment he ignored it — as well as any man could bear wanting a woman so much he could barely see straight. Leaning down, he kissed her slow and deep and openmouthed.

In other circumstances, with another woman, he might have tossed her onto the bed, shoved up her dress, and buried himself in her. The moment was the goal. This — she — was different. Whether she felt comfortable admitting it yet or not, Mary Campbell was going to be his bride. The goal was to give her pleasure, to make her crave him as much as he already craved her, and to claim her as his own. Forever.

Slowly he kissed and licked and nipped his way down her throat to her shoulders.

Looking up at her to see her head raised just enough to watch him, he licked one sweet, pink nipple.

With a gasp she dug her fingers into his hair, pulling him closer against her. "Arran," she said breathily, the sound deepening to a moan when he put his mouth over her breast and sucked.

God's sake, he wanted her. And he needed her to want him. Shifting a little to rest his weight on one elbow, he slid the fingers of his free hand down her stomach, danced lightly across her thighs and then parted her nether lips and slipped inside her. She jumped, but he kept his mouth on her breast and his fingers down below moving in the same tempo. And sweet Saint Bridget, she was warm and wet — for him.

Her breath came faster and shallower, and she writhed deliciously beneath his hands until with a shuddering groan she climaxed. With her hands clawed into his scalp he thought she might have drawn blood, but he didn't care.

"I'm sorry," she rasped after a moment of panting. "Did I hurt you?"

"Nae," he returned, finally lifting his head again. "Ye liked that, I assume?"

"Oh, yes."

"Good. And there's more, as well."

"I . . . My goodness. More?"

"Aye. We're only just beginning."

"Then you should remove the rest of your clothes, too." Her smile matched his. "I feel very naughty."

He kneeled again, pulling her into a sitting position in front of him. "Come here," he said, taking her hands and moving them to his waist.

She hesitated for a bit as if she didn't quite know what to do. Then, blowing out her breath in a soft O, she unbuttoned the fastenings of his trousers. The tug as she worked at unfamiliar buttons had him clenching his jaw. "I want to do this correctly," she said, her face setting into grim lines as she wrestled another button open.

"I dunnae think ye need to worry over that," he responded, carefully keeping any amusement from his voice and expression.

"I don't like not knowing what to do."

"Well, that's one of the lovely things aboot sex, lass. If ye stop thinking so much, yer body knows what to do. Sex has been aboot fer a fair amount longer than ye and me."

Her hands paused, and she lifted her face to look at him. "How can anyone simply stop thinking?"

"I'll have to introduce ye to my brother Munro. He's a prime example."

"Arran."

He covered her hands with his. "Just do what feels good to ye, Mary. We're here, and we're together; naught else matters." Drawing her arms up around his shoulders, he lowered his head and kissed her upturned face again. Tonight she tasted like sin, sweet and spicy and far too enticing for his peace of mind.

Reaching between them, he opened the last button of his trousers himself and pushed them down his thighs. Thank God. For a moment there he thought he might be permanently bent.

Mary, her arms still around his shoulders, looked down between them. "So that's what that does."

"It does more than that."

She reached one hand down to stroke the length of him. "I think you should show me, Mr. Fox," she murmured.

"With pleasure, Mrs. Fox." He scooted backward to sit on his backside. "Help me with my boots, will ye?"

She tossed her own dancing slippers aside, then knelt to grab his heel and pull. After doing the same with the other boot, she set them both aside and stripped his trousers down his legs and off. Now *that* felt better. And this was where they belonged — together. And whatever awkwardness she'd felt seemed to have vanished, because with a curious, aroused glance at his face she reached between his legs to curl her fingers around his cock and touch his balls. "All this goes in your trousers," she mused. "It doesn't seem comfortable at all."

"Well, in its resting state it's nae as impressive," he commented, beginning to wonder just how much a man could stand before he let loose and ruined the rest of the evening. "But if ye kick a man there, he'll definitely feel it. It'll drop him to his knees faster than a punch to the jaw."

"But how —"

"If ye dunnae mind, my lass, might ye save the anatomy questions till after I've had ye? I feel like I've been waiting a day past forever fer this."

Mary released him, pressing up along his chest to kiss him again. "Have me, then," she whispered.

She didn't need to tell him twice. Wrapping his hands around her back, he lowered them both down to the quilted bed again. Arran kissed her, running his hands along her slim, smooth body until he felt near to coming right there. That wasn't going to happen, though. He'd waited too damned long for this. He settled himself between her thighs, shifting her legs farther apart until the tip of his cock brushed against her.

"Now, Arran," she urged him, her breath coming faster again.

"It'll hurt ye fer a minute, lass. But I'll nae hurt ye again."

"I'm ready. Please."

Moving as slowly and carefully as he could force himself to do, he canted his hips forward and slid inside her, hot and tight. When he met resistance he paused, holding her lovely green gaze with his own, then moved deeper. Mary gasped, and he caught the sound with a kiss. Her fingers dug into his shoulders, but he held still, fully engulfed. Now she belonged to him.

"Relax, lass. Feel me inside ye."

Gradually her eyes half closed. "Dear heavens," she murmured.

With her fingers still restlessly kneading at his back, he slid out, then pushed back in again. "Does it still hurt, my bonny Mary?"

She shook her head. "No. It feels . . . Do it again."

That made him grin. "My pleasure." He pumped his hips into her, slowly at first, then harder and faster as her ankles locked around his thighs. Each motion felt like a statement — that she belonged to him, that he wasn't letting her go.

"More," she groaned, arching her back.

He obliged, again and again, then shifted his weight to free one hand so he could pinch and tug at her nipples. When she came he felt it, and with a grunt he joined her. For a long moment he held her, both of them shuddering.

Let the Campbells try to stop them now, if they would. Or the MacLawrys. Wherever this adventure took them next, it would be together.

CHAPTER TWELVE

Mary gazed into fierce light blue eyes above her and tried to gather up a single thought. The only words close to reaching her mouth seemed to consist of "more," "good God," and a plea for him to remain precisely where he was, inside her. She'd never felt so wicked, and so deliriously . . . happy.

With a slight, satisfied smile, Arran lowered his head for another of his breath-stealing, heart-stopping kisses. He settled onto his elbows, the shift of his weight on her — in her — exquisite, and reached up to pull the pins from her hair one by one.

"You — Is it always like that?" she managed shakily, shivers of pleasure running down her spine as he unbraided the long tail of her hair.

"Nae," he returned, his deep brogue rumbling through him and into her. "Ye undo me, my bonny Mary. Body and soul."

She didn't think she'd ever heard anything

so romantic. Coming from a man as self-assured as he was, it shook her to her core. "I'm undone, myself."

His smile deepened. "Good. Ye needed some undoing."

At the least, she knew now what he'd meant when he'd told her to stop thinking so much. Every sensation, every caress . . . It was all overwhelming. And at the same time she couldn't quite remember why she'd resisted him in the first place. From that first night they'd met, when he hadn't known who she was other than Lady Vixen, he'd felt exotic, forbidden, and very tantalizing.

"What's going through that mind of yers, lass?" he rumbled, sliding an arm beneath her and turning them so that he lay on his back with her looking down at him. "Ye're nae regretting this, I hope."

Regret? All she wanted to do was have at him again. But Crawford would know, and then everything would change. Everything *had* changed, already. But she couldn't say it was for the worse, whatever the consequences might be. "I don't believe I am," she said aloud.

"I feel like I've been waiting forever for ye to say that, ye know," he said with a chuckle. "Proclamation of undying love, or nae, it'll do fer tonight." He ran his palm down from her shoulder to her backside, cupping her arse.

"I want to do it again," Mary stated, kissing the base of his jaw as he'd done for her.

"Oh, we will." Lifting her as if she weighed no more than a feather, he set her next to him on the bed. "But nae tonight."

"No?" she asked, sitting up as he moved to the edge of the bed. "Why not?"

He picked up his trousers and shrugged into them, lean and well muscled and perfect. "Because ye want me."

Mary frowned. "What the devil is the logic in that?"

With a grin, he caught up his shirt and pulled it on over his head. "Tomorrow while we're riding, I want to look over at ye and know that ye're longing fer my touch, my bonny lass. I want ye to crave me the way I've been craving ye since before we began this wee journey. And I want ye to think aboot tomorrow night, when I'll have ye again."

A warm shiver ran down her spine and settled . . . there. "What if I've changed my mind about you by then?"

"Ye willnae." After he stomped into his boots, he returned to the bedside to cup the nape of her neck and favor her with a long, slow kiss. "I'll have ye every night between here and Scotland. And then ye can decide if ye still want to run to yer grandfather and yer old life, or if ye want a new life with me."

He set aside the chair that blocked the door, unlocked it, and stepped out into the hallway. With the door almost closed, he leaned back in. "Dunnae let that battle-axe say a cross word to ye aboot this. Blame me if ye wish; my shoulders are broad enough. I'll see ye in the morning, lass."

With that, he shut the door. Surely he was only teasing; he would return in a moment and strip off his clothes again to join her in his bed. She arranged herself on one hip, pulling her loose hair over one shoulder. It felt wanton, so hopefully it looked that way rather than pitiful or comical.

His bootsteps faded toward the stairs leading to the inn's common room, and didn't return. Mary frowned. He couldn't truly mean to leave her in this state. Yes, she felt delicious and satisfied, but at the same time, a restless want ran just beneath her skin. How was she supposed to think straight now? How was she supposed to make a logical decision about her future when he was all she could think about?

Huffing out her breath, she finally rolled

to the edge of the bed and stood to turn her gown right side out and step into it. With her room just across the hallway and most everyone still at the assembly she didn't bother buttoning it, or trying to tidy her hair. Crawford would be the only one worth fooling, and the maid would instantly know what she'd been about. And at this moment, she didn't even feel guilty about it.

She stepped into her shoes and then crossed over to her own room. Crawford stood from the writing desk and the book she had open there. "My lady, I didn't expect . . ." She trailed off, her already somber expression lowering even further. "Your parents will be so disappointed, Lady Mary. And I can only imagine what Mr. Calder's reaction will be."

"I don't belong to Charles Calder, Crawford. Not any longer. And stop chastising me. I wish to go to bed."

Pinching her lips together, the maid helped her back out of her gown. "You could tell your father that he forced himself on you, I suppose," she said after a moment. "You would also have to tell them that he kidnapped the two of us. I'll vouch for that, of course. And then hope that no child comes of this. MacLawry will . . . Well, we don't need to discuss him, but we might still be able to salvage your repu—"

"That is enough! For heaven's sake, listening to this is like having a spider crawl across my scalp. No one but us knows anything. Nor will they. Not until I speak to my grandfather and get this mess straightened out. And no one is going to hurt Arran."

That last part had somewhere become the most important, making certain that Charles Calder and her other cousins didn't harm a single black hair on Arran's handsome head. Of course he was quite capable of taking care of himself, but that wasn't the point. The idea that he might be hurt . . . It stopped her heart.

And a child? Why hadn't she considered that? All she'd wanted was Arran. To touch him, to feel his hands on her skin. Nothing else mattered. But a child? If she was pregnant, they would have to find a way to live peaceably. She would be able to have a family with him. To wake up every morning and not only see him, but see his eyes, his face, in a daughter or a son.

She shook herself. Tomorrow night seemed a very long time from now. Until then, she would settle for thinking hopefully unwanton thoughts and for praying that a fairy-tale ending could be possible for a

"Let me buy ye a pint, m . . . my dear Mr. Fox," Peter's voice came from the depths of the nearly deserted tavern.

Arran made his way over to the table. It was a lucky thing the footman had spoken up — he'd almost forgotten he wasn't a Scot. "I'll buy you one, my good man," he countered, signaling the tavern maid.

"Ye're a true, gentleman, y'are," Peter returned, his words slurring just a little. For a Highlander to be that far in his cups, he must have been going at this for a time.

"I thought ye were keeping watch," he said in a low voice, dragging the opposite bench closer and sitting.

"Just warming my innards. Ye've returned early from the dance, aye?"

"Aye."

Peter glanced up at him. "Should I nae ask ye more aboot that, then?"

"Nae, ye shouldnae."

Putting it in words could only diminish the evening, anyway. He'd been Mary's first, and he had every intention of being her only. She'd even left her logic aside for a moment, which left him hope that she would be able to choose him over her clan when the time came for it.

Walking out of that room with her sitting naked and disheveled and lovely was likely the most difficult thing he'd ever done. But as long as he was the pursuer, he remained uncertain of her own level of commitment. And with what would certainly lie ahead of them, she needed to decide for herself how far she was willing to go, how much she was willing to do. He knew what *he* was willing to do, but it would take both of them not only to survive this, but to make a future together. For God's sake, he'd intentionally not taken any precautions with her. She could be carrying his child, even now.

The maid brought him a mug and he downed it, blinking a little when the brew turned out to be a bitter beer rather than ale. He could be a father. A year ago with some lass from the Highlands the idea would have dismayed him; he was a Mac-Lawry of the clan MacLawry, and he couldn't afford to be so careless. Tonight, though, he felt . . . not precisely content, but satisfied. This was the path he was meant to tread, and he was with the woman who would walk it beside him. The only uncertainty was whether she'd yet realized that or not.

"Ye're quiet, Mr. Fox," Peter commented, working more methodically on his own

291

mug. "I do have Howard up in the stable loft keeping an eye on the road while I'm in here. I'll go oot again in a minute."

"I doubt anyone has figured out where we are yet, Peter. But I'm still not ready to stop looking over my shoulder."

"Ye should be looking in front of yerself, as well, ye know. She is a Campbell. Aye, she's pretty, but ye can nae trust a Campbell. She'll smile at ye while she puts a dagger into yer gizzard."

"My gizzard is safe. Mary wouldnae hurt me." Not physically, anyway.

"If ye say so. I dunnae trust either of those females." He sat back again and took another swallow. "So we're to keep strolling aboot this damned soft country and staying at these cozy inns while death comes hunting ye? Because even if they've nae found our trail yet, they will."

"Death may be hunting me, but I'd wager it's still looking in the wrong place." That was why they'd decided to avoid the North Road; once the Campbells — and Ranulf — realized what had happened, they would search along the quickest route north. Except that his odd little party was half a hundred miles west of it.

"If ye say so. I know yer brother, though, and he knows ye. How much will ye wager that he'll nae come to the conclusion that ye didnae take the easier road?"

That was a good point, dammit all. "Let's speed our pace a little tomorrow, just to be safe," he said. "We dunnae want to make it look like we're fleeing, but enough to get us to the Highlands by the end of the week."

"Aye. That's the best news I've had in a fortnight. Once we get there, though, do ye still mean to marry the Campbell lass?"

"I do, if she'll have me. I suppose it depends on whether she prefers being Alkirk's granddaughter to being my wife."

"Bah."

"Bah?"

"Ye've become too civilized, lad. A Mac-Lawry doesnae allow anyone else to decide the course of his life. He sees what he wants and finds a way to claim it. Tooth, claw, sword, rifle, or mind." He tapped a forefinger against his temple. "Just like yer brother's doing. If ye want her, take her."

Arran frowned even as a second tankard arrived to replace the first one. Its contents disappeared just as quickly. "Ranulf's turning himself into a Sasannach," he grumbled. "I want no kinship to that. Because he's nae laying claim to Charlotte; he's twisting himself inside oot to be what she wants."

"She proposed to him, ye know. He didnae bend a knee nor bow his head, from what I heard."

"He's bowing now."

"Why, because he's talking to the Stewarts and those Sasannach lords? How else could he purchase their land in the Highlands? I reckon those prissy lords are the ones bowing to him. And well they should. By the end of the month he'll own more of Scotland than Prince Georgie does. At least that's what Owen says."

What? Why hadn't he known that Ranulf was purchasing land? He was generally the one in whom his brother confided. Yes, Ran had asked for support, but Arran had thought the marquis had become set on making friends with the English lords because it pleased Charlotte for him to do so. Just as he'd decided to ally with the Stewarts to gain their trade contacts. He had no idea Ranulf had been purchasing English- and Stewart-owned land.

Peter began to look concerned. "Should I nae have said anything aboot that? I know his lairdship didnae want to argue with ye aboot spreading our cotters thin, but Owen didnae say it was a secret. And we all know we need the land, with us taking in Campbell and Gerdens and Daily cotters. So —"

"It's fine, Peter," he interrupted. Whatever

he'd missed, it was his own fault. Had he been that distracted by London? By Mary? And he'd accused Ranulf of losing his head over Charlotte. Far from it, evidently. His brother had been using his time in London to make more room for their own people, even the newly adopted ones. And now he'd gone and destroyed the truce with the Campbells — at a time that couldn't have been worse for any of this.

"Thank ye fer saying so, Mr. Fox," Peter drawled, looking relieved.

"Nae. Thank ye, Peter. I may have been a damned fool, and nae even realized it." And he would more than likely never be forgiven for it. But had it been worth it? He could answer that with every beat of his heart. If she loved him, it was worth it.

"Well, I'd best get back to watching the road," the footman said, rising a bit unsteadily. "With his one eye, that Howard's only half a lookout, at best."

Arran forced a grin. "Dunnae fall out of the hayloft. Ye'd send all the Highlands lasses into mourning."

"Aye. And half them Sasannach ones, too." Peter buttoned up his coat and pulled a pair of rough gloves from his pocket. "I nearly forgot," he commented, freeing an envelope from the tangle of gloves. "I saw

that female bringing this doon fer tomorrow's mail, and I thought ye might want a
look at it."

"Which female?" Arran asked, taking the
letter and flipping it over to see the Mathering House address neatly written across the
front.

"The square-jawed one. Crawford. I
thought she might be sending word of her
whereaboots to Campbell kin or
someaught."

"Aye, it's someaught." He didn't even
hesitate before tearing open the plain wax
seal. Whatever it was, Crawford was not going to be sending letters to Mary's parents.
Swiftly he unfolded it.

"Dear Lord Fendarrow," he read, his eyes
narrowing and growing anger making his
fingers clench into the paper. "On the
chance that my previous letter missed you, I
again inform you that Lord Arran Mac-
Lawry has forcibly taken Lady Mary and
myself from the Giant's Pipe Inn. We are
presently in the village of Wigmore, and will
resume traveling north in the morning. I
will once again do my utmost to slow our
flight, but our kidnapper is determined to
drag us into the Highlands. After that, it
will be too late to prevent this catastrophe
from being known. It may be too late

already. Please come in all haste! Ever your servant, Eunice Crawford."

"Peter," he said, keeping his voice low and even, "ye and Howard hitch up a fresh pair of horses. Then come up and help me get the luggage down. We're leaving in twenty minutes."

"Aye, m'laird. Might I ask —"

"This is a second letter. The Campbells know where we are. Or bloody near enough."

The footman's ruddy expression paled a little. "I'll see to it."

As Peter hurried off, Arran strode for the stairs. At Mary's room he shoved at the door, but it was latched. Balling a fist, he pounded. Hard. "Mary! Open the door!"

Inside he heard a smattering of sharp-voiced conversation, and then the door clicked and opened. "What's wrong?" Mary asked, sleepy-eyed in the white night rail he'd purchased for her.

If he'd been less angry, the way she looked would have completely distracted him. As it was, he wordlessly handed her the letter and then moved past her slender form into the room. "You," he growled, jabbing a finger at the battle-axe in her mobcap and high-necked night rail where she stood on the near side of the bed. "What did the first letter say?"

Her pale features grayed around the edges, but she kept her chin high. "I'm not speaking to you, you rogue."

"Call me whatever ye like, but ye *will* tell me aboot the other letter." Arran took a long step forward, using his height to force her to look up even farther, changing her stance from defiant to submissive.

It didn't seem to have any effect. "I am not employed by you," she declared.

"I dunnae —"

Mary pushed past him. "What did you do, Crawford?" she demanded, snapping the missive against her palm. "When did you send the first letter, and what did you say?"

The maid didn't alter her expression. "I am in the employ of the Marquis of Fendarrow. In his absence, I will do whatever is necessary to protect his reputation and that of his fam—"

"Arran, do you have two pounds?" Mary interrupted, turning her back on Crawford to hold a hand out to him.

Wordlessly he pulled two coins from his pocket and placed them into her palm. If she meant them to be set over the dead maid's eyes he would have preferred that she use shillings, but he couldn't disapprove the gesture.

Rather than throwing the blunt at Crawford, though, Mary turned and left the room. Immediately the maid started forward, but Arran took a step sideways to block her exit. "Ye're nae going anywhere."

"I will scream," she retorted.

"Scream till crows fall from the sky, ye witch. Ye'll still nae leave this room until we decide what to do with ye. And I favor putting ye in a hole in the ground and shoveling dirt over ye."

"I am only doing my duty. How dare you!"

"Yer duty. Bah. Ye've set an angry group of men after us. What, ye think they'll nae consider that Mary is ruined? Ye think she'll return to London and everything will be as it was?"

"I think this entire venture is all your idea, and your fault."

"Mayhap that's so, but she's in it now. And she's here because she didnae want the life her father decided for her."

"That is not her decision."

Mary topped the stairs again, her expression even grimmer than before. "I think ye have the wrong of that, Crawford," he returned, and faced his lass. "Is everything well, Mary?"

"Yes. Help me gather my things, will you, Arran?"

"Aye. We need to be oot of here before we're caught."

While Crawford, arms folded, continued glaring at them from one corner, they tossed Mary's new clothes and toilette items into the small trunk he'd purchased for her. She held back one plain green muslin, and crossed into his room to shed her night rail and pull it on. However much he would have liked to follow her to watch, he wasn't inclined to leave the maid unsupervised. Now was not the time for her to attempt again to convince Mary to return to London or to wait there at the inn for her father's arrival.

Peter trotted up the stairs, and Arran set him to watch Crawford while he hastily packed his own trunk. He carried it into the hallway and set it down. "There ye go, Peter. Get them loaded as quick as ye can."

"Aye, m'laird."

Mary approached again, and he moved behind her to close the trio of buttons running up her back. "Do ye have a preference over what we do aboot the battle-axe?" he asked, sending Crawford another glare. If Mary still wanted the maid with them he would agree to it, but only if she traveled bound and gagged and tied to her bedpost each night. And *that* he wouldn't compro-

300

mise about.

"I've seen to it," she said, a grim iron to her tone that he'd never heard before.

"If you continue on with him, my lady, you'll be ruined beyond anyone's ability to salvage. He's not only an enemy of your family, but he's a *Highlander,* for heaven's sake. A barbarian. It is my duty to guard you and your rep—"

"Not any longer, Crawford. Consider your employment terminated." She took a breath. "And you likely should have considered that I'm a Highlander as well, before you went about insulting all of us."

The maid's mouth opened and closed again, like a dying fish on a riverbank. "Your father hired me," she finally gulped out. "You cannot hand me my papers."

"I just did." Mary turned as the blacksmith with whom she'd danced earlier came upstairs, a hammer and lumber in his hands. "If you please, Thomas."

Crawford drew her hands up to her chest, an oddly girlish gesture for someone as severe as she was. Clearly she was mortified about being seen in her night rail by a stranger — though she hadn't so much as flinched when Arran barged into the room. "This — what do you think you're doing?"

"Making certain you cannot cause any

more trouble." The tavern maid appeared next, a tray holding a loaf of bread, a pitcher of water, and a glass in her hands. Mary took it with a nod and set it inside the doorway. "Goodbye, Mother Graves."

The blacksmith started to close the door, but Arran stopped him with one hand. He wasn't surprised that his logical lass had figured out a way to dispose of the woman, but he *was* impressed. "One moment," he said, not bothering to disguise his brogue any longer. Fendarrow knew where they were.

Stepping into the room, one wary eye on the fuming maid, he opened the wardrobe and removed the severe black muslin gown that remained there. With a squawk she leaped at him, but he beat her to the door and pulled it shut. Still screeching, Crawford shoved at it from inside. Arran put his shoulder against the wood while Thomas hammered the planks into place across the door frame.

"Whatever are we to do with her?" the tavern maid asked, sending the rattling door a nervous glance.

"Naught," Arran replied. "She has nae money to give ye and no clothes to wear. I imagine someone will come along tomorrow or the next day inquiring aboot us. They

302

can let her oot, if they choose. We'll be well into Wales by then."

The misdirection was fairly obvious, but hopefully the maid and the blacksmith were too distracted to notice. Mary wrapped her hand around his arm, and together they descended the stairs and left the Fox and Grapes. He remained as tantalized as the fox in that tale, but in his story no one was keeping him from his prize.

Outside the carriage he caught Peter by the arm. "I know ye dunnae approve of this madness," he said in a low voice, "but ye may have just saved us all. So thank ye, Peter Gilling."

Mary released him and stepped forward to plant a kiss on Peter's flushed cheek. "Thank you, Peter," she seconded. "You've given us a chance."

The footman doffed his floppy hat. "I couldnae have the Campbells riding us doon, begging yer pardon, m'lady."

"I couldn't have it, either," she returned, and stepped up into the coach.

"Take us north, as fast as ye can," Arran muttered. "We've nae the time to be subtle any longer."

"I'll see the two of ye to the Highlands or die trying, Lord Arran, curse me if I dunnae."

So with Duffy and Juno tied off at the back of the coach, they rumbled into the night. Their few days of leisurely travel were over; if they couldn't stay ahead of the Campbells they would lose their future together, and he would likely lose his life. And at this moment he honestly couldn't say which fate would be worse.

"I'm so sorry," Mary said from the darkness beside him.

He reached over and found her hand, drawing her up against his side. "Why are ye apologizing, my bonny Mary?"

Her hand trembled in his. "You didn't want Crawford along in the first place. I . . . I suppose I wanted to keep hold of a chance to get my old life back. But I never thought she would go behind my back like that."

"We didnae only upend our lives," he returned, tucking her beneath his chin. Her still disheveled hair smelled of lemons, fragrant in the cold dark of the coach. "We upended hers, as well. She was trying to put things back to what most benefited her."

"Will they catch us? My father and Charles, I mean?"

"I'm nae certain. It depends on whether and when they got that first letter, and how much Crawford knew aboot the road we meant to take."

"I think she knew a great deal." Mary squeezed his hand. "I don't want you to be hurt, Arran."

"I've nae wish fer that either, my lass. And nae wish to hurt any of yer kin."

"You didn't feel that way a few weeks ago."

Arran smiled grimly into the darkness. "A few weeks ago I only knew Campbells over the pointy end of a sword. And however I feel aboot most of yer kin, they *are* yer kin." He had no doubt that he could better than hold his own if it came to a fight; his years in the army hadn't gone to waste, after all. But the future he wanted for the two of them likely wouldn't be able to withstand him putting a ball through her father. That circumstance, therefore, needed to be avoided.

"You took Crawford's gown," she said a moment later, her voice stronger and steadier.

"Aye. I figured it might make her think twice aboot trying to climb oot a window. That was clever of ye, to barricade her into the room."

"I wanted to punch her in the nose." She shifted, and he could more feel than see her gazing up at him. "I wonder now if your sister and I weren't so different. I know you've always kept guards around her, and that your clan calls her the fairest flower of the Highlands. My father did hire Crawford, even though that would have been something my mother generally did. Perhaps she was meant to be my guard."

He thought about that for a moment. "She didnae precisely act the way my sister's maid, Mitchell, does," he said slowly. Perhaps Crawford had been more of a threat than he realized. That was a thought to keep him awake nights.

Mary sighed, her breath soft and warm against his cheek. "What are we going to do, Arran?"

"We stay together. That's what we do."

"That's a nice sentiment, but rather nebulous for a plan, don't you think?"

With a chuckle he found her mouth for a soft, slow kiss. He could live on those kisses, he was beginning to think. "Nae," he murmured. "It's the only thing that matters."

CHAPTER THIRTEEN

Munro MacLawry dismounted from his big gray gelding, Saturn. He didn't need a view of the sky to know the weather was turning, because the hair on his arms was lifting. Even so, from the front drive of Glengask Manor the black, roiling clouds were clear to see all the way across the valley.

"Storm by sunset, do ye think?" the lean man standing beside him asked, his gaze on the same view.

"Before that. Are ye staying fer dinner then, Lachlan?"

Lord Gray nodded. "Might as well. Cannae have ye roaming the halls alone like a great weepy ghoul."

"I'm nae weepy."

"Ranulf and Winnie have been away from here fer better than seven weeks, and Arran fer four. Have ye even heard from them?"

"Aye, here and there." Arran was the only one who wrote regularly, and even he'd been silent for better than a week. "Ye know more than I, dunnae? Isnae Winnie sending ye those fancy perfumed letters every day?"

Lachlan frowned, turning for the front door as grooms appeared to lead away the pair of mounts. "Ye know she stopped writing me."

"I'd fergotten. Likely she's found a handsome Sasannach lord to occupy her. Ranulf has — a pretty lass, from what I hear."

"Ranulf would never permit Winnie to marry a Sasannach who'd take her oot of the Highlands."

"A few weeks ago I'd have agreed with ye. But then I also would've wagered ye a hundred quid that Glengask wouldnae lose his heart to an English lass. They say being in England changes a soul." He didn't know any such thing, but it did serve to explain his oldest brother's actions. And if it gave Lachlan pause, so much the better. Because so far the viscount hadn't shown any sign of viewing Winnie as anything other than the pigtail-wearing sister of his good friends. But Ranulf seemed to want them together, so Munro meant to do what he could to help.

The door opened as they reached it, but rather than standing back to allow them entry, Cooper and his shock of red hair came out to meet them. "Ye've a note, m'laird," the butler said, holding it out. "Came by special courier. The lad said it was urgent. I was aboot to send William oot to look fer ye."

Munro took the missive. "We rode oot to see Duncan Lenox and his new bride."

"And his sisters," Lachlan added. "The oldest one, Sorcha, nearly fainted when Bear smiled at her."

"She didnae. And she's naught but sixteen. Now shut up so I can read this."

The address was in Ranulf's dark, spare handwriting. He broke Glengask's wax seal and unfolded it. At the first few words, though, he stopped, his blood freezing. "Ran's office, Lach. Now."

Lachlan fell in behind him as he strode down the wide hallway with its portraits of ancient MacLawrys, clan chiefs and warriors and statesmen, all of them with thick black hair and steely eyes, all of them sworn to fight to the death to protect Glengask and her people. Campbell haters, all of them.

"What is it, Bear?" Lachlan asked, closing the door to shut them inside Ranulf's spare, neat office. "Ye look green aboot the gills."

"I feel greenish. Listen to this. 'Bear, the

Campbell truce is likely broken past repair. I —' "

"That didnae last long," Lachlan commented. "But ye cannae be surprised."

"It's worse than that. 'I need ye to gather riders and head south to the border. Arran's on his way north in the company of Mary Campbell, Alkirk's granddaughter. Ye need to keep him from being slaughtered by the Campbells chasing after him, and ye need to keep him from marrying that woman AT ALL COSTS.' He capitalized that last bit."

"Sweet Jasus," Lachlan muttered, looking more than a little off color, himself. "A Campbell? *Arran?*"

It was the word "marrying" that caught Munro's attention. He could see Arran bedding the Campbell's granddaughter to thumb his nose at old Alkirk and his kin. But marriage? That didn't make even a madman's sense. Moving around Lachlan, he pulled open the door again. "Cooper! Fetch me William! And Andrew and Connor. And have horses saddled fer 'em."

"How many men are ye taking with ye, Bear?" Lachlan asked.

"Enough."

"I'll ride home and get my kit, then."

Munro blocked his friend from the door. "Nae. Ye know the words on the coat of arms. 'Always a MacLawry at Glengask.' Ye'll be staying here."

Lach frowned. "I'm nae a MacLawry."

"Yer grandmother was. And the clan knows it. I need ye here, especially if we're stirring up trouble."

After a moment the viscount nodded. "I'll agree to it only because of what this could set in motion, Bear. Because ye ken if ye run across any Campbells, it'll mean a fight."

"Aye. That's my hurry. If anyone's to murder Arran, it'll be Ranulf. Or me. Damned fool."

Perhaps he wasn't as razor-witted as Arran, but he knew well enough that if his brother had truly run off with Mary Campbell, they'd begun a disaster. He couldn't see a way through it that didn't include bloodshed. And more than likely the blood would be Arran's.

"Damned fool," he repeated.

Mary awoke from a dream in which her father became a great bear and slashed his claws through Arran's chest as she and Arran slept together in a cozy bed in a cozy cottage up in the Highlands. She sat upright, startled, and banged the back of her head on something.

"Ouch," Arran said mildly, rubbing his chin. "What woke ye, lass?"

They weren't in a cozy cottage in the Highlands. They were still in the badly sprung carriage fleeing north. And evidently she'd fallen asleep on Arran's shoulder, with his arms wrapped around her. Still, though, the terror of that moment, the horror of the . . . loss she'd felt, lingered. "It was just a dream," she said aloud, though it felt like far more than that.

No one in her family was a witch or a warlock, however — as far as she knew. No one could portend the future in dreams or tea leaves or tarot cards. And she seriously doubted her father could become a bear. An angry dog, perhaps, barking and howling at the moon, but if she had anyone as fierce as a bear in her family it would be her grandfather.

"Was I in this dream of yers?" he asked slyly, tucking a strand of her red-brown hair behind one ear. "Were we naked?"

"Yes, you were in my dream," she returned, still trying to banish the lingering cobwebs, "and no, we weren't naked. At least I don't think we were. We were in a bed with blankets over us."

"Together? Then I'm certain we were naked."

"Arran."

"What disturbed ye aboot it, then? It seems a fine dream to me."

"It was, until my father found us, turned into a bear, and clawed you to death."

"Well, then. That *would* be upsetting. Except that yer father's nae a bear and there are nae bears in Scotland, anyway. Nae any longer." He grinned. "Ye snore, ye know."

With an indignant laugh and truly grateful for the distraction, she slapped him on the knee. "I do not!"

"Ye do," he insisted. "It's a wee, delicate sound, like a lamb bleating."

"Well, you sound like an elephant trumpeting when you snore," she countered, because it seemed plausible.

"I didnae snore, because I didnae sleep."

Mary shifted into the far corner of the coach so she could take a look at Arran. Really, truly see him. His lean expression remained easy and amused, his sunrise-blue eyes darker but sharp in the dimmer light inside the coach. Beyond that, though, shadows swooped at the edges of his jaw and beneath his eyes, and she abruptly wondered when he'd last managed a good night's sleep. Likely not since they'd left London.

"Sleep now," she said, reaching out to run

a finger along his jaw. "I'll keep watch."

He studied her face as intently as she'd been looking at his. "Do ye regret this, Mary Campbell? Do ye wish we'd nae met?"

Vulnerable. That was how he looked. And if she chose to, she could wound him badly. "I've wondered about that," she admitted. "And I'm not so sure my circumstances would have altered all that much. The moment the truce began, my father went looking for Roderick — at my grandfather's behest, I assume. And if the truce had lasted long enough, I would have married him. If it hadn't, well, Charles practically sleeps on our front porch. Neither of them . . . light a spark in my heart." Not the way Arran did. "And I would have had no one to ride to my rescue."

She sighed, trying to think through what she wanted to say before she spoke the words aloud. "Before your family rode into London, my grandfather kept telling my parents to give me time. Eventually I would have had to choose someone of whom they approved, though, so I suppose it was all only an illusion of free choice. And I have a good idea now that my father would have pushed for Charles Calder, regardless of my opinion. After all, no one's spent more time or effort to ingratiate himself with my

314

parents than Charles has. He's lavished more attention on them, in fact, that he ever did on me."

"So ye reckon ye'd have ended up leg-shackled to him if ye'd never seen a Mac-Lawry, and whether I'd ever kissed ye or nae."

"I think I might well have. Without your presence, well, even though Roderick seems milder, I honestly wouldn't call him much of an improvement. And there would have been no one to ask what *I* wanted. There certainly wouldn't have been anyone to assist me when I said I didn't wish to marry Charles because he's cruel and a snake and I couldn't . . . tolerate him touching me the way you do." Nor could she imagine herself conversing with any other man the way she could talk to Arran.

"Then I have another reason to be glad I came to London," he said quietly.

She touched his arm again. It seemed vital to touch him every few minutes. "What about you, though? Do you regret that we met? You must have dozens of pretty Highlands lasses hounding you for a wedding. Deirdre, for example, is quite pretty."

"Mostly the lasses hounded Ranulf. There was some talk last year aboot him marrying a Stewart, but naught came of it. Whenever he'd pointed Deirdre at me, I would have fought him aboot it, and whatever mess I've made between Ranulf and me, I'll live with it. But in general, aye, there are lasses in the clan MacLawry who wish to be MacLawrys in fact. They'd take any of us, I suppose."

"I didn't mean because of your pedigree, though. I meant because of . . . Well, look at you. You're more handsome than any man I've ever set eyes on."

"Am I?" he returned, a slight frown furrowing his brow. "That has naught to do with me. I dunnae carry a mirror in my pocket. I only know how I feel. And I've never felt as alive as I do when I'm with ye. I wouldnae have wanted to go through my life withoot feeling that. Or without knowing ye. So nae, I dunnae regret meeting ye, my bonny Mary. Nae fer a second."

She sat back again, trying to hold in a sudden flood of tears. No one had ever said anything so splendid to her. If this was a fairy tale — and it was beginning to feel more and more like one — perhaps it was one of the few that could be true. Perhaps she could make a future somewhere with this dangerous, forbidden, devilishly handsome rogue. He certainly seemed to want to go forward with her.

If she could just look forward as well, stop

worrying over what her father and her grandfather and all of her friends likely thought of her now, stop thinking she was a traitor to her clan because she'd dared to defy orders in favor of her own happiness, this could be her grand adventure. *He* could be her grand adventure.

Arran tilted his head at her. "I thought ye'd at least give me a kiss fer my gallantry," he suggested.

She grinned at him. "Why is it that we can be fleeing for our freedom and our lives, and you still make me smile?"

"I'm a charming fella. And ye should kiss me. Now."

"Hm. I'll have to consider th—"

He lunged halfway across the coach and captured her mouth. Before she even had time to brace herself, he had her on her back. She wrapped her arms around his shoulders, settling into a long, deep, open-mouthed kiss that sent excitement swirling down her spine and between her legs.

"When do we need to change horses?" she asked, putting one hand between them and pulling his shirt from his trousers.

"In a half hour or so," he returned, breaking away from her mouth to look down at her. "Ye still need to ask me, bonny lass."

She swallowed. A proper lady would never

ask to be bedded. Of course, a proper lady wouldn't be alone with a man in a carriage fleeing for the Scottish border. A proper lady would be gathering her trousseau for a wedding she'd neither wanted nor agreed to.

"I want you, Arran," she murmured, brushing hair from his face.

His mouth twitched. "Ye want me fer what? Lawn bowling?"

"I want you for . . . sex."

He lifted an eyebrow. "Aye? Tell me more."

Her cheeks warmed. "I want you to take off my clothes and kiss me everywhere," she ventured, and was rewarded by a smile and his mouth trailing along the base of her jaw.

"Anything else, lass?"

Considering she could barely remember how to speak, Mary thought she was doing quite well. She drew a shaky breath. "I . . . I want you inside me, Arran. Now, if you please."

"Well, why didnae ye say so?" Rising up on his knees, one shoulder braced against the back of the seat for balance, he unbuttoned his trousers and shoved them down to his thighs. Judging by his jutting manhood, he wanted her as badly as she wanted him.

Last night he'd been slow and careful and

gentle. None of that seemed to be on his mind today. Rather, he seemed very single-minded about what he wanted. Being the recipient of his lust was quite thrilling, really.

Arran wrapped his hands into the bottom hem of her gown and gathered the material up, past her knees and over her hips. Then he went down again with his hands above her shoulders, spread her legs with his knees, and pushed inside her.

She gasped, the sudden sensation of his large cock filling her making her jolt into a sudden ecstacy of pleasure. Biting her lip to keep from crying out, she dug her fingers into the muscles of his back and arched against him.

Good heavens. They both still wore most of their clothes, and even so it felt like the most intimate, erotic moment of her life. When she could breathe again she pulled his face down for a kiss, their bodies rocking as he drove into her again and again. The world fell away until only the two of them remained, the only sounds the creaking of the carriage, their hard breathing, and his low exclamations of pleasure.

Faster and faster, deeper, harder, until with a moan she climaxed again. He followed immediately, pushing hard into her and holding himself there as he spilled his seed. This was the moment she'd already come to relish, when there were no doubts about the future or their present circumstances, or anything else. This . . . this was perfection. And they could only find it with each other.

Finally he lifted his head from her shoulder and kissed her again. "The part ye asked fer, with me kissing every inch of ye, will have to wait till we next find a proper bed," he murmured.

"I'll hold you to that."

A fist pounded on the roof of the coach, making her jump. "M'laird, coaching inn ahead. Howard wants to change the horses."

"Aye," Arran called out, the sound shuddering into her. "We could stand to stretch our legs and find someaught to eat."

Grimacing, he pulled out of her and rose up on his knees again to refasten his trousers. Not wanting to be caught on her back with her dress hiked up around her waist, Mary sat up and smoothed down her skirts. "How long have we been traveling?" she asked, finally pushing aside a curtain to see filtered sunlight lengthening the shadows of the trees to the east.

"A little better than seven hours. We'll have breakfast here and then push on north.

If ye want to change into yer riding habit we can travel on horseback until the next change of horses." He favored her with a wicked smile. "Or we could stay in here and make ourselves comfortable."

"That sounds delightful," she returned, "but I think I'd prefer to ride for a while. I swear the coach's springs are rusting away with every mile, if it had any to begin with."

"They may be," he agreed. "She's nae much fer comfort, but she does have some speed. And today I'm glad fer that."

In less than a minute they turned off the road and pulled to a halt. Still a bit shaky and out of breath, Mary waited until Peter opened the coach door and flipped down the steps before she emerged into the early morning chill. "Where are we?"

"Howard reckoned we're just south of Bunbury," Peter replied. "I told him that meant as much as the devil's laugh to me, so then he said we're aboot thirty miles south of Manchester."

Neither man looked particularly satisfied with that answer, either. And Mary wished she'd paid more attention to her geography lessons. "I believe that puts us approximately eighty miles south and west of York," she offered.

Arran's expression cleared. "Nae good

enough, but it's progress," he said. "I could say I wish now we'd taken less time to stroll aboot the countryside, but that would be a lie."

She knew what he meant. As much as they could have used the distance now, staying at quaint inns and going to the Wigmore assembly to dance had been the most magnificent set of days of her life. "How much farther to Fort William?"

"If we're as far from York as ye say, I'd wager aboot two hundred miles, lass. In this coach, on these roads, three days at the very least."

Just from Arran's tone she could tell what he was thinking. That it would more likely be four or five days, and that the rackety old coach wouldn't be able to stay ahead of the Campbells. They would be caught. "Arran, I —"

"Let's get someaught to eat, Mrs. Fox," he said, his smile not quite reaching his eyes. "I, fer one, am famished."

"So we're to wait until disaster strikes?" she asked, wrapping her hand around his sleeve.

"Disaster hasnae found us yet. And there are several roads leading north. We've nae been run down so far."

"I had no idea MacLawrys were such

optimists."

This time his eyes danced as he grinned, and that seemed like something of a triumph. All she'd done thus far in this flight was to insist that Crawford join them and then to shut the maid into a room when she'd finally believed the overwhelming evidence that the woman had betrayed them. So she had a balance of nought.

"Oh, aye," he responded, thankfully not reading her mind. "We MacLawrys still believe in sylphs and fairy tales. Or at least my brother Bear does."

The inn's roof sagged on the left side, and Arran had to shove on the door twice to get it open. All she could read of the hanging sign was Something Black Something, though from the faded drawing beneath she could guess it was Witch's Black Kettle. Or perhaps Cauldron. Whatever it was, the place didn't look terribly welcoming, and she edged closer to Arran as they stepped inside.

"The mail stage won't be by here until Monday," a low voice grumbled from the darkness. "You'd be better off waiting for it in Manchester." Evidently the innkeeper could only afford a single pair of candles, because that was the only light present. Nor did she see any windows that could be thrown open to let in the morning sunlight.

"We've our own transportation," Arran said in his faux accent, this time mimicking that of the unseen man in front of them. "We could use a change of horses and some eggs and toast."

"Can you pay for it?"

"Can you provide it?" Arran countered.

A squat, round man waddled out of the back of the common room. "I've a pair of horses that'll do for you, if you'll pay for the hay to feed the ones you leave behind until somebody collects 'em."

"And food?" Arran prompted, still not moving from the doorway. He had his free hand in his right pocket, Mary realized belatedly. Was he carrying a pistol? Did he expect an ambush?

"I'll poach you some eggs. No toast, though, because I've no bread. Three shillings first."

Arran released Mary and took a slow step forward, blocking her view of the stout man. "Do you have many people robbing you of poached eggs, then?" he asked succinctly. "Because I'm beginning to feel insulted."

"The next inn's just south of Manchester," the innkeeper said. "And they have poached eggs. And toast."

With that deceptive speed of his, Arran

flipped a coin at the man, who caught it just as deftly. "And some milk, if you please."

Grinning crookedly, the fellow waddled off into the shadows again. "I'll bring it out when it's ready. The tables with the candles are cleanest."

Once he'd gone, Arran led the way to the closest of the lit tables and pulled out the bench for her. "What was that about?" she asked.

"I wanted to see if he would try to keep us here."

"You thought this could be an ambush, you mean."

He sat down opposite her. "Anything *could* be an ambush. I'm just being cautious."

Mary couldn't help looking over her shoulder at the dimness behind her. "How long do you think we'll have before they do catch us? And don't say something comforting; tell me the truth."

Arran grimaced, his chivalrous, protective side clearly warring with answering her request for honesty. Gripping her fingers, he squeezed gently. "I dunnae, lass. I ken Crawford could have sent a letter two days ago, or four days ago from the Giant's Pipe. That note would have arrived in London better than two days ago. Figuring your

325

athair and Calder left within the hour, unless they were already on the road and a courier had to catch them up, at worst they could be aboot sixteen hours behind us. At best, thirty hours."

"That's good, then."

"By nightfall they could be twelve hours behind us, and by tomorrow night they could be as close as five. This coach cannae outrun men on well-bred horses."

A chill ran through her. "What if we left the coach behind?" He didn't have to finish the equation for her to know what it meant; by morning after next, the Campbells would be directly on their heels. And then . . . No. She didn't even want to think about it.

"Two hundred miles on horseback at a gallop, lass? Down bad roads?"

So Arran didn't think she could manage such a feat. That much was clear. But could she? She'd ridden for several hours at a time back at Fendarrow Park, but not for long at a gallop, and not for two or three days with very little rest. "Do we have an alternative?"

"Mary, this is someaught that once we decide, we cannae go back. I say we stay with the coach as long as we dare, then decide if we can make for the Highlands on horseback from there."

"I don't want us to be caught, Arran."

"Neither do I, lass."

"No. I mean I don't want to go back and marry Charles or be locked away somewhere for being defiant. I want to get to the Highlands, and I want to be there with you."

His expression eased a little. "I want those same things, bonny Mary. But if we flee at a run now, I dunnae think we'll last till Fort William. This way we still have time and room to maneuver."

Of course he meant that *she* wouldn't last, but at least he hadn't worded it that way. Once again, though, she lacked the practical experience to argue with his decision. There didn't seem to be anything meaningful she could contribute. And now she was slowing them down.

"When it's time to ride," she said, holding his gaze, "we will ride. I will not falter, and I will not slow us down."

He lifted her hand to kiss her knuckles. "I dunnae doubt it fer a moment. Ye are a Highlands lass, after all."

CHAPTER FOURTEEN

Arran barely noted the runny eggs that the unsavory proprietor of the nameless inn set before them. For all the attention he paid, he might as well have been eating straw.

She'd said she wanted to be in the Highlands. With him. And this time, he believed her. He heard it in her voice; Mary Campbell wasn't still looking for a way to reclaim her previous life, or to escape what would have been a disastrous marriage to Calder. Of course, there was still the chance that she was now in such a hurry to get away because that would keep her from actually having to choose between her family and him. If they were caught, she would have to make a stand.

With a quick, hard breath he choked down a last mouthful of breakfast. She'd never told him anything but her honest, true thoughts, so if he had any doubts all he need do was ask. And he would never do so —

because whatever her reasons, and however much she counted on circumstance and a favorable wind, she'd chosen him.

Therefore, all he need do was see to it that they reached the Highlands ahead of the Campbells. Once in Scotland they could marry without all the fuss English law required. And once in the Highlands, amid the valleys and mountains and rivers, anyone looking for them would have quite the task before them.

The part he didn't want to think about was that he wanted to give Mary a home, and that would be nearly impossible while they were being pursued. And while hiding would be easier in the chaos of renewed hostilities, his family — and hers — would be at the forefront of any conflict, and the idea that Ranulf or Bear might be injured or . . . killed because of him clawed at his heart.

If Mary's father had been more reasonable, and if Ranulf had been willing to listen for a damned minute, they might have found a peaceful path. For God's sake, it was a union of MacLawry and Campbell. It might have united the clans, instead of setting them after each other again. They'd all been stupid and foolish, but he had no intention of giving up Mary because of that.

"Let's get yer riding habit," he said, taking a last swallow of tepid milk and rising.

"Arran, if we're not going to beat my family to the border, what are we going to do?"

"At the moment I plan on hoping they're on the wrong road," he drawled. "If they do catch us, I suppose I'll be ready for however unfriendly they choose to be."

"You said you wouldn't hurt my father."

"I dunnae mean to. But I dunnae mean to let him drag ye back to Calder, either. And yer *athair* willnae be alone. In fact, he may not even be along. Calder's just as likely to have ridden ahead. Him, I dunnae mind shooting."

She stopped halfway around the long table. "You can't do that."

"I believe I can."

"He's the Campbell's grandson, Arran. If you kill any of them, they'll never stop hunting for us."

He looked at her for a moment. "I'm Glengask's *bràthair,* ye know. I'm his heir at the moment, unless he's already disowned me. Why isnae Calder worried aboot killing me?" he asked, then winked at her. Whatever needed to happen would happen. Deciding now which lines could or couldn't be crossed would only make him hesitate later. And that could be deadly.

Mary favored him with an exasperated smile. "I'm certain in Charles's mind you kidnapped me against my will."

"Which makes putting a ball through my head perfectly acceptable," he finished. "And here I am, unwilling to see my bonny lass weep." He put his hands on the table, leaning in close to her. "Have ye ever been on a fox hunt?"

She wrinkled her nose, which made him want to kiss it. "Yes, once. I didn't like it."

"I imagine the fox gave ye quite a run."

"It dragged us all over the countryside." She covered his left hand with her right. "But eventually the fox died, Arran. I don't like this analogy."

The inn door scraped open, letting a misshapen rectangle of morning sunlight flood the room. "The horses are harnessed, Mr. Fox," Peter said.

Well, that was poor timing. "They know we're running and close to where we are, Peter," Arran returned. "May as well give up on Mr. Fox."

"But I've just got to where I remember it." The footman took a deep breath. "The coach is ready, m'laird."

"Get yerself and Howard someaught to eat, first. Ten minutes, Peter."

"Aye, m'laird. Thank ye."

331

He returned his attention to Mary. "My point was that hunting a fox isnae a straight-forward matter. He's a sly fellow, a fox is. And my other point is that once we reach Fort William there's nae a man who can catch me. Nae in the Highlands." He grinned at her. "Up there this fox has a thousand dens."

She stood, kissing him on the cheek. "I will hold you to that. But I think we should hurry, anyway."

Back outside, Arran clambered up to the top of the coach and unstrapped the lid of Mary's trunk. Pulling out the riding habit and boots he'd purchased for her, he handed them down to her, then jumped back to the ground.

"I'd rather change inside the coach than somewhere in there," she said, indicating the inn.

"I dunnae blame ye." He pulled open the carriage door and helped her inside. "And I want ye to know I'd join ye in there if I did-nae have to keep watch."

With a smile she leaned out the door. "If you did join me I'd never manage to get dressed."

He tilted his face up and kissed her. "I ken ye wouldnae," he murmured, lust tug-ging at him again. Arran caught the front of her gown, holding her there. "Ye know ye're mine, lass."

Green eyes sparkled. "And you're mine."

Slowly he released her again. "Aye. That I am."

When she shut the door he leaned back against one of the coach wheels. Generally he enjoyed problem-solving. If Ranulf wanted to build a new school, he would be the one to find the location that would be the most easily accessible to the most children of the MacLawrys' cotters; he would hire the builders, and he would find a teacher who could tame — but not break — wild Highlands children.

But that had been before. Now the problem involved keeping away from Ranulf, along with all the MacLawrys and all the Campbells. And, if possible, keeping them from killing each other. The best solution he could think of would be a great-grandchild for the Campbell, with him and Mary wed and established somewhere neutral. Yes, he could likely bribe some Sasannach priest to marry them without the banns being read or a license procured, but a wedding of this import needed to be performed in Scotland, and by a Scot. Aside from that, in Scotland they wouldn't need a Canterbury marriage license at all.

All of that, though, hinged on the two of them actually making it to Scotland. And whatever he said about foxes and fox hunts, the odds of that did not look good. On his own he had little doubt that he could outride and outmaneuver the Campbells, and likely remove a few of them from the hunt permanently. But he wasn't on his own. And if Lord Fendarrow appeared and ordered Mary to return with him — and especially if he promised she wouldn't have to marry Charles Calder — Arran wasn't entirely certain she would refuse.

At the same time, for his pride or some other damned reason, he wanted to be what she *did* choose — and not simply because he'd really left her no alternative, either. He wanted to know that she wouldn't regret this, because *he* certainly wouldn't. Yes, he would miss his brothers and his sister, but he did not regret taking Mary for himself, whatever came of it.

"You look very serious," Mary said, from the coach's window.

"Do I?" he asked, stirring. "I was just noticing the morning. It's nae as stunning as the Highlands, but I'll admit it's pretty."

"Come in here and button me, will you?"

Arran straightened and pulled open the door. "Ye dunnae have to ask me twice, lass." If this adventure would end with him under the ground, he meant to enjoy every moment with Mary he had left.

When he stepped to the ground again, though, the smile on his face froze. The empty stable yard had found some occupants. Four of them. And none of the four looked particularly friendly. They also had their attention on him and the coach behind him. *Damnation.* Mary would have stepped down behind him, but he shifted sideways to block her exit. "When I move forward, shut the door," he murmured.

He heard her quick draw of breath, her hand lowering to his shoulder. "I don't recognize them," she whispered back. "I don't think they're Campbells."

And he'd thought she might caution him not to jump to conclusions, or to ignore the men and escort her back to the inn. Instead she'd caught onto the meat of the matter and simply given him the most useful piece of information. With a slight nod he stepped forward, and the carriage door closed behind him with a faint click. *Good lass.*

"Ye've found me on a fine morning, lads," Arran drawled, assessing muddy boots and worn jackets. Locals, likely drovers or farmhands. "What might I do fer ye?"

The one standing farthest from him spat

onto the muddy ground. "Heard your friends inside the inn. One of 'em called you a lord. Seems you're a long way from home, lord."

"Aye," the biggest of them grunted, grinning around a missing front tooth. "Ireland's a long way from here, lordship."

Arran sighed. "Aye. I agree: Ireland's a long way from here." Stupid thugs, they were — which didn't mean they couldn't hit hard, but it did comfort him somewhat. They weren't there on behalf of the Campbells.

Two of them looked at each other, as if they weren't certain what to do with a fellow who was both agreeable and unafraid of them. Arran gave an exaggerated shrug. With all the bile aimed at him by both friend and foe over the past week or so, a dustup seemed just the thing to help him work out a bit of pent-up frustration.

"Why don't you hand over your purse, lordship, and we'll let you go on your way?" the spitting man offered.

"Why dunnae ye come over here and take it from me?" Arran returned, and grinned.

Toothless charged forward like a bull. Sidestepping, Arran stuck out one foot, sending him headfirst into the door of the coach. With a dull thud Toothless went down. Spittle was right on his heels, followed closely by the other two.

Arran shifted, taking a fist to the jaw as Spittle slammed into his chest. Now it felt like a to-do. He sent an elbow into the ear of the lad on the left, then hefted Spittle off the ground to throw him feetfirst into the fellow on the right. That gave Toothless time to climb to his knees — until the coach door slammed open on his head and then neatly closed again. The big man dropped once more.

Sending a fist into the face of the next man to close on him, he took a blow to the left shoulder. If these lads didn't discourage soon, he was going to have to stop playing. He blinked blood out of one eye and dove in again. A heartbeat later he heard a gravel-voiced curse in Scots Gaelic, and the pile of them went over sideways. Peter Gilling, the old scrapper, flashed by him, Toothless heaved over his shoulder.

A pistol shot cracked into the air. For a frozen heartbeat Arran thought the Campbells had ridden them down, after all.

"That's enough, gentlemen!" Mary declared, tossing the spent pistol behind her into the coach and hefting a second one. "You've had your fun, and now you're getting my husband muddy."

Now *that* was a proper Highlands lass. *His* Highlands lass. "Ye heard the lady," he said aloud, straightening to dust off his trousers. "Thank ye fer the exercise."

The four lads stumbled back to the lopsided door of the inn, Spittle helped along with a swift kick to his arse delivered by Peter. Howard their one-eyed driver stood close by, a piece of lumber gripped in his hands. So Arran and Mary weren't alone in this, after all.

"Well, that was refreshing," he said, walking up to slide the pistol from Mary's fingers with one hand, and tug on the neckline of her gown to pull her in for a kiss with the other.

"You're mad, you know," she commented a bit breathlessly. "Everyone says you're the clever MacLawry, and there you were, grinning the entire time you were punching people."

"Aye. Fisticuffs is just a Highlands how-do-ye-do." The same smile still tugging at his mouth, he took a moment to gaze at her. "Ye're a *tapaidh* lass, Mary."

"All I did was strategically open a door. That's hardly brave, Arran."

"Tell that to the lad with the knot on his skull."

"Oh, very well." She smiled back at him.

"I know you likely wrestle bears and lions for amusement, but four-to-one odds didn't seem fair."

It seemed just about right to him, but she hadn't grown up with a pair of large brothers. "Let's get away from here before they find friends, and ye can spend the day telling me how manly I am and how fine the day looks with me riding aboot in it."

Mary chuckled, the sound warm as sunlight on his skin. "And you can thank me for keeping those men from breaking that handsome nose of yours."

Peter snorted as he brought their two horses over. "Everyone can admire everyone until the Campbells catch us up, or we can get back going north again."

Arran nodded. "Aye. North it is."

"This *is* pretty," Mary said, as she and Juno trotted over an old stone bridge, Arran and Duffy beside her. "I have a few second and third cousins about here, as I recall."

Arran sent her a sharp look, the jauntiness of his appearance somehow increased by the bruise on the left side of his jaw. "Somewhere close enough that anyone chasing us could find a hot meal, fresh mounts, and reinforcements?"

"Possibly."

Why hadn't she thought of that before? The pair of horses they'd harnessed at the last inn seemed better suited to the plow, which meant her clan was catching up to them even more quickly. She needed to out-think her family, as well as outrun them, and to stop being distracted by the lovely day and the handsome man beside her. Yes, he'd fought four men earlier, and given far worse than he'd received, but he'd done it to protect her. It was past time she did more than take in the scenery.

"There's also my aunt Morag somewhere north of town," she continued. "She married an English banker, and none of us have seen her in years. My grandfather said that Uncle Sean was more Irish than English, and that made him twice as unacceptable."

"Imagine what he'll say aboot us, Mary. Ye know he may refuse to see ye, whether they put me under the ground first or nae."

"Stop saying that!" she ordered, sudden horror tightening her voice.

He urged Duffy closer and reached over to touch her cheek. "I dunnae mean to die, bonny Mary. But it's a possible outcome. And if it happens, ye need to be ready. Ye need to be wise and choose the path that most favors ye."

Mary pushed his hand away with her own.

"Choose what?" she snapped. "Do you think you're a derby horse? If you fall I simply change my wager?" She clenched her fist tightly around the reins. "I already chose. If something happens to you — I . . . I won't allow anything to happen to you."

Of course that wasn't realistic; considering how little she'd done to aid her own rescue it was even laughable. But she was *not* going to prepare herself for his death, because even the idea of it was unacceptable. Unfathomable. It didn't matter that she'd known him only a short time. He'd become vital to her. Vital to her heart. Did he not believe that?

Arran's shoulders lowered. "I know ye chose. I apologize fer pushing at ye. Just . . . dunnae surrender to less than ye want. Ever."

That was it, then. He thought she would give in to her father and even to Charles if pressed to do so. If he wasn't there to protect her. Well. It wasn't anything she could prove to him, one way or the other, unless disaster struck.

"I hope you do the same," she said aloud, "if the MacLawrys catch us and put *me* under the ground." There. Let him see how much he liked hearing such nonsense.

"If one of mine harmed ye," he said in a

low, flat voice, "he'd be a dead man."

She didn't have to question if he was serious; she heard it in his voice. "Then we're agreed," she said briskly, a little shaken. "So let's stop talking about it."

He seemed inclined to listen, because for the next mile or so they rode in silence. Or in relative silence, rather. The squeaking coach behind them drowned out the songs of any birds or insects that might have been audible along the pretty, tree-lined lane. Howard kept saying she was just complaining about being so far from London, but Mary had begun to have her doubts that the vehicle would still be in one piece when they reached the Highlands. *If* they reached the Highlands.

"What's yer favorite flower?" Arran asked abruptly.

She sent him a sideways glance, and then a second one simply because he looked magnificent with the noonday light on his face and the wind ruffling his thick black hair. The MacLawrys thought themselves princes of the Highlands, Charles had said on several occasions. She was inclined to agree that they were. Or this one was, anyway. "Why?"

"Because we're to be married, if ye ever ask me to be yer dear husband," he returned. "I'd like to know what kind of flower ye favor."

Mary pursed her lips. No one could ever accuse Arran MacLawry of being predictable. "White roses," she said. "And purple thistle. I am a Highlands lass, you know."

With a grin, he closed in for a swift kiss. "I do know that."

"M'laird," Peter called from behind them, with his usual abominable timing.

Arran reined Duffy in as the coach rocked to a halt. "What is it?"

"Howard cannae keep his one eye open, and I'm near dead on my feet. Or arse, rather, begging yer pardon, m'lady."

"We cannae stop," Arran said, frowning. "I'll drive, and the two of ye can sleep in the coach."

"Nobody drives her but me," Howard grumbled, narrowing his one eye.

"I'll be gentle. I need ye ready to drive us after dark, Howard. I dunnae have the skill fer that."

Mary was fairly certain he was lying, but she nodded. "We'll need you at your very best tonight, Howard," she added.

"So you think you can charm me into co-operating, eh?" the driver muttered. "I suppose you can." He shoved down on the brake handle. "You certain you can drive a team, Mr. my lord Fox?"

"Aye. And I told ye to call me Arran."

The driver and Peter climbed to the ground. "I'm not grand enough to be calling lords and ladies by their Christian names. Now let's tie up those mounts of yours before I curl up here on the grass."

Arran swung down and walked over to hold his arms up to Mary. She took a moment to look down at him. If everything went as they hoped, in a very few days this man would be her husband. Heat simmered beneath her skin. He would look at her in just that same fond, amused way every day. She would fall asleep in his arms and wake in them in the morning.

"Ye keep smiling at me like that, Mary, and I'm like to burst into song," he murmured. "Come here."

She leaned into his arms, and he lowered her to the ground, bending his head to kiss her before he released his grip on her waist. "I'll ride up top with you," she decided.

"Aye. I doubt ye'd get any rest with those two inside, snoring." He flashed her a grin. "Besides, having ye with me will improve the view."

Peter tied their mounts behind the coach, and then he and Howard climbed into the coach, shut the door, and pulled the curtains

344

closed. With no perceivable effort Arran lifted Mary to the top right front wheel, and from there she pulled herself up to the high, narrow seat. He moved around the front, checking the horses' traces, then hiked himself up easily onto the seat beside her.

"*Can* you drive a coach?" she whispered.

"Aye. Or a wagon, more like." Arran gathered up the ribbons, released the brake lever, and clucked to the team. With a creak the coach lurched into motion. "When I imagined sweeping in to rescue ye," he drawled, "this was nae what I had in mind."

"You imagined rescuing me?"

"I'm here, nae?"

"But you imagined it first. How? What did you imagine?"

His jaw clenched, and for a moment she thought he wouldn't answer. The MacLawrys were a strong, wild, manly set, after all. If they had romantic hearts, they likely didn't make that known.

"It was more of a dream, I suppose," he said finally, clear reluctance in his deep brogue. "I rode up, stole ye from Calder while the priest and yer family stood with mouths agape, lifted ye up into the saddle in front of me, and we rode north faster than a flash of lightning. I found an abandoned castle overlooking a loch, and ye were mine and I was yers, and we lived happily ever after."

"I like your dream."

"So do I. We had naught to do with broken-down inns or badly sprung coaches, and our clans let us be."

She leaned against his shoulder. "Perhaps other than the part with the inns and the coaches, it can still come true."

Briefly he rested his cheek against her hair. "That's why we're here, isnae?"

"Yes, it is." And that was why they had to find somewhere safe and hidden from both the MacLawrys and the Campbells. Neither clan could see beyond the lines they'd drawn on the ground, and so neither of them could be allowed to find her or Arran.

He must have been at least as exhausted as the two men presently snoring below them, but Arran showed no sign of it as he drove them along at the fastest pace the broken-down coach and horses could manage. Even though her father at best was still hours behind them, Mary couldn't help glancing over her shoulder every mile or two all through the lengthening shadows of the afternoon.

Once again that was all she could do. One of her cousins — George Gerdens-Daily, as she recalled — had once taught her to drive a curricle, but she'd only been ten or eleven at the time and had run it into a hedge. So as much as she wanted to take the reins and tell Arran to try to get some rest, she knew quite well that that would likely lead to disaster. The best she could do, then, was to help keep watch and talk to him.

"So your oldest brother is Ran, Munro is Bear, and Rowena is Winnie," she said. "Why don't you have a family nickname?"

"Fer a time Bear tried calling me Book, I suppose because I like to read. But I gave Winnie a button every time she refused to call me that, and eventually he gave it up."

"You didn't want to be called Book?"

Arran shrugged. "It's nae a proper nickname if yer own *bràthair* takes a fortnight to decide what it should be. It either comes to ye naturally, or ye shouldnae be using it."

"How many buttons did it cost you?"

"I cut 'em off Bear's coats and trousers, so it didnae cost me anything."

Mary laughed. "That makes me wish I had brothers and sisters."

"I'd share mine with ye, if I could." He looked down at his hands for a moment, then straightened again.

She wasn't the only one giving up a life she'd otherwise been happy with. "I'm sorry," she whispered.

Frowning, he glanced sideways at her. "Sorry? Fer what? Fer being witty and lovely and honest? Fer making me look at the world with wiser eyes? Dunnae apologize fer that, Mary. It's what I love aboot ye."

Her heart stopped beating, then thundered to life again. *Love.* He'd said it so easily, as if it were something she should already have known. In a sense she supposed she did; a man did not upend his own life, abandon his family and his clan, and put himself directly in harm's way for a casual affair. But now he'd said it aloud, and that meant something, too. Had she actually done anything to deserve it, though?

She took a slow breath. "Arran, I —"

With a great crack the coach lurched out from under her. Shrieking, Mary grabbed for the seat to steady herself as they plunged sideways. Abruptly strong arms swept around her, pulling her against a hard chest. They careened against a wheel as the coach flipped onto its side and slammed into the road. She followed, curling against Arran as he thudded hard onto his back on the packed earth amid what seemed like an entire herd of screaming horses.

Mary rolled to her feet as luggage began falling around them. "Arran!" she shrieked, turning as she realized he hadn't followed her upright.

He lay faceup in the road, a thin line of blood trickling from his forehead and past one ear. The plunging, squealing horses had torn one harness loose from the shaft and were bucking in their traces less than a foot from him, but he didn't stir.

"Peter! Howard! Are you injured? I need help!" Dodging the horses, she grabbed for Arran's right boot, slid free the long blade he kept there, and edged in to saw at the remaining fastening.

The noise nearly deafened her, but all she could think was that Arran was injured and if she couldn't free the horses, he might be killed. The hard leather parted, and the horses, still harnessed together, stumbled forward and disappeared around a curve in the road.

She dropped the knife and flung herself onto her knees beside Arran. Anything might have struck him — the coach, a horse, the falling luggage. Whatever had injured him, he still hadn't moved. "Arran," she said shakily, taking one of his hands and squeezing it tightly. What was she supposed to do? What if he . . . *No, no, no.*

At the upturned side of the coach, the door flung open. More debris smacked into the ground around them. "Be careful! Arran's hurt!"

With a curse Peter clambered out of the coach, then held down an arm to haul up the one-eyed driver. The footman jumped to the ground and knelt down beside her. "M'laird Arran?" he quavered, leaning over Arran's still face and then slapping him lightly. "Lad? Can ye hear me?"

One light blue eye rolled open. "God's sake, Peter Gilling," Arran mumbled, "I didnae want to see yer ugly face looming over me."

"Oh, thank God," Mary stammered, and threw her arms around his chest.

Arran hugged her tightly before he released her again. "Are ye hurt, lass?"

"Just a few bumps and bruises, thanks to you." She kissed him, only relenting when he winced. That had been far too nearly a disaster. The idea that she might have lost him felt like a black, screaming mass in her mind that she couldn't penetrate. The thoughts and images of what might have happened simply wouldn't form, as if she would die if she thought about not having him in her life.

"Oh, my poor lady," Howard wailed, laying his hands on the coach's broken undercarriage. "What did they do to you?"

"Help me up," Arran muttered, and Peter

grabbed a hand and hauled him to his feet. "We didnae do anything," he said, then bent over with his hands on his knees. "Ye can see it there fer yerself. The front axle and the reach snapped."

"Aye," Peter agreed, dividing his attention between Arran and Howard. "Looks like the reach dug into the road. We're lucky we went over sideways and nae end over end."

"It was fine when I gave it over to you."

"Nonsense," Mary snapped, furious that anyone would be arguing with a man who'd just nearly died. "It's been creaking and groaning for the past thr—"

With a moan Arran went down on his knees and vomited up the remains of his breakfast. "Nae to alarm anyone, but I think I'm going to pass oot again."

Peter caught him by the shoulders as he went limp. "Let's get 'im off the road, lass. Howard! Get yer arse over here."

The two men carried him to the grass at one side of the road and carefully set him down again. Mary sat where she could cradle his head in her lap. "Peter, see to Duffy and Juno, will you?"

"Aye. I can do that."

"Howard, the team is still harnessed together. When I cut the traces they went up the road. See if you can find them. Take

Juno if you need to."

"I drive horses, my lady. I do not ride them."

"I'll look fer the team, Lady Mary," Peter said, leading the skittish mounts to the side of the road and tying Juno off to a low-hanging branch. "I'll take Duffy, though. I've ridden 'im before."

She nodded. "Very well. Howard, please move the luggage off the road, and find a blanket for Arran. I don't want him getting chilled."

The two men did as she asked. Trying to gather her thoughts back in, she brushed the hair from Arran's temple. The cut there was deep and still bleeding freely. Mary pulled a kerchief from her pocket, folded it, and carefully pressed it against the wound.

She knew Arran would say that they should hire another vehicle and resume the journey north as soon as possible. She also knew that he desperately needed a good night's sleep and a day or two of not being jarred about in a coach or on horseback. What they didn't have was the time for any of that.

At this moment her father and Charles Calder could be as close as six or seven hours behind them. With every moment they weren't moving, her clan drew closer.

And she did not want them any nearer than they already were.

Except for a few cottages scattered here and there, they hadn't passed any place where they could take shelter. The smelly fellow from this morning had said there was another inn just south of Manchester, but they'd turned farther west to avoid the town altogether. When she'd mentioned that she had relations close by, Arran hadn't wanted to risk her being recognized on the very slight chance that their pursuers didn't know precisely which road they were on.

She had relations nearby. Including an aunt who was as unpopular with the rest of the Campbells as she was likely to be if they survived this. An aunt she'd never met.

"Now this is a view I can tolerate," Arran said groggily, looking up at her with slightly crossed eyes.

"Hush," she said gently, and pressed down on his shoulder when he would have sat up again. "And stay still."

"We cannae stay here by the side of the road, Mary."

"Peter's tracking down the team."

He reached up and grabbed her arm. "Ye have to be safe, my lass. Take Peter and go find an inn where ye can hire another coach." With his free hand he dug into a pocket of his coat. "Have 'em send the bill here," he instructed, giving her a piece of paper as she tried to overlook the dismaying way his hand shook. "If ye cannae get a coach, purchase a seat on the mail stage. Keep traveling north. Peter will help ye get to yer *seanair.*"

She stroked his forehead. "I believe it was just yesterday that we decided we were staying together, no matter what."

"That was before a coach fell on my head. Mary, dunnae —"

"You'll just have to trust me, Arran," she said, more sharply than she meant to. "I seem to be in command of this little expedition now."

From his expression he wanted to say something about that, but instead he closed his eyes and nodded. "I do trust ye, lass. Just keep yerself safe."

She would keep all of them safe. How, she had no idea, but nothing would keep her from a future with Arran. Nothing.

"Howard, do you have a map?" she asked.

The driver straightened from dragging the last of the trunks over beside her. "That, I do," he said, producing one from his pocket. "I've never been outside London until this past week."

Mary unfolded it across Arran's chest.

354

"Where are we, precisely?"

"Dunnae be sticking pins in me," Arran rumbled, but kept his eyes closed.

"Precisely, I ain't certain. I was asleep when his lordship rolled us over, if you'll recall."

"It wasn't Arran's fault," she insisted. "Now show me where you think we are."

Grumbling under his breath, he squatted down beside her. "Here," he said after a moment, jabbing a finger into the map.

The road they traveled was so faint she could barely follow it even with her eyes. If Howard's estimation was correct, they were west and just north of Manchester. Trying to remember every half-heard mention of her aunt and the Sasannach banker she'd married, Mary traced her finger along a narrow country lane to where it dead-ended.

"We need to go here," she said.

Howard squinted his one eye. "In the coach that would take us an hour. On foot, two hours. Dragging Lord Arran, past sunset. If at all."

"I can walk," Arran said. "But unless that's an inn ye're aiming for, this isnae a wise idea. Ye need to keep heading north."

"Hush," she said again, putting her fingers gently across his sensuous mouth. "You're delirious. It's my turn to rescue you."

Hopefully she sounded confident. Inside she shook like a leaf on a windy day. But he'd saved her, and she was not about to let her family — her clan — hurt him or separate them. So she supposed she was about to discover just what it was she was capable of.

CHAPTER FIFTEEN

Either he was having a nightmare, or events had gone badly sideways, Arran decided.

He opened his eyes to see clouds and treetops, and for a moment thought he was still lying on his back by the road. But the trees were passing by, or he was passing by them, to an accompanying sound of wood scraping against dirt and stone. Moving his head slowly to be certain his aching skull didn't fall off and roll away, he looked sideways.

"Don't move," Mary said, leaning over from Juno's back to look down at him, clear worry on her face. "Are you going to be ill again?"

"I dunnae believe so," he returned, his voice dry and raspy. "Where the devil are we? What am I riding on?"

"One of the coach doors. Peter found the team, and they're much happier pulling you than they were the entire coach."

"I'm not much happier," Howard put in from somewhere behind — or rather in front of — him.

"I said you would be recompensed, Howard. Just keep them moving at an easy pace. No bumping."

Arran closed his eyes again, trying to gather a mush of thoughts back into something coherent. "We cannae travel to Scotland like this. And we're leaving a damned obvious trail, I'd wager."

"Nae," Peter said from beyond his feet. "I've got a bundle of branches Duffy's dragging. I dunnae think even that Daniel Boone lad from America could track us."

"Was that yer idea, lass?" Arran asked.

"I thought it might help obscure the marks the door is leaving."

He knew she had wits, but that was damned clever. When he shifted a little he felt a portmanteau beneath his knees, so evidently he was now a part of the luggage. This was not how he meant to make his way to the Highlands, and he was *not* going to be what got them caught. Grunting, he pushed with his hands, trying to sit up. Nothing happened.

"Ye didnae tie me doon, did ye, lass?"

"I didn't want you or the bags to fall off. Nor do I want you to get up and faint again.

Stay there."

"I didnae faint. I lost consciousness."

Her lips twitched. "State it however you wish, but stay where you are. We'll be at our destination within an hour."

"And what is our destination?" The dull thudding in his head kept growing louder, and he couldn't make out her answer. All he knew was that this was no way for a man to perform a rescue. Tied to a door and being dragged along the ground — it was humiliating. Devil take it, he'd beaten off four men just a few hours ago. He had the bruises beneath his newest bruises to prove it. When he managed to force his eyes open again, he would demand that he be allowed to walk.

Summoning every ounce of willpower he owned, he opened one eye. "I didnae quite hear ye, Mary. Where are we . . ." Arran trailed off as he realized he wasn't looking up at a late afternoon sky, any longer. A deep blue touched the western horizon, deepening to black the higher he looked. A minute ago he would have sworn he'd been in the middle of a conversation. How long had he been wading about in his own muddy mind?

For the first time, panic touched him. If he lost time with every blink of his eyes, he couldn't protect Mary. Just the opposite. His unplanned inability to act, to think clearly, was putting her in danger.

"Mary," he forced out, more loudly.

"I'm here," her sweet voice came immediately, and then she was walking beside his makeshift litter.

"Mary, ye need to go. I'll nae be the reason anyone hurts ye."

"This is my rescue, Arran." She glanced ahead, then motioned at someone in front of her. "Wait here for just a moment."

He grabbed for her hand, but she'd stepped away before he could make himself move. "Peter, go with her!"

"I am, lad," drifted back to him.

This time when he closed his eyes, he couldn't recall thinking anything except that he'd failed. Perhaps he'd been too rash to begin with. Perhaps he should have waited, lurked about in Wiltshire until the day of the wedding while he made his own plans, and then stolen her off to a ship and sailed to America. Perhaps the Highlands had been his life, his sanctuary, for so long that he'd been unable to let go of the idea that he and Mary would be safe there.

Of course if he'd failed to appear at Glengask after a fortnight Ranulf would have come looking for him. And the idea of Mary being trapped at Fendarrow with no allies, waiting to be locked into a marriage she dreaded — no. Waiting might have been wiser, but this was one time he was proud that he'd done what was right rather than what was wise.

If he'd feel that way in ten or twelve hours when the Campbells ran them down, he had no idea. But by God he wasn't going to let her go without a fight, even if he had to lie flat on the ground and keep one eye shut to shoot at the bastards. He'd claimed Mary Campbell in every way that he could. And his only true worry in all of this was that while he'd managed a sly comment that he loved her, he hadn't come out and said it directly. And that when the coach had gone over, he wasn't certain what she'd been about to say back to him.

He didn't want her gratitude or just her friendship. He wanted her heart.

With Peter standing at her shoulder and clearly uneasy at this little plan of hers, Mary struck the old brass knocker against the sturdy oak door. She wasn't certain which outcome would be worse — that this was the wrong door, or that it was the correct one.

"This is a very bad idea, m'lady," Peter

grumbled. "Laird Arran wouldnae like it."

"Laird Arran needs a bed and likely a doctor," she returned, pushing down her worry by counting the seconds of silence inside the house. Her breaking down and weeping on some stranger's front step wouldn't help him, and it wouldn't help *them*.

As she reached twenty the door rattled and cracked open. "The Mallisters aren't seeing anyone tonight," a mild-voiced older man said. The door began to close again.

Mallister. That was it. "I'm Mary Campbell," Mary said swiftly. "I'm looking for my aunt Mòrag."

The door froze. "Wait here." It clicked shut again.

All she wanted to do was put her shoulder to the door, push her way in, and demand assistance for Arran. For heaven's sake, he was lying out there in the cold with only a one-eyed coach driver to watch over him. But she knew quite well that patience would serve her better than brute force.

The cottage itself was almost comically innocuous, with a low, white fence covered with summer roses, a steepled roof, and a quartet of windows shuttered with pretty green and white curtains looking out from the ground and first floors. By Fendarrow standards it was tiny, smaller than the gatekeeper's cottage there. But for a pair of lovers looking to escape a powerful family or two, it seemed . . . perfect.

"What if they dunnae open the door again?" Peter asked gloomily.

"Then I'll think of something else." What, she had no idea, but he couldn't be allowed to know that.

The door swung open again, wider this time. A man and a woman of about her parents' age stood there side by side, gazing at her. The woman had the same light green eyes that Mary and her father shared, the same high cheekbones and narrow chin she saw in herself and her grandfather.

"Aunt Mòrag?"

"I . . . I go by Sarah now," the woman said, the merest trace of a brogue in her voice. That was how her father would sound, if he hadn't studiously flattened his vowels and reined in his *r*'s for so long that they'd become lost. "This is my husband, Sean."

Mary nodded at him, offering what she hoped was a friendly smile. "I . . . have a small problem, Aunt Sarah, and I need your assistance."

"We do not step into Campbell family business," her uncle stated, no Irish at all in his tone.

"I have a man outside your gate," Mary pressed, speaking quickly. Simply because the union she and Arran intended was frowned upon by the clan — clans — didn't make anyone else who happened to be out of favor her ally. That was up to her. "He was injured when our coach rolled over. I just need a bed for him for a night or two, until he recovers."

Aunt Sarah shook her head. "I stay away from the clan. Robert Daily has a house in Manchester, less than an hour from here. I'll give you the address. He can help you." She put her hand on the door. "You're very pretty, Mary. You remind me of me, in my younger days. I'm . . . glad I finally got to make your acquaintance."

Mary took a breath. "This injured man is Arran MacLawry. We . . . We are eloping. My father is likely less than ten hours behind us. I . . . I don't know where else I can go."

Her aunt's already pale cheeks blanched white. "A MacLawry?" she gasped. "This is precisely where your father will come if you're defying him! Don't you realize that?"

A tear ran down Mary's cheek, and she swiftly brushed it away. Arran had saved her from misery and offered her pleasure and happiness. She would not fail him now, when he finally needed her. "I do realize that. All I ask is one room, even a closet, where he can rest, and for you to say that you never saw us."

The banker looked over at Peter, who stood just to one side, his expression as serious as Mary had ever seen it. "And what of you, sir? Are you a Campbell? What's your part in all this?"

"I'm nae a Campbell. I wear the colors of clan MacLawry." He inclined his head. "And this lass and her lad, my laird, could use yer help."

Mary put a hand on Peter's arm, surprise and gratitude running through her. "I don't know what else to say that might convince you to help us. I cannot go anywhere else."

Aunt Sarah closed her eyes for a moment. "Come in, then. Sean, I —"

"I'll help bring in the young man," her husband interrupted. "And see what I can do to hide their transportation."

As Mary stepped into the house, trying to keep herself from collapsing in relief, the two men headed into the darkness. "All we have is a door, four horses, and two trunks," she said over her shoulder.

"A door?" Sarah Mallister led the way up the narrow staircase, Mary close on her heels and not wanting to give anyone time to change their minds.

"We salvaged it from the coach. When it rolled over, Arran struck his head quite hard. We were on the driver's perch, and he grabbed me. He kept me from being injured, and instead he . . ." Another tear trailed down her face, and she wiped at it impatiently.

How did Arran do it? He was strong and decisive and confident and good-humored, when he couldn't possibly have known what might happen to them next. And here she was, involving people from whom she should be staying well away — both for her sake and theirs — and all she could think of was how worried she was about Arran. Her Arran, out there in the dark where she couldn't watch over him.

Everyone always watched over *her,* protected *her.* Kept her from becoming acquainted with people she might otherwise have found . . . remarkable, simply because of the color of their plaids or the fact that they'd decided not to wear one. Well, now it was her turn to protect all of them, to see that no harm came to the people who'd chosen not to turn their backs.

"What's through there?" she asked, putting aside her doubts for a more opportune moment. She indicated a promising-looking door tucked into a corner of the hallway.

"Linens and winter bedding. If your father comes in here, he'll open every door, Mary." Her aunt frowned. "Fortunately, for a time I thought Sean or I might have to hide ourselves — until I finally realized that Walter considered my exile to be a worse punishment than being murdered."

A few weeks ago Mary would never have believed her father had such a vindictive side. But that was before she'd met Arran, and before she'd been shoved at Roderick MacAllister and then at Charles Calder. They continued on to a door halfway along the hallway. Sarah pushed it open, and they walked through what was clearly an unused spare bedchamber. As far as Mary knew, her aunt and uncle had no children. Had this room been meant for young ones? Or was it for guests who never came visiting?

She shook herself. She and Arran might be in similar circumstances, but they were different people. And there might yet be young Campbell-MacLawrys in their future, even now. They walked to the back of the room and pulled open yet another door, this one leading to a small storage closet. There Sarah stopped and knelt down, pushing aside a stack of hat boxes and a valise to reveal a bare, scratched section of floorboard. Putting her fingers beneath it, she lifted. A section of wall pushed upward, revealing a small, narrow room beyond.

"I'm going to hug you now, Aunt Sarah," Mary said, and knelt beside the older woman to throw her arms around Mrs. Mallister's shoulders.

"Goodness! It's unfinished, because we didn't feel the need to plaster or paint the walls. And there's no window, but once we get a lantern and some bedding in there, then you can hug me."

Together they pulled a careful selection of the winter bedding from the back of the linen closet, rearranging the storage so it didn't look like anything was missing. The hidden room was perhaps twelve feet long, but it was barely wide enough for one well-built Highlander to lie down in it. Even so, four people could squeeze inside in an emergency. And an emergency was precisely what she predicted.

At the sound of bootsteps on the stairs, Mary hurried back to the front of the house. Arran was on his feet, eyes shut and leaning heavily on Peter and Howard. She wanted to fling herself into his arms, the need so strong it made her hands shake. He was the reason she could be brave. And without him, none of this would matter.

Since pouncing on him now would send them all to the floor, she settled for carefully touching his right cheek. Seeing him so pale and unsteady hurt her heart. "Arran, can you hear me?"

"Aye," he answered, leaning into her palm. "Keeping my eyes closed seems to make it less likely I'll cast up my accounts."

"Then keep 'em closed, m'laird," Peter put in. "I've nae another coat to wear."

"Do you know where we are?" she asked, moving in to take Howard's place and draping Arran's arm over her shoulders.

"I can guess." He opened one eye to look sideways at her. "I dunnae like it, but I meant it when I said I trusted ye, my sweet lass."

"Good, because you're going to spend the next day or two sleeping behind a storage closet." She adjusted his solid weight, the way he leaned on her enough to tell her that he certainly wasn't ready to resume their flight north. "And this is my aunt Sarah."

He lifted his head a little more, the motion making him stumble. "*Tha mi toilichte do choinneachadh, Mòrag.* Thank ye fer taking us in."

Tears filled her aunt's light green eyes. "I haven't heard Scottish in a very long time," she said a little unsteadily. "I'm pleased to meet you, as well. And surprised." She cleared her throat. "My niece is very persuasive."

"Aye, that she is. Twisted me all up aroond her little finger, and I'm glad to be there."

"I've never met a MacLawry before. Your fellow called you my lord."

"He's Lord Glengask's younger brother," Mary put in.

"Ah. You're *that* Arran MacLawry."

"Aye."

Between the four of them they got Arran into the hidden room, which felt even smaller with the tall, broad-shouldered Highlander inside. More than anything Mary wanted to lie down beside him, to feel his soft breath on her cheek and know he would be well. But now she needed to see to the safety of not just the four travelers, but her aunt and uncle and their household, as well.

"Peter, please stay with him."

"Aye, m'lady. But he'd flay me alive if I didnae see that ye got some rest, yerself."

"I will. I'll be back in a few minutes."

Howard headed back downstairs to help Uncle Sean dispose of the coach door and to hide Duffy, Juno, and the team at a neighbor's property. Aunt Sarah's housemaid carried up a bowl of stew to Arran and Peter, while Mary and her aunt settled into the small breakfast room to eat.

"Thank you again, Aunt Sarah. Thank you so much. Will your servants . . ."

"There's only Susan and Levitt," she said. "They'll do as we ask. I suppose it's a good thing that we've thought about this day coming. Not you bringing a MacLawry into the house, but Walter Campbell appearing on our doorstep."

Uncle Sean walked into the room and sat in the chair beside his wife. "The horses are at the Finnegans'," he said. "They're not the nearest neighbors, but they'd fling themselves off a cliff before they'd tell the Campbells anything. And the coach door's at the bottom of the pond beneath some stones. That one-eyed fellow with you wept when we sank it."

Mary gave a brief smile. "It was his coach that rolled over. We hired it — or Arran did, rather — in London. Now we seem to have adopted him."

"So you fled London for Gretna Green, with your father on your heels?" Sarah asked, sipping at her tea.

"Not precisely." If anyone would understand her situation it was Sarah Campbell-Mallister, and the idea of having a female ally — especially after the disaster that was

371

Crawford — was very appealing. Taking a swallow of her own tea, she told them how she and Arran had met at the masquerade ball, their secret rendezvous, her grandfather's decision that she wed Lord Delaveer, the kiss, and her father's proclamation that she was to marry Charles Calder. When she described the way Arran had rescued her, her aunt actually put a hand to her chest.

The only thing she left out was the intimacy of her relationship with Arran, but she imagined that wouldn't have been too difficult to figure out. At any rate, they didn't ask her about it.

"Do you still intend to go to Alkirk and speak to the Campbell?" Sarah asked, and it took a moment before Mary remembered that her aunt was speaking about her own father.

"I think he's the only one who can stop the clan from hunting us down. My father certainly isn't willing to listen to me."

"Oh, my dear, I hope with all my heart that you're correct. I personally did not find him to be at all reasonable when I told him I wanted to be with Sean." Sarah sent her husband a fond look. "He gave me the choice of marrying someone of his choosing or leaving and never setting foot on Campbell property again."

And he'd evidently chosen Roderick for her. "That option would be perfectly acceptable to me," Mary said feelingly. A few weeks ago she might have felt differently, but choosing between clan Campbell and Arran was barely worth the moment it took to have the thought.

"I only wanted to marry a half-Irish banker, Mary. And I was his third daughter. You're the only living child of his firstborn son, and you want to marry the MacLawry's heir when he planned to use you to bring in the MacAllisters. He may not give you the choice of exile."

Worry skittered through Mary. In her life, in her mind, her grandfather had always been fair and levelheaded, and he'd always indulged her. It was one thing for her father to panic and shove her at the first clansman who asked. If her grandfather forbade her to marry Arran, if he ordered the clan to hunt Arran down . . .

When she'd initially asked to go to Alkirk, it had been with the idea that the Campbell would save her from Charles, that he would decree her life should be set back to where it had been before she'd met Arran. But now everything had changed. Now she didn't want to be parted from Arran MacLawry. She didn't want her old life back. She wanted a new life with the man she loved. The man she adored. The Highlander who'd shown her that life could be exciting and unexpected and passionate.

"I hope I'm wrong," her aunt continued after a moment. "Perhaps my circumstance was unique. But I thought you should be aware. If you'd left without me saying something, I wouldn't have been able to sleep ever again."

Setting her tea aside, Mary grasped her newly found aunt's hand. "I appreciate you telling me. It's given me some things to consider. Very carefully. But now if you'll excuse me, I'm going to go sit with Arran."

Her aunt and uncle exchanged a look. "We can put you in the maid's quarters with Susan. If your father appears it'll be a simple matter to get you upstairs again."

Mary stood, shaking her head as she did so. "Thank you, but it's far too late to preserve my reputation. And the only reason to do so would be if I intended to make a match with someone else. And I do not intend to do that."

Aunt Sarah stood, as well. "I'll walk you upstairs, then." Wrapping a hand around her niece's arm, she headed for the stairs.

"I want you to know that I understand

374

the trouble you and Uncle Sean could be stepping into, and on behalf of complete strangers."

Her aunt smiled, brushing at one eye. "Not strangers. Family who've only just met. And I'd be lying if I said there wasn't part of me that looks forward to besting Walter Campbell. I thought my brother would support me in anything. He did not do so." She leaned closer. "And if I may say so, your Highlander is very easy on the eyes."

"Yes, he is," Mary agreed. "And he's very witty, and even kind. I'd always been told that MacLawrys were devils, brutes, and barbarians." She smiled. "I will admit that he's something of a rogue." And thank goodness for that. If he hadn't been, she would be walking down the aisle with Charles Calder in the next few days.

At the top of the stairs, they stopped. "Though we are newly acquainted, I find myself wanting the best for you, my dear," her aunt said. "And that is why I have to ask if you've decided to wed this man because he saved you from an unpleasant match. Because he's forbidden and you feel tantalized or obligated."

"I asked myself that at first," Mary admitted. "In fact, I insisted that he agree to escort me to Alkirk solely to extricate me from my father's plans. But he . . . I don't want to live my life without him."

"Forgive me, but while I've heard you extolling his virtues in several ways, I haven't heard you say that you love him. And given these circumstances I would think that important."

Mary smiled a little. "I haven't used that word because I haven't said it to him, yet. And Arran should hear it first."

"My dear, I cannot argue with that. Barring your father's arrival, I will see you in the morning."

Kissing her aunt on the cheek, Mary slipped into the guest bedchamber and closed the door behind her. Then she gasped as a figure in a chair by the cold fireplace stirred.

"Come here, lass," Arran's low brogue came.

Oh, thank goodness. She hurried forward. "What are you doing? You should be lying down where it's safe."

"I had to sit up to eat some stew. I even choked doon a glass of whisky. And I'll nae lie doon to sleep again unless it's with ye by my side."

"Well, that's very romantic," she murmured, putting her hands on the arms of the chair and leaning in to kiss him slow and soft.

"Aye. I'm a romantic fellow."

Mary carefully sat across his lap, slid her arms around his shoulders, and kissed him again. The edge of uncertainty and uneasiness that had dogged her for the past few hours faded away in the warmth of his embrace.

When she settled her cheek against his neck and shoulder, Arran risked shutting his eyes again. He had the balance of a drunken sailor in a storm, but he was not going to hide in some priest hole while she faced uncertain allies. Aside from that, even with his eyes crossing, his ears worked just fine. And so he'd heard every word that she and her aunt had spoken outside the door. He wanted to ask her about it, but it wasn't the sort of thing he could prompt her to say. She either would of her own accord, or she wouldn't.

"Where are Peter and Howard?" she asked quietly.

"Our wee bairns are asleep in the hideaway."

She snorted softly. "I thought our bairns would be less . . . hairy."

Chuckling hurt his head, but he did it anyway. "I have a strong suspicion we'll nae be rid of Howard now that we murdered his coach."

"I like him. He grumbles, but he hasn't failed us yet." She stirred. "Now stop talking and let's get some rest."

"My head pounds less when I'm upright. I thought I'd spend the night here. The chair has a fine, high back to keep my skull from falling off and rolling aboot the floor."

"Well, I'm not sleeping in there with the lads," she said, indicating the hidden room behind them.

"I reckon ye can sleep atop the bed," he returned. "We can straighten up the covers if trouble comes calling." He remained fairly certain that the only question was *when* trouble would arrive, but with the coach overturned and his head bashed in, Mary had done the only thing possible to gain them some time.

Moving with exaggerated care, as if she thought he might break, she stood again and walked over to the bed. "You want me to sleep here?" she mused, touching the quilted coverlet. "All by myself?"

"Lass, dunnae tease me tonight," he protested, hoping that closing one eye would stop the room from spinning, then opening them both again when it didn't.

She regarded him for a long moment, her

silhouette lined with silver in the moonlight. "I won't lie down to sleep unless it's with you by my side, Arran," she said finally, and lifted the folded blanket from the foot of the bed. Then she dragged the other chair set on the opposite side of the hearth over beside his, curled into it with a sensuous grace that even a dead man would have appreciated, and pulled the blanket over both of them.

Well, it wasn't a declaration of undying love, but as she reached over to take his hand and twine her fingers with his, he decided that for tonight it was enough.

He awoke with a start, not certain what he'd heard, but knowing that something was amiss. Through the squint of his eyes he could see the first light of dawn edging into the east-facing window. Beside him Mary breathed softly. Ignoring the keen ache of his skull he held his breath, listening.

Then he heard it again. A horse whinnying, the sound immediately echoed by a second animal. The Campbells had caught up to them.

"Mary," he whispered, pushing to his feet and grabbing onto both arms of her chair to keep his balance.

She awoke immediately. "Are they here?"

"Aye. I think so, anyway. Wake up Peter.

Stay back away from the windows."

She rose with an ease that made him slightly jealous and moved quickly and quietly into the storage closet. Arran gathered up the blanket and refolded it before he set it back across the foot of the bed. His head felt clearer, but his left eye remained blurry. If they had to flee either on horseback or in a coach, he would likely find himself unconscious again. Thank God Mary had thought to seek out her estranged aunt.

"Do we bring oot the weapons?" Peter asked, tucking in his rough-hewn work shirt as he emerged from the closet.

"Nae. First we'll try Mary's way." He sent her a quick smile as she glided back into the bedchamber, then returned his gaze to Peter. "Move the chair back across the hearth, will ye? Quietly."

"Aye." The footman lifted Mary's chair and carefully carried it back where it belonged, even placing the feet back into the divots left in the blue carpet laid out there.

"Is everything else inside?"

Her green eyes wide with obvious worry, Mary nodded. "Along with some bread and water. Hurry, Arran. If it's my father, he *will* search the house for us."

Downstairs a door opened and closed

quickly. As much as he preferred a straight-up fight to sneaking about, this way held much less risk for the woman he loved. And he wasn't precisely at his best this morning. With one last look about the room, he motioned them toward the storage closet. "Let's go, then."

Going down onto his hands and knees to crawl through the absurdly wee opening made his head pound all over again, but he clenched his jaw and did it anyway. If nothing else, having a coach whack him on the skull would discourage him from drinking too much in the future; this particular aching head was not something he cared to repeat, no matter how fine or plentiful the spirits.

Once they were all inside, Mary nudged him out of the way and leaned out to pull the stack of hat boxes in front of the opening, then quietly lowered the door, closing them in. Even with the lantern lit it seemed dim, but he wasn't willing to risk any light being seen through some crack in the wall.

Sitting back, he shook the still-snoring Howard until with a sputtering curse the coachman sat upright. Arran favored him with a pointed look, and he subsided. "Bloody Campbells," he muttered. "Begging your pardon, my lady."

Evidently Howard was part of their clan, now. "From here on, we're quiet as church mice," Arran murmured, then took Mary's arm to draw her up against his side. With a slow breath, sending up a quiet prayer that everything would go as they hoped, he leaned sideways and blew out the lantern.

Settling in as comfortably as he could against the unfinished wall, he put his left arm around Mary's shaking shoulders. "I'll nae let anything happen to ye, lass," he breathed against her hair.

"I'm more worried about you," she returned almost soundlessly.

"As long as no one falls asleep and begins snoring, we have nothing to fear, I reckon."

In the past his family had once — or more than once — been accused of being Jacobites, of supporting James and then Bonnie Prince Charlie's claim to the throne of England. Some of his ancestors *had* been Jacobites. Because of that, most of the houses in the Highlands boasted so-called priest holes for hiding Scots being sought after by Sasannach soldiers. And now they were in a half-Sasannach household hiding away from the clans, including his own.

With his free right hand he reached into his coat pocket for the pistol he'd placed there. No, he didn't want to harm her father or any other Campbell, because that would hurt her. Neither, though, was he surrendering Mary. Not to anyone — Campbell, MacLawry, or Saint Bridget and all the heavenly angels.

Chapter Sixteen

Sarah Mallister sat on the edge of her bed and waited to be surprised.

As much as she would have preferred to be dressed in her finest gown with her hair pulled up and blush on her cheeks, the sun hadn't yet shown the merest sliver over the eastern hills. Under normal circumstances she and Sean would have remained in bed for at least another hour.

"Sean, don't pace," she whispered.

Her husband stopped halfway between the bed and the door. "Have you considered that perhaps we should be hiding ourselves behind that wall?"

"They've known for nineteen years where to find us. And frankly, I'm more looking forward to this than I'm worried about it."

Stepping more quietly, he moved over to sit beside her. "If we can manage it, I'd like to punch Fendarrow in the nose, myself."

She smiled, nervous anticipation running

through her. "I don't think a little suspicious hostility would be out of place. He's never bothered to come calling before, after all." Sarah took her husband's hand. "Just remember that this isn't about us. It's about protecting our young guests."

Of course her niece had only come calling because their coach had overturned and Lord Arran had been injured. They had literally had nowhere else to go. But they *had* come instead of waiting about to be caught, and she'd made the acquaintance of a brave young lady she would otherwise never have met. And a MacLawry. For goodness' sake, she wasn't certain even she would have had the courage to fall not just for a member of clan MacLawry, but for *the* MacLawry's younger brother.

Susan's knock came at the door, more strident than usual. "Come in," Sarah called, and the door cracked open.

"Mrs. Mallister," the housekeeper said a trifle unsteadily, "you have a caller."

"At this hour?" she asked, sending the servant an encouraging smile. She wasn't certain whether they could be overheard or not, but it was a small and quiet cottage, and so she would assume a visitor could make out every word she spoke. "Is it Mrs. Lester? I asked her to send me word when

Sally went into labor."

"No, ma'am. It's . . . It's Lord Fendarrow."

"What?"

"That's the name he gave me. And there are at least a dozen men with him."

"Good heavens!"

"Fendarrow? What the devil does your brother want of us?" Sean demanded.

"I have no idea," Sarah returned, not having to feign the trepidation in her voice. "Do you think something's happened to my father? Why else would he come here, Sean? It's been nineteen years!"

"We'd best go find out. Tell him we'll be down in a moment, Susan. I'm not meeting him in my nightshirt."

The maid curtsied. "Should Levitt offer them tea?"

"Not until I find out what he wants," Sean said loudly, offering her a reassuring smile.

Susan shut the door again, and Sarah let out her breath. "I'd nearly forgotten that I don't actually want to see him," she muttered, standing and hurrying for her wardrobe.

Her husband strode over to take her arm, turning her to face him. "Just keep in mind why he's here," he whispered, and kissed her. "I, for one, have no intention of allowing him to do to someone else what he did to you."

With a smile she kissed him back. "What he did to me doesn't matter, because he couldn't separate us. Now stomp angrily into your boots, and let's get this over with."

They hadn't had a chance to warn their guests that trouble had arrived, but Sarah hadn't heard as much as a squeak coming from down the short hallway. All she could do was presume that they knew, and that they'd closed themselves into the hidden room. The rest would be up to her and Sean.

Her hands shook a little as she shed her night rail and donned a plain green and yellow muslin, then brushed out her hair and pinned it into a simple knot. Sean dressed in his dark, conservative banker's clothes, and then together they left the bedchamber and descended the stairs.

Levitt hovered in the front entry, looking annoyed that he'd only had time to don his trousers with his night shirt hastily tucked into the waist. If given the choice the butler would have remained dressed all night, poised to greet their visitors. That, though, would have raised far too many suspicions, at a moment when they couldn't afford any at all.

"Mrs. Mallister, Lord Fendarrow is in the

front room," he said. "Two other gentlemen are in there with him. Another nine are in front of the house, watering their horses."

"Horses?" Sarah repeated, frowning. "He didn't come in a coach?"

"Not that I could see, ma'am."

She squared her shoulders. "Well. Let's go see what's brought Walter Campbell all the way to Manchester on horseback, then."

When she stepped into the sitting room her gaze went to the sharp-faced man with the slicked black hair who stood by the far window. The resemblance to a young Walter was striking. For a moment she felt like the eighteen-year-old girl who'd begged her older brother not to allow her to be cast out of the family. Sarah shook herself. This man might resemble the Walter she'd last known, but he wasn't her brother. A nephew, more likely. Perhaps the nasty Calder that her niece had described. She turned her head.

"You look older," a dry, precise voice said. Seated in Sean's favorite chair, a lean, gray-haired man crossed his ankles and gazed at her over steepled fingers.

So much for niceties. "What's happened?" she asked, facing him directly. "Is it Father?"

A muscle in his cheek jumped. "No. The last I heard, His Grace was well."

She nodded, swallowing. That couldn't

have been sympathy she fleetingly saw on his face. More likely he was worried that perhaps he'd guessed wrong about his daughter's whereabouts and he'd come here for nothing. "Then why are you here? I've kept my word; I haven't left Manchester since we purchased this house, and Sean only went to London last year for business."

"Stop prattling on, will you?" Walter pushed to his feet. "I'm going to ask you a question, and you are going to answer me completely and truthfully. If you lie, if you keep anything from me, I will know — and I will burn this house to the ground."

"I will not be threatened in my own house," Sean growled, taking a step forward.

"I'm not speaking to you," Walter commented, his gaze remaining on his sister.

Sarah was fairly certain this scene would have played the same way even if they hadn't been hiding runaways in their closet, even if they had been genuinely surprised to see a dozen Campbell clansmen milling around her house. She put a hand out, stopping her husband's advance even as the two younger men in the room moved up to flank her brother. "Ask your question, then," she said, her voice unsteady. "I have no reason to lie to you about anything."

"I don't know about that, Aunt Mòrag,"

389

the one who looked like a younger version of Walter said.

"Whose boy are you, then?" she asked.

"Your sister Bearnas's." He sketched a lazy bow. "Charles Calder, at your service."

"Don't bother introducing yourself, Charles," Walter broke in, his scowl deepening. "You won't be meeting her again."

"For heaven's sake, Walter, stop threatening us and ask your question!"

"Very well." For a bare moment he clenched his jaw, but she had no idea if it was anger or embarrassment or worry. Given her own experience with him, she tended to believe it was embarrassment. "A week ago my daughter, Mary, was kidnapped by Lord Arran MacLawry. We came across their wrecked coach last night, not five miles from here. And so my question to you, Sarah, is: have you seen them?"

She put a hand to her chest. "Mary? Oh, no! That's horrible! I — No, of course I haven't seen her."

"How would you know?" Charles Calder asked slyly. "You haven't seen her since she was two years old."

"Don't be ridiculous," Sean broke in. "We've spent nineteen years here, looking at the same neighbors. The last stranger to come through here was that fellow selling

Paris silks. What was his name? Something Chambers. And that was three months ago. And so yes, we would know if we saw a strange woman about."

"For the last damned time, banker, I am not talking to you."

Sarah stepped between her husband and her brother. "Sean is telling you the truth. If we'd seen anyone being dragged about by some man, I would certainly remember it."

"So she didn't come to find you and ask for aid?"

"If she did, I certainly would have done what I could to help her. Whatever's happened between us, I have nothing against your daughter. And to be taken against her will — she must be terrified. Have you gone to see Robert Daily?"

"No, I haven't. The difficulty I have with this," her brother said after a moment, "is that I don't see where else she could go but here. I daresay Mary would find it irresistible, especially after their coach rolled over. She would hope to find you sympathetic to her plight, and that you would harbor them until they could find other transportation."

"And then there was the blood we found there. One of them is injured."

She looked at her nephew, using every bit of wit she possessed to follow only the clues they gave her, to reach the conclusions she would logically come to given what they were saying. "I — This doesn't sound precisely like a kidnapping," she said hesitantly. "I thought you meant she would come here to ask for my help in getting back home."

Walter closed the distance between them and put a finger under her chin, forcing her to look up at him. "It is precisely what I say it is. Now. Are they here?"

Sarah met his gaze squarely. "They are not," she enunciated the same way he had, not having to pretend the uneasy quaver at the end.

"Then you won't mind if we look for ourselves." Releasing her, he angled his chin toward the depths of the house.

Her nephew left the room and headed back toward the small kitchen, while the second young man none too gently set Levitt aside and opened the front door, whistling. Immediately another half-dozen men, some of whom she recognized as her own relatives or husbands of her former friends and allies, tramped into her house.

"After what they've done to you, Sarah," Sean roared, his face flushing, "I will not have these . . . Campbells in my house!"

She turned around to face him, not certain

how much of his anger was feigned. Not much of it, she would guess. "Sean. Let them paw through our things. It's the only way they'll go and leave us be."

"Yes, it is," her brother agreed.

"And I hope *you* realize," she continued, facing the Marquis of Fendarrow again, "that I would never do anything — *anything* — that would give you reason to appear on my doorstep."

"Perhaps not." The second young man returned to the sitting room, and Walter walked over to the doorway. "And perhaps you would leap at the chance to cause me harm. Either way, Donnell here will keep you company while I go see what sort of life you've made for yourselves. At the least I imagine it will be amusing."

And yet you're the one whose daughter has run off with a MacLawry, she wanted to say, but kept her mouth shut. Instead she grabbed her husband's clenched fist and pulled him over to sit on the couch beside her. "I suppose we should be flattered that he thinks we're so clever," she muttered, knowing Donnell could hear her.

"I'd be flattered if he fell down the stairs and broke his bloody neck," Sean grunted.

She snorted. "If I ever had any doubts that I chose the right man to give my loyalty to, this has answered it. I really do hate the Campbells, you know."

"As do I. All but one of them." Slowly he uncurled his fist and grasped her hand in his.

"Thank you for that, but I happen to be a Mallister." And hopefully soon the one other Campbell for whom she had very recently developed a surprising affection would be a MacLawry.

If she'd had a pocket watch, Mary wouldn't have been at all surprised to see that four or five or six hours had passed since they'd taken refuge in their little hole in the wall. She didn't think she'd ever sat so still for so long in her life, but it still didn't feel like enough. She slowed her breath, tried to slow her heartbeat — which was quite difficult considering that the entire right side of her body touched Arran.

He hadn't moved, either, but she would never mistake his stillness and silence for helplessness. Danger and ready anger fairly radiated from him. She knew he had a pistol, and she knew he was listening for any reason to strike. The fact that he'd been unconscious twelve hours ago didn't seem to concern him, though she didn't think she would ever be able to forget the image of his still, pale face. And how . . . lost she'd felt at the idea of being without him.

It was as if she'd just discovered the sun with all its light and warmth, and then been faced with the prospect of never seeing it again. She needed to tell him that, but not here. Not now, when it might seem that all she wanted was his protection.

". . . think she'd actually come here?" Charles Calder's voice came from only a few feet away. She jumped, and Arran's arm tightened across her shoulders.

"That depends," her father's deeper voice returned. "If that blood belonged to Mary, they're likely nowhere near here. If it's Mac-Lawry who's been injured, well, I expected to see her sitting by the road considering the best way to apologize for all this. She's a clever thing, but she's not about to carry MacLawry about and risk taking responsibility for shaming me and betraying the clan."

So that was what her father thought of her. And a few weeks ago, his assessment would likely have been correct. She had become an expert in avoiding complications. What he hadn't taken into account was Arran, and how brave he made her feel. Yes, she'd come here for assistance, but she hadn't chosen to ask the help of her aunt because it was a way out of all this. She'd come because they needed a safe place to rest for a few days.

"I'm assuming I'll still be marrying her once we straighten this out."

Mary made a face in the silent dark. *Not bloody likely,* she thought to herself.

"The announcement's been printed, my boy. As far as most of London is concerned, she's at Fendarrow waiting for us to arrive for the wedding. I insist that you marry her. If she won't make an alliance for us, I will see that she doesn't make any further trouble." The marquis's voice came from nearer by; he must have been in the doorway to the storage closet.

"That's all I ask. Well, except for one other small matter. In all the rush to catch up to them, you haven't said what you mean to do about MacLawry."

Her father made a disgusted sound. "This wardrobe wouldn't look out of place in a barn," he commented.

"Well, it was purchased on a banker's salary," Charles said smoothly, amusement in his voice. Good heavens, he was a sycophant. Mary had known that before, but she hadn't actually listened to what a toady he was until now.

The marquis chuckled, and the stack of

hat boxes fell over. *No, no, no.* She felt Arran shift ever so slightly, and knew he'd moved the pistol into his hand. If that wall panel moved, someone was going to die.

"But MacLawry?" Charles pressed, his voice close enough that she could likely reach out and touch him.

"You heard his brother. Glengask is so anxious to keep this tattered little truce that he's ready to disown our large Highlander. It would be even easier if Arran simply vanished, don't you think? His family could invent tales about how he escaped to the Colonies to begin a new life."

"You're not suggesting we let him go, I presume."

"No, Charles, I'm not. I'm suggesting we tell everyone he chose to flee to America when we cornered him. And then the MacLawrys remain the aggressors, and the Campbells look both honorable and reasonable."

"Will Mary keep her mouth shut about it?"

"You'll be her husband. She couldn't say anything against you even if she chose to. Which she won't. That would make her responsible for ending the truce. Mary's too proper to want blood on her hands."

"You've been thinking about this quite a

bit, haven't you, Uncle?"

"Since we broke Crawford out of that inn, yes, I have."

This was not her father. This was not the man who'd purchased her hats, who'd danced the quadrille with her at Almack's, who'd said he was relieved that Glengask and her second cousin George Gerdens-Daily had arranged for a truce between their clans.

Whoever this man was, he'd speculated about whether or not she was injured only in terms of strategy. He promised again to give her to a man he knew to be nothing more than a social-climbing killer. And he spoke about murdering a man — the man she loved enough to flee her old, safe life — as if the only inconvenience was the fact that they would have to hide the body.

"Turn over the mattress, Charles. I wouldn't put it past them to hide under the bed."

Still chatting about the best way they could do away with Arran and get her to a church with the fewest people possible knowing anything had gone amiss, the ,voices faded toward the master bedchamber. Other than the sheer cold-bloodedness of the conversation, she was struck by their supreme confidence in the fact that they would catch her and Arran.

"Was that bastard your father, Lady Mary?" Howard muttered in his gravel-rough voice.

"Silence," Arran whispered in response, so quietly the word almost seemed to drift on the air. "They're nae alone."

Did he mean there were more men in the house? Or that there were men waiting silently in the room, listening for them? Mary shivered, her muscles already tight and aching. What if her father decided to stay the night? What if he slept in the room a dozen feet away from where they were hiding? They could be trapped there in the dark, unable to move for fear of making a sound, for days.

Warm lips brushed her ear. "When they dunnae find us, they'll have to move on," Arran breathed. "Your father has to catch us before we reach the border."

Evidently Arran MacLawry could read her thoughts. Not daring to speak herself, she settled for a silent nod. What he said made sense. If her father didn't find them here, he would have to assume they'd slipped away north again.

After what felt like another hour but must have been ten or fifteen minutes, the chair in which Arran had spent the night shifted and creaked, and booted feet left the room for the stairs at the front of the hallway. *Goodness*. How had Arran known? Had he heard an extra set of footfalls when the men first entered the room? Was there someone else still inside?

Farther away male voices mingled, her aunt Sarah's higher-pitched response cutting in every so often. Glass broke, but the conversation continued. How odd, that a woman Mary had met only fifteen hours earlier could hide and defend her when her own father couldn't be bothered to do so. And how surprising that a man she'd known only a few weeks had become more precious to her than her own clan. Than her own family.

A door downstairs shut soundly. Shortly after that, she was certain she heard hooves pounding down the hardpacked front drive. Was it over, then? Or had her father left someone behind to keep watch? *Oh, dear.* That was what she would have done.

"How long do we wait?" Peter asked, in the quietest voice she'd ever heard the footman use.

"Mòrag and Sean'll come tell us when they've well and gone," Arran answered.

"I hope it's soon," Howard put in. "I need to piss. Begging your pardon, my lady."

"Well, now I need to piss too, ye halfwit," Peter grumbled.

"*Church* mice." Arran's chest shook a little, and Mary realized he was chuckling silently.

After all this, after hearing men say they meant to kill him, after being in a brawl and then being struck on the head by a falling coach, he was amused. And just that thought lifted *her* heart, as well. Because if Arran could laugh, then she could certainly manage to muddle her way through beside him.

"I love you, Arran MacLawry," she murmured.

His arm around her shoulders jumped. "I may still be delirious, lass," he returned in the same tone, "because I think I heard someaught."

"You did, you rogue," she said, smiling in the darkness.

"Say it again, will ye, Mary?"

"I love you."

"And I love ye, my bonny lass. Ye've seized my heart, and I'll nae have it back from ye."

She reached over to find his face with her free hand, then leaned up to kiss him. Without him she'd been alone in the dark for a very long time. Arran had drawn her into the light. She felt it around her even now, light and warm and freeing. And with him in her life, she would never be in darkness again. Not even here and now.

"What's that sound?" Howard asked.

"They're kissing," Peter answered.

Arran laughed against her mouth, and Mary joined him. Not even the blackest dark could stand against them. Not when they were together.

Arran almost wished Fendarrow and his clan would ride back to the house. Because at this moment, dented head or not, he was fairly certain he could take on the entire Campbell clan with one hand tied behind his back.

Mary loved him.

He kissed her again, wishing Peter and Howard had found another hole in which to hide so he could be alone and naked with her. While he wasn't precisely at his best, he could likely manage that.

At the sound of rapid footfalls approaching he broke away from her mouth and firmed his grip on the pistol. "Be ready," he breathed. The hidden door slid up. Even the relatively dim light that entered their hole seemed nearly blinding, but he narrowed his eyes and lifted the weapon.

"They're gone," Sean Mallister said, ducking his head into the opening. "Left a man behind on the nearest hillside to keep an eye on us, I imagine, but I spotted him the moment he rode up there."

With a nod Arran pocketed the pistol again and motioned Mary toward the opening. "After ye, lass. Lads."

When the rest of them had exited, he put his head back against the bare wood of the wall and blew out his breath. That had been too damned close. He hadn't arranged the setting, but this was not how a Highlander dealt with trouble. And it was the last time he would hide from his foes in the dark.

Before anyone could crawl back in looking for him, he turned onto all fours, shut one eye against the throbbing, and exited the hidden room. The Campbells had left the hat boxes where they'd fallen, scattered across the floor of the storage closet.

"Let me help you," Mary said, putting a hand beneath his shoulder and pulling.

He could stand up on his own, but this gave him the excuse to hold her close against him. "Thank ye, Mary."

The spare bedchamber looked like it had been torn apart by wolves. The Campbells had even taken a knife to the mattress and ripped it open. Feathers littered the plain wooden floor and the blue rug before the hearth like white and gray leaves. And they'd done this not only to their own kin, but to a household that could ill afford to replace the items.

"This is inexcusable, Uncle Sean," Mary said, a tear running down one cheek as she looked about the room. "I will repay you for the damage. I promise."

"*We* will," Arran amended.

"I appreciate the sentiment," the banker returned, looking far less perturbed than Arran would have expected. "But it's not necessary."

Holding on to the railing, Arran trailed his small troop down the stairs. Now that he could see straight, he noted the tidy, simple rooms, the fresh flowers that seemed to take the place of expensive heirlooms, and the utter lack of family portraits on the walls. All these two people had was each other.

Sarah Mallister sat on the floor in the front sitting room as she gathered up bills and correspondence that had spilled out of a tipped-over writing desk. "Let me help you with that," Mary said, releasing Arran and hurrying forward to kneel beside her aunt.

"Where's the fellow ye spied?" Arran asked, facing Sean.

"Just up the hill on the far side of the

road. I'd point at him from the window, but I fear he has a spyglass. And if he does, he can see everyone coming and going from here for two miles in either direction."

"Unless he's a damned cat," Peter drawled, "he'll nae see us in the dark."

"Aye," Arran agreed. "But it's nae dark, so ye and Howard and bonny Mary stay away from the windows at the front of the hoose."

"I'll be in the kitchen," Howard said. "This house is too fancy for the likes of me."

" 'Too fancy,' " Sarah repeated with a rueful laugh. "Bless you, sir."

"I'm no sir, ma'am. Just Howard. Howard Howard."

Arran exchanged an amused glance with Mary as the coachman left the room, Peter on his heels. "I thought he'd just declined to give us his other name." He leaned back against the wall to help him keep his balance. "This couldnae have been an easy thing fer ye. We cannae thank ye enough fer giving us a moment or two to breathe."

"Please don't thank us, Lord Arran," Sarah countered, letting Sean pull her and Mary to their feet and then giving her niece a tight hug.

"It's just Arran to ye, if ye dunnae mind," Arran said.

"Arran, then. I don't care if they've broken a few things. You have no idea how long I've waited to stand up to the Marquis of Fendarrow. You gave me that chance. And I am very — *very* — grateful."

"But my father broke your things, destroyed your home, because of us."

"You gave him a reason to come calling. But he did all this" — and Sarah gestured at the torn couch cushions and curtains ripped from the windows — "simply because he could. Sean and I have no clan, no one to rally behind us or make anyone hesitate to do us ill. That was the price we paid to be together." She smiled, putting an arm around her husband's waist as he slid his arm across her shoulders. "And I would gladly pay it a hundred times over."

He and Mary were looking into a mirror, Arran realized. Not only could either or both of their clans cause trouble whenever they wished, but so could anyone who'd ever had a disagreement with or a grudge against either a Campbell or a MacLawry. *And yet.*

And yet. Sean and Sarah claimed they had no regrets, and he couldn't detect any sign that they were anything but sincere. "I wouldnae say ye dunnae have a clan, Mòrag," he said slowly. "Ye have us."

406

Mary smiled at him. If he'd required any proof that she was the only thing he needed, that smile provided it. He pushed away from the wall and moved forward, not stopping until he had her in his arms, her mouth soft and warm against his.

"We seem to have a clan, my dear," Sean said from behind them.

"Aye. Ye do." Arran lifted his head. "Whether ye want one or nae."

Chapter Seventeen

"We could stay another few days," Mary said, running her fingers down Arran's chest and then following with her lips. Beneath her cheek his heartbeat accelerated — because of her touch. Because of her. It was intoxicating.

"Your father'll double back if he doesnae catch our scent. And we've been here nearly three days already. We cannae risk more."

"But Sarah and Sean will be here when my father returns. I can't leave them to his cruelty when I've already seen what he'll do."

"I've an idea that might help them some." Arran slid his free hand around her waist and pulled her squarely atop him.

"What idea?" she asked, trying to concentrate on the conversation rather than on where his hands were now roving.

"Just a way to make it look fer certain like they had naught to do with us." He cupped her face in his hands. "Now. We've an hour before nightfall, my lass. Do ye want to keep chatting aboot our plans fer tonight, or do ye think we might do someaught aboot this terrible swelling I seem to have?"

She laughed. "Again?" Mary drew her hand down between them to curl her fingers around his terrible swelling. "I thought we just dealt with this."

Arran lifted his head a little to nibble at her exposed throat. "Ye keep encouraging the lad. Perhaps if ye put yer legs aroond my hips," he said, nudging her legs apart so she straddled him.

With her on top of him, her legs spread, she felt very wanton. Keen need flashed through her, heady and arousing. "Well, let's take care of that, then," she breathed.

"Kiss me first."

Lowering her face, her bottom up in the air, she kissed him hot and openmouthed. His cock brushed the inside of her thighs, and she moaned. Arran reached up, opening her with his fingers, and guided her down over him. Mary sat up, sinking down around him. Oh, this was exquisite. He'd been in control before, but this way it was her leading them. She could tease him, coax him, drive him as mad as he drove her.

Planting her palms against his chest, she

lifted up and slowly lowered herself again, then repeated the motion as he looked up at her, an aroused smile on his face. "Are ye trying to torment me, Mary?" Arran murmured, catching her breasts in his hands and gently pinching her nipples. "Come fer me, lass."

He pushed his hips up, filling her completely. With a gasping moan she shattered, flinging herself against him as he rocked up into her, holding her hips to deepen his upward thrusts. *Good heavens.*

As she regained control of her muscles she straightened again, bouncing up and down on his hard cock until he threw his head back and surged up into her. Then with a satisfied sigh she collapsed on his chest again. "You're very good at this, you know," she panted.

"Ye drive me mad, lass," he said, putting his arms around her. "I want to be inside ye all day and all night, but I lose myself with wanting ye."

If he was admitting to a lack of finesse or some such thing, she decided that him being in complete control of himself would likely kill her. She kissed his shoulder. "I'm never letting you go, Arran. Never."

His grip around her tightened. Legs and arms entwined, with him still inside her, ever leaving this bed would be the worst sin she could imagine. Ever leaving his side, being separated from him, would kill her. She knew that with as much certainty as she knew her own name.

"I changed my mind," he murmured. "We should stay here. I'm nae letting ye oot of this bed."

Mary chuckled. "What about my father doubling back to find us?"

He shrugged beneath her. "They've likely forgotten all aboot us by now. I say we take our chances and make our stand here."

"In this bedchamber?"

"In this bed. I told ye we're nae leaving."

"Excellent. History will record it as the battle of the feather bed."

His lean body shook with laughter. " 'They'd thought the bed mended, but by the end feathers flew once more.' Ye know, I'd wager we could split this mattress open again with just the two of us."

She deliberately rocked her hips, feeling his cock move inside her. "What are we waiting for, then?"

By the time they did leave the bed she was fairly certain feathers had begun drifting out of the knife hole she and Sarah had sewn shut the day before. Because it was growing dark and they didn't dare light a lamp, though, she couldn't be certain.

"I'll button ye," Arran said, moving around behind her and pulling her simple green muslin up over her shoulders. He kissed one bare shoulder blade, then closed the fastenings up her back. "Are ye ready fer what comes next?"

"I'm ready. As long as everything is where Uncle Sean says it will be, I have the easy task."

Arran turned her around and kissed her softly. "Nae. Ye'll have Howard Howard with ye," he drawled, running a finger down her cheek. "Only three eyes between ye."

Mary took a deep, slow breath. "We should be going."

"Aye." He gazed into her eyes for a long moment, then visibly shook himself. "Aye. Give me yer hand, then."

She did so, and he clasped it in his. Together they left the room and headed downstairs to find her aunt and uncle together with Peter and Howard all beginning a light supper in the small drawing room and going over their plans for the night once more. As she took her seat she wondered if their hosts knew what she and Arran had been doing upstairs. As Arran had noted previously, it was a very small, very quiet house. *Oh, dear.*

"Good evening," she announced, too cheerily, as she sat.

"Good evening, my dear." Aunt Sarah exchanged a look with her husband. "Sean says we'll have a late moon tonight. That should help you, shouldn't it?"

"Aye," Arran answered, taking the one remaining seat at the foot of the table. "It will. And the two of ye will have yer excuse fer not seeing anything amiss with our spy until morning."

"I still don't like the idea of coming to his aid at all." Sean passed a basket of hot bread down the table.

"If ye help him oot, Fendarrow willnae have any reason to disbelieve yer story. We'll nae cause ye more harm than we already have. I'll feed the fellow a tale. Ye just go along with it."

Peter, seated beside Mary, handed her a platter of roasted chicken. "Ye'd best eat generous, my lady," he said. "Ye'll need yer strength, and ye didnae get much rest upstairs."

Uncle Sean stifled a cough, while Aunt Sarah made a choking sound. At her left elbow Arran threw a piece of bread, which slapped Peter in the side of the head. "Ye idiot," he said, without heat. "Dunnae embarrass my bonny lass or I'll leave ye here

413

to walk back to Scotland."

"I apologize, my lady," Peter said dutifully.

"That isn't necessary." Mary took a large piece of chicken and passed the platter on to Arran. "I'm quite famished, actually." She favored the footman with a grin.

They reviewed the plan Arran had set out once more, though Mary didn't think she would feel any calmer after a hundred rehearsals. She just wanted it to be over with — and she wanted not to have to go through it at all. Or rather, she wanted Arran not to have to go through with his part.

"I know you need to leave," Sarah commented, "and I know why, but part of me still wishes you could stay."

"I wish that, too," Mary returned. "Perhaps when we're settled there will be some way you can come and stay with us."

Sean nodded. "I would like that. And I know Sarah would. We have our friends here, but it's good to have family again."

Mary knew what he meant. And even under the very best possible scenario, neither she nor Arran was likely to have any more contact with their families. They'd both turned their backs on arranged marriages and destroyed potential alliances, and they'd more than likely shattered a very delicate, flimsy truce. Sarah and Sean could well be all they had. And the odds of the two couples ever seeing each other again were actually very small. But since tonight they all seemed to be pretending that everything would be perfect and splendid at the end of this journey, she supposed she could say they would all spend Christmas together and everyone would agree.

At the end of the meal Susan came and cleared the dishes while Peter and Howard retrieved their luggage and brought it down to the kitchen by the back door. Nervous anticipation ran through Mary. It was time to go.

Arran shrugged into his heavy coat, pulled a pistol from the pocket and checked it, then returned it again. He'd said he meant to do his utmost not to kill anyone, and she certainly believed him. But her father and Charles and the rest of them were beyond angry, and she'd heard with her own ears that they meant to kill Arran. No matter what, that was not allowed to happen.

"I'd be happy to lend you a hand, Arran," her uncle said slowly. "Waiting here and doing nothing doesn't sit well with me."

"Ye'll nae be doing naught," Arran returned, bending down to loosen the knife in his boot. "Ye'll make certain the lad on the

hill sees ye down here so he knows it wasnae ye up there."

"I understand. I still don't like it."

"I ken yer meaning, Sean. But this is best
fer all of us." With a grimace he offered his
hand. Sean shook it. "And ye, Mòrag. We
cannae thank ye enough."

Aunt Sarah smiled, then stepped forward
to embrace the big Highlander. "Don't you
dare thank me. When you find somewhere
to stay, just send us your address. Please."

"We will."

With that, Arran and Peter headed to the
back of the house. Mary followed; she
couldn't not do so. "Arran."

He stopped in the middle of the kitchen,
then took a long step back to her. "Give me
ten minutes," he said, leaning down to kiss
her. "Within five after that ye'll know if we
got hold of him or nae."

"How will I know if you didn't get hold of
him?"

"He'll be bellowing fer help."

She forced a smile. "Just please be careful."

"Peter and I know what we're aboot, lass.
This is one lad. Dunnae ye worry yerself."
He flashed his devilish smile. "I cannae die
till ye've asked me to marry ye, anyway."

She grabbed his lapels. "Then I'm not ask-

416

ing you yet."

"Yet," he repeated, touching her cheek, then slipped out the kitchen door and into the darkness.

That was that, then. Ten minutes to wait and listen for something to go wrong, and then she and Howard would be off to collect the horses, find the wagon Sean had arranged to leave close by for them, and then wait again for Arran and Peter to join them.

Squaring her shoulders, she walked back to the front of the house. In the sitting room her aunt and uncle hadn't waited, but were busily lighting every candle in the room and throwing more logs onto the roaring fire. "Not so much," she said quickly, stopping in the doorway so her shadow wouldn't be added to the two already filling the room. "If it's too obvious that you're choosing this moment to be seen, Arran's plan won't work."

"Oh, dear." Aunt Sarah swiftly blew out half the candles. "How do we do this without it looking intentional, then?"

Mary thought for a moment. Arran hadn't mentioned any of that. "You should dance," she decided.

Sean lifted an eyebrow. "Beg pardon?"

"Yes. Do a few turns of a waltz, then just . . . be there together. Be happy that your house is back in order and the Marquis of Fendarrow didn't burn it down."

It wasn't only that they needed to appear relaxed and at ease, but she wanted a last moment to see them happy. Because if they could still be content and in love after nineteen years on their own, then so could she and Arran.

"And what about you, my dear?"

Mary wiped a sudden tear from her eye. "If you could spare a moment to come here and embrace me, that would be very good."

"I can do that." With a damp smile of her own, Sarah left the sitting room to hug her tightly. "You write to us," she said fiercely. "Let us know how you're getting on."

"I will," Mary promised. "I'm so glad that I met you. Both of you."

"Likewise, my dear Mary." With a last squeeze Sarah let her go and returned to the sitting room.

If Mary had needed any proof that she and her life had changed over the past weeks, the smile that touched her face as her aunt and uncle moved into the center of the room answered it. Sean hummed an off-key waltz, and the two of them began to dance. The realization that such small things could make a paradise was so odd, and yet so very, very vital.

She backed away slowly, then turned to head down to the kitchen. "Are you ready, Howard?"

"If you can take that satchel, my lady, I'll pull the other trunk outside."

She slung the satchel over her shoulder and followed him out the door. It was her turn, now.

Arran crouched behind a half-buried boulder and waited. Down below the cottage sitting room lit up like morning, then dimmed to a more normal glow. He didn't know if someone had knocked over a candle and set a chair on fire, but the light did catch the attention of the Campbell seated on the ground two dozen feet from him.

The lad couldn't have been more than eighteen — a wee bairn who shouldn't have been left on his own, much less looking for the trouble that Arran MacLawry represented. Damn Fendarrow. Wherever Mary had gotten her nerve and her wits, it hadn't been from her father.

The spyglass rose, pointed down at the cottage for a long moment, then lowered again. As he risked another glance down the hill, Arran abruptly stilled. With the repaired curtains hanging partly open, the sight of Mòrag and Sean Mallister twirling in a slow waltz made him smile. The dance had likely been Mary's idea, and he couldn't conjure any image that spoke more of ease and contentment.

He waited another minute to be certain Peter was in position on the other side of the stand of trees, then began moving forward. After a lifetime of hunting deer and grouse and rabbit and then four years of killing Frenchmen, the instincts of stealth and silence were second nature to him. But this time he didn't intend to kill. And the only reason for that was somewhere in the dark below, waiting for him.

When he was close enough to share the lad's cold leg of mutton, he launched forward. Grabbing the fellow around the neck, he lifted and shoved, planting him flat on his face in the dirt. "Good evening," he drawled, setting his knee into the middle of the lad's back.

Peter appeared, grabbing up a rifle and pistol from beside the tiny fire and stomping on the spyglass. "That was nicely done, m'laird."

"Thank ye."

"MacLawry," the lad gasped, his voice muffled against the ground.

"Aye. MacLawry. Now ye tell me what the devil ye're doing up here, when I saw the

420

rest of the Campbells ride oot two days ago."

"I'm . . . I'm watching the cottage," he squeaked, no note of the Highlands in his unsteady voice. Another Sassannach-raised Scotsman whose blood had thinned to water.

"The cottage." He gestured. "That cottage? Why?"

"Why?"

Arran ground his knee between the lad's shoulder blades. "I've been hiding in some fellow's barn fer three days, so I'm nae in a mood fer ye nae to answer me. Why are ye watching that cottage?"

"It's — he — Fendarrow's sister lives there. He thought Lady Mary might have brought you here."

"A Campbell lives there? And Fendarrow thinks I'd set foot in a Campbell hoose? I'd sooner burn it to the ground. Ye're all daft. The whole damned lot of ye."

Peter produced a length of rope and made a show of uncoiling it while the young fellow squirmed like a spit fish. "I'm Fendarrow's nephew," he squealed. "If you . . . If you kill me, you'll be breaking the truce!"

Arran cocked his head. "Didnae ye get word, lad? I kissed yer cousin. The truce is already broken."

"No it's not! I mean, there's some confusion about that. No blood's been spilled yet, I don't think."

That was something, anyway, though he imagined it was only a matter of time. A very short time, if Fendarrow had his way. "And yet ye were sitting here with a rifle beside ye," he said aloud. "Were ye hoping we'd ride doon the road so ye could blow my head off? Or Mary's?"

"Not Mary's! She's not to be hurt."

"Ah. But I am, eh? Dunnae ye think that would break yer truce?"

"He's an *amadan,* fer certain," Peter put in. "So are we hanging him?"

"God's sake! No!"

Arran sighed, winking at Peter. "What's yer name, Campbell?"

"Fergus. Fergus Campbell."

"My brother has a dog named Fergus." With a last shove between the shoulder blades, Arran stood. "Let's string up the dog, Peter."

"N—"

Arran hauled him upright and cuffed the lad in the face. He'd told Mary he wouldn't kill, but the idea of this bairn pointing a weapon in their direction, of what might have happened to Mary if he'd missed his shot, dug a hole of worry into his gut.

"M'laird?"

Shaking himself, he gave Peter a quick nod. Together they bound Fergus Campbell's feet together and hands to his sides. Then Arran threw the end of the rope up over a sturdy-looking oak branch. The lad looked ready to wet himself, but Arran didn't have much sympathy for him.

He stepped in front of the boy. "When ye next set eyes on Fendarrow, ye tell him someaught fer me."

"What . . . What shall I say, then?"

Stating that he wasn't so easy to kill would have been supremely satisfying, but it also might remind the marquis of the conversation he'd had with Calder in the cottage. Arran wasn't about to risk the Mallisters' safety over a boast. "Ye tell him that his only grandchildren will be half MacLawry, and ask him if that's reason enough to make peace."

"I —"

Arran shoved a rag into Fergus's mouth before the lad could finish his bleating and tied it in place. "Now. We're going to haul ye up into that tree. I'll . . ." He looked around as Peter ransacked the small camp. "I'll throw that shirt of yers over ye so if ye're lucky Fendarrow's sister will see ye up here and come get ye doon. And ye remember what I said. And that I could've killed ye and I didnae."

He tucked one of the lad's spare shirts into the rope so the white material would flap about in the breeze, and then he and Peter hauled him a good fifteen feet into the air. "Can we spin 'im?" the footman asked. "He's the reason I had to sleep with a sow and piglets fer three days."

"Nae. If he spews sick he'll likely choke to death on it."

Once the rope was tied off around the trunk he and Peter gathered up the lad's things and destroyed any items that would help him on his way. "Do we take his horse west with us?" Peter asked.

Arran stifled a smile. For a fellow who couldn't read a word, the footman had a grand memory and quite a sense of the dramatic. "Nae. I'll nae be called a horse thief on top of my other sins. Leave it here. But cut the cinches on the saddle. I dunnae want him deciding to ride us doon. If I shoot him, Mary'll frown at me."

The figure in the tree began making sobbing sounds. Saint Bridget, Fendarrow leaving him here had been like leaving lambs to guard for a wolf. It was a very good thing for young Fergus Campbell that this wolf was in love with his cousin.

He hoped the lies he'd spun would be enough to protect the Mallisters. There wasn't much else he could do except force them to join his little troop, and that would hardly be doing them a favor. He found himself wishing he could talk to Ranulf to arrange a way to make their lives easier. His brother was no longer an ally, though, as mad as that notion even seemed.

The name MacLawry had made him enemies. It had also granted him power and respect. While he'd had the clan at his back, no one would have dared enter his house and destroy his possessions. Now, though, he had no clan. And except for the fact that he was bigger and younger and more physically imposing than Sean, he and Mary would be just as vulnerable as the Mallisters.

His dream of making a home in the Highlands with her lay directly before him now, nearly close enough to touch. He was strong and capable — he knew that. But no one man save perhaps William Wallace himself could stand against every Campbell and MacDonald and MacLawry and their allies. Was he leading Mary into nothing but a nightmare, then?

"M'laird?" Peter said, dropping the remains of Fergus Campbell's saddle beneath the weeping tree.

"Aye." He shook himself. "Let's fetch Mary before the dog unties himself."

They headed back down the hill and turned east up the road. This was the course he'd set. If it meant living a smaller, more cautious life, then he would adjust to that. Because with Mary at his side, he didn't *feel* smaller. He felt ten feet tall on the inside. But that was feelings. What mattered was whether he could keep her safe. And happy.

A mile down the road he spotted the light wagon with its well-worn team, Duffy and Juno tethered behind it. Howard had pulled them off the road into the deep shadows of a stand of elm and pine. London hack driver or not, the man had a good instinct for survival.

As they approached, Mary climbed down from the wagon seat and ran toward him, her skirt hiked to her knees. Sweet Saint Bridget, she was lovely. And he wanted her to have a happy life. "Mary," he breathed, and pulled her into his arms.

"Is everything well?" she asked, embracing him.

"Aye. Young Fergus Campbell is now a flag of surrender."

"Fergus? What in the world was my father

thinking, to bring a nineteen-year-old boy along for a murder?"

"I'd rather ask what yer father's doing planning a murder with his daughter so close to danger."

She looked up at him, her expression curious and her light green eyes silver in the starlight. "If you ask that, I would ask if you think his daughter is so simpleminded and weakhearted that she doesn't realize what she's doing and what the consequences are."

And just like that she reminded him why he loved her. Mary Campbell wouldn't be dragged anywhere against her will, even by him. They were here together. He would guard her and protect her and provide for her, but she was by no means helpless or naïve. She came from a clan, the same as he did, and she knew now what life outside of it could be like. What did she think of it, though?

"And if ye asked that, I would ask if ye could stand to live the life the Mallisters do."

Mary pulled his face down and kissed him. "I could, but we won't. Sean Mallister isn't a Highlander. He's civilized and mild. You're a barbarian devil warrior. If you think my father would have the courage to threaten to burn us out without an army behind him, you —"

He stopped her words with another kiss. "I'd nae face *ye* withoot an army at my back. Ye're a fierce Highlands lass, ye are."

"That I am. And don't you forget it."

Peter set his rifle on the driver's seat and climbed up beside Howard. "Ye know, there's a small chance that fella could wiggle free from those ropes. I'm only saying that because the two of ye seem to be too busy kissing to remember we're fleeing someaught."

"I've nae forgotten." Arran helped Mary into the wagon, then climbed up after her. They could ride on horseback in the morning, but he didn't care to risk one of their mounts breaking a leg in the dark. "Ye ready to see Scotland, Howard?"

"I'm ready to give those bloody Campbells a chase. Begging yer pardon, my lady."

"No need, Howard," Mary said, as they rocked back onto the narrow road. "I'm looking forward to escaping the Campbells, as well."

Peter clapped Howard on the shoulder. "Ye've lost yer coach, ye've had to hide from damned Campbells, and now ye're driving a farmer's wagon. Why havenae ye fled back to London, Howard Howard?"

The driver shrugged. "I suppose I'm curious to see what happens next. Most people I drive a mile or two and then they go on their way and I never set my eye on 'em again. Since I met you lot I've helped rescue a lady, hit a fellow with a club, lost my coach, dined with proper gentry, and been farther from home than I ever thought to see in my life. It'd be a privilege to see Lord Arran and Lady Mary wed."

When Arran met Mary's gaze, even in the starlit dark he could see her smiling. He took her hand. "Perhaps ye could stand in fer the bride's family, Howard. Ye are part of our clan, now."

The wagon nearly ran into a hedge. "I'd be honored. Truly."

Mary leaned her head against Arran's shoulder, and he tucked her in against his side. Perhaps he could keep danger away from her, but he was abruptly seeing Ranulf's actions in agreeing to a truce with the Campbells and bringing in the Stewarts, in addition to his dancing about with Sasannach lords, in an entirely new light. Because his primary concern was no longer defending clan MacLawry. It was doing whatever was necessary to protect his bonny, bonny lass.

"I love ye, Mary," he murmured, resting his cheek against her autumn-colored hair.

"I love you, Arran. In a day or two I may even ask you to marry me."

He laughed. "I do hope so."

CHAPTER EIGHTEEN

"Any sign of them?" the Marquis of Fendarrow asked, as Charles and another nephew, Arnold Haws, stomped into the Manchester Arms. Why he'd been cursed with a single daughter when his siblings had been blessed with multiple sons in addition to gaggles of girls, he had no idea. Had his son William lived, the circumstances today would have been completely different. He could simply have disowned Mary, turned his back on this mess, and stayed in London.

"Nothing," Charles answered. "Traffic headed in both directions on the three nearest roads, but no one's seen anyone resembling Mary or MacLawry."

"I'm thinking they wrecked that old coach deliberately, to slow us down," Arnold added, gesturing for a glass of whisky. "They had another vehicle waiting, and they're already in Scotland."

From the low grumbling that circled the

inn's private room, Arnold wasn't the only one to have come to that conclusion. The lads wanted MacLawry blood, and the longer he kept them waiting here, kicking their heels and drinking whisky and beer, the more frustrated and unruly they became. Which meant when they did find MacLawry, they weren't likely to listen to anything the lad had to say in his own defense — but neither would they heed *him*. Of course that could keep him from being blamed when someone shot the bastard. It could also lead to something bloody and public that he would never be able to turn into the mysterious disappearance of an extremely troublesome fellow. Yes, he was walking a very fine line, and some blasted news would be welcome.

"How long do we wait here, Uncle?" Charles asked. "Wherever MacLawry is, he's still breathing. And that does not sit well with me."

"And you think it sits well with me, Charles?" Walter snapped back. This was *his* chase, and *he* would control the outcome — whether he wanted it to appear that way or not. "Do you think I'm pleased that a MacLawry ruined an alliance and took my daughter, and that he's been doing God knows what to her for over a week?"

"No. Of course not."

"Then stop making ridiculous statements. I believe they are still nearby. However, if we haven't heard anything by this time tomorrow, we will divide our numbers and take all three roads north."

His nephew had narrowed his eyes, and the abruptly sinister expression reminded Walter that Charles had the reputation of being a rather deadly opponent. "If they reach Scotland ahead of us, they'll likely marry, my lord."

"And if they do, you'll be Mary's second husband. I assume you'll have no objection to marrying a widow, if the dowry's favorable enough."

"I do not. But if they marry and sign a register, MacLawry's death will have to be made known or I won't be able to marry her at all."

Fendarrow hadn't actually considered that. Once MacLawry and Mary signed the church register at Gretna Green or wherever they were headed, they would leave behind a written record. And convenient though it might be, the Campbell would not approve the burning down of a church to obliterate a piece of paper. He glared at Charles for a moment. Perhaps Arnold would have been a less demanding choice for a son-in-law.

"Not if we give a generous enough donation to the priest," Walter's youngest brother, Angus, spoke up. "Something worth a page of a register, say."

Walter nodded. "Precisely." As long as the equation ended with Arran MacLawry dead, he didn't particularly care how complicated or expensive the route might be.

Two more of his lookouts had returned, and four others had gone out, by the time the damned lazy innkeeper brought luncheon into the private room. Considering he'd rented the entire Manchester Arms, the service should have been a bit more . . . grateful. This was why he detested the countryside. The northern countryside, in particular.

The door linking them to the common room slammed open. Half the men with Fendarrow reached for weapons before Fergus Campbell stumbled into the room. His clothes were ripped and dirty, his face bruised and caked with mud.

"Fergus," Angus said, striding forward. "What the devil happened to you, son?"

"MacLawry," the boy panted, collapsing into a chair.

"You saw him?" Charles demanded, lurching to his feet.

"Is he dead?" the marquis added. With

any luck their troubles could be over. All that remained would be to collect Mary and dispose of anyone else accompanying her.

"He attacked me. From behind, the dog." Fergus took Arnold's glass and drained it, then began sputtering and coughing.

"Then he *was* at Sarah's house. She lied to me." The marquis scowled. Evidently she hadn't believed his threat to burn her cottage down. A low anticipation ran through him. All these lads would see that he was ready to succeed the Campbell. That he wasn't someone to be trifled with.

"No, she didn't lie," Fergus replied, when he could speak again. "MacLawry wanted to know why I was spying on the house. He didn't know a Campbell lived there. And Mallister's the one who saw me up on the hill this morning and cut me down. I might have been there for days if he hadn't spotted me."

"What do you mean, 'cut you down'?" Angus Campbell asked, his expression lowering as he eyed his son.

"MacLawry and the other Scottish fellow tied me up and hung me in a tree all night. He said they'd been hiding with pigs in a barn, trying to figure out how much we knew about their whereabouts. They kept waiting for me to stop watching the road, but they couldn't wait any longer because they were worried you would double back."

"Ha. I *knew* they were still close by."

"He . . . He gave me a message for you, Uncle Walter."

"What message?" Fendarrow asked slowly. Threats? A boast that MacLawry couldn't be stopped? He hoped so; that would give his men whatever incentive they still required to end the life of the bastard.

Fergus cleared his throat. "He said to tell you that your only grandchildren would be half MacLawry, and to ask you if that would be enough to convince you to honor the truce. To make peace."

The marquis looked up to see Angus gazing at him, a hand on his son's shoulder. That was supposed to weaken his resolve, then? The idea that Mary could already be with child? Reminding him that MacLawry had ruined her? "He asks me to make peace after he steals my daughter. Ridiculous," he finally said, knowing he needed to make some statement.

"He couldn't know if she's pregnant," Charles said in a cold voice, "even if he has attacked her. Forced himself on her. And there won't be any MacLawry grandchildren, Lord Fendarrow, if there's no Mac-Lawry husband."

With a deep breath, Walter nodded. This wasn't about grandchildren, or even about alliances. Not any longer. It was about cementing a line of succession for the Duke of Alkirk, with him at the front of that line. "This is why you'll be my son-in-law, Charles," he said. "Now get the damned horses saddled."

The speed with which everyone jumped to do his bidding was rather satisfying. Only Angus gave him an uncertain look, and Angus was a second son, six years his junior. What he thought only signified if it happened to agree with the opinions of his betters.

As of this moment only one thing mattered; catching Mary and MacLawry before they reached the border. And failing that, Arran MacLawry would die just as easily on his native soil. But there would be no half-MacLawry grandchildren. He wouldn't allow it. And for bloody certain the Campbell would never allow it.

"Ye cannae blame 'em fer nae wanting to do a straight swap fer the horses," Peter said, helping a stableboy back a fresh pair of bays into the traces.

"I suppose a farmer's wagon isnae the most elegant of vehicles," Arran agreed, his attention on the road off to their right. "And the grays wouldnae make a meal fer a starving dog."

"How much did we have to pay?" Mary asked in a low voice, though of course she hadn't paid for anything, herself. Not with only seven shillings in her reticule. No one else needed to know the state of their finances, though, particularly with the wilder, less populated countryside they were now passing through. The edge of the Lake District was stark and lovely, but it was also full of caves and valleys known to be the hideouts of highwaymen. Arran might enjoy a brawl now and then, but she didn't fancy a fight that would slow down their flight north.

"Three quid," Arran returned, taking the cloth-wrapped roast ham the innkeeper's son brought out to them. "But I'm sending the bill to Fordham."

They'd sent several bills to Lord Fordham, and while she trusted the viscount firstly because Arran did and secondly because he'd enabled them to exchange the notes that had led to Arran rescuing her — and everything since then — she had to wonder if his generosity had a limit. After all, even if they intended to repay him, which they did, it wasn't likely to happen anytime soon.

Since they were already spending money they didn't have to hand, she supposed they might have acquired a second coach. The cart, though, actually enabled them to move more quickly and attract less notice. It was also much less comfortable even than Howard's rackety coach, and she'd spent most of yesterday afternoon huddled with Arran under his heavy coat while rain nearly washed out the road. Mary smiled to herself. Despite the weather, she'd never had so much fun beneath a coat before.

"What's got ye smiling, lass?" Arran asked, placing the meal up behind the driver's seat.

"I was just wondering if I should purchase a coat of my own, or if we should continue sharing yours."

"My vote is fer sharing," he returned with a grin, then stepped up into the bed of the wagon and pulled her up after him. "Though I dunnae want ye getting a chill. The next village we pass through, we'll find ye someaught warmer to wear." Arran glanced over his shoulder again, then patted Howard on the back. "Let's be off, lads."

"How close do you think they are?" she asked in a low voice, as the wagon jolted through the rutted stable yard and back onto the road.

Arran shrugged. "I cannae see 'em, but I can feel 'em. Like a storm coming. Or perhaps it's only that I'm expecting trouble."

"That's not encouraging, either way." She leaned toward the driver's bench. "Can we go faster, Howard?"

The fresh team accelerated into a canter. "For a time, we can. I'll push 'em, but I don't want them bottoming out in the middle of nowhere."

With the midday still overcast and soggy, Mary was beginning to wish she'd asked Arran to barter for a coat or a blanket, after all. But it wasn't just the weather. She wasn't certain if it was his statement about having a feeling, or the knowledge that they were drawing near the Scottish border. Something, though, seemed poised to strike. And that something was likely her father and another dozen angry Campbells.

Arran cleared his throat, making her jump. "I've a yen fer a good Highlands song," he said. "Peter?"

"Aye. Someaught to chase the gloom away."

Mary sent him a dubious look, but Arran was smiling. "That'll give the Campbells pause, I wager. Whatever ye please, Peter Gilling."

"You don't think they'll hear him?" she whispered.

"Nae. With this rolling land he'll echo like a banshee. And they're likely to spy us before they hear us, anyway."

Then, as she was looking about for something to jam in her ears, the sweetest tenor she'd ever heard began, and she froze. "Twa Bonnie Maidens," a song even she knew despite her limited visits to the Highlands, soared up around them.

There were twa bonnie maidens, and three
    bonnie maids,
Came o'er the Minch, and came o'er the
    main,
Wi' the wind for their way and the corry for
    their hame,
And they're dearly welcome to Skye again.

"Ye think we're nae in enough trouble already, that ye choose a Jacobite song?" Arran said, but he was chuckling and already tapping his foot.

Come along, come along, wi' yer boatie
    and yer song,
My ain bonnie maidens, my two bonnie
    maids!

For the night it is dark, and the redcoat is
    gane,
And ye are dearly welcome to Skye again.

By the second chorus she and Arran were
singing along, and she thought his fine, rol-
licking baritone seemed even more delicious
than it had in Wigmore. Perhaps he wasn't
Bonnie Prince Charlie returning to the
Highlands in the guise of a maid, but he
was a Highlands prince returning home.
And she was going home, to a place she'd
only ever been allowed to glimpse.

Even Howard attempted the last chorus,
which nearly made Peter fall off his seat. "I
think ye might be part Scottish, Howard
Howard," he proclaimed, chortling.

"I like the tune," the driver admitted,
humming as he turned up the lapels of his
coat against the chill. "Will you teach it to
me, Gilling?"

"Aye. Dunnae sing it in London, though.
They might hang ye fer it."

"I actually had a thought that I might try
to make a go of it here," Howard returned
after a moment. "I left nothing behind but
a room in Whitechapel I shared with three
other lads, and a drawer full of clothes
which they've likely divided among themselves by now."

Mary had never considered whether he might have a wife or children waiting for him back in London. The fact that he didn't was small excuse for her thoughtlessness. All she could conjure in her defense was that he'd seemed to belong with them from the beginning, and he'd never mentioned anything he needed to return to.

"I dunnae expect we'll have a grand hoose, Howard," Arran said slowly, removing his coat and tucking it around Mary's shoulders. "But when Peter returns to his duties at Glengask, I reckon I'll have plenty of work fer two men to do. Nae driving though, more than likely."

"I've always had a yen to try my hand at farming, my lord. I'd be honored to join you if you've a place for me."

"It's settled, then." Arran crushed Mary to him in a tight hug. "I told ye he was ours," he whispered, chuckling.

She stifled a laugh in the warm folds of the wool coat. However odd the entire conversation, the notion that a London hack driver would become a Scottish cotter to a pair of exiled aristocrats made as much sense as anything else.

"I've been thinking some thoughts myself, Laird Arran," Peter said abruptly. "My task as given me by yer brother was to look after ye. And so I think I might continue with seeing ye and yer lady safe."

"Ye grew up aroond Glengask, Peter. I dunnae want to take ye away from that."

"And ye grew up inside Glengask," the footman countered. "I reckon I like this wee clan o' yers, and so I'll be staying. And that's the end of that."

"As ye say, then."

Arran's light blue gaze remained on the horizon. Mary could guess what he was thinking; they both came from large, powerful clans. And now with Peter joining them, and counting her aunt and uncle, they were six. She leaned up and kissed him on the cheek. "We're not alone," she murmured.

He blinked, looking down to kiss her mouth in that possessive, toe-curling way of his. "Nae. Our clan's grown again by a third just in the past five minutes."

She was fairly positive that they would be adding yet another to their number in just under nine months, but she would wait to tell him that until she was absolutely certain. That was a conversation for just the two of them, anyway.

Aside from that, he already had enough weight on his broad shoulders to break most men. Arran, though, could still laugh and sing and hold her. And heaven help anyone who tried to come between them.

The last time Arran had come through here he'd been heading south, stopping only to rest Duffy and seize an hour or two of sleep when he could no longer keep his eyes open. He'd made it from Glengask to London in just over four days. Ranulf had written a letter, and he'd mentioned a Charlotte Hanover four different times. And *that* had sent him flying south, ready to stop a match between the chief of clan MacLawry and an unfit Sasannach lass.

At the time it had made sense; their mother had been English, and after their father's death she'd swallowed poison rather than be trapped in the Highlands with four children. As far as Arran had been concerned, one Sasannach was very like another, and clearly Ranulf had lost his mind.

It had taken far too long for him to realize that Ranulf wasn't mad. He was in love. And to keep his lady safe, he'd done things he might not have previously contemplated. Arran had chided him for it, had argued that Ranulf wasn't using his head. And then he'd met Mary, and berated his brother for not understanding his position or the connection *he* had with *her. Idiot.*

If it hadn't been far too late, he would

have apologized to Ranulf, both for the mess he'd left behind and for the way he'd chosen to view Charlotte. He understood now. Of course Ran hadn't wanted him hanging about Mary; stirring up trouble with the Campbells was precisely counter to the safety he'd been trying to create for Charlotte.

But Ranulf wasn't the only MacLawry in love. And Arran was not about to allow anything — or anyone — to come between Mary and him. Not even his own family.

All he could do at this moment was hope that one day Ranulf would come to the same understanding that he had. If not, well, it would be a damned shame. And he still wouldn't spend a moment regretting the past few weeks and this woman beside him. She was his clan, and making her happy had become his new purpose.

A low, crumbling stone wall appeared along the horizon ahead of them. It dipped along the valleys and topped the hills, nearly six feet high in some places, and no more than two stones set atop each other a few yards beyond that. At the road it stopped, only to begin again immediately on the other side.

"Who owns all this land?" Howard asked, from around his pipe. Evidently he either drove the horses, or he puffed a pipe. At least the man knew what he enjoyed.

"It doesnae mark one man's land," Arran said, waking Mary from her light doze so she could see it, as well. "It marks the end of the civilized world."

Mary lifted her head from his shoulder, the withdrawal of her warmth leaving him chilled. "Hadrian's Wall. My goodness. We're nearly there."

"Aye. Only seven or so miles to the border and Gretna Green beyond." Frowning, he took her hand. "I wanted to marry ye in a proper Highlands ceremony, but it's another hundred and twenty miles to Fort William. I dunnae think we can risk waiting that long."

"We'll nae even reach Gretna Green by nightfall, m'laird." Peter flicked the reins, and the team jumped into a gallop.

"Slow 'em doon, Peter. No sense spending 'em fer no good reason." Every instinct Arran possessed wanted him to send those horses flying, but they would still never beat the sundown. "Keep yer eye oot fer a good place to hide us off the road until morning. If ye pass by the village, that wouldnae be a poor idea."

"You think they might be waiting for us there?" Mary asked, worry sending her sweet voice lower and quieter.

He'd heard that same timbre far too often since they'd met. And he wanted with all his heart to promise her that once they married she would never have to worry about anything ever again. That was a naïve dream, though. And whatever he was — devil, barbarian, rogue — he wasn't naïve. And he wouldn't lie to make her feel safe, when any such tale could be deadly for both of them.

"It's possible," he said reluctantly. "This isnae the only road north. Nor is it the fastest."

"It *is* the most rutted," Howard put in helpfully.

"And the muddiest," Peter added, nodding.

"That's enough help, lads. Thank ye." Frustrated and troubled as he was at the notion that Walter Campbell and Charles Calder might well be sitting on their arses inside some warm tavern waiting for them to arrive, the two men seated on the driver's seat gave him . . . hope. Neither of them had to be there, and yet both of them refused to leave.

"If they are already at Gretna Green, could we find the next village north?" asked Mary, who filled him not just with hope, but with excitement and contentment, arousal and satisfaction, and somehow caused it all to make sense with every precious beat of her fierce Highlands heart.

"Aye, we could, but it would add more hours fer them to catch us, and they're just as likely to have lads waiting there, too."

He gazed at her for a long moment as the setting sun lengthened the shadows of Duffy and Juno behind them, turning them into great, mythical beasts. And then there was Mary, a faerie princess even in his rough wool work coat and her hair in a simple, bronze-tinted knot.

"What's got you smiling, Highlander?" she asked, her own mouth curving up at the corners.

Arran kissed the upturned corners, and then the soft, sweet middle. "I've an inkling of an idea," he drawled, hoping silently that if he was truly about to suggest something mad, it would be mad enough.

"What is your idea, then?"

"I'll tell ye when we've stopped." And when he'd had time to think it through, tried to talk himself out of it, and braced himself for her to do the same thing.

They continued on past twilight, slowing the team to a walk when it became too dangerous to race through the dark. After

449

an hour or so a small group of twinkling lights came into view on their right.

"Gretna Green?" Mary asked in a hushed voice, as if she thought her father might be lurking just around the next hedgerow.

Of course he could well be doing just that. "Aye," he returned in the same tone. "Another mile or so, Peter."

"Aye, m'laird."

"I'm afraid we'll be sleeping oot in the cold tonight, my lass."

"I don't mind. You're very warm."

Arran allowed himself a frown in the darkness. "I mind. And I'm sorry. This wasnae how I imagined us spending the night before our wedding."

Mary hit him in the arm. Hard.

"What the devil was that for?" he demanded, remembering at the last moment to keep his voice down.

"Stop acting as if you're the only one responsible for us being here," she snapped. "Do you think I wrote that note to tell you where I would be because I hoped you wouldn't come looking for me?"

"Nae. But I had to convince ye to come along with me."

"Because I forgot there was a difference between being comfortable and being happy. Just as there's a difference between being uncomfortable and being unhappy. I'm here because I want to be here, so stop apologizing because the road hasn't been easy."

Arran narrowed one eye. "So ye're saying ye're uncomfortable but happy, I presume?"

"That is precisely what I'm saying. And don't think I haven't noticed that you spend the nights keeping watch, or that you're shivering right now because you've given me your coat. Are you unhappy?"

"Nae. I'm only . . . worried that I'll nae be able to give ye everything ye should have."

"You are what I want, Arran. Anything more is just . . . buttermilk."

"I beg yer pardon?"

"Buttermilk. It tastes pleasant, but it's a great deal of work and I could certainly live without it, without even giving it a second thought."

"I cannae help wanting to protect ye and purchase ye pretty, silly things, Mary."

"You *are* protecting me. You've already saved me. And purchase me pretty things if you like, if we can afford them. But I don't *need* them. I *need* you." She shifted around to look him squarely in the face, though he didn't know what she could see in the dark. "Have I made myself clear,

Arran MacLawry?"

What he hadn't realized in all this was that Mary Campbell was as occupied with looking after his best interests as he was with looking after hers. Having her in his life made him happy. Why would that be any different for her? "Aye," he said aloud. "I reckon I understand ye."

"Good."

He grabbed her by the lapels of her oversized coat and tugged her up against him. "And now ye understand this," he growled. "Ye're mine. If ye're sad or hurt or angry or lonely, ye'll tell me aboot it. Ye'll nae keep it to yerself because ye think I'd be happier nae knowing. And if I choose to make it my business to see ye happy, ye'll just have to put up with it. Have I made myself clear, Mary Campbell?"

She smiled and kissed him softly on the mouth. "Aye."

"Och. Now I've a tear in my eye," Peter said from in front of them.

"Ye'll have my boot in yer arse if ye dunnae find us a place to spend the night, ye heathen."

With that incentive they found a promising spot a half mile or so farther on, just over a hill from the road. Arran jumped to the ground to guide the wagon into a stand of trees, and then helped hobble all four horses by the small stream running along the base of the hill.

That done, and with an apple smuggled to Duffy for putting up with him for being such an *amadan* when he'd last come this way, he sat on the ground against a wagon wheel. Mary sat beside him, handing over a piece of cold roast ham. "It's all I could wrestle from the lads," she said, indicating the two men seated across from them.

"Nae true, m'laird," Peter protested. "We gave the lass half the carcass."

"I'm teasing, Peter."

"Lass," Arran said, brushing a strand of her long, curling hair from her face, "ye know there's a good chance yer family or mine or some other fools looking to make trouble may decide they cannae let us be."

She nodded. "We may not be able to remain in Scotland."

Of course she'd already realized that. "I've heard that Virginia is a fine, fertile land," he said slowly. "With milder winters than up in the Cairngorms."

"Ye mean we have to be Yankees?" Peter asked.

"Do they have ale there?" Howard lifted the bottle they'd purchased from the inn. "And whisky?"

"Aye. They also have horses, I hear. And fiddles."

"Well, if someone there can play the pipes and they have some good tobacco, then what are we waitin' fer?" the footman announced.

"We're waiting because we're Highlanders," Mary said, removing Arran's jacket and putting it over his shoulders, then shifting to sit between his legs and lean back against his chest. "We'll make a go of it here, first." She took his arms and pulled them around her shoulders.

"I'm yer blanket now, am I?" he muttered, kissing her hair.

"You're my everything," she whispered back, tilting her head back to kiss his chin. "Now. Tell me this plan you have for tomorrow."

Arran grinned. If his lady didn't so much as blink an eye at the idea of traveling across an ocean to make a new life, she certainly wouldn't be troubled by a bit of subterfuge. As she said, they were Highlanders. And so with a bit of the luck that had been journeying with them so far, in twelve hours or so he would be a married man — and not a dead one.

CHAPTER NINETEEN

"This is the worst idea in the history of bloody bad ideas," Peter complained, turning his back on Arran. "I said I'd be a Yankee, but this is going too far."

Arran shot Mary a quick grin, then fastened the buttons running up the footman's back. "I dunnae fit in the battle-axe's gown. Ye do. Now shuck yer trousers."

Peter turned around again, his face going scarlet beneath the matronly gray bonnet they'd liberated from Crawford. "Nae in front of Lady Mary," he grumbled, and stalked behind the wagon.

"Coward."

"I didn't dress in front of *him,*" Mary said, tucking her oversized shirt into her taken-in trousers and wishing she'd had time to do a bit more sewing. "It's only fair."

"But ye didnae dress in front of me, either, and that's nae fair. Let me look at ye, lass."

"That's laddy, if ye don't mind," she

ventured, lowering the timbre of her voice as much as she could.

With only her small hand mirror to view her appearance, she would have to rely on him. But she thought she looked very like a lad of fifteen or sixteen, clad in handed-down, altered brown trousers, the clearly cut-down coat of some other undescribable brown color, and the worn shirt that had once been white.

"I wish Howard's shoes fit ye better," he said, and took her around the waist. "I know I willnae mistake ye fer a lad."

"Will anyone else, though? That is the question."

"Here. Try this." He set his floppy-brimmed straw hat over the tight knot of hair she'd put at the top of her head. "And dunnae smile. Ye're far too lovely when ye smile."

Well, that was very nice. "Howard's coat is too small for you," she returned, tugging at the lapels. "But with his cap on, you do look less like you." She met his gaze, his light blue eyes the precise color of the sky this morning. "Is this going to work?"

"I'd be happier if we didnae have such a fine day," he commented, glancing toward the clear sky. "It's a good omen fer a wedding, but I'd like it better if we had cold and rain so we could bundle ye up a bit more."

"Arran, you're a . . . large, strapping man. If they're inside that church, they'll recognize you."

He shook his head. "They'll nae be inside the church. That's one thing all Highlanders agree on. A church is sacred and holy. If they're in Gretna Green, they'll be watching the ootside of the building. And they'll be looking fer a proper lady and a handsome, roguish Highlander. Nae two farm lads and their mother bringing flowers to the church."

"I'm beginning to think we might just declare ourselves handfasted."

He grinned. "And so we are. But we need to sign that church register as husband and wife. It's proof, and evidence, and it's in Scotland. And once the church is involved, both the Campbells and MacLawrys will have to be a bit more . . . careful in the way they proceed."

She knew that, of course. A church wedding would provide an additional layer of protection for both of them. That was always his aim — to keep her safe. But it would keep him safer, as well. Their marriage would be recorded. No one would be able to make him simply disappear, as her

457

father had been planning.

Arran ground his fine Hessian boots into the earth, scuffing and dirtying them beyond repair, then pulled them on. They couldn't hide his height or his broad shoulders, but in ill-fitting clothes and a worn hack driver's cap and dreadful-looking boots, he would at least raise some doubts. Together with a younger brother and a frumpy mother, perhaps he would go unnoticed altogether. Not by Mary, of course.

"I hope ye dunnae expect me to clean those ever again," Peter said, gesturing at Arran's boots as he hobbled around the side of the wagon.

"Nae. They're done fer."

"Well, what do ye think?" The footman spread his arms and made a slow turn. The dress fit him reasonably well, especially with the extra cravats they'd stuffed into his bosom. Mary had lengthened the dress as much as she could, and though it was still only at Peter's ankles, if he hunched over a little it didn't seem overly short.

"Try saying good morning," Arran suggested.

"Madainn mhath," Peter said, his voice high and squeaking.

"Lower. Crawford didnae have a dainty voice. Sound like her."

"Madainn mhath," the footman repeated, his voice half an octave lower.

"Aye, that's better. Why are ye speakin' Gaelic?"

"Because yer dear mother's Scottish. She prefers nae to speak English."

Arran frowned at him. "The Campbells speak Gaelic, ye know."

Mary put a hand on Peter's shoulder and pulled the bonnet forward just a little so that it shadowed his face without looking obvious. "Not all of them do. But I think it's a fair idea, Peter. We are in Scotland, after all."

"Practice walking, both of ye," Arran instructed, returning to the wagon.

She wasn't surprised to see him checking the knife in his boot and tucking another into his waist at the back of his coat. As she and Peter navigated their way around the wagon in unfamiliar shoes, she kept her gaze on the man she meant to marry. A pistol went into each pocket, and after he and Howard pulled the trunks off the wagon he wedged a rifle under the driver's bench.

"For a man who doesn't mean to kill, you're exceedingly well armed, Arran," she noted.

"That's because I dunnae mean to be dead, either." He narrowed his eyes. "Ye sway yer hips too much, lass. It makes a man take notice. Use yer toes more."

"If I walk aboot in these contraptions much longer, I'll be crippled," Peter said, coming to a stop.

Mary took a deep breath, anticipation still winning over nervousness in the battle going on inside her chest. "Peter's correct. We've practiced enough."

Arran's shoulders rose and lowered. "Aye. Howard, ye wait here with Duffy and Juno and the trunks. If we dunnae return, sell 'em and get yerself back to London, or wherever else ye wish to go."

"I know the plan." Grimacing, Howard offered his hand to Arran. "Best of luck to you both. I'll be here when you *do* return."

Peter clapped the hack driver on the shoulder. "Ye're a good man, Howard Howard. Now let's get on with it. Help me into the damned wagon."

Once Peter had seated himself and arranged his skirts, Mary handed him the bouquet of thistles and daisies they'd gathered. Arran climbed up to the driver's bench and then leaned sideways to offer her a hand up. Keeping in mind that she was a spry, trouser-wearing young man, she stepped up and clambered onto the seat.

"Are ye ready fer this, lass?" Arran asked

her. "It's nae a brilliant plan, but it's the only one I can think of that doesnae have us trying to avoid the Campbells fer another three days."

"I'm ready. And I like your plan."

He grabbed her shoulder and kissed her. "And now *I'm* ready."

With a whistle he got the team moving and carefully maneuvered the wagon over the hill and back onto the faint road. Then they turned south for Gretna Green.

Mary's hands felt clammy, and she fought the urge to clasp them together. Instead she lowered the brim of her hat a little and slouched on the hard seat. She and her brother were bringing their mother to the church to lay flowers on their father's grave, and to pay their respects to the pastor. And that was all.

"Do we need names?" she asked abruptly.

"If I ever have lads, I mean to name 'em Angus and Duncan," Peter said from behind them in his oddly pitched voice.

"Then I'm Angus Gilling and ye're Duncan Gilling, lass," Arran provided. "And ye're Una Gilling, Peter."

"Ye named me after Laird Glengask's dog, didnae?" the footman grumbled. "Una. Saint Bridget."

"It's a fine Scottish name."

Mary knew what Arran was doing; with his usual good humor he meant to keep them at ease as long as possible. Considering that any weapons were likely to be pointed at him, she could only admire his courage — and do her damnedest to see that the plan succeeded.

For all that it remained on the lips of every young pair of English lovers who felt the need to elope, Gretna Green was something of a disappointment in daylight. It barely qualified as a village at all, with perhaps a dozen houses along the lane, a single tavern, and a blacksmith's forge. According to rumor the smith could also perform weddings, but she and Arran required the church.

And then the quaint little building came into sight at the top of a gentle rise just above the village. The butterflies in her stomach turned into bats. And not just because they might well be driving into a trap. Choosing to marry Arran was the most momentous decision she would ever make in her life. Perhaps she shouldn't have been as certain as she was, but she simply couldn't imagine *not* spending the rest of her life by his side.

"Three horses at the rear of the tavern," Peter whispered.

"I don't suppose it could just be three men breaking their fast." Mary kept her gaze straight ahead, even though more than anything she wanted to turn around and see if she recognized the horses.

"Could be," Arran said. "Two more horses under the trees up here. Two, nae, three men. Relax, my bonny lass. Ye can be curious of strangers. Dunnae pretend ye dunnae see 'em."

"Why are you so . . . proficient at this?" she whispered.

He shrugged, keeping the team at their leisurely walk up the slope. "Anyone nae wearing yer clan colors could mean ye harm. I grew up with that." With a sideways glance at her, he sent them past the waiting men and circled the wagon so they were facing back down the hill. "I also got myself caught behind French lines once," he went on conversationally. "Had to steal a corporal's uniform and pretend to be French fer three days."

"I never knew that, lad," Peter said from behind them, his tone surprised and alarmed.

"I didnae tell anyone. Ranulf . . . He had enough to worry over withoot adding that. Whoa, lads." He pulled up the ribbons and set the brake.

Good heavens, they were there. Twenty feet from the small, whitewashed church. And beneath the trees only ten feet farther away stood three men, all looking at them. Her breath caught. One of them was her cousin Arnold Haws. *Oh, heavens.*

"Help me with Mama, will ye, Duncan?" Arran said, hopping to the ground with that easy grace of his.

Yes. She was Duncan . . . something. Gilling. Duncan Gilling. Escorting his mother to the church to see the pastor and lay flowers. Swallowing, she climbed down, trying not to look too ungainly.

The men, five of them now, moved closer, but from what she could hear of their low-voiced conversation it was mostly snide comments about dirty peasants and ugly Lowlands women. Poor Peter.

Moving around to the rear of the wagon, Mary allowed herself a curious glance or two from beneath the brim of her hat, glad she'd let Arran rub some dirt on her face. She lifted a hand to Peter, and with Arran at his other arm the footman descended clumsily to the ground.

"Are those Sasannach?" Peter asked in Gaelic, his voice still not quite feminine.

"Are they, Angus?" Mary seconded when Peter squeezed her arm. He'd been a soldier too, she remembered. Two warriors, two Highlanders, both ready and able to protect her.

"I dunnae, Duncan. They're none of our affair."

With Peter between them, holding one hand around her arm and the other gripping the flowers, they walked in what she hoped was an unhurried manner up to the church door.

"Can we talk to them?" she heard herself ask, and she glanced over her shoulder at the group. No Charles Calder, and no sign of her father. Perhaps their luck was holding out.

"Nae," Peter answered. "I dunnae want ye learning their ways, Angus. Into the church with ye, and be polite to the Father."

"Aye, *màthair,*" she answered.

And with that they walked through the Gretna Green church doors and closed themselves inside.

Peter kept her by the door while Arran strode forward, checking all the pews and then walking through the side door into what must have been an office or a vestry. "What if the priest isn't here?" she whispered, her stomach clenching at the thought.

"If he's nae here, I'll marry ye myself,"

465

Peter stated.

To her immense relief, Arran returned a minute or so later, a tall, thin man with cloud-colored puffs of hair above either ear in tow. "This is Father Leonard," he said, gesturing at the black-robed man. "He's agreed to marry us."

The pastor stopped just beside the first row of pews, his very high forehead furrowing in a frown. "We see a great many couples here," he said, Scots in his voice, "all eager to begin their new path together. Some marry for love, and others for wealth. And no offense to you, madam, but I need to ask why this strapping young man has chosen to be wed to you."

Mary blinked, then realized how they all must appear to poor Father Leonard. She stepped forward and pulled off her hat, then pulled the pins from her hair. "It's me the strapping lad is to marry, Father," she said.

The pastor looked relieved. "Ah. Now it makes sense. Come forward, child. And though it's not my place to ask, I assume you two are marrying against at least one of your family's wishes?"

"Aye," Arran answered. "And Peter, remove yer bonnet. We're in a church."

"Begging yer pardon, Father," the footman said in his normal voice, untying the bonnet and pulling it off to set it on one of the pews beside Arran's and Mary's hats.

"Good heavens," Father Leonard said faintly, staring at the stocky man with his worn face and ample bosom. Then he shook himself. "Well. To each his own, I suppose. You'll be the witness then . . . sir?"

"Aye. But I'm nae a sir. Gilling's the name, Father. Peter Gilling."

"Very well. Let's begin then, shall we?"

Mary started up to the front of the church, then stopped, surprised, when Arran held up one hand. "Just a moment, if ye dunnae mind, Father. The lady's nae asked fer my hand, and I'll nae be swayed until she does." He folded his arms over his chest, eyes dancing in the light cast through the stained-glass windows.

The bats in her stomach became giant geese. Part of her hadn't even expected they would reach the inside of the church. She'd completely forgotten that he wanted a proposal from her. Clearing her throat, she stepped forward, her boot heels tapping on the hardwood floor.

"I'm not feeling very eloquent at the moment," she said, looking up at his face and very aware of Peter and Father Leonard standing well within hearing.

"I didnae ask fer eloquence," Arran returned softly, reaching out to touch her cheek. "I just want to hear ye say the words and know ye mean them as much as I do."

She captured his hand, holding it tightly in hers as she faced him. His fingers shook a little, she realized; he was not as calm about this as he pretended. That actually bolstered her somewhat. She blew out her breath. She didn't need to be flowery or effusive or dramatic; he would say yes. All she need do was ask.

"Arran."

"Aye, m'love?"

She gazed into his eyes the blue of Highland mornings, and everything simply faded away. No one else in the church, no trouble waiting outside. Nothing but Arran and her, holding hands in the multicolored sunlight.

"I should never have met you," she began slowly. "We should certainly never have conversed. But we did. And from that moment you made my life adventurous, terrifying, amusing, and all the other emotions that had never touched me before. Just for that, I would love you. But you also saved me, not just from a marriage I didn't want, but from a life I found perfectly comfortable, perfectly ordered, and perfectly dull. You are my friend and my love, and I don't want to spend another day without you."

She wiped a tear from her cheek with her free hand. "Will you marry me, Arran?"

His blue, silent gaze seemed to see all the way to her soul. "By God, lass," he finally murmured. "I only expected that last part. Ye are my beating heart, and every other part of me that keeps me on this earth. Aye, Mary. I'll wed ye. I'd like to see anyone try to stop me." He took her other hand. "And I'll ask ye the same question, my bonny lass; will ye be my wife?"

"I will. Happily."

Father Leonard blew his nose into an embroidered handkerchief. "I don't generally get to witness that part," he said briskly, then motioned them to stand before him at the altar.

"Where do ye need me, Father?" Peter asked, handing Mary the bouquet and then using the hem of his gown to wipe his eyes.

"Where you are is fine." He cleared his throat. "We are gathered here today in the sight of God to unite these two souls in holy matrimony. The Good Book says —"

Shouting erupted outside. And it didn't sound friendly. *Oh, no.*

Beside her Arran was as still as granite. "Father, I'd be grateful if ye'd get to the meat of this ceremony and have us sign yer register."

"I . . . Is that ruckus about you?"

"More than likely. Peter, block the door."

"Aye, m'laird." Hiking up his skirts, the footman hurried to the rear of the small building. "Dunnae worry. I can still witness ye."

"If ye please, Father Leonard."

"Oh. I — very well. Do you . . ."

"Arran Robert MacLawry," Arran supplied.

"MacL . . . Oh, dear."

"Father," Mary put in, as the shouting and yelling and angry talking grew nearer and louder. "Please hurry."

The pastor closed his eyes for a heartbeat. "Do you, Arran Robert MacLawry, take . . . Mary to be your lawfully wedded wife? To honor and —"

"Aye. I do. Forever."

"Ah. And do you, Mary . . ."

"Mary Beatrice Campbell," she said.

Father Leonard turned gray. For a moment she thought he meant to faint. And then what would they do? "*Good heavens.* Do you, Mary Beatrice Campbell, take Arran MacLawry to be your lord and husband?" He leaned closer. "Shall I forgo the rest?"

"If you please. And I do, with all my heart."

"Then by the power vested in me by God and the Church of England, I pronounce you husband and wife." He glanced toward the line of windows. "Saints preserve us all. Kiss your bride, lad."

With a slight, fond smile Arran cupped her cheek, then leaned down and touched his mouth to hers. The soft, gentle gesture made her ache to her toes. "You're mine now," she whispered.

"And ye're mine. The father skipped the 'let no man put asunder' bit, but no one will sunder us, Mary Beatrice MacLawry."

She kissed him back, holding his face in both hands. "No, they will not."

"You'd best come sign the register," Father Leonard said, his tone uneasy. She couldn't blame him for his worry, now that he knew the MacLawrys and Campbells were involved.

Inside the vestibule first Arran and then she signed the thick book, and then Arran traded places with Peter so the footman could make his mark as their witness. Once Father Leonard had added the date and his own notation and dusted the ink with sand, she shook his hand.

"Thank you, Father Leonard."

"I'm . . . You're welcome, my lady. May God protect and keep you. Truly."

Back in the main part of the church Arran had his back pressed against the door, his arms outspread. "Lass, do ye want to be a boy again, or shall we assume they've found us oot?"

Swiftly she pinned her hair up again and handed Peter his bonnet. "We make them earn it," she said, the steel in her own voice surprising her. "I'm not simply surrendering."

He nodded at her. "I'd nae go against ye, my fierce lass," he returned, putting Howard's hat back on his head. "Together?"

She took one of Peter's arms, and he took the other. "Together."

CHAPTER TWENTY

Arran shoved open the church's double doors. The two men standing just outside stepped back, startled.

He likely would have been wise to cut them down before they recovered. Instead he put his arm around Peter, as if protecting the old woman the footman was pretending to be. "Step careful, *màthair,*" he said, not quite able to bring himself to apologize to the two men.

"What are they yelling aboot?" Mary asked, in a fine imitation of his own brogue.

"I dunnae ken, *bràthair,*" he answered truthfully. If the Campbells were certain they'd found their quarry, stealth from them would have seemed the better choice. He eyed one of the men as his troop maneuvered around them. "What's amiss, then?"

The man frowned, actually taking another step back. "I . . ." He sent a glance at his companion. "John?"

With a disgusted snort Peter urged them forward, and the clearly baffled men let them pass. Surprised they'd made it even that far, Arran kept the three of them at a slightly accelerated walk toward the waiting wagon. If he could get them back north through the village, they had at least a slim chance of returning to their hiding place by the stream.

"Stop them, you halfwits!" came from farther down the hill.

Everything happened at once, but at the same time Arran seemed to have the clarity to make note of every moment, every action. The Marquis of Fendarrow topped the rise, spurring his horse as he caught sight of them. Another, larger group of riders charged up from the east, scattering Campbells as they came. In fact, they wore Mac-Lawry colors.

Bear, he realized, even as he moved forward to put himself between Mary and the weapons that seemed to be appearing everywhere. He might have been relieved to see his mountainous younger brother, except if Ranulf had sent him, they weren't allies. Not any longer.

"Stay back!" he bellowed, pulling a pistol from each pocket and leveling them at the nearest group.

The Campbells skidded to a stop, but didn't lower their own weapons. Peter produced a blunderbuss from somewhere Arran didn't care to contemplate, and the footman swung it around to gain them some room on the other side. No one had yet opened fire, but it would happen — and it would happen soon.

"Back to the church," he growled.

"Father Leonard just barred the doors," Mary said from directly behind him. He felt her hands at his back, and then she had his spare knife in her grip.

"Against the wall, then," he amended, "so they cannae come at us from behind."

"Arran!" Bear called, leaping from his big gray gelding and bowling over three Campbells as he strode forward.

Cursing, Arran shifted one of his pistols, aiming it at his brother and praying that hotheaded Munro wouldn't press the issue. "No closer!"

"What the devil do ye think ye're aboot?" Munro demanded, barely slowing his approach.

"Stop, Bear! I will shoot ye!"

His brother finally stopped, a look of baffled anger on his face. "The hell ye will, Arran."

"You damned MacLawry, get away from

my daughter!" Fendarrow swung down from his horse but approached much more cautiously than Bear had. There was no sign of Calder, and that troubled Arran.

"And I'm telling ye to stay away from my wife!" he snarled back.

The pushing and shoving around them changed to a roar. They were watching the resumption of a full-out clan war, he knew, MacLawrys against Campbells. And the first man to die would signal the last moment of peace he and Mary would ever find in the Highlands.

Abruptly Mary moved up beside him. "You're too late!" she yelled, flinging off her hat and shaking out her hair. Thank God she'd done that; he didn't want anyone mistaking her for a lad and shooting her by accident.

"Come away from there, Mary! Now!" her father shouted back.

"No! Arran and I are married. You can't kill him and pretend it never happened, because all these men know it now!" The point of her knife flashed as she gestured.

"We dunnae want to hurt anyone," Arran took up. "But by God I'll nae let anyone between us!"

"Strike if you wish the truce to end," Mary continued, as fierce as any Highlands war-

476

rior and lovely even in a coat and trousers. "But you will all have to face the wrath of my grandfather, the Duke of Alkirk. The Campbell."

"Will they now?" a new voice came from the edge of the clearing. Dry and cool, it made the hairs on the back of Arran's neck prick.

"Good God," Mary whispered. He risked a glance at her, to see that her flushed cheeks had paled to an alarming degree.

The nest of Campbells stirred, moving aside as someone passed among them. Bobbing heads, downcast eyes, and a bit away from them, the stiff-spined Fendarrow looking like he'd swallowed a bug. A tall man with snow-white, close-cropped hair, straight shoulders, and sharp eyes deeply set in an angular face stepped into view. Arran didn't need to see the diamond pin in his lapel or the green and red plaid of his kilt to know precisely who he was.

"Yer Grace," he said, lowering both pistols. The mad shooting might have been avoided, but unless he was greatly mistaken the situation had just become much more dangerous. "We thought to meet with ye in a few days, in the Highlands."

"I received word that ye and my granddaughter were heading north. Yer brother and I seem to have come to the same conclusion — that ye would come here. Especially with Fendarrow on yer heels."

"I knew they were coming to Gretna Green, Your Grace," the marquis said crisply. "There was no need for you to travel all this way."

"Aye, this looks very orderly," Bear commented, his rifle lowered but still in his hands.

"I dunnae care who came from where," Arran stated, wishing Mary would move back behind him again, where he could put himself between her and any gunfire. "Go and make yer peace or yer war as ye will. Mary and I are wed. All we ask is to be left alone."

The Campbell came a few steps closer. "Are ye mute now, Muire?" he asked, using the Gaelic version of Mary's name. "Does this MacLawry speak fer ye?"

"No, I am not mute, *seanair,*" she returned, "and yes, in this he does speak for me."

"And together ye decided to flee north and risk war? Ye decided together to throw an alliance with the MacAllisters back into *my* face and set all the Highlands into a rage? Perhaps ye should speak fer yerself."

"We didn't decide to flee north," she

countered. "I kissed Arran and everyone saw us and Lord Delaveer walked away, and the next day Father declared that I was to marry Charles Calder instead. Arran rescued me from that, and we headed north so I could ask for your assistance."

"Ah." Alkirk flicked his gaze to Arran. "Ye wanted my assistance as well, did ye, MacLawry?"

"Nae. I wanted yer granddaughter. But I gave my word I would see her to yer door, whatever happened between us."

"It seems a wedding happened between ye. Withoot my permission."

Arran regarded him coolly. "Aye."

"And if I'm nae mistaken, ye were to wed Lady Deirdre Stewart before ye began this wee holiday."

Of course the Campbell would have heard about a potential alliance between the Mac-Lawrys and the Stewarts. What angered Arran was the way the duke referred to their flight as a holiday, as if it had no significance. As if it could be easily done away with. "So I was. We've neither of us done well by our clans, I suppose. But if ye think ye can put a stop t—"

"Arran." Reaching sideways, Mary abruptly gripped Arran's arm with her left hand. "I love him, *seanair,*" she broke in, "and none of you left us any choice but to go behind your backs. We came to Scotland so no one would be able to part us."

"There are still several ways to part ye, my dear," Alkirk replied coolly.

Her fingers tightened convulsively. *That was damned well enough of that.* Arran broke away from her and walked up to the Campbell, ignoring the weapons bristling in his direction as he approached. "So ye think to stand here like a great bully and frighten yer own granddaughter? Ye think she hasnae been frightened enough over the past weeks, from her parents trying to barter her away and then promising her to a coldhearted weasel, to a gaggle of armed men chasing her all the way from London? Mary adores ye, and ye're aboot one sentence away from trampling her respect fer ye into the mud. From all she's told me aboot ye, I expected . . . better."

"I dunnae answer to a MacLawry. Especially one who's poached my kin. I could put a ball betwixt yer eyes and nae even blink."

"I'd make ye blink, I reckon," another, more familiar voice said. A big bay Thoroughbred cut through the clearing, stopping beside Bear. Ranulf swung to the ground and continued forward on foot, his gaze on Alkirk and an angry, bristling Fergus pacing beside him like a massive gray hellhound.

"Saint Bridget," Arran swore. "We came here to get away from the lot of ye."

"Then ye chose a poor way to go aboot it, *bràthair*," Glengask shot back at him, his voice clipped with fury.

"Nae. *Ye* did. Ye call a truce, and then all either of ye do is try to increase the size of yer armies so ye can get back to killing again. And then ye clobber us, fer what? Fer being yer best chance fer a true and lasting peace? What do ye want, then? Peace, or more blood spilled?"

"That's enough, Arran."

"Aye, it is. Kill us, kill each other, or shake yer damn hands. Those are yer choices. Mary is my wife. Ye'll have to murder me to separate us." He dropped his pistols onto the ground. "I'm finished with yer proud nonsense."

"Glengask, control yer brother. He began this, by stepping where he wasnae permitted."

Arran felt Mary walk up behind him more than he heard her quiet footfalls. The knife clattered to the ground beside his pistols, and then her hand caught his. Almost without thinking he twined his fingers with hers.

"We began this latest mess," she said, her voice shaking a little, "and we are ending it. If you kill Arran, you may as well kill me, because if you don't, I will. And you'll be killing your great-grandchild as well, *seanair*. A bairn who would be your best excuse for peace in a hundred years. For both clans."

As he listened, Arran's heart stopped and then began roaring like thunder in his chest. He faced her, ignoring the stunned faces of the onlookers. "Are ye carrying my bairn, lass? Why did ye nae tell me?"

"I wanted to wait until we were somewhere safe," she returned quietly, tears in her moss-colored eyes. "But I don't know if we will be."

Instinctively he pulled her into his arms, tilting her face up to kiss her tears away. A bairn. A child. *His* child. His and Mary's. And if nothing changed — and it looked like a very good chance that nothing would — not only would he be unable to ensure that he would be present to see the young one grown, but the babe had only the slimmest of chances of surviving a clan war. He lifted his head again.

"Tell me what ye want, then. Both of ye," he said. Because whatever his own plans, the MacLawry and the Campbell were the ones with the power, the ability to put things right or allow them to crumble into bloody dust. "What's the price for ye to stop hounding us, so I can hold my bairn in my arms and nae fear that he'll lose his father to this stupidity the same way I lost mine? Tell me. Please. If it's in my power, I will see it done."

Ranulf cocked his head. Gazing intently at Arran, he slowly reached down to pat Fergus on the deerhound's growling, low-held head. "Off, Fergus."

The dog sat on his haunches, clearly not pleased with the order, but obeying anyway. Arran, though, kept his head high and his arms tightly around the sobbing Mary, both to comfort and protect her. He wasn't a damned dog, after all, to blindly follow his brother's orders. Not any longer.

"That tune ye're singing is different than the one ye blasted at me in London," Ranulf finally said, his tone neutral.

Arran nodded. "Aye, it is. And I'm aware that I put ye in a bad spot, and that I judged ye unfairly, as well. I thought ye were bowing to the Sasannach and turning us into merchants to please yer Charlotte. It wasnae aboot pleasing her, though, was it? It was aboot making a place where she could be safe."

The Campbell was studying the three of them like a cat studied a mouse. With the knife in his boot Arran figured he could still set his claws into the old man if it came to it, so he returned the duke's gaze evenly. Hopefully Alkirk realized that calm and reasonable didn't mean helpless, and that he'd meant every word he'd said. This was the clans' — both of them — last chance. If nothing could be resolved, then he and Mary would be leaving as swiftly as they could reach the coast. Or they would die here and now. There was no other option for them if the chiefs couldn't see beyond their own stubborn noses.

"So ye want peace, do ye, Arran Mac-Lawry?" the Campbell uttered.

"I do. They say ye and my father were friends once, Yer Grace. Ye must've wanted peace yerself, at least fer a while. And now it's time fer ye to decide if ye want Mary in yer life." He looked at his brother. "And are ye done with me, Ran? Ye said ye were. Because honestly, once I brought Mary to Alkirk my next task would have been to purchase us a berth on a ship bound fer America." Yesterday that wouldn't have been strictly true, but now everyone knew where they were and what they'd done. Hiding away had become a much more difficult proposition.

"You aren't listening to this rogue, are you, Father?" the Marquis of Fendarrow snapped, stalking up to the small group at the center of the clearing. "MacLawry, Campbell, or . . . Jones, he had no right to make off with Mary against my wishes. And yours. We had plans. The MacAllisters will never trust us again."

"And yer grand solution was fer Mary to wed Charles Calder?" the Campbell returned, lifting an eyebrow. "Do ye think I want that lunatic closer to becoming chief of this clan than he already is? I suppose ye thought him a pup to lie at yer feet and worship ye." The duke snorted. "Mary's got the right of that; if she'd come up to see me I'd have put a stop to it."

The marquis flushed. "I'm sorry you didn't approve of my choice. She embarrassed all of us, and I didn't care to give her a chance to make things worse by dallying with a MacLawry. She couldn't wed him if she was already married, and Charles offered to help." He gestured at Arran. "You cannot want Glengask's heir this close to your throne, either."

Mary lifted her head, her face streaked with tears. "*I* want Arran," she said simply.

"I won't be without him. So banish me like you did Aunt Sarah, and we'll be away from here."

"You *were* there," her father growled, narrowing his eyes and clearly seeking a target to vent his own frustration and embarrassment. "I warned her that I would burn her out if she lied to me."

"Mòrag took ye in?" the Campbell interrupted, his sharp voice cutting through his son's blustering.

"Arran was injured when our carriage broke an axle," she returned. "Don't blame her; she didn't wish to allow us in. She's done everything possible to go unnoticed by any Campbells. And my father took a knife to her mattresses and her curtains and broke her precious things, just because she couldn't do anything to stop him."

"Well now," Alkirk said slowly. "It seems my own hoose isnae quite in order." He looked over at Ranulf. "Ye sent Munro here to protect Arran from us, didnae?"

Ranulf nodded. "I did. That's why I rode up here, as well. Whatever I may think of Arran's actions, he's my *bràthair*. No one harms him." The Marquis of Glengask sent an unreadable glance at Arran, then stepped directly up to the duke. "What do ye say, Alkirk? Do we see where these two intend to lead us, or do we stay mired in our own bog until there's nae a man left standing?" With that, he held out his right hand to the duke.

Arran sucked in a hard breath. In all his imaginings, he'd never thought to see Ranulf actually offer peace. And certainly not without turning it to some strategic advantage for the MacLawrys. But there he stood, surrounded by a closing circle of Campbells and MacLawrys, each man of whom would be looking for any sign of weakness in his clan chief.

The Campbell gazed at Ranulf. If he ignored the hand, the best Arran and Mary could hope for was exile. If he turned his back, blood would spill here. Arran could feel the shudder that went through Mary and he tensed, ready to move.

Finally the Duke of Alkirk took a half step forward and clasped Ranulf's hand with his own. *"Guaimeas,"* he said. "Peace." He returned his attention to Arran and Mary. "We've a wedding to celebrate."

The men around them roared, echoing the word in English and in Gaelic. *Peace.* "Thank God," Arran murmured, and kissed his Mary. She dug her fingers into his arms, kissing him back with a passion that made him want to fall to the ground with her.

"You did it," she whispered against his mouth.

"Nae. *We* did it. I told ye there's nae a man could stand against ye when ye get that fierce look in yer eyes."

She smiled. "I meant every word of it."

"As did I."

"Well," the Campbell said, "we've shaken hands on it. Now I'd like to speak a word with my granddaughter and wish her well."

Arran didn't much like that; all of these people had been nothing but trouble for weeks. But Alkirk *had* shaken hands, and in the Highlands that was more binding than any law. "That's fer Mary to decide," he said aloud, reluctantly releasing her.

She nudged him in the shoulder. "Go make amends with your brothers," she muttered, and walked away a few feet to speak with her grandfather.

At least she hadn't told him to apologize, but he likely needed to do so. For some of it, anyway. He'd pointed a loaded weapon at Bear, for God's sake. Squaring his shoulders, he walked up to where they stood. "I'm sorry I pointed a pistol at ye, Bear," he drawled.

"*That*'s what ye apologize fer?" his younger brother rumbled. "Ye disappear, we hear that ye've kidnapped the Campbell's favorite granddaughter, and then ye go and marry her, and ye apologize fer a pistol." Shaking his head, Munro wrapped him into a hard bear hug. "I thought we'd lost ye, Arran."

Arran hugged him back. Bear might have a short and heated temper, but he was also generous to a fault. Today he would call himself lucky that he'd found the generous part. "So did I, fer a moment," he returned.

"Ye married a girl in trousers. And Peter Gilling's wearing a dress."

"Aye," Arran said, straightening again. "It's been a long day."

"And it's nae noon yet," Ranulf commented. "Why didnae ye tell me how much ye cared fer the lass?"

"I tried to tell ye. Ye didnae want to listen." Arran took a breath. "I ken now that ye were trying to find a way to protect yer own lass, and me being after Mary didnae help ye any." He grimaced. "I misunderstood. I apologize fer that. But I'll nae apologize fer escaping Deirdre Stewart. If ye dunnae wish to forgive me, so be it, but I wanted ye to know."

"I should've listened harder to ye, Arran," Ranulf returned. "Love's a damned tricky bastard."

"Aye. I'll agree with —"

Something slammed hot into his upper arm. Half a second later the sound of a pistol discharging echoed across the hillside. Arran staggered sideways, his shoulder on fire. Ranulf grabbed him as he went to his knees, while Bear stepped between them and the sound and lifted his rifle.

He heard Mary scream, and then she was on her knees beside him, tugging on his coat and ripping his sleeve. "Who did this?" she shrieked. "Who did this?"

"I thought we had a plan," Charles Calder's voice came. Arran looked over Mary's head to see her cousin drop the spent pistol and pull a second one from his pocket. "Arran MacLawry disappears, we bribe the priest to burn one of the pages of the register, and I become Fendarrow's son-in-law."

"Put that down!" Mary's father ordered.

"Someone's going to do as they said, even if it's only me." He lifted the pistol, aiming it at Arran — and Mary in front of him.

Grabbing her, Arran flung her to the ground, offering Calder his back. Even if he wouldn't live to see his child, she would. She had to.

Another shot shattered the air. Arran tensed, waiting for a ball to pierce his spine. Nothing. Still holding Mary down despite her struggling to rise, he looked over his shoulder.

Charles Calder lay in the grass, moaning and holding his left thigh. To either side a dozen weapons were aimed at him, but only the one the Duke of Alkirk held was smoking. Slowly the Campbell lowered it again. "No damned nephew of mine will begin a war I just ended," he declared. "Get him doon to the blacksmith and press a hot iron to that. Make certain it hurts, lads." Then he handed over the pistol and approached. "Ye're nae dead, are ye, MacLawry?"

"Nae. Ye're nae going to poke *me* with a hot iron, are ye? I think a bandage would do me better," Arran said, sitting up with Mary's help. "Thank ye."

The Campbell nodded. "Let's get ye doon to the tavern and patched up. Arnold, go have the innkeeper drag oot his best whisky, and take someone with ye to find a proper gown fer Mary."

"I'll see to it, Your Grace."

"And find us a piper. We cannae celebrate a wedding withoot pipes."

"Right away, Grandfather."

Climbing to his feet, Arran let Mary pull his good arm across her shoulders. "I can walk, ye know," he murmured.

"Perhaps I just want to be in your arms,"

491

she whispered back, smiling. "I love you, Arran MacLawry."

"*Tha gaol agam ort,*" he returned. "I love ye, my sweet, bonny lass."

She leaned her head against his. "We have a great deal more than a wedding to celebrate, don't we? A child, the first peace in four hundred years between our clans, gaining our families back . . . Have I missed anything?"

Arran kissed her on the temple. "I dunnae believe so. But tonight I'll only be celebrating the fact that ye're mine. Forever. Everything else is . . . buttermilk."

Mary laughed and kissed him back, his fierce Highlands lass.

The employees of Thorndike Press hope you have enjoyed this Large Print book. All our Thorndike, Wheeler, and Kennebec Large Print titles are designed for easy reading, and all our books are made to last. Other Thorndike Press Large Print books are available at your library, through selected bookstores, or directly from us.

For information about titles, please call:
    (800) 223-1244

or visit our Web site at:
    http://gale.cengage.com/thorndike

To share your comments, please write:
    Publisher
    Thorndike Press
    10 Water St., Suite 310
    Waterville, ME 04901